LIGHT

in the Company of Women

LIGHT

in the Company of Women

KEITH MAILLARD

HarperCollins*PublishersLtd*

First Edition

Canadian Cataloguing in Publication Data

Maillard, Keith, 1942-
   Light in the company of women

ISBN 0-00-223894-2 (bound)   ISBN 0-00-647533-7 (pbk.)

I. Title.

PS8576.A34L53 1993   C813'.54   C92-095387-5
PR9199.3.M32L53 1993

93 94 95 96 97 98 99 ❖ RRD 10 9 8 7 6 5 4 3 2 1

For Mary

BOOK ONE

I am just an ordinary man, without any special ability in any direction.

-Theodore Roosevelt

It is a melancholy fact that childhood, so short when compared with the average span of life, should exert such a strong and permanent influence on character that no amount of self-training afterward can ever completely counter it.

-Consuelo Vanderbilt Balsan (formerly the Duchess of Marlborough)

1

On a fine spring afternoon in 1908, Sarsfield Middleton looked down from the roof-top of the building that housed his father's photography business and saw one of the oddest sights that had ever greeted his eyes: a tall, angular man in the street below was playing an Irish jig on a whistle. The peculiar fellow wore an excessively rumpled suit made of some dull green fabric; he moved with a comical, slack-kneed, shuffling gait that was more of a dance than a walk; and he had attracted half a dozen laughing children who followed along behind him, leaping at his heels. It was a picture straight from a story book, and Sarsfield wished that he had one of his cameras set up to capture it. He watched until the strange man, still leading the whooping children, vanished like an hallucination at the corner of Short Market Street.

"Queer go," Sarsfield thought, and turned back to arranging his printing frames. On fair days he always did his printing-out on the roof, ostensibly so that the direct sunlight would speed the process, but actually so that he could be assured of being alone; his father had long ago given up climbing the narrow ladder from the room below.

That morning had been a busy one. In a little more than a month all the high schools in the Ohio Valley would turn loose their new graduates upon the world; and long-standing custom required that "every Sally or Johnny about to embark upon the rocky road of life"—as their advertisement in the *Raysburg Times* put it—be captured forever in a studio portrait. "Short of cash? Don't let that stop you," the advertisement (written, as always, by Sarsfield's father) proclaimed; "At J. C. Middleton's we have a price range for every pocket." Now Sarsfield had twelve frames laid out in the sun on his work bench; there was nothing left for him to do but watch the images of the Sallies and Johnnies darken and then, when they were ready, to carry them back down to the darkroom and immerse them in running water; so, still bemused by the odd sight he had just seen, he stepped back to the edge of the roof.

There was no sign of the man with the whistle. The street, which had been quiet only a moment before, now was suddenly bustling with Saturday shoppers; under the brilliant sun, each appeared wonderfully drawn—particular and exquisite. The sky was the vivid color it ought to be and seldom was in Raysburg; the light was so intense it hurt his eyes. Then, looking out across the roof-tops, Sarsfield saw the heart-stopping gleam of the Ohio River; reflecting back the sky, the water was blue as steel. The new graduates could go to the devil, he thought; it was a perfect day for color photography. He could not imagine how the light could get any better.

Late the night before Sarsfield had been awakened by the discreet creak and rattle of his father's rubber-tired sulky, had been kept awake for another hour as his father had stumbled, apparently aimlessly, around the house in the dark. These three-in-the-morning perambulations of his father's were not unusual, but they always filled Sarsfield with a fuming indignation such as is only possible for an idealistic young man of twenty-five when faced with a recurring example of mortal foolishness,—particularly when the fool in question happens to be one's own father. Unable to fall asleep again, Sarsfield had lain in bed thinking that the biggest fool, after all, surely was none other than himself. He was a first-rate professional photographer and a Harvard man to boot; his color process was second to none; he could find employment easily enough in New York or Boston; he could, for that matter, hitch his wagon to the rapidly rising star of George Eastman who appeared to be well on his way to putting one of his Kodak cameras into the hands of every citizen in America. There was, in short, no earthly reason why Sarsfield had to go on working for his father in this brash, dirty, backward, money-grubbing town—his home town—of Raysburg, West Virginia. If he had an iota of gumption, he'd pack his bags and leave on the next train. *So why didn't he?*

But he could never find an answer to that question. And, while Sarsfield had lain there in the dark worrying about it, he had felt a good stiff breeze spring up; eventually his bedroom window curtains had begun to flap like banners. Then, instead of dying out with the dawn, the breeze had blown right on through into the day and was still blowing. "Of course," Sarsfield thought, "That's what did it!": the smoke from the mills was nowhere to be seen. Even the persistent dense white fumes from the Top Mill in the north end of town had been blown away. The day looked as bright and sharp as a freshly minted penny. It even smelled good.

The street below was filled with a parade of vehicles: traps and buggies of every description. A farmer, who should have known better, had mysteriously got himself turned sideways at the end of the market and was blocking the flow of traffic; his chickens were protesting, but no one else appeared to be: the day was obviously too fine for that. Even the elaborately attired young ladies in the old-fashioned landau with the top down (Sarsfield, amused, recognized his pretentious cousins, Bedelia and Lenore, beneath their parasols) were waiting patiently; so was their black driver, a broad grin on his face, as he watched a couple of fellows from the saloon bound out to assist the old hay-seed in putting things aright. These worthy gents doffed their hats to a cluster of schoolgirls in gleaming muslin frocks, then seized and gentled the farmer's horse, hauled her around and aimed her the right way: "There's your soup ticket, you old rascal!"

The street was alive with sounds. The colored shoe-shine boy was calling out for customers; another lad was crying the paper's headlines— "Night riders along the Ohio! Tobacco warehouse burned!"—and, out of sight, probably all the way down by the wharf, an automobile motor sputtered and died,—accompanied by a chorus of groans from the spectators that these cantankerous machines always attracted. For a moment Sarsfield heard a snatch of the Irish jig again; the odd man with the whistle sounded impossibly far away by now; then the strangely melancholy tune was lost amongst the voices of the street. And finally, arriving into this lively setting as perfectly timed as an actor to his cue, was Sarsfield's father—J. C. Middleton, the photographer himself, "Jack" to his cronies—the businessman and investor, impeccably dressed as always, a gardenia in his lapel, his black eyes flashing in his long, white face above the huge brush of his black moustache, striding up Short Market Street like a lord, his gold-headed walking stick flashing in the sun; and Sarsfield knew what the boys in the saloon would be saying: "Here he comes, old Jesus Christ Middleton."

Sarsfield watched his father stop to have an additional glimmer of shine added to his already perfectly blacked boots. As drunk as Jack had been at five o'clock in the morning, it was a minor miracle that he was appearing in public at all; but, from the look of him, he was at the top of his form, in the most buoyant of good spirits. Jack trimmed and lit one of his fine Havana cigars, studied, with obvious satisfaction, the sign he'd recently had made and affixed to the front of what he, but no one else in town, called "The Middleton Building." Despite the fact that he had only one son working for him and the other was barely twelve years old and had yet to learn one end of a camera from another, Jack's pretentiously large sign read: J. C. MIDDLETON AND SONS, PHOTOGRAPHERS, EST. 1873. And, about the time that Sarsfield was wondering how long it would take his father to notice him on the roof, Jack looked up, laughed, called out in his ringing voice that could carry a mile: "What're you doing up there, you puppy? Hump yourself, *hump* yourself, boy, there's a dollar to be made!"

Sarsfield did not know whether to laugh or cry. He had heard exactly those theatrical phrases hurled at him as long as he could remember and was sick to death of hearing them. He had been looking forward to having the shop peacefully to himself all afternoon; and he did not know what was worse: his father in a foul mood or his father in a cheerful one. But, on the other hand, if his father were to assume responsibility for the afternoon's portraits, perhaps Sarsfield could sneak back up onto the roof for an hour and take some color pictures of the bustle in the street below.

Jack, however, had obviously no intention of doing any portraits that afternoon; he strolled into the shop like a baronial visitor, paused in the front to rag their clerk ("Ah, Miss Calendene, 'tis a delight to see you, as always. The very picture of loveliness to greet our customers on this splendid afternoon—"); and, still talking, trailing inconsequential blather behind him like his cigar smoke, approached his son—who had climbed down into the studio to meet him; and Sarsfield got a strong whiff of tonic and burnt hair, knew that his father had stopped for a singe in the barber shop at the end of the bridge; and neither Miss Calendene nor Sarsfield had been supposed to notice the airy, magical moment, like a sleight-of-hand demonstration, when Jack had dipped into the till and helped himself to all the loose cash.

"So who are you doing this afternoon?" Jack said, glancing through the appointment book. "Oh, the old Southerner's daughter, eh? Little Emma—just about ripe by now, I'd say"; and Jack conjured up an imaginary young lady under the skylight, let his broad hands drift up to caress her bosom: "Forgive me, my dear, but I must adjust your dress the better to catch the light—"

When Sarsfield thought of Emma, the youngest of the Rossiters, all he could imagine was a little girl in pigtails. "She's just a child," he said.

"But you know what these mountain folk say, don't you, Son?"— and Jack, a man of many voices, fell into a passable imitation of a down-state West Virginia accent: "If she's old enough to bleed, she's old enough to butcher."

Before he could stop himself, Sarsfield burst out with: "Really, Father, draw it mild!"

"You priss! You're a copy of your mother." Jack slapped Sarsfield on the back hard enough to rattle his teeth, and then, laughing, was gone.

Since Sarsfield had come back from Harvard, he had been running the business single-handed; but when he suggested to his father that, perhaps, he should be drawing a salary, Jack always replied: "What the hell are you talking about, you puppy, the business is yours!" Jack hardly took a picture these days; he certainly had not made a print in months. But Jack's defection from photography, Sarsfield thought, was not a great loss to the art. Jack's ability to focus a camera was directly related to the amount of whiskey in his veins; he never measured the light but guessed at his exposure and compensated in the printing; he never timed anything but counted in his head ("Naught, one half and one, one half and two—"); he never measured his chemicals, but mixed them in as they felt right ("that's it, son, you take your Ferri-Cyanide of Potassium about the size of a pea, and then your Hyposulphite about the size of a baseball—"); he was indifferent to the temperature of the water; he would rather fiddle around to try to repair something than take the trouble to get it right in the first place ("Oh, we can save that one; we'll just soak it in corrosive sublimate for a while—"); he was as totally ignorant of the chemistry of photography as any mediæval alchemist ("Now you see, son, your bitter Gold Salt needs to be sweetened up with your Sugar of Lead—"); he piled on the flash powder with a lavish hand and more than once had blown away the backdrop behind his terrified sitters. Everything Jack did was, to sum it all up, a matter of feeling and not of science. Oh, Jack could, on occasion, muddle his way though to a brilliant picture; but, to save his soul, he could never make two prints in a row that resembled each other.

"But to give the devil his due," Sarsfield thought, "he did teach me everything he knows." The process, however, had not been an easy one.

As soon as he had started school, Sarsfield had begun to come into the shop on weekends in winter and on the long, hot afternoons of his summer vacations to learn the business. For five days in a row Jack might spend hours answering all of his son's questions, demonstrating camera work or a darkroom process, carefully, step by step, the very personification of patience; then, on the sixth, he might greet Sarsfield with: "Get out of my way, you little son of a bitch!"

Sarsfield had long known that he did not much like his father; for nearly as long, he had been certain that his father did not much like him; the last three years had, of necessity, thrown him into close, daily intercourse with the man, and Sarsfield no longer felt singled out by his father's dislike: he had concluded that Jack Middleton did not much like anybody. Oh, his father was affability itself; Jack had dozens of cronies and pals all over town. He could walk into any saloon, and the boys at the bar would begin chuckling at the mere sight of him, eager for the torrent of words that—after a shot or two of bourbon whiskey, chased with a pint of good foamy steam lager—would begin to pour out of him like a geyser. "Where's he get it?" they'd say; "It never dries up!"—as Jack would launch into one of his standard declamations:

"Now, gentlemen, let us consider a thick-headed tribe of German peasants growing hops in the ancient, venerable, stinking swamps of East Hesia, for generations passing their days swilling beer and gobbling sauerkraut, red-faced and sweating in their fertile fields, which, for pestilential miasmas, would put to shame anything studied by the good doctors who disinfected the route of our great canal. One day something as singular as an idea appears in the mind of one of these muddled Lutheran oafs; and he crosses the broad seas to America's distant shore to establish his race in the green and rolling hills of Pennsylvania—" That particular opening (and Sarsfield knew them all) was the general introduction to Jack's vilification of his in-laws, the Eberhardts; and then, taking his own sweet time, Jack would move from the general to the particular until he had heaped insult on every Eberhardt in Raysburg, West Virginia, without ever mentioning the fact that the Eberhardts comprised the wealthiest family in the city. And, eventually, one of the grinning yokels at the bar, amazed that anyone short of a United States senator could be as purely and ridiculously and *pointlessly* garrulous as Jesus Christ Middleton, would say, quoting Mr. Dooley in the paper: "Aye, you could waltz to it."

Oh, Jack Middleton was amusing all right—so long as you weren't a member of his family. Sarsfield could remember with painful vividness dozens of nights in his childhood when he had been awakened by his father's ringing, declamatory voice, had crept downstairs, hidden behind the sofa, and watched while his parents played out an oft rehearsed scene like something from an old melodrama.

"When these two ill-fated blood-lines did mix to produce their tainted offspring," Jack shouts out, grinning like a demon, "the pompous German fool out of the Eberhardts and the beribboned, bedecked, social climbing, cross-eyed half-wit out of the clown-like Raineys—"

"Jack, please!" Sarsfield's mother hisses. "You'll wake the whole house."

"Yes, the Raineys," Jack bellows (now referring to the Ohio Valley's oldest and most respected family), "that gaggle of Scotch-Irish cretins serving as bound servants in the tidewater plantations of East Virginia; those blonde-haired, wall-eyed idiots who fled westward to settle in the fastness of our own impenetrable mountains—"

Sarsfield's mother approaches cautiously, as though to a horse that's been known to kick. Jack pushes her hands away, steps back, takes up an oratorical stance. "Who distinguished themselves by their abilities to live solely on corn," Jack proclaims, gesturing broadly to the empty chairs as though they had suddenly become packed with dozens of avid spectators, "whether in solid or liquid form, you understand, makes little difference—Yes, the Raineys, who for generations bred with each other and with whatever else was handy, pedigree or color—or indeed species—being no impediment—"

Sarsfield's mother begins to weep. "Jack, for God's sake!"

"When these effusions of doubtful blood did mix like the products of two sewers to give rise to a daughter, why—yes, why! I ask you—was it my lot to marry the woman? Were there not other maidens more fair? Yes, there were. Were there not other—" and here Jack grinds to a halt. His face goes slack. He steadies himself with a hand on the wall. As though noticing her for the first time, he stares at his wife who has fallen onto a chair and is sobbing as though her very heart will break.

Then, hours later, Sarsfield's mother guides her husband, stumbling and groaning, to bed. Back in his own bed Sarsfield can still hear occasional, sudden bursts of words erupt from his father: "This woman, who,

by the cultivation of all the right people, including, of course, encyclo-
pedia salesmen, chautauqua lecturers, and clergymen of whatever
denomination, did rise to social prominence—"

"Jack, please be quiet!"

Sarsfield had spent his boyhood trying to please his father; and now
that he had arrived at a stage in his life when he no longer cared
whether he pleased his father or not—when, in fact, he had come to
understand that there was nothing he could *ever* do to please his
father—he felt as though he had lost something, some precious boyhood ideal. The loss left him with a sad emptiness that, as yet, he had
found nothing to fill. He would never forget the long strolls he and his
father used to take together; he would cling to his father's hand and
stare, fascinated, at the gleaming arc the gold head of Jack's walking
stick made in the air. And then, after a perambulation sufficient to give
father and son a good thirst, Sarsfield would always find himself seated
on the bar in one of Raysburg's many saloons, a sarsaparilla or a grena-
dine soda in his hand, listening, as Jack, aided with stronger beverage,
spun out his fabulous yarns. For a little boy trying to make sense of the
world, it was often devilishly hard to distinguish what parts of his
father's stories were true and what were not.

One of the tales Jack loved best to tell was how everyone in town
was mystified by him when he first arrived. "Who *is* that strange feller?"
he would say, speaking in a voice meant to represent the Greek Chorus
of Raysburg citizenry back in 1873. The boys at Howell's Livery Stable
(Jack claimed) took him for an Englishman. That's right, only an Englishman would be so crazy as to drive up in a rig that would have been
an embarrassment to an old Jew and then, when you came over to ask
him what he wanted, address you as "my good man." And didn't he
have an English accent, and, after all, wasn't Middleton an English
name? "That's what they do over there in England," Jack would say,
imitating the backwoods stable boys, "them fancy families, you know.
They ship the youngest sons over here to get 'em off their hands. And
did you see his clothes, dirty as they was? Why you'd have to pay five
dollars to get a suit of clothes as good as that." (And here, Jack always
laughed at his own joke.)

The old Dutchman in the farmer's market took him for one of them
high society Yankees come down from New England to make trouble;

but the darky who blacked Jack's boots held that the man must be a Duke at least. The gent in the general store who sold Jack half a dozen of the best of Karl Eberhardt's stogies was left with the impression that this handsome lad must be straight from the drawing rooms of London. But Mrs. Clancey, when Jack appeared at her boarding house, didn't have to speculate. ("She knew me all right," Jack said with a wink.) "Sure, he's a fine young Irish gentleman," she said. (And Jack, raising his voice into a fluting falsetto, did her accent perfectly.) Why, as soon as he arrived, wasn't the first thing he required a bath? And by the Mother Mary and the Carpenter, didn't he have a sweet, cultured, Irish voice? And didn't he change his clothes, not only his linen but even his suit? Indeed, he did, and he stepped up to the table with his chin fresh shaven and his moustache waxed, and there, affable as you please, made conversation with everyone present, and you could see he was to the manner born just by the way he used his knife and fork.

Then, laughing again, pausing to look his listeners in the eye for emphasis, Jack would make a speech that never varied; falling into a modest, self-deprecating tone, he would say that when he'd come to America, he'd put all pretensions behind him—that he did not expect it to matter a damn to anyone that he was one of the Middletons of Wicklow whose land was given to them by Queen Elizabeth herself. (But, Sarsfield wondered, if Jack *were* one of the Middletons of Wicklow— whoever the devil the Middletons of Wicklow might be—why had Jack "lost touch" with them so completely? In all his years of growing up, Sarsfield had never seen a letter arrive with an Irish postmark. "Given by Queen Elizabeth herself?" Sarsfield thought. "The old humbug!")

As angry as Sarsfield could get when he thought of his father, the man might still, however, at odd moments, enlist his sympathy. Sarsfield's favorite story, the one he hoped he would always remember, was of Jack's arrival in the Ohio Valley. Jack had driven a wagon over the National Road—a lunatic's adventure to be sure (as Jack, himself, always styled it); but Jack had just attained his majority, by God, had just arrived in America, by God, and was full of himself and wanted to see what he could see. He had been on his way to Columbus, or—who knows?—maybe even Saint Louis. Jack had bought a good old dray horse named in the predictably idiotic American manner "Betsie," bought her and the wagon with her from a drunken tinker in Baltimore, loaded up his cameras and equipment, and headed west.

It was a hot day with a taste of rain in the air. Jack was alone on the road as he had been for most of his journey; he drowsed with the leathers on his lap as the scenes through which he had passed continued to unfold themselves before his closed eyelids:—sylvan groves so dense that not a sun mote relieved the gloom; vast prospects of mountain ridges folding back behind yet more mountain ridges, the valleys between hazy with purple mists, as though of some mysterious fairyland; long stretches of the old, dusty pike—overgrown now with grass—upon which snakes lay about like so many ropes, sunning themselves, and in so great a profusion that Jack could not avoid running his wheels over them; silent taverns, long ago fallen into picturesque ruin;—for yes, the heyday of the National Road was long past; and, if expeditious transportation had been his primary concern, he should have ridden on the Baltimore and Ohio Railroad—as, apparently, everyone else was doing. And Jack may have been the only traveller on the road; yet, in every sleepy, silent, ramshackle village through which he passed, he had, to his continuing good fortune, encountered garrulous American peasants mad to see pictures of themselves; and he had been trading tintypes for meals and lodging all the way from Baltimore.

He slept a bit, woke, and found himself crossing over yet another of the stone bridges so solidly constructed that they might have been built by the industrious Romans at the height of their imperial power. The valley was gradually widening out. The road had been wending its way around the base of yet another lofty hill; now it turned and aimed itself toward the summit along a steep ascent which appeared to have been cut through solid rock. Jack saw a high, circling hawk against a rapidly thickening bank of clouds; and he felt an uncharacteristic melancholy settle over him, for the first time since leaving Ireland asked himself if he were not a total damned fool to strike out with such blithe insouciance into this raw, sprawling, naïve country in which people didn't know what an Irish gentleman was, having never laid eyes on one.

Jack kept at hand a flask of spirits to assist him in such moments (he said, with a wink); and now he helped himself to a long drink. A tickle of rain was lashing up in the west. The lower edge of sky looked as though printer's ink had been poured into it. Jack took a second drink, paused with the flask in his hand, and discovered that he was experiencing an inexplicable though profound stirring of emotion. For the first time he genuinely *saw* the place where he was, saw it as clearly as if it were framed, upside down, on his ground glass. "It's very like Wicklow," he thought. "By God, it is. Put up some stone fences, and this could be the very place—County Wicklow." He slapped the leathers, called out, "Step along there, girl. Move lively, my sweet." He did not yet know where he was going; but he was suddenly in a fierce hurry to get there.

Jack attained the summit of the hill and discovered a little shack which had once been a tollgate for the National Road; directly in front of it, an ancient, white-bearded character was seated in a rough-hewn chair, smoking a pipe made from a corncob. A few minutes of conversation were sufficient to establish the fact that this worthy had once collected the tolls; what remained mysterious to Jack, however, was why he was still there years after his function had passed away. "Nice view," the old man said.

Since ascending the crest of the hill, Jack had perceived a distinctly unpleasant quality to the atmosphere. "I mean no offense by the question," Jack said, "but could you hazard an opinion as to the origin of the terrible smell hereabouts?"

"Smell of money," the man said, "from the mills."

"Indeed? And with what endeavor are these mills engaged?"

"Why, iron, Son. Iron."

Jack bid the old gentleman a good night; he proceeded only a few yards and was suddenly staring down upon the roof-tops of a prosperous town. It was, he would discover, Raysburg, West Virginia. And then, as he followed the steep streets on down toward Main, as he passed the lamp lighter busy at his work, the long-threatened rain struck. And, following the line of least resistance, Jack found himself urged on toward a great dark curve, out at the edge of things and below the city, where the gas lamps of the down-town were reflected, burning white and yellow against the rain in the slate-gray sky;—and, as his tired mare felt her way over the cobblestones on down the hill, he found that the mysterious line of darkness, lights reflecting yet further back, vague and diffuse, like a scattering of weary jewels, was the great uncoiling form,—obscured by night,—of the Ohio River.

While Sarsfield was thinking of his father, Jack wasn't thinking of Sarsfield at all, for now Jack was striding under the brilliant sun like a conquering king down the main street of the town, of *his* town—Raysburg, in the state of West, by God, Virginia. For thirty-five years he had been doing business here; and the thirty-five years had been good to him. He had built the Middleton Building (fully electrified); he owned the land on which it stood. He had built his stately home on the Island—with its imposing front portico and belvedere overlooking the water. And, as well, Jack owned pieces of a steel mill, a glass plant, two railroads, and, of course, stock in the good, old, reliable Eberhardt cigar works. Jack had every right to be pleased with himself: he had made his first money in the terrible seventies when most Americans had not had two nickels to rub together. Then he had married crafty old Thaddeus Eberhardt's younger daughter, and his father-in-law had taught him to put his money where it would do him the most good: when Thaddeus had said to buy, or sell, or sell short, Jack had bought, or sold, or sold short; and Thaddeus had never been mistaken yet,—or never mistaken for very long. Jack had weathered the depression of the nineties; the panic of last October had scarcely touched him. Recently he had begun to buy real properties; he owned three splendid tracts out the pike, and, by God, wouldn't they be worth a pretty penny in ten years! Now he was buying tenement houses down in Hunkyville, a guaranteed investment: the wretched refuse of Europe's teeming shore had to live somewhere, did it not?

A hopeful newsboy was dogging his steps. "Vanderbilt dog whipped by mastiff!" the lad called out; "Wright Brothers fly a mile!"

But Jack's attention had been caught by a jaunty female form in a navy blue suit. She looked up; and he saw, under an enormous hat drowning in ribbons, the face of a girl he knew from somewhere or other. "Mr. Middleton," she said. He doffed his hat and turned to watch her walk away; and she knew he was watching her—the vixen! He could see it in the way she moved her hips. She gathered her skirts high, stepped off the curb, and showed him a brief glimpse of shapely limbs well above her ankles, trim as could be, flashing between her oxfords and a hint of sky-blue petticoat. Gleefully, he imagined slapping her soundly on her splendidly turned backside. "Hot blood in your old veins yet, Jack, you dog!" he told himself.

"President's daughter puts tack on chair!" the newsboy called out; "Visitor sits on tack in House of Representatives!"

"She didn't!" Jack said.

"She did," the newsboy said. "Read all about it."

"Here, you rogue." Jack handed over a nickel. "Imagine," Jack thought, "the president's daughter—a grown woman and married to boot.

Why, the whole lot of them must be mad as hatters!" He could never resist any gossip about the president or his family; there was no one on the globe Jack hated more than Teddy Roosevelt: a traitor to his class, to the Republican Party, and to the hard-pressed American businessman.

The thought of the speed with which Roosevelt was ruining the country called for a drink; Jack turned toward the nearest saloon and was nearly run down by a young lout going hell-for-leather on a wheel. "Watch it, you old swell!" the boy yelled; and, just at the moment when Jack was about to shout after him a well-phrased comment about his probable parentage, there suddenly, from no identifiable direction, came the sound of an Irish tune played on a whistle. Jack stood, listening. Although it was fast enough to dance to, it was a melancholy tune—a dark tune indeed.

Jack plunged into the saloon, toyed with the notion that it was too early in the day to drink anything stronger than beer, dismissed the notion as contemptible, ordered a whiskey, drank it down, and found himself engaged in a discussion with the bartender about the unmitigated evils of labor unions. "That Gompers is a mad dog," Jack said urgently, "rabid and vicious.—Could I have another, if you wouldn't mind, please, Patrick, you villainous Hibernian."

"By Jesus, you're right," the bartender said (just as he would have said to any of his regular customers who expressed an opinion dead opposite to Jack's), and filled Jack's glass. "You give 'em an inch, they'll take a mile."

"Well, there you are. These men call themselves labor leaders, but I'll name them for what they are—anarchists—and they've inflicted an evil on this country that can never be repaired. Roosevelt may think he can control that vicious pack of mongrels, but no one can control them, throw scraps and bones as they might. Already they've destroyed the apprenticeship system in many of our great industries, and what choice do we have but—"; and here Jack stopped in mid-flight for he had just seen, like an apparition, a man in a crumpled suit of an odd green hue pass by the saloon door playing an Irish reel on a whistle.

"I'll be damned," Jack said. "Who is that?"

"I couldn't say as I've heard the man's name spoken, but sure if he isn't just off the boat."

Both men listened to the bright, piping lilt as it receded in the distance. "Plays well," Jack said.

"Faith, does he not? He plays like an angel."

Jack downed his second drink quickly and stepped out into the blazing sun; it had suddenly struck him that he wanted to have a word with the Irish whistle player. But, turning slowly, looking up and down the street, he could not see a trace of the man. Listening hard, he could not hear a note. The odd fellow might as well have vanished into thin air. Jack rose to the challenge. "I know this town inside and out," he thought; "there's nowhere in Raysburg he can hide from me!"

The town that Jack Middleton claimed as his own had always been a junction,—first for river traffic, then for the National Road, most recently for the Baltimore and Ohio Railroad;—and most Americans, if they traveled, knew Raysburg as a place they had passed through on their way to somewhere else. Trapped between the river on one side and steep hills on the other, the town had spread itself along a line running from the Top Mill in North Raysburg, through the bustling downtown, to South Raysburg where the factories and mills again appeared, and continued—all the way down the river, open hearths blazing twenty-four hours a day like illustrations for Dante's hell. Directly west from the down-town, linked by the grand Wire Suspension Bridge ("the longest single-span suspension bridge in the world," residents proudly proclaimed), across the "front river," lay Raysburg Island with its gracious old homes and acres of farm land; the western side of the Island faced the shallow, slow moving "back river"; the Bridgeport bridge led from the Island to the state of Ohio.

When Karl Eberhardt arrived in the eighteen-thirties (coming not, as Jack claimed, from "East Hesia" but from the historic, old, fortified city of Wittenberg in Prussian Saxony), Raysburg was already distinguished by smoke; as the century wore on and the number of mills increased, so did the proliferation of noxious fumes; by the time of the Civil War, a dense, acrid cloud was pressed perpetually down over the city. Walls of new buildings were begrimed within days; clothes left too long on the line were yellowed; the river absorbed the smoke and the effluence from the mills and turned a mucky brown; in winter the unpaved streets by the mills turned to clinging mud two feet thick, and the smoke made fogs dense as clabber. In the mills Welshmen and Irishmen worked twelve hour shifts for pennies; they poured and puddled molten iron in heat well over a hundred degrees; their wives and children worked in the cotton mill; they crammed together in tiny rooms, without fresh air, slept on dirt floors alive with moss, ate rank pork and bread and molasses, and died at forty. But it was equally true, as Jack Middleton said, that "this has always been a hell of a good town for a man to make a buck," and Karl Eberhardt, who was a trained cigar maker, did not go to work in the mills; with amazing rapidity, he went from selling cigars on the street, to making the cigars himself, to hiring other people to make them for him, to owning the plant that made them, to owning the holding company that owned the plant.

Karl did not confine his interests to cigar manufacturing, but put his money into any venture that appeared likely to turn a profit; early in his career he evinced a fondness for ironworks and began to buy up mills, furnaces, and foundries up and down the river. The Civil War was a godsend: when the ironclad steamships, the *Merrimac* and the *Monitor*, met at Hampton Roads and fought it out to a stand-off, there arose a sudden, insatiable demand for iron plate. Karl owned puddling furnaces and rolling mills that could manufacture good, heavy wrought-iron plate an inch thick; he sold so much iron plate to the Federal Army and Navy that, during the course of the war, he was able to acquire three other mills; the return of peace saw Karl emerge as Raysburg's premier ironmaster—as well as owner, or part owner, of so many, and so diverse, other businesses that it was said that only the Lord God Almighty Himself knew exactly what Karl Eberhardt owned. Karl built a mansion on a hilltop far outside the city and told his elder son, Thaddeus, to go and search for iron ore.

When Karl died in 'eighty-four, the Eberhardt interests were so extensive that each of his two sons inherited millions. Thaddeus had sought and found iron ore; the Eberhardt family owned the largest underground mine in the Lake Superior district; Thaddeus rapidly converted his father's Raysburg Iron Works into the Raysburg Iron and Steel Company, moved into the Eberhardt mansion with his five children to establish the line known as "The Raysburg Eberhardts," and there settled down to pursue his dream of destroying utterly all of his competitors in the valley. Henry, younger by ten years—and restless—saw his chance in the crash of 'ninety-three; he sold most of his local interests to his brother, sailed into the New York market with immense capital, and bought when everyone else was selling; by his wild daring and sheer ruthlessness, he established himself as one of the premier financiers in America; in 'ninety-six he removed to New York and established the line known as "The New York Eberhardts," a family that, at this very moment, was busy pushing its way into the social circles dominated by the Astors and the Vanderbilts. So, if in a brash, booming, go-getter's Northern mill town, money is society, then the Eberhardts were the highest society you could get.

But, although Western Virginia had split off from the Confederacy and Raysburg itself had been fiercely Unionist, there remained an uncrushable spirit to the place that was Southern; and to the Southern sensibility, blood has always counted for more than money; and blood is measured by longevity; and, therefore, no blood in Raysburg could possibly be any better than that of the Raineys. The first of them, Josias Rainey, had been settled on the Island long before George Washington had passed by on his survey. The Raineys had never been noted for displaying any interest whatsoever in written records (or, for that matter, literacy, Jack said), so the exact date when old Josias arrived is uncertain, as is the exact number of his wives or children; what is certain is that the Raineys flourished in the valley (largely, Jack said, because of the alacrity and tenacity with which they slaughtered the indigenous Indians). The clan laid its mark everywhere: Raysburg itself had originally been called Raineysburg; there was a Rainey Road out the pike and a Rainey Street on the Island (which some of the older inhabitants still called Rainey's Island), a Raineysville twenty miles down the river on the Ohio side, and, just short of the Pennsylvania line, a hilltop called Rainey's Point where some Rainey had held off the Indians, or, perhaps (Jack said), they had held off him.

After Josias, the most notable of the Raineys had been the great hero of the Revolutionary War, Kyle, who had ridden with "Light-Horse" Harry Lee. In the centennial year, the Raysburg chapter of the DAR had commissioned from a local stonemason, well known for his funerary angels, a statue of the great Kyle. The choice of this particular historical personage for commemoration (so Jack said) was perhaps influenced by the fact that Mrs. Thaddeus Eberhardt, nee Rainey (Jack's future mother-in-law), had been president of the Raysburg chapter of the DAR for the past fifteen years. All the leading citizens of the town subscribed to the worthy cause (even, with considerable reluctance, Jack himself); and the statue, done in marble, was to stand before the city court house. At the unveiling, a muscular young man was revealed; he was dressed in knee britches, clutched a sabre in one fist, and stared with anguished fixity into the distance. Beneath him the words were boldly carved: KYLE RAINEY. IN THE PURSUIT OF LIBERTY. To Jack the figure appeared hardly to be in pursuit of anything at all—his feet were too firmly planted for that;—but, from the solidity of his stance and the thickness of his sabre, he was obviously (Jack said) about to commence the butchering up of a side of beef.

His curiosity aroused, Jack had sought out Aunt Phemia Rainey, who, at the age of one hundred and one, must surely have remembered the great Kyle. "Well," the old lady said, "I 'spect Uncle Kyle rode with somebody; and if he did, I 'spect he killed as many men as he could lay hands on."

She did, indeed, remember the great Kyle. A bachelor gentleman, he had raised pigs on the south end of the Island, had lived well into his nineties, wore knee-britches his whole life (at least the stone-mason had got that right) long after the style for them had vanished, had, like many of the Raineys, one wandering eye, drank ferocious applejack, hot, seasoned with dried peppers. A year or two before he died, he was arrested for attempting to shoot, with a flintlock rifle, the Indians who were passing through Raysburg on their way to meet with the Great White Father in Washington.

The Raineys appeared to have spent the entire force and energy of the family in the single burst of the great Kyle; after him, a peculiar lassitude descended on the family; and the Raineys nowadays did not do much of anything. The Raineys never displayed the slightest interest in commerce or industry; they owned neither a mill nor a mine; all the Raineys believed in was land. The Raineys still owned three quarters of Raysburg Island; most of the businesses in down-town Raysburg stood on Rainey land and paid rent to the Rainey family; when old Karl Eberhardt decided to build himself a dwelling as big as anything he remembered in Germany and required a hundred acres of the finest land well outside of town to build it on, he had to buy the land from the Raineys. By their sheer persistence, the Raineys had become the most respected blood-line in Raysburg society. But if a visitor from out of town were to stroll around Raysburg Island, turn his back on the majestic homes of the north end and walk south along the unpaved road lined with great Lombardy poplars, he would soon find himself in a setting as agrarian as anything in down-state West Virginia. Because no one bothered to put up fences, our visitor might wander out of one of the well-kept gardens into a wild patch overgrown with hollyhocks and meandering pole beans; he might wend his way through a dozen pecking chickens and a few odd ducks; and then he might encounter a white-bearded fellow in his shirtsleeves—a garrulous, ancient, wholly unprepossessing figure sitting on a rocking chair on the back porch of a run-down farm house staring out at the river; and our visitor would have no way of knowing that this was Daniel Rainey—who owned more land than any other man in the valley.

So, as long as he stayed in Raysburg, Sarsfield thought, he would always know exactly who he was; he had grown up knowing it: with Daniel Rainey as his great-grandfather and Thaddeus Eberhardt as his grandfather, there had never been a possibility that he would grow up without knowing it. And then, to top it all off, there had been his father to tell him, from the earliest age that he could comprehend the words, that the Middletons of Wicklow were not merely society, but *aristocracy*, that one good Middleton (Jack, for instance) was worth more than both the tribes of the kraut-gobbling Eberhardts and the corn-swilling Raineys put together.

But Sarsfield was sick of knowing exactly who he was. When Thaddeus Eberhardt and Daniel Rainey died, Sarsfield would inherit some money from the one, some land from the other, but, at the moment, he had neither; and the preoccupations of the Eberhardts and the Raineys seemed a thousand miles from anything that preoccupied him. And, as for his father—well, all he ever got from him was more blather; he was sick of his father's stories. Sarsfield felt that every time he tried to find his way in life there were old men, and dead men, dragging him down. It had been over forty years since the war, but the bitter old men were still waving the bloody flag; and Sarsfield was sick of the bloody flag, and particularly sick of the glorious dead. He liked his grandfather Eberhardt well enough as a man, but he hated everything he stood for. Sarsfield was sick of financiers and their watered stock and cornered markets and monopolies and trusts. He was sick of the money-mad plutocrats who skinned honest farmers and businessmen and working men to line their own foul pockets. If the unlimited promise of America were to be fulfilled, then the vast exuberance and energy of this most favored of all nations must be harnessed and guided; and the man to do it, as far as Sarsfield was concerned, was the man who was in the right place at the right time—in the White House: the young, vigorous, outspoken Teddy Roosevelt.

But, oh, my God, how slow everything was! Sarsfield was sick of the ward-heelers and tub-thumpers who turned out the Republican vote, sick of the mill owners, sick of the "go-getter" businessmen, sick of his grandfather Thaddeus Eberhardt's great Raysburg Iron and Steel Company that dominated everything in town. He was sick of walking into the shop every day and seeing his father's photograph of that nonentity, President Rutherford B. Hayes, looking back at him with watery, bewildered eyes. He was sick of his father's pronouncements about sound money and expansion and profit. He was sick of hearing his father rant about anarchists and socialists and the imminent collapse of the American republic. He was sick of his father.

With yet another good whiskey under his belt, Jack was sauntering south on the trail of the mysterious whistling Irishman. He was sure he saw the man duck into Nolan's—the lanky, unkempt figure in his crumpled suit of that oddly greenish hue was unmistakable;—but when Jack looked, all he could see were the regulars lined up at the bar. Then, as he stepped out into the sun again, Jack heard the sad, rhythmical whistle all the way down by the railroad tracks. How could the damnable fellow have got so far ahead of him? Jack quickened his pace.

Since he had been a child, Jack had loved the tunes of the Irish; his father's tenantry—however stupid, stubborn, superstitious, backward, and traitorous they might have been—had all of them, to a man, been endowed with the gift of the music; and, to this day, whenever Jack met a wandering Irishman who could play, he always invited him home to take a meal with the help and play a few tunes in the kitchen. (Let no man say that Jack Middleton was not a patron of the arts!) A strange lot, the Irish: they'd call you "Sir" for ten years and on the eleventh have a rising and try to burn your house down around your ears. But they had made a place for themselves in America—there was no doubt about that: strong backs and thick heads were always in demand. Why, your bartender, your janitor, your garbage collector, your cop on the corner—chances are, like as not, he'd be a Paddy from the bogs. The signs reading "No Irish Need Apply" had all but vanished these days; and your Paddy even made a passably good Republican. Yes, the Irish were fitting in just fine. Now it was the Wops and the Dagos you had to watch.

Jack arrived at the B and O line, looked right and left but saw no sign of the elusive green man; annoyed, Jack turned and started back the way he had come. At the foot of Sixteenth, the sappy temperance people had put up a huge billboard reading: SALOONS CANNOT RUN WITHOUT BOYS. HAVE YOU ONE TO SPARE? Within a stone's throw of the sign were four saloons; the long walk had given Jack a thirst; he chose the nearest and stepped inside, felt a minor disruption in his bowels, called for a beer with an egg in it. "Seen anything of an Irishman playing a whistle?" he asked the barman.

"Sure did, Mr. Middleton. He was in here not ten minutes ago. I guess he was headed back up town."

"To hell with him," Jack thought and sipped his beer. Directly over the bar some benighted soul laboring under the misapprehension that he could handle a paintbrush had (years ago, judging from the layers of grime) daubed a huge painting of a satyr pursuing half a dozen nymphs; as badly executed as the figures were, the poor fellow had obviously had a love of the ladies, had endowed them with big, ample backsides and bosoms like watermelons; and Jack was suddenly reminded that it had been months since he'd paid a call on the good Mrs. Smith. "Perhaps tonight," Jack thought. "Yes, that might be the very ticket."

Just on the far side of the county line, only a few hundred yards beyond the interest of the Sheriff, Mrs. Smith had, back in the wild seventies, built herself a house; she had, in fact, established her business about the same time that Jack had established his; but he had not begun to avail himself of her hospitality until ten years later when he had found himself married to Thaddeus Eberhardt's darling daughter;—and, imagining his sour, graying wife, Jack resolved that, yes, tonight was the night for a drive. Once on the National Road, he could give his mare her head; he loved galloping along in the twilight knowing what awaited him: after the turn off at the top of the hill, after the little rattle-trap bridge over Rainey's Creek, after the last breathless dash down the last two miles of dirt road, he would leap out of the sulky, turn over the reins to the darky who sprang up to meet him, step across the veranda, and Mrs. Smith herself would already be there in the doorway, saying: "Why, Jack Middleton, how nice to see you again." Then, in a drawing room more comfortable, more sumptuously furnished, than that in any hotel this side of New York, he would recline at his leisure, in his shirt sleeves, with his feet up, while Mrs. Smith's girls brought him— well, damned near anything that took his fancy: a glass of whiskey, a cigar, a pint of beer, a plate of ribs. Oh, by God, that's how a man should spend his time!

There was no red lantern for Mrs. Smith, no bucket-house piano player; her bully boys stayed out of sight unless they were needed; when they did appear, they were as polite as deacons. Money was never mentioned—and, indeed, never changed hands; later, you would receive a discreet note and then make a deposit to Mrs. Smith's account. No, sir, there was nothing of the South Raysburg cathouse for Mrs. Smith. In her drawing room you might find your-self chatting with a mill owner, a banker, a judge, the mayor of Rays-burg himself. You could, after you had satisfied your baser needs, return to civilized converse with your peers and, perhaps, a gentle-manly game of poker; or, if you weren't in the mood for company, there were alluring side rooms, each decorated in a different exotic style, where you could be alone. And the girls?—Well, that was it, wasn't it? And Jack drank deeply.

None of your starved, consumptive little chickens for Mrs. Smith; her girls were round and voluptuous with flesh enough for a man to get a grip. Styles might change from year to year; but Mrs. Smith knew what the gentlemen liked; and, in her establishment, the styles never changed. She kept her girls so tight-laced they swelled out in the arse and teat like big, wonderful, pink balloons; she kept them in the high-est possible lacquered French heels; they minced around in tiny steps, bent at the waist, everything sticking out and wiggling like cream pud-ding. They were scented like roses, like lilacs, and wore plenty of paint. "That's right," Jack thought, sucking up the last of the foam, "a whore ought to look like a whore!"; and he felt a gratifying stiffening in his good, reliable cock. There was that new one, that blonde Dutch girl from the farms of Pennsylvania (she had run away with a drummer who had left her on the street in Raysburg, so she had been damned lucky to end up at Mrs. Smith's and not in one of those two-bit cribs down-town); my God, she had been blessed like the pride of a dairy farm, that one; and Jack could span her waist with his hands; and all he had to do was point her at it and she'd have old John Peter out and be giving him a wash like a cat with a kitten. "Oh, Lord," Jack prayed fervently, "I'll pass on Zion, just send me a good whore!"; and Jack didn't know how he could constrain himself to wait till nightfall, he was so hot and full of steam, thinking about those big, fat, pink peach halves of her backsides that simply begged to be grabbed and slapped, and how, once they began to engage in serious business, that big, blonde cow could fornicate like a mink.

Jack was out on the street, striding away, up town, his cane swinging; he had already covered four blocks when it occurred to him that he was (good Lord, how did it happen?) the slightest bit unsteady on his feet. The sun was suddenly too hot, too bright; and he was sweating like a nigger at a pole raising; and, suddenly, he heard, quite close to him, an Irish jig played fast on a whistle, dancing feet keeping time to it. He stepped inside; and, by God, he was right back in the first saloon where he'd started. It was too dark in there, full of shadows; he could not, for a moment, make anything out. Then he saw one of the oddest sights he had ever encountered: that strange, lean Irishman was playing a jig and dancing to it. The boys were pitching pennies at him. Jack had not seen anyone dance like that since he had left Ireland; and he had never seen anyone dance to his own tune. He fumbled in his pocket and threw the man a quarter.

From deep in his shadow the green man gave Jack a nod. Jack found himself leaning against the bar with a whiskey in his hand that he could not recall asking for; and the man in the shadows finished his tune to the applause of everyone. "You're a good man yourself," the bartender called out; Jack even called out, "Good man!" and then wondered why he'd done it.

The Irishman gathered up the change, walked directly to Jack, and offered his hand: "Ah, 'tis a fine sunny afternoon, is it not, Captain Jack? I see you're after taking a whiskey. Will you take another?"

"I will," Jack said. He felt muddled, confused; he wished he could lie down.

"Quinn," the man said; and Jack felt a chill of apprehension. "It's a common enough name," Jack thought; "there are thousands of Irishmen named Quinn."

"I'm pleased to meet you, Mr. Quinn," Jack said; "You play marvelously well. May I call you by your Christian name?"

"Faith, if it isn't the same as yours. John—Sean, we'd call it back home."

"Here's to you, Sean Quinn," Jack said.

The man looked back with oddly compelling eyes blue as a deep-bottomed lake. "*Bas in Erin*," he said; and then, after a moment, Jack remembered that it meant: "May you die in Ireland."

2

At the very moment when Jack was taking his glass of whiskey with the peripatetic Irishman, his wife, Alice, was resting on the glider on the back porch of the Middleton home, taking a cup of tea flavored with the fresh mint that grew wild on the banks of the river. Alice was deeply immersed in the romantic world of Marie Corelli,—so immersed, in fact, that when she momentarily raised her eyes from the page before her and looked down across the sloping lawn, the sunlight gleaming on the Ohio River might as well have been a painted backdrop, so less compelling was it than the lovely, pink-and-mauve cobweb of sentimental phantasy spun by her novel. Alice Middleton suffered from a nervous condition that had constrained her, some years before, to abandon all but the most subdued of activity; today, however, she felt better than she had in weeks; and something about the fine, high drama of the tale, with its setting in the drawing rooms of London, reminded her (she could not have said precisely why) of her formidable mother; and she wondered if she were not, perhaps, feeling strong enough to pay a visit to the Eberhardt mansion. But then she considered that she would have to summon Mrs. O'Hara and request that Mr. O'Hara prepare her carriage; and then she would have to change her tea gown for a proper afternoon *toilette* (which would have to include veil and parasol to ward off the hot afternoon sun that she knew, from previous experience, might cause her to have a relapse); and then she would have to endure the forty minute ride out the pike; *and then she would have to sit and talk to her mother*; and—Oh, it was all simply far too tiring to contemplate! She would, instead, in the cool of the evening, write her mother a long letter. Her daughterly duties thus concluded, she drew her bottle of nerve tonic from its hiding place at the bottom of her sewing basket and added several drops to her tea cup. She sipped, tasted the familiar, consoling flavor of licorice, and returned to Marie Corelli. Long ago Alice Middleton had determined to take what pleasure she might from each passing day, so she no longer wasted her time brooding over the events of a marriage from which there was no escape short of the blessed peace of heaven; but, if she had been compelled to tear her attention away from her novel long enough to consider, once again, the twenty-six years she had spent with the man, she should have said that marrying Jack Middleton had been the biggest mistake of her life.

Alice Eberhardt had been a slender, pretty, delicate child who had been taught obedience from her earliest years and thus had received the full imprint of her mother's shaping will,—for Mrs. Thaddeus Eberhardt (nee Amanda Rainey), who had been thwarted by her first daughter, was not about to be gainsaid by her second. The elder girl, Mathilda, might as well have sprung straight from her mother as a pure Rainey, so little did she evince any of the Eberhardt blood; and, indeed, as Mathilda came of age and confronted her mother, the inflexible Rainey will met the inflexible Rainey will—with a consequence like a reenactment of the recent, great conflict between the states. Mrs. Eberhardt won many a bloody skirmish; but Mathilda, with the staying power of youth to her advantage, in the end won the war. A big, plain, healthy girl, Mathilda "did not care a packet of pins" about proper deportment, polite society, fashionable attire, or, in short, any of the plans her mother had laid for her; she married beneath her, bore five children, all of whom lived, and by now had become a robust, loud, laughing, jolly grandmother whose inexorable calls upon Alice (made on the first Monday of every month) sent her younger sister to bed for days.

Alice, however, had received a proper education: she had been guided and constrained at every turn. Unlike her elder sister, Alice had not been overseen in her earliest years by a round, gentle, colored girl, but rather by a strict nurse-maid imported from England; and later, the shy child had been further instructed by a severe, gray, spinster governess from Boston. At fourteen, the demure Miss Alice had been sent to an exacting, old-fashioned boarding school with an excellent reputation for the most thorough "finishing" of young ladies; at eighteen, the fashionable (some said "affected") Miss Eberhardt had returned to Raysburg and had been given a proper "coming out" ball—the most elegant the city had ever seen. Alice Eberhardt was a beauty; none would deny it. She was also a lady of such profound refinement that few of the eligible young men of the city could be induced to come within ten feet of her; and no one could envision a proper match for this paragon. But, when Alice Eberhardt married John C. Middleton in the spring of 'eighty-two, those who professed themselves surprised (or even shocked) should not have been. The energetic, garrulous Irishman may have arrived in town with nothing more than a few dollars and a cart full of cameras; but, in less than ten years, he had built a most lucrative and flourishing business; and the Eberhardts admired nothing if not the ability to make money. Jack's fondness for the bottle had not yet become apparent; when he was in polite society, his manners were impeccable; and, in fact, there were many who claimed that they had never, on the commonplace streets of Raysburg, encountered a more elegant and polished gentleman. That Jack was so foreign, so courtly, so *European* made him attractive to Alice:—he was so very like the characters in the British romances she read in the privacy of her room.

Within the first weeks of her marriage, Alice discovered that the crude animal needs of the male sex were far more beastly and intolerable than she had imagined even in the most naïve moments of her girlhood; but whether Jack Middleton's were worse, better, or the same as those of other men, she had no way of knowing, for there were some things a lady could not discuss with anyone—except, perhaps, her mother; and, in her most airy flights of phantasy, Alice could not imagine discussing this particular matter with her mother. It took Alice considerably longer—several years in fact—to discover that there existed a profound difference of opinion between herself and her husband concerning the obligations imposed upon one by having been born to the highest level of society. Alice, in the absence of any intelligence that might have convinced her otherwise, had assumed that she and Jack, once married, would immediately take up their proper responsibilities,—that they would entertain on a lavish scale, move amongst the right people, educate their small son as befit a gentleman, and, in short, set an example for the lower classes. But Jack, for his part, did not give a hang for anything that called itself society in this provincial "hick" town; his own blood, he believed, was better than any to be found in the Ohio Valley—if not, indeed, in the entire United States of America;—and, moreover, if social standing had any meaning at all, it had to mean exactly what it had meant to him back in Ireland: that he could do anything he damned well pleased.

Sarsfield, as soon as he was old enough to take cognizance of the world around him, was aware of the conflict between his parents. He had memorized his mother's motto—"prestige demands responsibility"—from such an early age that he seemed always to have known it. People in genteel society, she said, must live up to the best and finest traditions. Charm of manner, wit, consideration of others, tolerance, and, above all, tact, she said, are the marks of true ladies and gentlemen. "Boys, as they grow older," she said once—and only once—but in a such a quiet, fear-laden voice that Sarsfield was chilled to the marrow, "are subjected to terrible, terrible temptations," and, with that, she took Sarsfield's hands into hers, drew him close, and stared directly into his eyes with a look of profound melancholy that he could never forget: "Just remember, you are never alone, Sarsfield, *never*! *The eyes of Our Lord are always upon you.*" She taught Sarsfield that the most important thing in life is to maintain the old standard of Christian morality, good manners, and self-control. Her own manners and self-control were perfect: Sarsfield could not recall an occasion upon which she had ever raised her voice to him.

Jack Middleton's voice, however, was raised most of the time. Jack shouted at his family, at the servants, at strangers on the street. Jack was capable of oaths so extraordinarily vile that Sarsfield's blood froze in his veins; and, if his mother were present, he blushed with shame upon her behalf. Just as his wife did, Jack had much advice to pass on to Sarsfield—most of it delivered at the top of his lungs. "This here's America, boy," he would yell in a mock West Virginia accent, "and the only thing that counts is the almighty dollar!" He taught Sarsfield that the most important thing in life is to take care of yourself, because nobody else is going to do it for you; and Sarsfield learned quickly enough never to ask his father's help in anything, for Jack would always respond with the words: "You know what the mountain folk say, don't you, son?—*Root, hog, or die!*" Sarsfield had memorized his father's motto—"in business, you don't have friends and you don't have enemies; you only have customers"—from such an early age that he seemed always to have known it. "The dollar, the dollar, the dollar, the dollar!" Jack would chant, his entire teaching boiled down to these two words, as he beat time on the back of his son's head; then, seizing Sarsfield under his arms, spinning him through the air, and settling him, finally, atop his shoulders, Jack would cap it all with a gleeful shout: "*In God we trust, all others cash!*"

Sarsfield did his best to please both parents, but it was not easy. Jack would ignore his son for days; but then, with no warning, he would spring upon Sarsfield with a game that never varied. "Put 'em up," he would yell; "Come on, you little bastard, fight me like a man!" There was no escaping; Jack would pursue his son until he cornered him and then proceed to pummel him with light, stinging blows. Sarsfield could not avoid this game by crying, or hiding, or screaming; he learned that the only way out was to swallow his tears, make tiny fists, and fight back. The sport would continue until Sarsfield had been driven into paroxysms of infant rage; when he had at last been goaded into attacking his father with blind, murderous fury—punching, kicking, howling, biting—Jack would finally relent, burst into laughter, and say: "That's it, son! That's the way a man fights—*no holds barred!*"

These mock fights left Sarsfield utterly exhausted; he would fall into bed, sleep for half a day, and wake to find himself back in his mother's domain where he was expected to speak in a voice just above a whisper and to walk carefully on his toes so that the heels of his shoes did not make a distressing clatter on the floor. The seamstress who made his mother's clothes also made his; his standard attire was a jacket and a plaited kilt skirt; he remembered having dozens of these outfits, in serge or wool for "every day" and velvet for church. Boys were supposed to wear dark colors; and he remembered olive, prune, navy, Van Dyke brown, and the usual plaids. The jackets were trimmed in fancy braid and sometimes finished with smoked pearl buttons or satin nail heads; and these costumes were completed far too often with a ribbon bow and matching sash. The over-all effect created by his costume, particularly when combined with the ringlets curled into his long hair by his mother's maid, might well, in Raysburg, West Virginia, have proven fatal to a little boy other than Sarsfield. He, however, had been trained by his father and quickly devised a foolproof method of communication with other little boys who, it seemed, did not care a hang about manners and self-control: when one of them said a harsh word, or, for that matter, even appeared to be *considering* saying it, Sarsfield instantly delivered his left fist (for he was a "southpaw") into the center of the offending face. Mothers on the north end of the Island wondered how on earth that polite little Middleton boy who went about in skirts could also have become the acknowledged king of bloody noses.

As odd as it might seem, Alice Middleton was convinced that her son had been cursed with a constitution as delicate as her own. Little Sarsfield suffered from terrible nightmares from which he awoke sobbing; he would stare wildly about, not recognizing his mother or nurse, and often would continue in this frightening state for hours afterward. Old "Doc" Anderson, who had attended the Eberhardt family for thirty years, examined the boy; the diagnosis was congestion of the brain brought about by nervous exhaustion; a quiet, sheltered life was recommended. This was exactly the news that Alice had expected; she was appalled at the frequency with which Sarsfield was becoming embroiled in fisticuffs with other little boys on the Island (she somehow managed not to notice that he usually emerged victorious from these encounters); and she had, by then, resolved—secretly—to protect Sarsfield for as long as possible from the disgusting, low, animal-like crudities of the male sex.

Citing Doc Anderson as her authority, Sarsfield's mother restricted his playmates to his girl cousins. Having an aunt, three uncles, and a great-uncle of the Eberhardts; so many Rainey aunts and uncles that it took him years to sort them all out; more distant relatives amongst the Staubs; and aunts and uncles by marriage amongst the Revingtons and Ebelings; Sarsfield was confronted with a plethora of girl cousins. His favorite was his great-uncle Henry Eberhardt's petted daughter, Julia—a giggling, lively little sprite two years younger than himself. Julia was the most excessively beribboned, ringleted, flounced, and petticoated of any of the girls; to Sarsfield, she was as magical as a fairy princess—and she made him laugh; to Alice, little Julia looked and acted exactly the way a little girl *should* look and act and was, therefore, the ideal, heaven-sent playmate for her son. It was arranged that Sarsfield and Julia should spend much of their time together.

Jack Middleton, meantime, believed that there was nothing what-soever wrong with his son that getting him away from the pernicious influence of his mother would not cure. Jack, however, had weightier matters on his mind than the rearing of children; the advice he gave his son, he himself took; and in the pursuit of the dollar, he was so little at home that Sarsfield continued largely under his mother's tutelage.

When he turned six, Sarsfield was permitted to abandon his plaited skirts for short pants or, until he rebelled, the hateful velvet Fauntleroy costume worn with lace collars and patent leather slippers; and he was sent, not to the new public school on the Island where, as his mother claimed, he should not have received a proper education, but out the pike to Miss Crawford's. Housed in the old, antebellum Crawford family mansion, this was a venerable Raysburg institution that functioned primarily as a finishing-school for society girls but also accepted a small and select number of boys at the grammar school level. There Sarsfield proceeded at a break-neck pace through the *McGuffey's Readers* until he could soon enjoy unaided the works of Louisa May Alcott and Susan Coolidge; he learned to write a highly adorned hand that could effortlessly transform capital letters into birds and flowers, to memorize and recite poetry with the appropriate dramatic gestures, and to comport himself in a manner that would have been proper to a young gentleman in the lovely lost decade before the war,—as remembered fondly and inaccurately by his maiden-lady teachers, the youngest of whom was sixty-two.

Luckily for Sarsfield, Miss Crawford's was also blessed with the presence of the horse-faced, mannish Miss Sarah Winnette, who recognized in the shy boy a passion for science equal to her own and taught him so much of mathematics, chemistry, and physics that his grounding in these topics could scarcely have been improved. He also, by the time he turned twelve, had learned to dance the quadrille and the "german," construe simple French, distinguish at a glance fine muslin from shoddy, play the piano badly, comprehend the enormously complicated etiquette of paying calls, and know whether or not a young lady were dressed properly for any given occasion—and if she were not, exactly in what details she had failed.

When he was in the company of women, Sarsfield did his best to live up to his mother's oft repeated adage that children should be seen and not heard. If he sat quietly without speaking and pretended to be absorbed in a toy or a picture book, the ladies would forget about him and say many fascinating things. Listening carefully, he began to figure out how the world was put together;—and, with his family, that took considerable figuring out. Drinking was never mentioned, yet Sarsfield knew that his father drank; he even learned to differentiate amongst his father's various drunken states: when Jack's face was flushed purple and his jaw was grimly set, Sarsfield knew that he was about to hear the hated words: "Put 'em up, you little bastard!"; when Jack was singing in a raucous baritone louder than the hoofbeats of his galloping horse, Sarsfield knew that he could expect an hour of rough affection ("Come here, Sars, my little man, and tell me all about yourself!); when Jack was lying on the front lawn or crawling about in the rosebushes, Sarsfield could—at least most of the time—talk him into the house and into bed; but when Jack had "the black mood" on him, the only thing for it was to stay out of his way or Sarsfield would find himself knocked halfway across the room. The doings of ladies of questionable virtue were never openly discussed, yet Sarsfield knew that when his father vanished for days at a time, he was visiting with someone called "Mrs. Smith,"—just as he knew that this woman's name must never be spoken aloud. And Sarsfield knew—from Jack's pained, sweating white face and his hair-trigger temper—when his father was sober. Jack sober was worse than Jack drunk; Jack sober was the worst of all possible worlds. Luckily, Jack never stayed sober for long.

The year that Sarsfield turned twelve, there had been a storm brewing up between his parents for months. Ostensibly it was over whether the Middletons should follow the exodus of the other society families from the Island and remove out the pike. Sarsfield's mother held the opinion that the Island was rapidly becoming a place where genteel people would no longer wish to raise their children; Jack said that was ridiculous,—that if it was good enough for the Raineys, it was good enough for the Middletons, and, moreover, his money was going into business expansion and he had none left over for such a hair-brained scheme. This dispute, however—like all the disputes between the Middletons—was about a far more serious question than whether or not to leave the Island; it arose from the long-standing difference of opinion between Jack and his wife about the responsibilities of their social position. He had, at first, given his wife free rein to play the socialite, Jack said, and in this, he had made a deadly mistake; he had allowed her to have her own maid—as well as a housekeeper!—to gad about town in her own carriage, to spend a king's ransom on her wardrobe, to send their son out to Miss Crawford's to be turned into a molly-coddle when the Jefferson Public Grammar School should have been plenty good enough for him; but now, by God, enough was enough! What did she think, that he could go down and pull dollars out of the river like so many catfish?

As these arguments became more bitter and frequent, Jack was seen to be drinking more than ever. Then, in the fall of 'ninety-five, Jack suddenly "dried out" and remained sober for the longest period Sarsfield could remember. Shouting in his best orator's voice, Jack harangued his wife day after day about her profligate expenses. He abused the house-keeper, and she quit. Jack appeared to have given up sleeping: till three or four in the morning Sarsfield could hear his father's huge, ranting voice. Jack counted his wife's frocks, shoes, gloves, presented her with an itemized list, and said, in a deadly tone: "Would you be so kind, my dear, as to account for this untoward, insane, and decadent expendi-ture?" Jack was up at dawn screaming at the maid. She quit too. Sarsfield and his mother tip-toed about like wraiths.

One evening Sarsfield's mother was preparing to go out to her liter-ary club. "Where the hell d'you think you're going?" Jack demanded; and, just as if somehow he might not have noticed that she had gone out every first Thursday of the month for years, she explained it to him.

"That is the most thoroughly moronic proposition I have ever heard," Jack said; he was speaking quietly, and that was worse than if he had been shouting. "You? Read a book and comment upon it? Good God! *McGuffey's First Reader*, perhaps. That I might believe. 'The cat is on the mat.' Yes, you might manage that.—The problem, my dear Alice, is that I have been far too lenient with you all these years, and you are giving yourself airs. To begin with, the brain of a woman is somewhat less considerably developed than that of your average cricket; and you, my dear, in particular, are one of the most vicious, depraved, and cretinous of your entire devious, dim-witted, traitorous sex.—I forbid you to leave this house."

Sarsfield's mother, as much of a lady as she might be, was not half Rainey and half Eberhardt for nothing: she dressed and prepared to leave. Jack stopped her at the front door and slapped her full in the face. Sarsfield sprang to his mother's aid. His father seized him, and—kicking and pummeling him the whole way—dragged him out to the carriage house where he thrashed him with a harness, shouting out: "This is my house. Do you hear me? *Mine!* My land. My money. *And you're my son,* you wretched little bastard!"

This was not the first instance in which Sarsfield had been similarly disciplined by his father; but this was the most violent occasion;—and this time Sarsfield resolutely refused to cry. Jack, however, wept buckets, shouted out to the hired man that he would have his mare and he would have her *now*, leapt into his sulky, and galloped away into the night.

Jack was gone the better part of a week. He came back in the middle of the night to discover that his wife had locked him out. He smashed the bay window, crawled through it, cutting himself on the broken glass (Sarsfield, following his father's progress from hiding places in shadows, saw the blood splattered on the rug), kicked his way through his wife's bedroom door and shouted at her that he would not have it,—he would not be kept out, he would, by God, be master in his own house.

Cursing himself for a coward, Sarsfield hid in his room; he heard his father yelling at his mother; he heard falling furniture, breaking glass; and he heard the sickening, dull smack of heavy blows,—heard his father begin to make sounds that were far more frightening than the ranting voice they had replaced: terrible grunting noises like those torn from the guts of a ditch-digger when exerting himself against the resistance of hard clay. Sarsfield's mother began to shriek in a way he had never heard before—as though she were suffering the very agony of the damned; then her screams gradually abated and were transformed into a heart-broken sobbing. Sarsfield heard his father storm out of the house; then he lay in bed for hours listening to his mother weeping. He wanted to do something, say something to her; but, nauseated and terrified, he remained where he was, the blanket pulled over his head. The following morning, Sarsfield's mother appeared heavily veiled; but Sarsfield could see that her entire face was misshapen and discolored, that one of her eyes was swollen entirely shut, that her lip was split. She took Sarsfield to the Eberhardt mansion where they stayed a week.

Grandmother Eberhardt—who had been Amanda Rainey—was an enormous woman who wore the most opulent, thickly decorated dresses with pearls; she had the Rainey wandering eye, and she had always scared Sarsfield half to death. He was withdrawn into a distant corner, pretending to look at a book, when he heard her say to his mother: "He may be a rotter, Alice, but you married him. A woman's place is with her husband. *Now you go back and live with him.*" Nine months (practically to the day) from the night that Jack had crashed through the bay window, Sarsfield's little brother was born.

The baby was named Kyle Rainey Middleton. The choice of name, Sarsfield thought, was a perfect example of Jack's devilish jokes. No one could possibly object; Grandmother Eberhardt might even be pleased that the great hero of the Rainey family was being remembered; but, at the same time, the new little baby had been given a name that would make him, for ever after, the butt of his own father's cruel humor.

Sarsfield could not understand what had happened; it was as though *nothing* had happened: the state of his parents' marriage appeared to be exactly what it had been before. Could it be, he wondered, that this was how things were to be lived after one has grown up?—that, after the most painful and unspeakable of events have transpired—events that should have inexorably altered the course of one's life forever—then one simply forgets and goes about one's business as though one's life has been altered not in the least? Is that what his mother meant by "tolerance and tact"—bearing the unbearable? He studied his parents to see if he could ascertain any profound change in them. His mother, of course, was constrained by her condition to pass many months in her bed; Sarsfield visited in her room and waited for her to speak about what had happened, but she never did so. Jack was drinking, or not drinking, as the case might be, just as he had done before; if he felt any remorse, he did not show it.

Since he had been a child, Sarsfield had often experienced difficulty falling asleep; now he began to suffer from what could truly be called "insomnia"—a curse that was to plague him for years to come. He took to barricading his bedroom door with furniture—against what he could not have said, for he did not, by any stretch of the imagination, expect his father to attack him in the night. He remembered Doc Anderson's words (for he had heard them often enough repeated by his mother) and lay in bed, wide awake, sure that if he were not soon to enjoy a good night's sleep, he would begin to experience congestion of the brain. He prepared everything he might need: an handkerchief folded under his pillow in case he should have to blow his nose, a glass of water on the bed table, a chamber pot under the bed. He often, just at the point of drifting off, felt a terrible sense of suffocation, so the window had to be raised high; he often fancied that a terrible, dark spectre had, at precisely the moment when he had not been looking, slipped by him to hide in the closet, so the door must be opened wide and lit by a student lamp. If he neglected any of these preparations, insomnia was assured. If nothing else worked, he found it calming to solve long problems in physics, geometry, or trigonometry.

The only bright spot in Sarsfield's life was his cousin, Julia Eberhardt; she also attended Miss Crawford's, so he saw her every day. Julia was ten now and could no longer be called by her nursery name of "Cricket"; they fell into a game in which they played to the hilt all the rules of genteel deportment, addressed each other as "Miss Eberhardt" and "Master Middleton." They strolled arm in arm like grown-ups; they always chose each other in dancing class; he read fairy-tales and poetry to her, helped her with her arithmetic. In the wonderfully long, sunny days of the summer vacation, they played together at Aunt Ida's or at the Eberhardt mansion where they were given ponies to ride; Julia loved to gallop and stuck to her pony like a burr. Julia also loved to run; she still wore her skirts quite short, and when Sarsfield closed his eyes, he fancied he could still see her slender white legs flashing beneath a flurry of petticoats. In the evenings the Eberhardt cousins—the number varied from as few as six to as many as fourteen—produced elaborate theatrical spectacles on the small stage, complete with curtain, which had been built for that purpose in the carriage house. Julia was a natural actress who threw herself deeply into whatever rôle she assumed; playing prince to her Rapunzel, Sarsfield opened his eyes and was astonished to see that she was shedding real tears to restore his sight.

Sarsfield and Julia were so obviously smitten with calf-love that they were a source of amusement to the ladies sipping their tea on the verandah; but the cousins were so young that it occurred to no one that they should be chaperoned, and they wandered alone throughout the grounds of the entire Eberhardt estate. Standing by the small trickle of Rainey's Creek, they held hands one evening as the sky turned a golden pink, then turned to look into each other's eyes as they discovered themselves lost in a strange, breathless moment unlike anything either of them had ever experienced heretofore. "Let's play at kissing like grown-ups," Julia suggested.

Sarsfield had never seen grown-ups kissing, so he did not know quite how to go about it; he bent and brushed his lips against her cheek. Julia had certainly seen grown-ups kissing and knew better; she turned her head and pressed her lips into his. He would have thought that gesture would have concluded the business; but Julia threw her arms around his neck and played out the kiss she had once seen transacted between her mother's maid and the gardener. Sarsfield was halfway between twelve and thirteen; he felt a desperate stirring of his emotions; a vital force swept through him that was at once the sweetest thing he had ever known and the most painful; he was badly frightened and held on to her all the harder because of that. He would not have said that what they were doing was "naughty"; nor would he have called it by the more seriously grown-up word "bad"; once Sarsfield had sipped from a glass of his father's and had known instantly that such liquid fire was not for children;—such a kiss was not for children. He released his hold on her; she clung to his hands. He did not know what he could possibly say to her; but Julia, to his surprise, expressed precisely what he was feeling: "Oh, Sarsy, *that's not playing, is it?*"

Walking back up the hill to the Eberhardt mansion, holding her small hand in his, he was certain that he loved her more than anyone—perhaps more than life itself. "I shan't kiss you again until we're married," she told him.

In the fall of 'ninety-six, Jack summarily announced that his son's days of playing with girls were over; he put Sarsfield into long pants, informed him that he need no longer trouble his Eberhardt relations with his presence, abruptly withdrew him from Miss Crawford's, and,—appearing to have forgotten every word he had ever uttered about "untoward expenditures,"—sent him to the far more costly Raysburg Lancastrian Academy where, Jack said, the little molly-coddle was sure to receive a proper education—and high time too! Sarsfield's mother was still suffering her long convalescence; a nurse-maid had been engaged to care for little Kyle, and Alice did not leave her room; if she had any objections to the new regime Jack had imposed upon Sarsfield, she kept them to herself.

Nothing in his life heretofore had prepared Sarsfield for the Academy: in the blink of an eye, he passed from a world comprising entirely girls to one comprising entirely boys. New students at the Academy were traditionally subjected to a brutal "ragging"; but Sarsfield was singled out for treatment that was particularly cruel and unrelenting. All the boys had nick-names; and Sarsfield was at once dubbed "The Little Lord"—often with the vile epithets "Miss Middleton" and "sissy" added for good measure. A sentence he had uttered in all innocence during his first days was used thereafter to torment him; whenever he stepped through the main doors of the school onto the walk leading to the grassy pitch where football was played, he could be sure of hearing from another boy, who would immediately have struck a pose of languidly effeminate foppishness, the hateful line: "Oh, dear me, I *do* believe the day shall prove to be raw-ther inclement." His carefully prepared lessons were torn from his grasp and ripped to shreds before his eyes; his cap and shoes were stripped from him and thrown into the urinals; dozens of times a day he was knocked sprawling. When he remonstrated a boy with the words, "Oh, don't be such a blasted ass," the entire class took up the phrase and gleefully chanted it back to him in the accent he had delivered it: "Blahsted ahss, blahsted ahss, blahsted ahss!"

After some weeks of this treatment, Sarsfield surmised that once again his mother's advice about "manners and self-control" did not "fit the bill"; and once again he began to take recourse in his good left fist. As soon as it was discovered that The Little Lord would fight, the "ragging" began to abate; but each morning Sarsfield had to steel himself to face the day ahead. Twice he was flogged for fighting, yet he knew that he could not stop fighting—that he must be prepared to swing "at the drop of a hat." He was sure that he would forever prefer the company of girls to the company of boys; he missed Julia terribly; alone in his bed at night he wept; life, it appeared, was a cruel affair indeed.

Arch Kimbell was the largest boy in Sarsfield's class. A handsome, strapping lad with flashing dark eyes, Arch had the misfortune to have been born of a father who was the owner of a dry-goods shop; and so the Academy boys, scions of Raysburg money and already vicious snobs, had, behind his back, dubbed him "the Counter-Jumper"; not one of them, however, had the courage to say it to his face, for Arch, in the first week of the school year, had quickly and thoroughly thrashed a lordly Sophomore. Since then, no one had ventured to cross him. For reasons neither of them could have explained, Sarsfield and Arch Kimbell hated each other upon sight. As the grandson of Thaddeus Eberhardt, Sarsfield automatically was allied with the other boys of genteel birth against this interloper whose father was a common tradesman; Sarsfield was so eager to be liked, that he welcomed the alliance; but he soon found himself forced into a ghastly position from which he could find no means of escape: he was being dared to confront this mature, self-assured boy who, although no older than Sarsfield, already had shoulders that looked as broad as a stevedore's.

After several sleepless nights, Sarsfield decided that he would rather be beaten senseless by the huge lout than go on interminably at the Academy without a friend, so, one morning before classes began, he threw down the gauntlet: "How's your trade these days, Mr. Counter-Jumper? Got any new muslin in the shop?"

"We've got some fine new muslin, Miss Middleton," came the response, "want to make yourself a petticoat?"

Sarsfield swung at that; but, for the first time in his life, he did not connect; the bigger boy had expected the blow and easily dodged out of the way. Sarsfield flung himself bodily at his opponent; the rules of Queensberry were abandoned upon the instant for the rules of Kilkenny: the two fell upon each other with a fury the likes of which had seldom been seen at the Academy. Sarsfield was flat on his back, his head being pounded into the dirt as he endeavored to get his thumbs somewhere near the other boy's eyes, when, suddenly, it was all over. He saw hanging over him the round, florid face of Mister Sloan, known as "Old Gutbuckets"—the venerable personage who had taught the boys their history and boxing for twenty years. "Middleton, eh? Fighting again, eh? Well, well, well. You've been warned, sir, indeed you have."

The Academy had her most ancient, hoary, and venerable of traditions—as indispensable for the atmosphere of a proper boys' school as the hundred-year-old ivy growing on "Old Main"—and one of them was that serious fights must be settled properly: in the ring with gloves on. The matter was concluded that day after classes had ended; Sarsfield was too frightened to show it; he entered the first round as though in a trance, was knocked down repeatedly. Not only was Arch Kimbell some fifty pounds heavier and several inches taller than he was, but Sarsfield was confronting a natural athlete who moved with the speed and grace of a wildcat; it was, as the boys crowded around the ring were saying to each other, "no match at all."

Between rounds, Sarsfield gulped water and told himself that if he did not do *something* he would be slaughtered like a lamb; he came back swinging, and, oblivious to the blows that were landing on his face and arms, "clinched" again and again, to pound his opponent's hard belly. He kept hearing old Sloan's voice: "Break, sir, break! Stand and fight, sir!" Sarsfield stood and tried to "slug it out"; he was struck with a solid right cross, sent sprawling. He pushed himself to his knees; the ring seemed to be wobbling under him; blood was streaming from his nose. He regained his footing, was knocked down again as the round ended. "You've shown us you're game, sir, throw in the towel," was whispered into his ear. Sarsfield shook his head.

These matches must continue, so the tradition had it, until one of the boys cries enough; to stop the fight before then would be unthinkable.

Sarsfield would not give up; it was not something that he had decided to do; it was just something he did—he knew not why. He lost count of the number of times he was knocked down; his eyes were rapidly swelling shut; the blood from his nose could not be staunched; eventually he was so blown and beaten that he could no longer raise his arms. Each time he was struck to the floor, he forced himself to his feet, pushed himself in the direction of the other boy (Sarsfield could no longer quite remember who the other boy was or why he was fighting him) and tried to swing.

Old Gut-buckets was just upon the point of breaking precedent and stopping the fight when Arch Kimbell burst into tears. "I won't hit him again, sir!" he cried out. "It's not right, and I won't do it." Arch wrapped his arm around Sarsfield's shoulders, dragged him to his feet and supported him. "Jeeze, kid," he whispered, "you're game as they come!"

"I do believe, gentlemen," Gut-buckets Sloan proclaimed, "that this fight is a draw."

Sarsfield and Arch Kimbell became the best of friends. Each could not quite recall exactly why he had formerly disliked the other. Sarsfield saw Arch as a paragon of the manly virtues; Arch considered Sarsfield to be the perfect gentleman; and their intimacy grew at such a pace that soon neither could imagine how he had managed to live his life for nearly thirteen years without the other in it.

Arch envied Sarsfield's social position; but further acquaintance tempered this envy and made him appreciate his own people all the more. Arch was genuinely "tickled" by Jack Middleton and pronounced him "a card," was awed by Mrs. Middleton and claimed that, until he met her, he had never understood what the word "lady" meant; but he also secretly thought Sarsfield's family "a bit queer" and would not have traded places for all of Thaddeus Eberhardt's millions. He was sure that if he, like Sarsfield, had been forced to spend seven years at Miss Crawford's with a bunch of silly girls, he would have killed himself. He resolved to stand by Sarsfield and "show him the ropes." Sarsfield found Arch's parents (unlike his own) everything that ordinary American parents ought to be: Mrs. Kimbell was round and jolly and produced vast quantities of food at a moment's notice; Mr. Kimbell was a gentle soul who was determined "to give this great boy of mine every advantage." It was costing Mr. Kimbell nearly every cent he made to send Arch to the Academy; when Sarsfield considered this sacrifice, he felt humbled. He resolved to stick by his new friend through thick and thin. Together, these two were ready to take on the world. They took on the Academy and made their mark there.

In the winter of 'ninety-six, Uncle Henry and Aunt Ida Eberhardt removed to New York; and that was the last Sarsfield saw of his cousin Julia. By then he had resolved to forget his childhood, so he put thoughts of his cousin firmly out of his mind. The Academy aided him in this resolve: the vigorous life there left him with little inclination for brooding over the past. Gut-buckets Sloan taught the boys that boxing was a science; Sarsfield and Arch worked-out under the old man's watchful eye. They shadow boxed, sparred, punched the heavy bag and the light; they exercised with Indian clubs and barbells, threw medicine balls at each other; they ran around the track, puffing like steam engines. Sarsfield was too light to be any credit to the football team; but he was an enthusiastic participant nonetheless. At his scholastics, he continued to excel in mathematics and science but, with everything else, muddled through as best he could.

At the Academy the study of literature was considered an onerous but necessary duty: a proper gentleman was expected to have read enough to have acquired a certain "polish," but he was not supposed to have much enjoyed the experience. The boys slogged through the easier plays of Shakespeare in editions from which the improper speeches of gate keepers and grave diggers had been carefully expurgated—and read, from other eminently dead or moribund authors, selections so refined and uplifting as to sink at once any young, spirited, male reader into the profoundest of stupefaction. On their own Sarsfield and Arch devoured "penny dreadfuls" like peanuts, moved on to popular romances and adventure tales, and discovered at last those two most compelling yarn-spinners of the day: Kipling and Richard Harding Davis. They pronounced Kipling a "genuine stem-winder," but they adored Dick Davis—who, in his broad-shouldered, square-jawed, immaculately groomed, vigorously chivalrous person embodied everything they longed to become. Rotogravure pictures of Davis adorned their walls; they studied his writings like sacred texts; from Davis,—and from the clean, fine, brave young men of his fiction,—they learned that a gentleman always dresses for dinner, treats the ladies with the utmost gallantry, and loves America with all his fervent heart. Thus primed, when the warship Maine blew up in Havana harbor in the winter of ninety-eight, they were "keen" for war.

Then, like a character from a Davis novel, an aristocratic young swell from New York resigned his position as under-secretary of the navy, organized a regiment known as the Rough Riders, and led a "bully" charge up San Juan Hill. Sarsfield and Arch added pictures of Theodore Roosevelt to those of Davis on their walls—the whole surrounded by Gibson girls. "Oh, it was a splendid little war!" they repeated, parroting what they had read in the papers; the boys longed for another equally splendid one (perhaps next time somewhat larger)—when they would be old enough to fight in it. Arch, by then, was rapidly becoming the mainstay of the football team; Sarsfield slugged his way to the bantam-weight championship of the school. The boys had also acquired other estimable skills: they could spit and "cuss," smoke cigars without turning green, walk down Main Street with the proper Academy swagger, and drink their beer like gentlemen. Sarsfield had, to his amazement, grown to like the Academy; this new, manly life absorbed most of his time; what he had left, he gave to photography.

When he was sixteen, Sarsfield read the theories of James Maxwell on color vision and wanted to see if they worked. He set a vase of flowers in the light of a window and made three long exposures through filters of each of the primary colors. He then borrowed three magic lanterns from his father's stock, covered their lenses with the same colored filters, projected his positive slides onto a white wall, and adjusted the images so that they were aligned. Sarsfield felt an electric thrill run through his entire body; he stared for over an hour. The buttery orange of the marigolds, the ardent red of the roses, the delicate shades of the bluebells, the soft whites of the baby's breath, the tranquil greens of the ferns—it was muted, a bit ghostly, but there it was: *a full range of natural color captured by photography!* Finally, when he allowed himself to believe what his eyes were telling him, he called in his father to see it. "I'll be damned," Jack said; he, too, stared at the image for a long time. "Well, you know what the problem is, Sarsfield?" he said, finally. "How the hell are you going to sell it to anybody?"

After he had swallowed his disappointment at his father's reaction, Sarsfield had to admit that Jack was right: to have any commercial interest, the process had to yield a print. He read everything he could find on color and light and began his experiments with color printing. He dimly perceived that he had discovered what could well be his life's work.

By the time that Sarsfield's little brother Kyle had turned three, much of Alice Middleton's lost vigor had returned, and she had begun to take up the abandoned threads of her social life. Sarsfield was pleased to see his mother reappear as the fashionably dressed matron he remembered from his childhood; she resumed her "at-homes" and afternoon calls, her whist games and club meetings, and her charity work. But the better his wife's health became, the lower sank Jack Middleton's spirits—until he was deeply plunged into "the black mood."

Jack took to drinking openly at home, which he had never done before: he would arrive late at night already "well oiled" and then sit for hours on the back porch in the cool nights of that long Indian summer of 'ninety-nine—and on into the frosty autumn—his glass and bottle of bourbon on the table at his right hand, staring out at the river. Through his open bedroom window, Sarsfield could hear snatches of the conversation Jack carried on with the ghostly assembly of invisible tormentors who, by three in the morning, would have invariably joined him: "The hell you say! I won't have it; I won't take another minute of it—No, by God!—Oh, this night that covers me, black as the pit—No, a thousand times no! It matters not how strait the gate, how charged with punishment—For am I not the captain of my fate, the master of— the master, the master—By God, I'll be the master here—the master here, the master here—All of you can go to hell!"

One evening Sarsfield was walking into the drawing room when the sound of his parents' quiet voices through the partially opened door stopped him; he could not make out his father's words, but Jack's hissing tone was exactly the same as that he used to address his demons; then Sarsfield heard his mother suddenly exclaim in a voice bereft of all human dignity: "Oh, no, Jack. Oh, God, no! Oh, please, Jack!—You could not be so cruel. Another child would kill me!"

Sarsfield was so affected by what he had heard that the hair on his entire scalp prickled and he instantly lost the ability to think of anything whatsoever. A brave young man, he decided later, would have stayed, and watched, and waited,—and perhaps intervened; but that is not what he did. He walked out of the house and up Front Street and across the Suspension Bridge to town. He did not walk quickly but plodded steadily forward as though he were crossing the continent; he did not stop until he had reached the top of Raysburg Hill. He felt as sickened as if he had eaten tainted meat: perspiration rolled from every pore; his head was pounding; he shook as though from a mid-winter chill.

Supporting himself on a tree, he knelt and, to his shame, vomited. Then, at last, he found that his brain worked again: thoughts were crashing down upon him fast and thick as hail stones. He knew that it was his duty to do something; but, for the life of him, he could not figure out what it was he could do; as a gentleman, he could not even discuss the matter with Arch, or with any of his relatives—or with anybody. "What would Dick Davis do?" he asked himself. "What would Theodore Roosevelt do?" He never did figure out what either of these excellent gentlemen might do; what *he* did was walk home, go to bed, get up the next morning, go to school, and do his best to forget all about it. But the shame clung to him and troubled his sleep with nightmares.

Sarsfield was never able to guess exactly what had befallen his mother in his absence, for she remained in her room and would see no one for nearly six weeks afterward; when he finally, early in the new year, received the intelligence that his mother was in the family way, he heard it from the housekeeper.

Alice Middleton's labor with her third child was long and difficult; it commenced several weeks early and continued for an afternoon, and a night, and on into the second day. A trained nurse was engaged to attend Mrs. Middleton around the clock; Doc Anderson called frequently—and departed, each time with an air of pessimism more profound than the last. Finally, near ten in the evening, the child was born alive; Alice—at least for the moment—was also still alive. Because he received news of the birth while watching a production of *Twelfth Night* at the Virginia Theater, Jack named his new daughter "Olivia"; a summer baby, she was not expected to live; and her mother, so the doctor said, "clung to life by a thread." But Alice surprised everyone by hanging on day after day; and then, gradually, she began to improve; by the Fourth of July, she was pronounced out of danger. The baby, Doc Anderson said, might have a small chance of survival if she could but last until the cool days of autumn.

Sarsfield was standing in the far corner of the drawing room pretending to look out the window when Doc Anderson told Jack that his wife was suffering from acute neurasthenia brought on by the severity of her labor. "Her nerves have never been good," the doctor said in his low, hypnotic tone. This stooped old man with sad eyes who stood stroking his long, gray beard with tobacco-stained fingers had attended Alice since her own birth, had attended her ever since, and so spoke with the voice of authority: "She was always such a high-strung, excessively emotional girl, not strong—no, not strong at all—Perhaps there is some taint in the blood—"; he suggested that madness was not unknown amongst the Raineys; and Jack nodded sagely. "Perhaps if she should have exercised the full force of her will against this morbid influence—" the doctor droned on, but then shook his head, indicating plainly that it was too late. Only years of bed-rest might restore Mrs. Middleton to some semblance of health, he said; she must be kept from all stimulation; he prescribed a soothing nerve tonic.

Sarsfield resolved to detach himself, so far as was humanly possible, from the life of his family; he would consider himself a visitor from a distant land; and, in this way, he would not allow himself to be affected by these strange people amongst whom he had found himself trapped by a mere, trivial accident of birth. He had set upon some serious work,—which he could not accomplish at the shop, where he was oppressed by his father's presence, nor in his room at home, where the constant crying of his new baby sister grated on his nerves like nails on a blackboard;—so he appropriated the woodshed behind the house, and there he whiled away the days of his vacation by making color prints from an intaglio process. He produced a series of pictures of flowers, none perfect, but each slightly better than the last. He began to construct a camera that would—through a system of prisms and mirrors—make simultaneously all three of the exposures required for a color photograph.

Sarsfield's mother lay in bed week after week, refusing to see anyone but the housekeeper, the doctor, and, infrequently, her mother; Jack took to dining at his club, so Sarsfield ate in the kitchen with the help. In the evenings he always met Arch at the end of the bridge; they strolled through town, stopped in the soda fountain to flirt with the girls, or bought a bucket of beer and sat on the river bank to drink it. They had reached the age at which they felt enormously old and wise; their phantasies of only a year before—of filibustering in Latin America or of taking up the romantic profession of journalism—had been put behind them like discarded boyhood hoops or slingshots. "Say, kid, you know what I've decided?" Arch said one night, "I'm going to go in for medicine."

"Capital!" Sarsfield replied; and then, out of deference to this important announcement, he carefully chose his words to match the tone and diction of their fictional heroes: "How clean and fine of you! You'll make a jolly good sawbones, old man."

"Well, one wishes to do one's bit, you know," Arch replied in kind, "to leave the world a better place than one found it."

"Oh, *rather*!" Sarsfield exclaimed and slapped his friend on the back in the wordless affection of young men; he had particularly appreciated Arch's use of the word "one." Then, this weighty exchange having been concluded in language that befitted it, they fell back into their normal mode of speech. "Yeah, you'd be a shine at it, all right," Sarsfield said; "Guess you'll be going down to the university, huh?"

"I want to go to Harvard," Arch said quietly.

"Harvard!" Sarsfield stopped stock-still; Arch might as well have said "heaven."

"Yeah," Arch replied in an embarrassed tone, "sounds like a queer notion for *me* to have, don't it? But—Well, you see, I've got this uncle in Pittsburgh, old bachelor gent, and he thinks I'm the cheese.—He's the one put the bee in my bonnet. He was a Harvard man, and he says he'll say a word for me in the right places and even help out with a few bucks, and—Well, my old man says he's been broke so long sending me to the Academy, he may's well be broke another four years, and—" Arch took a deep breath and then burst out with: "Say, kid, you've got to come with me!"

"Lord," Sarsfield said, "my old man wouldn't hear it for beans!"

"Ain't there some way you can get 'round him?"

"Maybe. I don't know.—Good Lord, Arch, Harvard! Wouldn't that be swell?"

Seniors at the Academy were kings of the castle; having survived the miseries of their previous years, they could now lord it over the younger boys; and, moreover, it was only a matter of months before they would be graduated and gone forever—leaving behind them hazings, floggings, punishment duty, the Colonel's morning lectures on the duties of Christian gentlemen, the deadly hours in study hall, their Academy nick-names, and Latin. Filled with huge self-satisfaction, Sarsfield, Arch, and their friends swaggered arm in arm through the streets of Raysburg, singing: "I don't give a damn for any ole man who don't give a damn for me!"

Arch and Sarsfield both wrote the Harvard entrance examinations; and both were accepted. "That's it, kid," Arch said; "You've got to come with me." Sarsfield could not imagine anything that would have pleased him more; the moment he had heard the name "Harvard" pronounced, he had longed to go there with all his heart; now he had to convince his father. Sarsfield prepared a speech about how much more useful he would be to the photography business if he had made a serious study of chemistry, light, and optics. Jack howled like a dog run down by a buggy: "What d'you think, I'm made out of money? You're bleeding me white, the whole damned lot of you! *Harvard?* I'll have none of it. Do you hear me? None of it!"

It was exactly what Sarsfield had expected. He sat down and penned a long missive to his grandparents.

A messenger summoned Sarsfield to the Eberhardt mansion. He was told that Grandmother Eberhardt awaited him in her rooms. His heart in his throat, he approached the old woman enthroned in the over-size rocking chair that had been constructed to accommodate her ever increasing girth, and inquired after her health. "My health is perfect," she said in the abrupt, testy manner of the Raineys. "My health is *always* perfect." One of her pale blue eyes was aimed directly into his; the other appeared to be examining the wainscotting. "And your mother is no worse, I trust?" she asked him.

"No worse, Grandmother. Much the same."

"And the baby?"

"Flourishing, Grandmother. Ole Doc Anderson says she'll live."

"So I understand. Well, I'm glad of it. Your mother's had sorrow enough in her life, I dare say.—Sit down, boy. Yes, yes, there! Don't fidget. Good heavens, I can't think when you fidget like that!—Your grandfather and I read your letter—quite carefully, I can assure you. Several times. And—Sarsfield, you don't much like me, do you?"

Sarsfield could not find any safe reply to that; but, before he could speak, his grandmother continued: "Oh, say anything you want, I know you think I'm an old battle-ax; I've always liked you well enough, so I don't give a damn what you think.—Listen to me, Sarsfield: I'm going to talk to you plain. Your father's blood may be as blue as an ink-well, but he's—no gentleman!"

"I would not care to dispute you on that point, Grandmother," he responded after a moment of deep consideration.

"No? Well, you've got good Rainey blood in your veins, boy, and I'll say that for you—and good, reliable Eberhardt blood too—yes, good German blood—and one of these days I guess you'll be glad of it. Listen, boy, just because your father's a no-good rotter, doesn't mean you have to be a no-good rotter too. Your grandfather will see you through at Harvard—No, no, you don't have to say anything. Good grief, boy, sit down!—Your grandfather understands that there are certain expenses that must be incurred by a gentleman, so don't stint yourself;—but see that you're not profligate either. Don't drink more than a single glass of whiskey at a setting, and don't ever play cards for money; and, Sarsfield?—Fast women and fast horses, avoid them like the very devil—"

"Grandmother, I really have to say how deeply—"

"Yes, yes, you're welcome, I'm sure. Not another damn word, Sarsfield. It's all in the family. Now you just go off to Harvard and get yourself a proper education."

And that is exactly what Sarsfield did.

3

When they first arrived at Harvard, Arch and Sarsfield felt like West
Virginia "hill-billies" who have wandered barefoot into the big city for
the first time. "Lord a' mighty," Sarsfield exclaimed in a parody of a
mountain man's voice, "whar the hell are we, Archibald? 'Pears we died
and gawnta heaven!"

"Ain't that the truth of it, Sarsafrass!" Arch replied in kind; and
the young men fell to laughing and slapping each other on the arms;
they were so delighted to be exactly where they were that nothing
could dim their pleasure. Their rooms, which consisted simply of a
narrow bedchamber and a study (two desks, a fireplace, and a broad
window-seat), appeared to them sumptuous, palatial,—infinitely
desirable; their professors, even at first glance, were obviously mon-
sters of erudition; their classmates seemed, to a man, the most elegant, enormously sophisticated young "swells" ever known to
Christendom (and they talked exactly the way they were supposed to
talk—like the characters in British novels). The friends were so
excited they could not sleep; in the middle of the night, they walked
in circles around Harvard Yard, gawking at the ancient buildings of
the university; but they scarcely had time to get their bags unpacked
before a larger event impinged upon their lives.

At a reception at the Pan-American Exposition in Buffalo, President McKinley had been engaged in one of his favorite political pas-
times: the shaking of hands. Each citizen who had been waiting in line
to see the president had received, as usual, a cheery word, a warm smile,
and a firm handshake ending in a brisk jerk that had sent the recipient
rapidly on his way; McKinley had so perfected the art that he could
shake fifty hands a minute. A young, crazed anarchist named Leon Czolgosz waited his turn and then shot the president twice in the stomach.

For a week the nation waited. Harvard men bought up copies of
each new edition of the papers, rushed back to the campus to stand

around in clusters muttering about this terrible event; the accounts were so wildly contradictory that no one trusted them; some said that the president was recovering nicely, others that he was at death's door. A brooding sense of destiny hung in the air—a stillness as though all were holding their breath. Czolgosz readily admitted his foul deed; in his written statement he said: "I done my duty. I didn't believe one man should have so much service and another man should have none." One bullet had been deflected; but the other had passed through the president's stomach; McKinley had undergone surgery; and, after a few days, it was generally thought that he would survive; he had, so it appeared, eaten some toast. Sarsfield would remember for the rest of his life that it was a Saturday—a brilliant autumn day with crisp air that stirred the blood like wine—when he and Arch heard the news: the surgery had not been successful after all; the president's stomach had not been functioning. McKinley had tried to sing "Nearer My God to Thee"; then he had slipped away. The president of the United States was dead.

The young men devoured the special edition, threw it aside; they walked, they knew not where. "A great man," Sarsfield said, "a kind, good man,—a true Christian."

"Yes;" Arch replied, "no doubt about it. A credit to his nation."

Somber and dazed, they sat in a Cambridge saloon and drank a pitcher of beer; they felt for William McKinley what most Americans did: a deep fondness. They genuinely mourned him. Then Sarsfield looked up, saw that his friend's eyes were on his. He allowed himself to smile; and then he said, quietly, the name that was now in the forefront of both of their minds: "Roosevelt."

That September of 1901, Sarsfield would say, looking back years later, marked a dividing line between the old age and the new. The time of the old men, tried and true, their characters shaped by the terrible intestine war, was over; now was the time for young men to march into the future. McKinley, like a needle-point sampler reading "Home Sweet Home," had embodied all the virtues of the old, small-town, rural life; he had been kind, genial, conservative, cautious. Teddy Roosevelt hit the White House like a whirlwind; he was pugnacious, wildly enthusiastic about everything under the sun, radical and daring. Cartoonists had a "field day" with him: he was drawn countless times, in the midst of some vigorous activity performed at break-neck speed, his teeth and

glasses gleaming, shouting out "Splendid!" and "Bully!" Teddy was just
the man to lead the new, booming, restless, rapidly expanding nation
into the fulfillment of her infinite promise; he appeared to be getting
more done in a week than had been done in the last forty years. And
Sarsfield, moreover, had left Raysburg and his family behind for the first
time; he felt as though he had escaped some dark, oppressive fate; he
could never quite believe his excellent good fortune,—he was so deeply
delighted to be at Teddy's *alma mater*,—at Harvard! It was the first day
in Eden, the dawn of the world, the beginning of everything sparkling
and spanking new; and Sarsfield felt that he, at long last, was truly
living in the twentieth century.

Neither Arch nor Sarsfield had ever been out of Raysburg before,
and they found their new freedom wildly intoxicating; they walked for
hours on the streets of Cambridge, then rode the street-car into Boston
and walked for hours there. They looked at historical buildings; they
looked at the graves in Mt. Auburn Cemetery; they walked along the
Charles and looked at the gentle water and the trees; they looked at the
shops and the centers of commerce; but mainly they looked at the girls.

The ladies back home suddenly seemed quaint, old-fashioned, coun-
trified; here in the big city, the socialites were grander, the "bachelor
girls" jauntier, the school girls daintier, the ladies of the *demi-monde*
naughtier; the two young men could not begin to get their fill of looking
at them. The year before, skirt lengths had risen as high as the ankle
bone; but now, as though frightened by their own temerity, they had collapsed again to the ground;—at least so it was decreed in fashionable circles, and so it was done by those who cared about such things; but many
young, sprightly Boston girls wore their skirts shorter than anything
Arch and Sarsfield had ever seen off the stage. The friends made bets as
to how short skirts could get; then, early in their freshman year, in a
"dive" by the fishermen's wharf, they lost their hearts: "Look at *that*
rainy daisy!" Arch said, awe in his voice, "I guess she's won the cigar."

Sarsfield was already looking at her: a singularly handsome girl, tall
and athletic, with tresses so pale that she had to be of the peroxide per-
suasion, with what was obviously paint on her cheeks and lips, she ran,
laughing, from table to table delivering the pitchers of beer; Sarsfield
had never seen skirts that short on a full-grown woman (they must
have swung along nearly six inches above the sawdust!); and beneath
them twinkled an exquisitely well turned set of ankles and a pair of

tiny, fast-moving feet clad in wonderfully bright red boots. As red, liter-
ally, as late cherries, those boots lodged themselves in Sarsfield's
memory and would not go away. What a subject for a color photograph!

Her name turned out to be Mae; and she was not at all averse to a
night on the town with two young swells from Harvard: "Why so shy,
fellahs? I seen you in here rubbering at me every night. I don't bite, you
know." Sarsfield's intentions were photographic; but Arch had something in mind more amorous—which got him exactly nowhere at all:
"Say, Archy, soft pedal that stuff, can't ya? I ain't the kind of girl that
gives it away in a doorway." Mae had a beau who was out to sea; and
she guessed she'd marry him one day; but, in the meantime, a girl had
to have a bit of fun, didn't she? Arch and Sarsfield split the cost of the
endless procession of cherrystone clams, dainty ices, French pastries,
cold cuts, caviar, paté, and truffles that passed down her throat. When
Sarsfield asked if he could do her picture, she said: "Sure."

He wanted to capture her in her natural habitat; the owner of
the establishment said he did not mind so long as his commerce was
not interfered with. Just before he had left Raysburg, Sarsfield had
completed his one-shot color camera; an intricate arrangement of
German mirrors and prisms divided the light passing through the
lens onto three photographic plates; the entire device was only
slightly less large than a steamer trunk. He set it up on a tripod in
front of the bar and suggested, hesitantly, that Mae might consider
posing there. He had chosen the middle of the afternoon of a brilliantly sunny fall day; the broad saloon windows faced west, and the
entire establishment glowed brilliantly. But his color filters cut the
light to his plates by a good half, and Sarsfield needed all the illumination he could get; he decided to make a long exposure and aug-
ment it with magnesium powder.

The question was how best to arrange his flash-pans; but, as Sarsfield
studied the situation, Mae, just to get into the spirit of things, jumped
onto the bar and kicked up her legs, showing, momentarily, the flounced
edge of some undergarment. The customers sprang to their feet and
began yelling encouragement. Caught between the fear of missing an
absolutely splendid picture and a desire to get the lighting right—and, it
must be admitted, somewhat muddled by a pitcher of beer,—Sarsfield did
not bother to measure the flash powder, but piled it on lavishly just as he
had seen his father do. He dumped about six ounces on a pan behind the

bar as a back light, a good eight ounces on each pan in front of the girl, and at least twelve ounces on the pan above the camera. Running now (the men were chanting "Mae, Mae, Mae!" and banging their glasses on the tables), Sarsfield connected a wire to each pan, connected them all to the dry cell battery and the switch that would,—if the properties of electricity did not fail him,—set the whole works off at once. Arch, watching, was laughing so hard he threatened to topple over.

Sarsfield threw the cloth over his head and focused the lens until Mae appeared sharply on his ground glass. All around him he heard a wild roar of pandemonium; some of the men were suggesting, in crudely effective language, that they would like to see somewhat more than Mae had yet shown them. Grinning, she hiked up her skirts to display her lace-trimmed bloomers. A yell went up that would have shamed a Republican nominating convention; when it subsided, Sarsfield shouted out the usual photographer's order that everyone understood at once: "Hold it!" Mae froze, grinning at the camera; the men in the saloon froze. Sarsfield squeezed the bulb to open the lens. He had not had time to get out his stop watch; and he began to count in his mind just as his father had taught him: "Naught. One-half-and-one, one half-and-two—" At twelve seconds, he began to sense that his time was running out: soon someone would move and ruin the exposure. He felt perspiration pouring down his sides. At twenty-four seconds, he knew that he couldn't expect the formidable, breathless immobility in the saloon to persist even a second longer; he gave Arch the sign to set off the powder.

Sarsfield had not, of course, been at Krakatoa when the volcano exploded. Sarsfield was sure, for ever after, that the volcano could have had nothing on his flash powder. Broken bottles and glass were flying everywhere. Men were diving for cover under tables. The camera on its tripod legs, seemingly with a life of its own, was cake-walking away with alarming speed; Sarsfield leapt after it, seized it just a foot short of the ground. Even then the air was still full of flying debris; an enormous cloud of smoke hung over everything. Arch was convulsed on the saw-dust howling in a spasm of inhuman laughter. For minutes afterward the entire establishment reverberated like the inside of a wash tub struck by lightning. "Gee, fellahs," Mae said, "that better be some swell picture!"

Sarsfield and Arch had to empty their pockets to pay for the damage. The next morning, suffering "the cold gray dawn of the morn-ing after" (huge draughts of soda water helped), Sarsfield had to admit that, as much as he did not care for the idea, he was—at least partially—his father's son: oh, Jack Middleton would have been proud of him all right! He developed his plates to the fullest; but, despite the sunlight and the gargantuan amount of magnesium he had exploded, his negatives were thin, so he decided to use an oil-based transfer process to print them; getting it right took him most of his free time that fall. Arch watched as Sarsfield transferred layers of gelatine to the ground, registered them, rolled them, and gently peeled back the cloth support; they would both hold their breath, hoping the gelatine would not disintegrate. "Explain it to me again, old man," Arch would say, "Maybe I'll take it in this time."

"Look, it's as simple as can be," Sarsfield would reply, "your blue filter withholds blue light and allows all other light to pass. And all the other light that's passing is everything that *isn't* blue. And everything that isn't blue is red and green; and red and green makes yellow. So when you print the negative that was made through the blue filter, you make a yellow positive out of it."

Then Arch would laugh uneasily, and Sarsfield would see in his friend's eyes, once again, a total incomprehension.

As tedious as it had been to make, the final result was delightful. There was Mae, captured by photography—her merry grin, her exquisite calves, her white lace bloomers, her cherry-red boots. Sarsfield did not realize until he had framed it and hung it on the wall what a spicy image it was; his classmates came to stare and snicker. They all believed that it was an oil painting. He could not convince a single one of them that it was a photograph.

Late in the fall, Sarsfield received a letter from Aunt Ida Eberhardt inviting him to pass several days with her family in New York during the Christmas vacation. Sarsfield wrote back inquiring if he could bring Arch with him; because of the close relation that existed between himself and his aunt, Sarsfield thought that such a request would not be taken amiss; and, indeed, his aunt replied by the next post that of course they would be delighted to know Mr. Kimbell.

"Now hang on a minute, kid," Arch said; "Who are these people— 'Uncle Henry' and 'Aunt Ida'? I haven't got your relatives straight."

"Well, Uncle Henry's actually my great-uncle—my grandfather Thaddeus Eberhardt's younger brother. Seems odd, but I can't remember that I ever met him—but I've always been close to my Great-aunt Ida. She's splendid; you're bound to like her. And maybe my cousin will be there—" Sarsfield was not certain what he felt about the prospect of seeing Julia again after all these years; but perhaps he should not worry about it: the last he had heard of her, she was attending a fashionable boarding school in France.

"So this Uncle Henry," Arch persisted, interrupting his friend's train of thought, "he's in the iron and steel business like your grandfather?"

"No; he's a financier—took his share of the Eberhardt money and went into the stock market with it—made a fortune, I guess—back in the nineties when everybody else was losing his shirt. They call him 'The Gray Wolf of Wall Street'—"

"And we're going to go pay a visit to 'The Gray Wolf of Wall Street'?" Arch said with a laugh, "Lord save us!"

When they arrived in New York, the young men descended from the train at Grand Central Station and stood on the platform, well back from the bustle of the afternoon crowd, casting their eyes about for the Eberhardts' man who, it had been promised, would meet them. "How will he know us?" Arch asked.

"Don't we look like Harvard boys?" Sarsfield replied. They had both adopted the Harvard costume of sweater and wide-hip trousers, and, with their luggage at their feet and the air of lost souls, could not have appeared, Sarsfield thought, any more conspicuous than if they had been wearing signs with their names printed on them. They had also adopted Harvard manners and speech—which, like their clothing, were so new to them that they both secretly feared that the callow Raysburg boy beneath might show through and betray them at any moment.

"I shouldn't have come," Arch said in a funereal voice, repeating what he had been saying during the ride down from Boston.

"Don't be an ass," Sarsfield told him.

"It's bound to happen—we'll get invited somewhere, to some blamed party or dance or something—and somebody, sometime, is bound to say: 'Oh, and tell me, Mr. Kimbell, what does your father do?'"

"And you'll give them that big, genuine smile of yours and tell them all about the dry-goods business; and if they hold that against you, they're not worthy of your friendship."

"Sars, that's all well and good for you to say," Arch replied in a tone that betrayed his anxiety, "but I really—" and he stopped in mid-sentence, his mouth hanging open.

Sarsfield followed the direction of Arch's eyes and saw the vision that had so thoroughly disrupted his train of thought: a lady of such an elegant and highly polished appearance that the crowd of ordinary folk was instinctively parting before her. The two young men watched avidly as she strolled down the platform in their direction—her chin in the air, bearing herself with the self-assured insouciance of the true thoroughbred. Men were staring at her, thunderstruck; but her manner was so regal that not one of them hazarded a comment. The friends exchanged a glance and held their breath: yes, indeed, she was coming their way, and would, so it appeared, pass directly in front of them.

As she approached, Sarsfield saw that she was younger than her manner suggested—scarcely out of girlhood. He studied the details of her *toilette*. She wore a superbly tailored Eton jacket in navy blue velvet, piped in black scallops; her matching skirt was of precisely the length most fashionable at the moment and just escaped brushing the ground; beneath it, he could make out the twinkle of patent leather. In her black-gloved hands she carried what, at a distance, had appeared to be a cane, but now, upon closer inspection, proved to be a furled, beribboned umbrella of exquisite slenderness; her hat, with a sweep of feather, sat upon her head at a piquant angle; and she was lightly veiled. It would have been enough, Sarsfield thought, that she was so stylishly turned out, that her deportment was so chic and self-assured;—but she was, he saw, beautiful to boot. Her features were small and lovely as a cameo's; her complexion was an inwardly glowing alabaster; her enormous, thick-lashed eyes, even at a distance—and through the fine, black net—carried like beacons. But the feature that in all likelihood startled the onlookers in the train station more than any other was her waist—which was the smallest that Sarsfield had ever seen short of the exaggerated lineaments of a fashion drawing.

Now, *mirabile dictu*, she had stopped directly in front of him and was smiling. "Sarsfield," she said, "how lovely to see you again."

For a single, dizzying moment Sarsfield felt as though he had entered into a fairy-tale kingdom of magical, miraculous happenings; and then he saw, following several steps behind this princess, a large fellow in livery who was obviously the Eberhardts' man; and then he remembered those dazzling dark blue eyes (how could he have ever forgotten them?). A wave of emotion swept through him so profound that he could not name it; what had he expected, that she would remain a child forever? He mastered himself, assumed his heartiest voice, and exclaimed: "Why it's Julia—Julia Eberhardt! How splendid of you to meet us!"

In the carriage they discovered Julia's maid, but, to Sarsfield's surprise, no sign of a chaperon. As they rolled along, Arch—wholly unlike himself—sat as silent and unmoving as a wall; he gave Sarsfield a woebegone look. Julia was chatting gaily: "A proper young lady should have awaited your arrival at home—I daresay that's what you're thinking—but as I'm not 'out' yet, I may still behave like a child and beg for treats and drives to the train station.—Have you been to New York before, Mr. Kimbell?" Arch stammered that he had not; and, doing her best to put him at his ease, she began to point out the sights.

Sarsfield, to his growing annoyance and alarm, found himself just as speechless as his friend. Out of the corner of his eye, he studied Julia's profile. Was this his little playmate? Memories of Julia began to flood his mind; he had done his best to forget her; but, so it seemed, he had not succeeded. "Say something," he told himself; "Say anything, no matter how stupid—it doesn't matter what!"

"By Jove, Julia," he began; and that sounded all right; that sounded like a Harvard man, all right. "I just remembered the last time I ever saw you. It must have been just before you moved to New York. It was at Grandfather's lawn party; and you rode the pony—"

"Oh, my childhood sins come back to haunt me," she exclaimed; "I shall never, it seems, live down that little escapade!"

"How old were you? It seems to me you couldn't have been more than—"

"Eleven," she said; and, turning to Arch, she began to narrate the story: "My Uncle Thaddeus had relegated the children to the stables. Ponies had been saddled; and we had been instructed to ride them. This device, you see, was meant to keep us occupied and well out of the way—which did not suit me in the least. I had been so longing to see the ladies in their finest—and, naturally, to show off my new frock— which I fancied to be just as grand as could be. So, when my turn came, I jumped the fence and rode straight up the hill—"

"You should have seen her, Arch," Sarsfield said, "this little pixie of a girl all in lace, grinning like a chessy cat—and here she comes at a full gallop, right up through the guests and Grandfather's darkies—and there was no stopping her! Right around the side of the house she goes—bucketing along as fine as you please—and up the steps!"

The picture of the little girl on the pony was deeply emblazoned in Sarsfield's memory—along with all the light and color of that special day: Sarsfield, at thirteen, had been wearing long pants for the first time to that annual affair; he had, by then, spent his first year at the Academy and was just entering his second; he had been doing his best to act like a grown-up young man. He had not seen Julia since his father had forbidden him to play with his Eberhardt cousins; he had been looking all over for her—had been told that she was down the hill with the other children. Then he had heard the pony—the lap-a-ta, lap-a-ta of the hoofbeats;—and, along with all the other guests, he had turned to stare. Julia in her pink-and-white taffeta dress, ribbons and petticoats flying, urging on the pony with a tiny, patent leather slipper, had appeared like a swift messenger from the kingdom of childhood he had thought to leave irrevocably behind him. "What on earth were you thinking, Julia?" he asked her now.

"That revenge is sweet," she said with a smile.

"She rode that pony directly into the house," Sarsfield continued, "and down the front hall—and *right into the drawing room!* Then black George finally caught the reins! You should have seen my grandfather— You know how fat he is, Arch? Well, he was puffing along behind and laughing the whole time. 'Capital!' he kept yelling out. 'Capital!'"

"I'm delighted to hear that someone was amused," Julia said; "My father, when he heard of it, most certainly was not."

By now the carriage had turned onto Fifth Avenue and was proceeding down "Millionaires' Row," where, in the depression of the nineties, Henry Eberhardt had purchased a vacated mansion—so it was said, for a song. Arch had been smiling dutifully at the proper moments in the course of the story; but Sarsfield could see that his friend was far from having been put at his ease; and the sight of the monumental, three-storey ædifice that was the domicile of the New York Eberhardts (Arch said later that he had thought that it must be the great city's post office) once again plunged Arch into a stony silence.

When the friends were alone in their room, Arch threw himself onto his bed and exclaimed: "Can I leave now, please? Can I catch the next train back to Boston?"

"Oh, the devil!" Sarsfield said.

"You know, old man," Arch said, his eyes fixed on the ceiling, "the only times I was ever at your grandfather's mansion was when I was making deliveries for my father—to the servants' entrance! Hang it all! Riding her pony into the drawing room!"

"Arch, listen to me: you're a gentleman and a Harvard man—and second class to no one. So buck up!"

"Oh, Lord, I'll do my best, kid," Arch exclaimed, "but you gotta give me some time to collect myself."

Sarsfield descended to the first floor in search of his cousin. He was glad to have heard that his Aunt Ida was not at home that afternoon; he was, thereby, freed of the necessity of going to her directly; he was glad that Arch had remained behind. All he could think about was Julia. Casting his mind back, he could not recall a time when he had not known her; he remembered her as a four-year-old who would never stop playing when bidden to do so and had to be carried off to bed, howling, slung over the shoulder of the large, placid black maid; he remembered her as a six-year-old who had insisted upon wearing yards and yards of the most elaborately flounced petticoats so that when she spun, fairy-like, her skirts would sail up and out in perfect, swishing, frothy circles. Julia, her mother said, had been, from the day of her birth, blessed—or cursed—with "a mind of her own"; her mother had called her "Cricket" then, because she was always jumping. He remembered Julia—of course he remembered her!—as a ten-year-old, thin as a grass stem, full of mischief and apparently inexhaustible energy; and he remembered how kind she had always been;—even as a tiny girl she had been kind—a virtue not usually found in a child: when Sarsfield withdrew, as he sometimes did, into moody silence, she brought him bon-bons and tarts and always managed to draw him back into the game. And he remembered their kiss. She would be sixteen now; he could not quite believe that she had been transformed into such a polished young lady as he had seen at the train station.

He found her in the garden still attired in her elegant walking costume. "How lovely," she said when she saw him; "I was hoping you would join me—"

Sarsfield could no longer hold back the enormity of what he was feeling—and spontaneously exclaimed: "Hello, Cricket!"

Her carefully acquired façade of the society lady fell away at once—like a dropped curtain; she stepped forward, seized his hands, and, with the warmest of smiles, said: "Hello, Sarsy."

Sarsfield stood, holding her elegantly gloved hands, looking down into her eyes; and he did not know what to do next: they were no longer children, and he could not, for the moment, find a proper rôle to play with her. She must have been feeling something similar; they stood, holding hands, looking into each other's eyes, for so long that Sarsfield saw the light change around them as clouds drifted out from under the sun. The light was brilliant and white; a delicate pattern of blue shadows—the shapes of winter branches—was cast upon his cousin's unveiled face.

She rose on tip-toes and kissed him lightly on the cheek; he released her hands. She continued to look at him, her upturned face like an open flower; then she sighed. "Oh, dear," she said and stepped back. Sarsfield still could not find a single word to say.

He saw her regain her composure. "Let's put aside our nursery names," she said, "and at least *pretend* to be grown-up—'Cricket,' indeed! No one has called me that since I was—Oh, you have no idea the effect it had upon me—hearing that. I can see that I shan't be able to dissemble with you, dear Cousin; you will always be able to say: 'She can't get away with that nonsense with *me*—why, I've known her for years!' And, of course, I'll be able to say the same about *you*.—Come on, Sarsfield, let me show you the garden. It's supposed to be a splendid example of, ah—whatever it's a splendid example of."

He followed her farther along the path between the clipped hedges. She had become, again, the young society lady of the train station. "But where is Mr. Kimbell?" she asked him.

Sarsfield felt an inexplicable pang of jealousy. "In our rooms—suffering stage fright," he said.

"What does he think, that we're going to roast him for dinner?"

"No; only that his origins might not be lofty enough—"

"Oh, piffle! Does he think we don't know who the Kimbells are? We're from Raysburg, after all. Mama used to buy yard goods from his father. If we didn't want to know him, we wouldn't have invited him, now would we?"

"I'll tell him that," Sarsfield said; and he fancied that he had just seen in his cousin's eyes a look of cool, detached scrutiny directed toward him; but then she smiled, and he could not be sure that he had not imagined it. Again she walked ahead of him; he continued to follow, wondering why her presence seemed to be having such an exhilarating effect upon him. "I have been *so* looking forward to meeting you again, Sarsfield," she said, glancing back.

"Oh?" he replied.

"Have you thought of me at all?"

He had, over the intervening years, done his best *not* to think of her; but he said: "Of course I have."

"Liar," she said softly.

Her tiny waist was adorned with a narrow patent leather belt; in the front it was cut into a V-shape to match the "Marie Antoinette dip" of her skirt; now he saw that in the back it sported a neat, pointed "postillion" which rode above the beautifully rounded sweep of her for all the world like a clever little tail. He knew—and it was a sudden, unheralded knowledge that struck him like a lightning bolt—that she aroused the full force of his virile energy as no girl had ever before. He was astonished: this little girl with whom he had shared his childhood? It didn't seem possible! And, inexplicably angry with himself—and with her—he said: "I'm surprised you remember *me*."

"Don't be silly," she said. Then she stopped abruptly, turned toward him. "We must stop this right now," she said firmly. "We're about to begin flirting with each other—Yes, we are; I can feel it beginning to happen, and I won't have it!"

Sarsfield felt that the ground had been cut out from beneath his feet. She offered him her hand, and he took it. "You have been at Harvard, and I have been in Paris," she said, "and we have become—oh, quite quite grown up, have we not? But what were you feeling when you called me 'Cricket'?"

He could think of nothing but to answer her honestly: "That I'd found my old chum again."

"Oh, yes!" she exclaimed. "That's right. That's exactly what I felt too. Oh, let us not lose that moment, Sarsfield! Can't we take up where we left off and be chums again?—And chums must be honest with each other, and never never lie—not even harmless little white lies—and chums must, oh!—tell each other *everything*!"

Dinner that night, Sarsfield told Arch, most definitely required formal attire. "You sure 'black tie' will do it?" Arch asked. "You sure it doesn't call for a white tie?" He was staring apprehensively at his partially dressed image in the glass.

"Heavens, no," Sarsfield replied.

For at least the tenth time a pearl stud shot from between Arch's broad fingers to vanish beneath the dresser; Sarsfield, who was already fully dressed, retrieved it. "Here, let me," he said, taking over his friend's shirt front. "White tie's for evening weddings, balls, receptions, formal dinners, and the opera," he said.

"But isn't this a formal dinner? You said 'formal attire.'"

"Yes; but not 'white tie,'" Sarsfield said with a laugh.

"Oh, Lord! Do we wear gloves?"

"No; of course not."

"Why 'of course'?"

"Because we're not going out anywhere, because gentlemen do not wear gloves into the drawing-room—and certainly not to the dinner table."

"How the deuce do you learn all this stuff?" Arch cried in an anguished tone.

"You grow up knowing it," Sarsfield said, "and if you don't, you listen to your friends who do.—Come on, stop fussing; you look splendid—absolutely correct. Now just relax and be yourself."

In the east drawing room Sarsfield was surprised to find only Aunt Ida—who greeted him with obvious pleasure; and, just as Sarsfield had known she would, his aunt at once turned the full power of her charm upon Arch. It was not so much a matter of what she said but of how she said it—of the warmth of her smile, the graciousness of her manner, the easiness and lack of malice in her laughter.

Ida Eberhardt had always been Sarsfield's favorite aunt; he had known her and liked her as far back as those distant days when, still dressed in skirts, he had accompanied his mother on her afternoon calls. It had not been customary upon these occasions for society ladies to bring their children with them—not even small boys as well-behaved as Sarsfield—and he had often been made to feel unwelcome,—but never by Aunt Ida; he could remember engaging her in long conversations and trusting her in a way that he had not trusted other adults. The habit of easy confidentiality had persisted over the

years and ripened into that rare mutual understanding that is sometimes shared between a woman and a boy when there is some thirty
years between them.

"All of my men are quite fled," she was saying now; "Both of my
Henries—Junior *and* Senior—appear to be detained down-town on
business, and Arthur, so it seems, is 'stagging' with his chums from
Princeton, so you gentlemen must content yourself with the distaff side
of the household. Will you take something, Mr. Kimbell? Sarsfield?
Whiskey, or one of these 'cocktail' things?"

Arch was staring openly at the furnishings of the room, at the
Celtic crosses, the turquoise woodwork, the intricate floral wallpaper;
Sarsfield tried to catch his friend's eye, but Aunt Ida took command of
the situation, covered over Arch's gaucherie by saying: "Oh, I see
you're admiring our decorations, Mr. Kimbell. Some famous artist—oh,
why can't I ever remember the man's name?—spent months, simply
months, doing it up for me. That frieze, you can see, is copied from the
Bayeux Tapestry—"

"Oh, it's capital, Mrs. Middleton," Arch exclaimed somewhat too
forcibly, "just, ah—capital!"

Aunt Ida laughed as though Arch had just uttered the most
piquant of witticisms; and, happily, the butler arrived with their
drinks. Aunt Ida had never lost her West Virginia accent (as Julia
had); and Sarsfield saw Arch smile at the sound of her soft, southern
vowels. "Now where *is* that daughter of mine? I can see that she's
resolved to make us wait for her.—I trust that you boys—oh, I'm sorry,
you're Harvard *men*, aren't you?—but I trust you'll forgive us if we're
'putting on the dog' a bit, as the folks back home would say. It might
seem odd for such a small number, practically all of us family—but
Julia insisted that it's the *done* thing in New York, so we must be right
and proper with all the bells on—"

"How else should I get to indulge myself in vulgar display?" Julia
said, her timing so perfect that Sarsfield wondered if she had not been
waiting just outside the door for a perfect "cue" line. "After all," she
said, "I'm not 'out' yet."

Sarsfield had risen at the sound of her voice; Julia entered as
though into a crowded ballroom, with a bearing of vast hauteur. Sarsfield, delighted with her play-acting, walked to meet her, offered her his
arm, and escorted her across the room. Aunt Ida had chosen for the

evening a handsome but simple black gown and no gloves; Julia, however, had arrayed herself in a pale pink gown that, with its demure high
neck, was girlish enough, but, with an old-fashioned bodice tight fitted
to show off the curves of her bosom and wonderfully small waist, was,
perhaps, not quite suitable for one who had not yet made her début; her
hair was elaborately dressed; and she wore white evening gloves. Beautiful young girls, Sarsfield thought, have so often been described as
"radiant" that the adjective has lost all meaning; seeing his cousin as
she was now fully restored the word to its original force.

"Julia, good heavens!" her mother exclaimed before she could stop
herself, "that gown was meant to remain in its box until spring." Then,
recovering herself, she said: "Just look at her, Sarsfield—there are times
when I can't believe she's mine. You know, I sometimes wonder if it
isn't a mixed blessing to be quite as beautiful as *all that*—"

"*Merci du compliment, Maman,*" Julia replied in an ironic tone and
dropped a curtsey; she glanced wryly at Sarsfield.

"Just who *is* the hostess here tonight!" Aunt Ida said. "Julia, you are
very close to being in bad taste.—Obviously no one has ever told this
naughty girl that it's bad form to outdress one's mother. Poor Cin-
derella—no ball for her. Now, gentlemen, what ever shall I *do* with her?
Riding off to the train station without a chaperon because her poor
mother wasn't at home to stop her—"

Sarsfield led his cousin in a promenade around the room as though
there were a dozen appreciative guests looking on. Aunt Ida laughed,
said to Arch: "New York society is not nearly so impenetrable as it used
to be a few years ago, but it is still quite impenetrable enough; and Julia
is determined to make her mark—Yes, *you*, you terrible girl! Oh, such a
fuss that's going to be made over her—she must simply *blaze*!"

"*Alors, Maman, il n'y a que le premier pas qui coûte.*"

"Oh, do speak English, Julia, for heaven's sake! If you become any
more affected, you will drive me to absolute distraction." And, turning to the young men, Aunt Ida told them: "When I was a girl,
Boston was considered quite far enough to go to get oneself 'finished';
we didn't go sailing off across the Atlantic at a moment's notice and
then go fluttering around after all these oily, vulgar little European
noblemen in the hopes that someone would make us a princess—"

"I've met a few of those American princesses," Julia interjected,
"and they can keep their titles."

"Well, I'm delighted to hear you say that."

"But an English duke, however—"

"Oh, you're impossible!"

Presently dinner was announced; and the company proceeded to the dining room. The table could have sat easily a hundred people; four covers had been laid at one end. The gentle light of shaded candles provided the illumination thereon; the remainder of the vast room was shrouded in a deep gloom relieved only by side gas brackets with the jets turned halfway. Set on a mirror disk, a low, silver jardinière filled with two dozen perfect *gloire de Paris* roses decorated the table; Sarsfield saw Arch staring down at the six forks, at the goblet of still water and the tumbler of sparkling, at the array of empty wine glasses, at the large, simply folded napkin with bold monogram; then Sarsfield saw his friend give him a look that conveyed the thin edge of panic. Sarsfield smiled reassuringly. The butler and a footman in livery, silent as wraiths, poured a white wine with a bouquet delicate as alpine flowers and served oysters on the half shell. Sarsfield took up his oyster fork and looked to make sure that Arch had followed suit.

"Is this grand enough for you, my dear?" Aunt Ida asked her daughter.

"*Oui, Maman, cela va sans dire.*"

"Julia! Please. No more French.—You see, gentlemen, teaching her manners appears to be a lost cause. So tell me, Mr. Kimbell, are you enjoying your first year at Harvard?"

Arch took a long pull from his wine glass and stammered out that Harvard was "first-rate, ripping, and capital." But, with the soup (a stately lobster bisque), sherry was served, and with the fish (an excellent brazed hake, lightly garnished), the first bottle of icy champagne was poured foaming into the waiting glasses; and, by then, Arch was amusing the ladies with the tale of Mae and Sarsfield's exploding flash powder. Aunt Ida wanted to hear all about how Sarsfield made photographs in full color; Julia was intrigued by Mae's short skirts and cherry-red boots; and so, by the end of the third course, the ice had been well broken and all sense of constraint had vanished.

Sarsfield was seated next to his cousin, and—like a magnet seeks a loadstone—he felt her presence even when he was not looking at her; often, when he turned toward her, he found her shining, sea-blue eyes already turned toward him as though she had anticipated his movement.

She had, by now, removed her gloves; and her bare, white arms appeared touchingly child-like. She caught him studying her, asked: "Will I do?" in a dry, ironic tone.

"Oh, yes!" he said.

Across the table, Arch was growing more expansive with every sip of champagne. "Now you must tell me about New York society, Mrs. Eberhardt," he exclaimed with disarming simplicity; "Is it really as grand as it's cracked up to be? Is Mrs. Astor really the queen of the city?"

"Oh, Mrs. Astor—" Aunt Ida said, shaking her head.

"She's like a fat, ugly old spider at the center of the web," Julia interjected, "but her grasp of the strands is slipping—"

"Oh, Julia, don't be such a little cat! But, yes; she is old, and some-what feeble now. She can no longer dictate what's what—"

"Thank heavens," Julia said. "She would have kept us out if she could. She finally sent her card—when was it, Mama?"

"Just this last season. She's actually quite an amiable old soul. But it took us five blessed years—Well, I suppose that's not so bad. In the old days, we would not have got in at all.—Luckily, Mrs. Van Gort brought us along a bit—"

"She had to," Julia said; "Cher Papa was too useful to her hus-band—"

"Julia, please."

"But why mince words, Mama? Money is the ticket; everyone knows that—and they just can't keep us out any longer. They need us."

"Yes; I suppose they do.—So now we're 'in the push' as they say; and Henry and I will have to go to the famous Astor 'crush' in January—"

"And get to see the old toad in her diamonds—"

"Oh, you're simply terrible. Forgive her, gentlemen; she'll say anything."

"I'm just jealous, Mama. I want to see the old toad before she dies—and all her famous diamonds. But I won't be 'out' yet."

"You'll be 'out' soon enough—quite soon enough for your poor old mother."

A second bottle of champagne was opened to accompany the dainty stuffed mushrooms. Arch was of the variety of young men of large and robust constitution for whom substantial food washed down with ample drink provides an impetus to conviviality; and it was now apparent that he was succumbing to the charms of the ladies and the exotic nature of the setting in which he found himself: like many another small town American, he was dying of curiosity about the details of the luxurious life of high society. "How did you find it when you moved here, Mrs. Eberhardt?" he asked; "Was it a shock? Were you dazzled by it all?"

"I'm not sure that I shall ever feel quite at home here," she replied. "Much of what is done in New York strikes me as vulgar—"

"Mama was a Revington," Julia said, "and *so* genteel—"

"Oh, not all that genteel—but we were an old family in the valley, and I was raised to believe that one did not—well, display one's wealth in quite the forceful way that it is done here—"

A substantial port arrived with the roast; and, for the next few minutes, the young men were entertained with tales of wealth forcefully displayed: the immense palaces built in New York and Newport, the glittering balls, the Worth gowns, the yachts, the jewels, the motor cars,—culminating in the story of an affair at Mrs. Astor's at which the table had been covered with sand and the guests provided with small, sterling pails and shovels so they could dig up the buried party favors— which were diamonds, rubies, sapphires, and emeralds. Sarsfield saw that Arch was avidly hanging upon every word.

After the roast, the pace of the dinner slowed and became meditative. "Society back home is such a rough and ready affair," Aunt Ida said. "Yes, I do still think of Raysburg as my home—but, as queer a place as it is, at least I understand it—"

"Queer," Arch said, "how would you say Raysburg's queer?"

"Well, you take the Raineys," Aunt Ida replied. "Everyone would concede that they're the oldest and best blood in the valley; the amount of land they hold is simply astonishing, but they have no polish at all; they live like farmers—not even like gentry but like plain West Virginia farmers. It would never occur to Dan Rainey to host any sort of social function; why, he weeps and curses every time a penny passes from his fingertips. And my husband's people, the Eberhardts—"

"Here it comes," Julia said with a smile.

"Well, why should you be the only one who is permitted plain speech? The Revingtons were well established—"

"In the cut nail business," Julia interjected.

"What of it? Everyone's money has to come from *something*, doesn't it?—well established when Karl Eberhardt was still selling cigars on the street corner."

"Now we're going to hear how old Karl was nothing but a German peasant," Julia said.

"Well, he *was* nothing but a German peasant—with a genius for business and a single-minded passion for acquisition."

Sarsfield's ears pricked up at that; he had always been fascinated by the history of his own family, and the founder of the Eberhardts, his great-grandfather Karl, was still a shadowy figure to him; as the frozen lime punch was served, he encouraged his aunt in her recollections of Raysburg's great ironmaster. "The first time I was ever at dinner at the mansion," she said, "the old man sprang suddenly up from the table—without a single word of apology—and strode across the room and out onto the veranda where he leaned himself over the railing and blew his nose.—Yes, he did!—quite without the aid of a handkerchief—a most tremendous honk. And then he simply strode back in and sat down again and fell to eating—and I do mean 'fell to'—Later Henry told me that the old man's manners had improved considerably; in the old days he wouldn't have bothered to leave the table."

"I've heard that story a thousand times," Julia had whispered to Sarsfield; but, nonetheless, she encouraged her mother brightly: "What did you *do*, Mama?"

"What could I do? I sat there and ate my dinner like a good girl should;—but I don't want to paint your grandfather as a total boor. He was a simple man; he never had a doubt about what life was all about: you grabbed as much as you could get, and you hung onto it for dear life. But he was kind too; nothing was too good for his children—or their wives, I might add. I imagine he wanted us to—well, we were supposed to be like one of the noble families he'd known as a child back in Germany. The Eberhardts were supposed to grow and flourish, become ever wealthier—own more land, build more mansions, marry other wealthy families, forever and ever—"

"And that's exactly what you're doing!" Arch exclaimed.

Julia laughed; Sarsfield looked closely at his aunt to see if she had been offended; she did not appear to be, but she hesitated before speaking. "Yes," she said, "I suppose it is."

The pheasant and salad were complemented perfectly by an urbane red wine of a markedly persistent character. Julia, of course, was drinking nothing but water; Aunt Ida, though no teetotaler, was drinking very little; so the greater part of the wines had been consumed by the gentlemen. Sarsfield, to his alarm, saw that Arch by now had drunk enough to become reckless. "It appears to me, Mrs. Eberhardt," he said, "that what we're talking about is an aristocracy—an American aristocracy—"

"Oh?" Aunt Ida said with a dismissive gesture. "I suppose you could call the very old New York families a kind of aristocracy—"

"And then the Astors pushed their way in," Julia said, "and then the Vanderbilts—and now *us*. That's what you mean, isn't it, Mr. Kimbell?"

"Yes," Arch said with a broad, ingenuous grin, "that's exactly what I mean."

"Well, Mama, what do you say to that?" Julia said, laughing.

"I would say that it's time for the next course, wouldn't you, you terrible girl?—Oh, Sarsfield, whatever shall I do with her?"

The easy friendliness of the conversation had been dimmed somewhat by the previous exchange; and Sarsfield felt a faint but unmistakably tension in the atmosphere—like the uneasiness before a storm breaks. The artichokes passed unheralded by any additional beverage, as did the *marrons glacés*, but the cheese and fruit brought forth a powerful Tokay which Arch drank with obvious relish.

"I often wish we had never left Raysburg," Aunt Ida said, sighing; "Here one must be so careful to do the right thing—always—but it's devilish hard to know what the right thing is. If we'd stayed in Raysburg, I'd know, but here—Times are changing *so* fast. Just try to make up a dinner party: the lovely young couple you had last month will turn out to be divorced! And then there are all the flirtations—You can't seat so-and-so next to so-and-so because—haven't you heard?—their affair is quite over! And you didn't know they'd been involved in any affair in the first place—"

"Ava Astor," Julia said, "she was a Willing, you know!—got herself photographed in *Vogue* playing tennis—"

"Good lord!" Sarsfield said with mock astonishment.

"That's right," Aunt Ida said, "and comment was made upon her athletic figure—and a few years ago, such a thing would have been simply impossible!"

Julia and her mother then vied with each other in supplying the young men with further amusing examples of the changing times—divorces and scandals and gossipy tid-bits of outrageous behavior; by end of dinner, the conversation had again grown so lively that

Aunt Ida suggested that it would be a shame to disrupt it; setting custom aside, the ladies accompanied the gentlemen to the drawing room. "We're all good Raysburg folk here," Aunt Ida said, "the niceties of deportment can go to the devil for the night—smoke by all means; yes, yes, please do."

The young men helped themselves to the absent Henry Eberhardt's cigars; by now Sarsfield was certain that his friend had a point to make; he'd seen Arch do this before: grab at an idea and hang on like a bulldog until he bit clean through it. He tried to catch Arch's eyes but with no success. "Excuse me, Miss Eberhardt," Arch said to Julia, "earlier in the evening you made a comment that I find really interesting: 'Money's the ticket,' you said, 'everyone knows that.'"

"Oh, did I say that?" Julia replied with a brilliant smile.

"Yes, I believe you did—And, well, ah—in Europe the aristocracy arose from force of arms and attained a *political* power; they had social responsibility that went with the position—but this new American aristocracy—Well, look, Miss Eberhardt, if the only criterion is money, where's the responsibility?"

If Sarsfield had not been, just at that moment, engaged in studying his cousin, he would have missed the flick of her eyelashes—the most infinitesimal of gestures—that betrayed her inner response; but then she said in a bright, tinkling voice: "I am sorry, Mr. Kimbell, but I have no opinions on such weighty matters. No; I'm not prepared for discussions with Harvard men. I'm only an empty-headed girl—and a thoroughly silly one. All I ever think about are my frocks and gowns—I have never had a serious thought in my life; and I'm unlikely to have one now."

Sarsfield saw his friend pondering these words: Arch had drunk too much; the stubborn, bulldog set of his jaws proclaimed that he was not about to let go. "If you'd never had a serious thought in your life, Miss Eberhardt," he replied to her, "you wouldn't be able to say that you hadn't."

"Now *you're* being silly, Mr. Kimbell. I won't allow it. I've cornered the market on silliness, and you shan't have any."

"So *that* is how she flirts!" Sarsfield thought—and felt a stab of jealousy so fierce he might well have been skewered on it.

Instead of taking up the game that Julia was offering him, Arch looked around the room, a baffled and unhappy expression on his face;

he appeared to have rediscovered, suddenly, exactly where he was. "Forgive me, Mrs. Eberhardt," he said to Aunt Ida, "have I said anything wrong?"

"No, you have not, Mr. Kimbell," Aunt Ida replied, and then turned to her daughter: "A young man such as Mr. Kimbell has every right to ask us such a pointed question, Julia. I'm sure that what he has said is what many people think—but don't have the honesty to put into words—"

"Indeed?" Julia said, "well, then *you* answer him, Mother."

"If we have more money than most people," Aunt Ida said, "then we should have more responsibility than most people."

"Spoken like a true Revington," Julia said.

"Julia, this is not a joking matter—for once. No; it is not."

"*Pardonne-moi, Maman*, shall I go to my room?"

Aunt Ida expelled her breath sharply and cast her eyes toward the ceiling as though calling upon divine intervention. Sarsfield cleared his throat and said: "Society *implies* responsibility."

"Thank you, Sarsfield," Aunt Ida said, "my point exactly. And, really, after all, the only thing that counts is breeding—and all the money in the world can never buy that!—Would you care for a liqueur, gentlemen—some brandy?"

"Brandy and soda would not go amiss, thank you," Sarsfield said; he saw that his cousin had searched out his eyes. She was flushed; he could not read her smile. The conversation was restored to safe ground; and nothing of consequence was said for the remainder of the evening.

"Give me a hand, kid, I'm reeling!" Arch said as the young men climbed the stairs to their rooms; "Did I disgrace myself utterly?"

Sarsfield was not himself untouched by the alcohol; he steadied his friend with one hand and himself with the other on the banister. "Not utterly—you barbarian!"

"Not too subtle.—Lord, you should have kicked me when I started in on the American aristocracy and all that guff—"

"I couldn't kick you," Sarsfield said, "I was too far away.—But nobody took it amiss," he added, although he was far from certain of that.

"I just can't get over the money that's being flung about," Arch exclaimed, "there seems to be no end to it! What d'you suppose that little spread cost them?—Oh, I know gentlemen aren't supposed to discuss such matters, but I'm just a counter-jumper under this 'tux,' and—what? Fifty beans a head?"

"More," Sarsfield said, laughing.

"Seventy-five?"

"The wines were all imported—more."

"Good God, old man, you can't mean it!"

"Shhh," Sarsfield said, propelled Arch into their sitting room with a good push and shut the door firmly. The gas had been lit for them and a fire made up.

Arch threw himself into a chair and kicked off his shoes. "I like them, I've got to admit it. Their sense of humor saves them.—Your aunt's really a grand lady, and your cousin—she's a daisy, all right!" and then he broke out into a chuckle. "By Jove, Sarsfield, she's so tight-laced I kept expecting her to snap in the middle like a wine glass! How on earth could she eat anything?"

The comment was so apt and embarrassing at once that Sarsfield could do nothing but join his friend in laughter. "Well, she didn't eat all that much, actually," he said; "I don't know, maybe it's considered part of a proper education in those fashionable French boarding schools, or maybe it's just some queer fancy of Julia's." He was not about to admit to his friend that he found his cousin's severely constrained figure as lovely as an image from Gainsborough. "She's half a child still," he said; "She's only sixteen."

"But beautiful," Arch said, "wheww! And bright as paint, and all that blessed money. She really is going to marry a duke, isn't she?"

"I expect so—if she wants to marry a duke. She's not as empty-headed as she would have you believe—"

"Oh, I know that. Give me some credit, old man; d'you think I'm thick as all that?—But she wasn't about to get into a debate with me, now was she?"

The friends retired; and Sarsfield heard Arch, the instant he laid his head upon the pillow, begin to snore. But Sarsfield closed his eyes and felt the bed wobble under him like a raft on the river. "Middletons should never drink," he told himself; and he lay there hanging on just as though he were being swept downstream.

There was something about all of this—the Fifth Avenue mansion, and the plethora of servants, the absurdly elaborate dinner, and, of course, his splendid cousin—that felt absolutely natural to him: he could live in this luxuriant, artificial life, he thought, as easily as a cat-fish in the Ohio. At the same time, something about it revolted him—just as much as it obviously did Arch—and he wanted to flee—not back to Harvard, but home to West Virginia where he belonged. He could make no sense of this inner conflict; he was too tired and full of food and wine to think about it.

The bed made a lurch, and he caught it just in time. Then, without being conscious of having done so, Sarsfield had already floated into that strange kingdom that lies just between sleeping and waking; like Huck Finn, he was being swept along to the south; he heard frogs and crickets, saw Julia on the bank in her elegant walking costume. She raised her veil and waved at him in an odd gesture that was like a salute. He was afraid he had lost her, but then she was on the raft with him; he saw her as a little girl in petticoats, and he called her "Cricket," and on down the dark river they went, not toward the Mis-sissippi but out across the great, sleeping, dark continent itself; and, his excitement growing, he called out to her: "Julia, this is how we will bind together all the streams of the nation!"—which was the last he would remember of this soft journey, for he had been carried away into the very darkness of sleep.

The next morning Sarsfield awoke to a fierce pounding in his forehead, sat up and saw that Arch was awake ahead of him. "Hock and soda water!" Arch called out, the only quotation Sarsfield could ever remem-ber from Lord Byron; Sarsfield could not manage even a chuckle.

The young men made themselves presentable and shambled down-stairs; there they were directed into a sunny room on the east side of the house where the family took breakfast. Aunt Ida, in the best of spir-its, awaited them; and they were compelled to make the acquaintance of Julia's brothers. Sarsfield had never met the boys heretofore because they had been, from their earliest years, sent to eastern boarding schools. Henry Junior—"Henty," as he was called—was a formal young man some five years Sarsfield's senior, who, by way of greeting, elevated his chin approximately one inch and bared his teeth. Arthur, the Princetonian, was exactly Sarsfield's age; and his relaxed, pleasant greeting was in marked contrast to his brother's artificiality. Henry Senior—wiley old Henry Eberhardt, "the Gray Wolf of Wallstreet"—was nowhere in evidence; either he had never returned the night before or, if he had, he must have crept out at dawn; no one referred to his absence, but considerable joking speculation was offered as to when Julia would put in an appearance.

Breakfast was well underway when Sarsfield saw his aunt suddenly change color; she opened her mouth to speak but then, apparently, thought the better of it. Sarsfield turned and saw that Julia had, once again, made a grand entrance; but this morning she was still wearing her lounging robe; automatically, he rose to his feet; Arch took his cue from his friend and rose also;—then Henry Junior and, with considerable reluctance, Arthur followed suit.

All eyes were turned to Julia. Her negligee garment was of gold and jade-green crêpe figured in a deep scarlet, trimmed with an enormous scarlet rosette and trailing innumerable scarlet ribbons; there was no sound but the the rustle of the crêpe as she approached, the skirt rippling behind her along the Oriental; she greeted the company with a dazzling smile. It was Henry Junior who broke the silence: "Julia!" he said in a shocked tone, "you are not *en famille*."

"Oh, dear; oh, dear," Julia said, not in the least abashed, and proceeded to the sideboard where she lifted the lids of the chafing dishes to see what was offered. "Sarsfield is my own sweet cousin," she said, "and he and Mr. Kimbell are like brothers, so that makes Mr. Kimbell my cousin too—" and added, in an affected manner that was a perfect mockery of her elder brother's: "quahte, ah—in a spiritual sense, doncherknow?" Then, reverting to her own accent—dryly amused—she said: "So as to *famille*, I would say that makes me quite sufficiently *en*—"

"You're no longer in West Virginia, Julia," Henry said, staring like a storm cloud at his sister. "Mother, say something to her—"

"She understands the point," Aunt Ida said with some annoyance, "so I suppose that's all that matters—"

"This is intolerable," Henry Junior said, his fingers rigidly gripping the back of his chair.

"Oh, oh, oh," Julia replied and began helping herself to scrambled eggs. Sarsfield stared, fascinated, as one of Julia's feet, in a tiny gold slipper with a high Louis XV heel, appeared momentarily under the edge of her robe.

"Will you leave, or shall I?" Henry asked her through clenched teeth.

"It appears to me, Henty, as you are the one who is offended, then you should be the one—"

"Arthur!" Henry said abruptly, signaling to his younger brother to accompany him out of the room. Sarsfield looked at Arch significantly; if Arthur left along with Henry Junior, they would have no recourse but to accompany them.

"Oh, Henty," Arthur said, "give it up!" and to his mother: "I don't see that what Julia's wearing is so hanged important we should miss our breakfast over it!"

Aunt Ida, at last, intervened: "Sit down! All of you. Yes, you too, Henty. You are embarrassing our guests—and I would have thought that making guests feel comfortable in our home were more important than insisting on the niceties of—Good heavens, sometimes I do wish we'd stayed in West Virginia! Julia, you shall please dress properly for breakfast in future—"

"*Oui, Maman*," Julia said.

"There, I've told her," Aunt Ida continued, speaking to her elder son, "now *do* sit down."

Julia chose the setting next to Sarsfield's; and, before he could turn away, he saw, as her robe languidly drifted a half step behind her, in that moment before she gathered it to her and closed it with one slender, white hand, that she must sleep in her stays. He felt the blood rise to his face, looked up and saw that her eyes, sparkling with amusement, were on his. "Good-morning, Sarsfield," she said, "I trust that you had a pleasant night."

Arch and Sarsfield passed the next hour by strolling in the garden and smoking the cigars they had found in the humidor in the library; the day was cold, but brilliant and clear. They walked on in a circle, past hedges and rosebushes,—past yet more hedges and more rose-bushes back to whence they had begun; neither of them said a word. Sarsfield was dying of curiosity to hear what his friend thought of the performance at breakfast, but he could not—and he did not know why—quite bring himself to ask. "Good tobacco," he said.

"First-rate," Arch agreed, taking the cigar from his mouth and studying it critically, "Havana, wouldn't you say?"

"Yes; I'd say so. Must be Havana. Nothing but the best for Uncle Henry." Sarsfield thought he could see something like suppressed laughter glinting in his friend's eyes. "Anything on your mind?" he asked.

"No; nothing in particular.—Lovely morning."

"Couldn't ask for a nicer."

After a few moments, Arch said thoughtfully: "I've never been in New York before, and—just like any other 'hick from the sticks'—I guess I'll do the sights. Yep; guess I'll hop a street car—take in the Statue of Liberty, see how the Flatiron building's coming along—"

"Arch!"

"Yes; old man?"

The friends stopped, turned, and looked at each other; Arch was grinning openly now. "Well," he said, timing his words like an actor, "seems to me she's *still* riding her pony into the drawing room."

Sarsfield was inexplicably angry, but, after a moment, found himself laughing. "Yes, indeed, sir," Arch said looking away at the brilliant sunlight, puffing meditatively on his cigar, "I do believe I shall take in the sights.—I daresay you can find some way to amuse yourself—*eh, old man?*"

"For God's sake, leave off, will you? Tell me what you're thinking."

"Two's company, three's a—"

"Don't give me that!" Sarsfield exploded.

"I've never in my life seen anybody so smitten," Arch said with a smile.

"I am *not* smitten!"

"Oh?"

"Maybe a little," Sarsfield said grudgingly.

"Uh-huh."

"You don't approve, do you?" Arch hesitated; and Sarsfield said: "Go on. Let's hear it."

"OK, kid, you asked for it. If you're still capable of rational thought, you might pause and inquire of yourself from time to time what sort of animal she might ride into the drawing room—after she's a married woman."

Arch, true to his word, set off to see the sights; and Sarsfield spent another half-hour brooding in the garden. He could not decide whether he was smitten or not;—oh, he knew that he still felt an enormous affection for his cousin; but perhaps it was a familial sort of feeling. Yes, she fascinated him, amused him; yes, he found her utterly beautiful—but *smitten?*—with all that implied? He never did arrive at a conclusion; eventually he went in search of Julia as though to test his feelings by a direct confrontation with the object of them. She was nowhere to be seen—not in any of the rooms on the ground floor—and he hesitated to search the upper levels, so he was reduced to inquiring of the inscrutable butler, who told him: "I'll see if she's in, sir," and returned in a few minutes to say: "Miss Julia will be down directly, sir. Please await her in the drawing room."

Sarsfield could not now imagine what he had been thinking the night before; no, he could not live easily in such a life as this; if he had to live surrounded by servants, he would, he was sure, go speedily mad. But presently Julia appeared in an elaborate tea gown; and, the moment she came bursting into the room with an energetic rustle, he felt a peculiar sense of relief. He had been wondering what he could do with her for the day; and, after they had sat awhile exchanging pleasantries, he suggested a photograph. Julia at once became as animated as a child offered a treat; her air of sophistication fell away, and he was astonished to see her actually clap her hands. "Oh, wonderful, Sarsfield!" she exclaimed, "I was hoping you had brought your camera with you! I'll do you a Pre-Raphaelite, shall I? I'll borrow the costume Mama wore to the Van Gorts' party last summer.—I'll do you one of those Rossetti 'damozels' who looks as though she needs a good dose of salts—intense, and brooding and just so utterly *spiritual*—" And, to make her point, she at once struck the very pose.

While Julia retired to prepare her costume, Sarsfield constructed his setting. In his earlier search for her, he had come upon a room done in Gothic; the high, vaulted ceiling with its elaborate pattern like blue polka-dots, the diamond-shaped panes of the French doors, the stained glass above them (a stylized peacock spread his fan)—created a romantic atmosphere like something from a Walter Scott novel and, he thought, admirably suited his theatrical cousin. Sarsfield tied one end of clothesline around the neck of the marble Cupid who, high on his box-like pedestal, appeared to be spurning poor Psyche's advances, the other end to the sash above the French doors; he draped the line with fresh linen sheets to act as a reflector. Through the leaded glass, the sunlight on fresh snow entered—brilliant and intense. "Perfect!" he thought, and, driven by a rapidly mounting excitement, paced up and down while he again awaited his cousin's appearance.

The moment she stepped slowly into the room, he saw that she did not look even remotely like a Rossetti "damozel,"—that the entire point of the photograph must be, for her, to display the smallest possible waist. For his camera, Julia had exceeded all demands of current fashion—and probably the limits of good taste, certainly that of good sense. Assisted by two maids, she approached cautiously, her movements so restrained that she appeared to have been transformed into a person wholly unlike her usually vibrant self;—and her waist looked so small that Sarsfield, in all seriousness, was sure he could have put his collar around her and fastened it easily. (The scientist in him wished he could take a tape measure to her). It was as though she were indeed, just as Arch had put it, in danger of breaking in the middle like a wine-glass stem; fully aware of that danger, her face white—absolutely bloodless—she stepped gingerly across the intricately inlaid floor and took up a stance by the French doors. She was in a state, Sarsfield thought, that a boy back in West Virginia would have called "trancified." He aligned her on his ground glass; he was not at all sure that he liked seeing her so utterly passive, so fragile; looking at her was giving him a sensation like seasickness.

With printing-out paper Sarsfield measured the light falling onto Julia's face, timed the arrival of the first perceptible darkening of the silver. He calculated his bellows extension. He wanted to drown his negatives in light, so he would make a three minute exposure.

"Do hurry, Sarsfield," Julia said with a slight, thrilling smile. "I do not wish to die a martyr to beauty."

She wore her lovely hair down (it was nearly dark as sable) and a jeweled circlet on her forehead to match the period implied by her mother's fake mediæval costume done in a cold blue; but the cut of the gown was unlike anything that would have been seen in the twelfth century (and quite the opposite of the flowing robes favored by the Pre-Raphaelites): the girdle fitted so smoothly and tightly over her corsets that Julia's maids must have sewn her into it. Given license by the theatrical nature of the photograph, she had used paint on her lips, giving them the fervent hue of rosebuds; and they presented the only color anywhere to be seen on her face—until one came to the electrifying energy of her huge, deeply blue eyes. By now Sarsfield felt himself to be fully compelled by the artificiality of the image she had created; for his part, he would do his best to capture it.

"You are," he said, speaking with the most sonorous voice of authority he could muster, "the most beautiful girl I have ever seen in my life." With such words does the photographer bring his subject to life; but, as he spoke them, he also knew that they were true.

Forgetting that Rossetti damozels were supposed to look melancholy, Julia again produced that eerie smile; it raised the hairs on the nape of his neck. He squeezed the bulb—and held it. The three-minute exposure created an interval quite separated from the normal flow of time. Both Julia and Sarsfield were scarcely breathing; each was staring with immense fixity of purpose at the other. Sarsfield released the bulb, felt the vital force drain from his body. He knew that he could not make another exposure. Julia was wilting visibly; he held out a hand to her, and she took it.

The negatives were first-rate. Contradicting the custom that photographs could not be hung on the wall, Julia hung the final print, gilt-framed, in the main hallway where anyone entering the house through the great glass doors of the front would see it. Sarsfield had not titled the work, but Julia's friends aptly nick-named it "The Snow Queen," proclaimed it as good as any of John Sargent's paintings; and, by next season, Sarsfield discovered that he had become the photographer most in demand by the girls in Julia's set. His mother's voice whispered that, if he were a gentleman, he would present his photographs as gifts; but the spirit of Jack Middleton won the day. They "paid through the nose."

4

By the time that Arch and Sarsfield arrived at Harvard, the innovative
changes that the great educator, President Eliot, had begun in the seventies were already in place; under his administration, students were
offered an unprecedented freedom of choice in their studies. Sarsfield
attended classes in chemistry, physics, and higher mathematics; Arch
struggled with medicine—beginning with anatomy and histology, was
soon to be heard at all hours muttering various of the ancient verses
used by medical students to remember their body parts. ("On old
Olympus' topmost top, a fair-haired German viewed a hop.") Sarsfield,
delighted to have a first-rate laboratory at his disposal, began work to
improve the speed of his emulsion. He was also pleased to discover
that he could, should he wish, write his senior thesis on the chemistry
of color photography.

The social life of the university, however, remained much as one
would have found it in the years before the war; the student body still
largely comprised wealthy young men, most of them from Boston; and
these worthies still considered athletics, drinking, and club activities
far more important to a proper education than scholarship. Arch, from
the moment he set foot on campus, was courted by members of the
football team and the rowing squad (one look at him was enough to
bring them around to feel his muscles); but he kept insisting that he
had come to Harvard to better himself, not to play; and he was dismissed as a "dig." Sarsfield was much more of a regular fellow; he had
the air of a gentleman about him; he would not really have minded
joining a club or two, would actually have enjoyed the prestige of
belonging to the DKE's, or even the great Porcellian; but, somehow, he
never got around to doing anything about it. So Arch and Sarsfield
worked out in the "gym," boxed a bit, enough to keep in shape, and
collected a few friends, enough to feel at home—a number of "odd
ducks" like themselves.

One activity to which they devoted as much of their time as could be managed was the pursuit of the ladies. "You can have your New York socialites," Arch said; "they're a bit too rich for my blood." So Arch and Sarsfield made a habit of "picking up" the bachelor girls of Boston—who seemed totally different from any girls he knew back home, and, indeed, made Sarsfield realize, in a way he had not heretofore, to what extent Raysburg was still a small town. Raysburg had a dozen or so "society" girls (Sarsfield's cousins), a large number of "good" girls (the daughters of bankers and shop-keepers), a class of girls his mother would have styled "common as dirt" (their families raised pigs and chickens on the Island), and then, at the very bottom of the heap, the totally foreign immigrant girls whose fathers worked in the mills. What Raysburg did not yet have were working girls like those in Boston—brash girls, sharp and "sassy," who strolled the streets in the evenings, or loitered about in "spas" (which, back home, would have been called "soda fountains"); girls who wanted to meet young men just as much as young men wanted to meet them. Sometimes a glance and a smile was all it took for Arch and Sarsfield to fall into step with a couple of beauties, slide into a conversation as relaxed as if they had known each other since childhood, and keep walking with them right on through to good-night.

After classes, Arch and Sarsfield would rush off to wait for the latest pair to get off work; they bought their girls dinners of sausages and beer, or took them to the theater or the penny arcade or the Vitagraph shows. Sarsfield loved these girls; he loved their humor, their brassy slang, the way they could achieve a bright, stylish appearance on pennies; he loved to be invited back to their rooms to share a dinner of spaghetti and wine drunk from toothbrush mugs; he loved to hear their stories of the working world; he loved the way these girls jumped into life with both feet,— the way they were determined, by hook or crook, to get ahead. Arch did his best to kiss them—and succeeded often enough to be pleased with himself; Sarsfield, always the gentleman, photographed them. Their pictures—in color—spread over his walls; classmates trooped in, as though to a gallery, to appraise the latest additions; comments were offered, not upon the art but upon the subject matter; and Arch and Sarsfield were proclaimed "a right pair of queeners."

"For the first time in my life," Sarsfield declared, "I feel like I'm living sixty to the minute!" and then asked rhetorically: "Who needs sleep?" Many nights Sarsfield contented himself with only three or four hours; Arch, whose larger, more robust physique required longer periods of rest, dragged about, red-eyed and yawning; in the middle of the night, the young men ate pie and drank vast quantities of coffee at "The Hole in the Ground," or strode up and down in Harvard Yard to "clear the cobwebs." But when he finally did go to bed, Sarsfield often could not fall asleep; and then he would watch the slow increase of dawn at the window and, with the detachment of a scientist, examine his own mental state. This was not the terrible insomnia he had experienced in high school; gone was the sense of some childish hob-gob-blin lurking in a shadow; being away from Raysburg and his family, he concluded, was doing him a world of good. And, in those long, intro-spective moments, he would always find his thoughts turning at last toward his cousin Julia.

After Christmas, Sarsfield had written Julia a short note; she had replied at once with a rapid, cheerful letter; and so they had fallen into a vigorous correspondence. Sarsfield hated composing letters, but he wrote to her every few days; her replies were delightful improvisations that appeared to have been penned non-stop in a matter of minutes. Her prose was filled with French phrases, incomplete sentences, fre-quent underlinings, and punctuated only with dashes and exclamation points; sometimes he would receive two or even three of these short, slap-dash missives in a single post.

In the spring, Arch and Sarsfield received formal invitations to Julia's "coming out" reception; and, as well, Sarsfield received a note from Julia herself begging him to come to New York a few days before-hand. "I have a bad case of the nerves," she wrote, "I am simply perish-ing with terror—oh, mon cher Cousin, do come to my aid—like a good, sweet knight—and hold my hand!" Arch replied with his regrets, told Sarsfield, at first, that if he did not keep his nose to the grindstone, he was sure to "flunk," but added later, in a more candid moment, that he was not prepared "to rub shoulders with the likes of the Astors or the Vanderbilts." Sarsfield did as he had been bidden; on the train to New York, he discovered, to his surprise, that he had his own "bad case of the nerves." He was disappointed to be met only by the Eberhardts' footman; but, the moment he stepped inside the house, there was Julia herself. Laughing, pouring out a giddy stream of words much like the way she wrote her letters, she rushed to him as though he were her oldest and dearest friend and seized both his hands; he felt again that curious relief which he experienced in her presence.

"I must go to your mother," he said.

"No; not yet! She'll forgive you.—I need you to advise me, dear Cousin. No; really, it can't wait." She was leading him up the stairs and into a study he had not seen before; he gathered that all of this fuss had something to do with her father, but he could not yet make sense of it. "—at the very last minute! To London! What a wretched, beastly thing to do, don't you think so?"

"What? Your father's gone to London?"

"Yes; that's what I just said. On his beastly business—He left yesterday."

"You mean, I still don't get to meet your famous—"

"Hang it all, Sarsfield, you're not going to meet him; nobody's going to meet him.—He's not going to be here! Don't you see?—And he's 'bought me off,' the way he always does—" She had closed the door firmly behind them, saw his apprehensive look, said: "Oh, don't be so silly. We don't need a chaperon." She swung away a row of books to reveal a small, hidden wall safe; she knew the combination, in a trice had the thick, steel door open and was drawing out a tray covered with black velvet.

She set the tray down on the great mahogany desk. She sighed; and then, for the first time since Sarsfield had arrived, she forced herself to speak slowly; and she chose her words with some deliberation: "My feelings for the great Henry Eberhardt are—frequently not of the warm, familial nature one would expect from a dutiful daughter."

Sarsfield smiled uneasily. "You want to back up and start over, Julia. I don't know what's—"

With an abrupt, annoyed gesture, she whipped the velvet from the tray; revealed were diamonds—a set of ear rings, a "dog collar" necklace, a bracelet, and a "stomacher" of diamonds—the largest diamonds Sarsfield had ever seen, so many of them that he quickly gave up his attempt to count them. He and his cousin, both struck speechless by the cold fire before them, stared first at the glittering stones, then at each other. "That's supposed to make up for it," she said, "for his absence—Oh, it's not as though he hasn't done this to me before—"

"By Jove," Sarsfield said, and heard how fatuous his words sounded even as he uttered them: "there's a lot of diamonds here."

She giggled. "Oh, Sarsfield, what a perfect thing to say!"

They stared at the diamonds another moment; and then she said in a grim voice: "Two hundred thousand dollars, or maybe three hundred—I'm not exactly sure."

"Julia, please, don't joke—"

"I'm not joking."

Sarsfield walked away to the window where the spring sunlight was penetrating the small panes of leaded glass; he needed that moment to compose himself. The wealth represented by those cold stones would have bought all of Raysburg Island with money left over, would have supported dozens of families in comfort for the rest of their lives, would have—but he gave up his speculation; he could not figure out what he was feeling. He heard Julia saying: "Father overestimated my waist by a couple of inches. The man at Tiffany's had to knock off a few thousand dollars' worth to get the blessed thing to fit."

He had to laugh at that; he turned back to confront his cousin. "Débutantes are not supposed to wear jewels at their coming out," she said. "It's considered tasteless."

"Yes; it *is* tasteless."

"He obviously expects me to wear them."

"Don't do it."

"Are you sure?"

"Yes."

"Thank you. I won't wear them—" and then she exclaimed in an anguished voice: "Oh, Sarsfield, I've never felt like an heiress before, *but that's what I am!* I shan't be able to marry anyone unless he's filthy, filthy, *filthy* rich; how else could I believe he really liked me?"

The evening reception that occasioned Julia's début was held in the ballroom at Delmonico's. She wore a tulle gown made by the house of Worth, that venerable institution which had, for decades, dressed European royalty and American heiresses. Worth gowns were known for their opulence and conservatism; Julia's was the most virginal of white, as befitted a débutante at a *bal blanc*, and even more conservative than usual; the cut of it made no concession whatsoever to contemporary style, and it could have been as easily worn in the nineties as in the new century; the old-fashioned lines of it, with a tightly fitted bodice, were perfect to show off Julia's equally old-fashioned figure—laced to a degree that the women of Aunt Ida's age had not seen since their own débuts. Julia wore the *de rigueur* white evening gloves—they were smooth as a second skin and extended practically to her shoulders—and no jewels whatsoever. The *décolletage* was the most extreme permissible within the bounds of good taste; and Julia's long neck and smooth shoulders—snow-white and flawless— were exposed to the view of the world for the first time in her life. This was still very much the era in which women were expected to be ample—even plump;—and Julia certainly did not exemplify that particular ideal of feminine beauty: there was a delicacy to her—in the tender curve of the nape of her neck, in the small points of her shoulder blades, in the hollows beneath the fine lines of her collar bones— that was very nearly too childish for the gown; but Sarsfield saw her as a paradigm of all that is fine-bred and feminine and tenderly young. As she moved through the ballroom, she created a hush, a small circle of silence before her; and Sarsfield could not imagine any young man in his right mind not falling instantly in love with her.

Sarsfield passed the evening in a haze of apprehension—unwarranted, as it turned out, for it was said afterward that it could not have "gone off" better: all the right people were there. As he danced with her, Julia whispered in his ear: "Don't be obvious, but look toward the corner—it's Jack Ass himself!"

"Who? What?" Sarsfield said.

"Jack Astor, silly, the old toad's son! He's probably just come to *look* at me."

Neglecting his studies, Sarsfield remained in New York so he could, chaperoned by Aunt Ida, escort Julia to the Vanderbilts' ball the following weekend. Now that she was "out," Julia wore yet another Worth gown, this one highly decorated—a silk taffeta in pale gold, printed with roses and trimmed in guipure lace—and with it, all the damnable diamonds. To his amazement, Sarsfield heard from the sophisticated crowd a perfectly audible gasp as they entered the ballroom.

Sarsfield returned to Cambridge in a dark and sour mood; he had never understood before just how wealthy Henry Eberhardt must be; Sarsfield himself would inherit, at the most, a few thousand dollars from Thaddeus Eberhardt; but he would never be "filthy, filthy, *filthy* rich." He threw himself into his work; and then, much too soon, the school year was over. He invited Arch to stop over in New York with him but Arch declined.

Julia and her mother were preparing for the Newport season; Sarsfield was the only young man within anyone's knowledge who actually enjoyed going to fittings. He and Aunt Ida sat in the fake Louis XV chairs at the dressmaker's as Julia appeared in her various summer "outfits" and posed for them. Although he could not have said precisely how he came by the knowledge, he always knew exactly what was *à la mode*, exactly what looked best on her: "No, not the pink—try the peach," he would say, or: "You can wear your skirts just a hair shorter than that." His aunt and cousin lauded his taste and soon began to defer to him. "It so helps to have a man's opinion," Aunt Ida told him.

Sarsfield and Julia sat holding hands in the garden behind the house. "Why so gloomy, Cousin?" she asked; "Look at the trees! Spring's in the air, birds are singing—You're with me—"

"I've got to go home."

"No, you don't. Come to Newport with us."

"Oh, Lord, Julia, I'd love to do that, but—No, I've got to go home."

By the middle of June, Sarsfield felt as though he had been back in Raysburg so long that he might as well never have left; little there had changed: his father was still drinking and spouting his oratorical nonsense; his mother still lay abed reading her novels; the summer heat was oppressive as it always was; his brother and sister were older, that was all. Sarsfield paid a duty call upon his grandparents, reported upon his first year at Harvard; they seemed pleased enough. Arch was helping out in the dry-goods store, and Sarsfield was assisting Jack at the shop; in the evenings the young men walked along the river bank, drank beer, commiserated with each other, and slapped at mosquitoes. Sarsfield's old insomnia returned; just at the point of dropping off to sleep, he would sit bolt upright in bed, fighting for breath, oppressed by the sense of some terrible dark spirit lurking just beyond his field of vision. Julia might well have been a distant, fairy-tale princess he had met once in a dream.

By August, Sarsfield could no longer bear to remain in Raysburg going through the motions of "learning something useful for a change"—as Jack Middleton styled his son's impressed labor at the shop. He ignored his father's howls of outrage and went to Newport.

Henry Eberhardt had commissioned, from a distinguished society architect (noted for the extravagance and massiveness of his *Beaux Arts* style), a summer home; Henry had specified that the building should compare favorably to those already built at Newport by the older New York families—such as the famous Vanderbilt "Breakers." No expense had been spared; the work had been completed by the previous year; and Julia and her family had been there all summer. The Eberhardts' "cottage," copied from a palace at Versailles, was styled "Seacourt," but Julia called it "Daddy's Pile"; nearly fifty servants were required to maintain it. Julia escorted Sarsfield on a tour of the formal French garden, the stables (which housed not only a half-dozen of the finest carriage horses but several motor-cars), and, finally, the house itself. Passing through the ostentatious dining room with its high walls of pink Numidian marble, Julia said: "—and this intimate little corner, as you can see, is perfectly appointed for the casual family breakfast"; then, leading Sarsfield through the vast ballroom with sculpted walls done in gold leaf, she said: "and here, in this quiet, tasteful chamber, one might, of an evening, invite a few of one's closest friends to stave off ennui with a modest dance—"

"What's your mother's line about 'wealth forcibly displayed?'" Sarsfield said. "By Jove, this is, ah—"

"Isn't it, though?"

"And am I finally going to get to meet your illustrious father?"

"Afraid not. The 'Gray Wolf' can't seem to tear himself away from New York—*Business*, don'tcherknow?—and, of course, his Florodora girl.—Oh, yes, he does have one; he shopped around and bought the best one he could find. I got a glimpse of her once, quite by accident. Yes, she *is* lovely—a classic beauty actually. Sometimes I wish Mama would divorce him, and *in New York* to make a public spectacle of it— but she never will. Good heavens, Sarsfield, could you imagine being married to a man like that!"

They strode along the Cliff Walk overlooking the sea, and Sarsfield heard Julia express for the first time the full depths of her resentment of her father. "He's a crude man," she said, "for all of his surface polish. In the bosom of his family—upon the rare occasions when he manages to *be* in the bosom of his family—he will tell you, once again, for the thousandth time, just as though you had never heard it before, the tale of how he got to be so very much richer than Uncle Thaddeus—"; and she assumed a tone imitative of her father's dry, pompous voice: "My dear older brother may boast all he wishes of his service to his country—sentimental poppycock! No such nonsense ever swerved *me* from *my* duty, I can assure you—"; then, in her own voice, she added: "His duty, you understand, is the making of money: thus he serves his family, his country, and the world."

Julia had stopped walking she was looking fixedly out to sea. Sarsfield studied the white cameo of her exquisite profile. "Remember Mama's favorite story of Grandfather," she said, "how he blew his nose over the railing? Well, Papa's favorite story of Karl Eberhardt is this— He asked his father once if he should devote himself exclusively to the manufacturing of iron, and the old man replied: 'Oh, no, Henry'— 'Heinrich' he called him—'you must put your money where it will do you the most good!'—*Cher* Papa always delivers that maxim in German, and it's the only German I have ever learned. I've often thought that if we had a coat of arms, it should say that—"

She turned to Sarsfield with her brilliant smile: "The Eberhardt arms: smoking mills rampant on a field of dollar signs, with the motto boldly inscribed beneath: *'Streue die Gulden wo sie am besten gedeihen!'*"

During the two weeks Sarsfield spent at Seacourt, Sarsfield and Julia engaged in an endless conversation, interrupted only when they slept; even in company, each had eyes only for the other; and it appeared that they would never exhaust the mutual desire to share their innermost thoughts and feelings. Julia was a surprisingly active girl (more of a "sport," he thought, than he was); in the daytime she gave up her old-fashioned "wasp-waist" French corsets for modern ones of a gentler design, and they played lawn tennis, or strode along the Cliff Walk, or climbed into Julia's little electric runabout (she had named it "Angelica") and went buzzing out to the golf course to engage in that gentle game which had recently become "all the rage" in polite society. They bathed on Bailey's Beach, attended gay luncheons—followed by bridge parties, musicals, teas, and receptions. Their evenings were spent at grand dinners and glittering balls. Julia, showing not the least sign of fatigue, could dance till three and then rise at nine to propose a long walk before breakfast. Sarsfield photographed her on the tennis court in a dazzling white dress, on the beach in a bathing costume, in the formal garden of Seacourt in her crisp shirtwaist and elegant walking skirt, in the gold ballroom in gowns by Worth and Doucet. Late at night they met secretly, and, quiet as thieves, crept into the billiards room; her brothers had taught her the game, and she beat him more often than not.

That Julia should be so "taken up" by her male cousin did not pass unnoticed in the staid atmosphere of Newport; and more than one eyebrow was raised; but Julia appeared to be utterly unaware of the fact that she and Sarsfield were fast becoming the subject of some not inconsiderable gossip; and, for his part, Sarsfield was so enchanted with her that he threw his normal caution to the winds. In the quiet, brilliant light of perfect mornings, deeply engrossed in each other, the cousins strolled for hours above the murmuring sea.

Having heard Julia's frank talk about her father, Sarsfield found himself—hesitating and stumbling over the words—telling her what he had thought he could never tell anyone: something of *his* father's despicable treatment of his mother. He could not, of course, speak of the most sordid and unhappy of the details; and he couched the whole in language he deemed appropriate for the ears of a young lady; so, when he concluded his tale, the events had been as expurgated as the editions of Shakespeare he had read in high school; but, nonetheless, the telling of it had been a strain upon him. "And I—I did nothing," he said, feeling again the full shame of it.

"I don't understand, Sarsfield," she said after a time. "What is it that your father actually—*did?*"

The question struck Sarsfield mute; and he could only look at her with his misery written on his face. "He had been drinking?" she asked. He nodded. "He was inebriated—badly inebriated?" she asked. He nodded again. "And then—?" she prompted him.

"I'm sorry, Julia, I should not have—"

She stamped her foot. "I won't have it! I thought we were chums.— You must speak plainly. You must tell me *everything*." And that, of course, was what he could not do; he knew by now that he had been the greatest of fools even to have raised the topic; he could not find any genteel and acceptable way to elaborate upon it. "Did he strike her?" Julia asked. He could no longer bear to look her in the eye; he turned away and nodded.

Then, as though he were hearing words spoken by another, he heard a strangled voice emerge from between his clenched teeth: "He struck her with his fists. He struck her as he would have struck another man."

"Oh!" Julia exclaimed.

They stopped walking. Close below them, the sea murmured on quite as though nothing remarkable were occurring. Looking down,

Sarsfield saw, glistening in the cheerful sunlight, bright pools left by the receding tide; he saw in them periwinkles, tiny crabs, and starfish. This pleasant perspective mocked the turmoil he was feeling: he was so light-headed that he feared he might faint; everything he had ever been taught told him that now he must stop; he had, indeed, gone much further than he should ever have dreamed possible. Julia caught his hands and said: "Oh, how terrible. How utterly terrible."

After some moments had passed, she asked: "Was this often, was it—"

"Twice," he replied; and then, before he could forestall the words, he heard himself say: "You see, I have a brother and a sister."

Julia stared at him with a look of total incomprehension on her face; then he saw the truth of the matter flood into her eyes. She did something he had never seen her do before and would never see her do again: she closed her right hand into a fist, pressed her knuckles firmly into her mouth, and bit down.

"I'm sorry," he said. "I shouldn't have told you. Can you ever forgive me?"

She took her fist from her mouth and gasped; he realized that for several seconds she had not been breathing; he saw that her teeth had imprinted a neat row of indentations upon the smooth surface of her glove. "Oh!" she exclaimed "Oh!—*Such things are not possible.*"

They walked on for quite some time without speaking. Suddenly she burst out with: "God help me, Sarsfield, I should have been a shopkeeper's daughter—a barman's daughter—for then I would know more of life than I do now! What else have I never heard? What else is totally beyond my comprehension?—Oh, I hate it with all my heart, to be so—so ignorant, so naïve!—Oh, and you must have felt—so utterly—You must have suffered so!"

Again he could only nod mutely; but then he added: "But I did nothing."

"What could you possibly do?"

"I don't know, but I could have—I should have been able to—" As he tried to continue, he discovered that he had lost the power of speech.

"You were just a child, Sarsfield!"

"Not the second time. I was sixteen."

"And that isn't a child? What do you think you should have done?"

"I don't know."

They had walked a mile or more from the house; they turned now to walk back. "I'm not a boy," she said, "but—Listen to me, Sarsfield, there is *nothing* you could have done."

The brilliant sun and the pleasant surroundings seemed a mockery to Sarsfield, so plunged was he into a state of despondency. Julia took his hand; and, as they walked on, she began to narrate an experience of her own. At first he listened with only half an ear; but soon he became engrossed in her tale.

"After I rode the pony into the drawing room," she said, adopting a tone so archly aloof that she might have been talking about someone other than herself, "which so many people—including you, *cher* Cousin, found so amusing, I discovered soon enough that my father was not amused. It was, he said, 'the last straw'; and shortly after that, a small boarding school in New York was found for me. Up until then *cher* Papa had taken hardly any notice of me, for, you see, I was not a *boy*—and, therefore, not one of God's elect—but suddenly he took my education to heart. My mother protested, but, you see, there was nothing she could do.—And so I was forced to sit silently and listen while my father told the head-mistress and several of the teachers that I was a disobedient, willful, thoroughly unruly child—and that they might inflict upon me any discipline they saw fit—no matter how often or how severe—and that his only requirement was that, when I was returned to my family, I should have been thoroughly schooled in proper deportment. I was utterly humiliated—having to sit and listen to this;—perhaps you can feel something of how humiliated I was—but there was nothing I could do.

"I learned to dissemble, Sarsfield. Had I not done so, I should have suffered even more than I did.—It was often said to me that I had no one to blame but myself; but I knew then—and nothing I have learned since has changed my mind—that I could, with justice, blame certain others far more than myself. I often thought of running away—but to go where, to do what? So you see, there was nothing I could do.—I learned to behave exactly the way they wished—and with a smile! Oh, it was a valuable lesson, I assure you. And I resolved that later, so far as I could, I would do exactly as I pleased;—and when I was returned to the bosom of my family, all pronounced me a paragon of maidenly virtue. I begged so sweetly to go to France that I was sent to France; and France suited me;—and since then—I generally get what I want, Sarsfield.—And you're a man and have much more freedom than I, so use it. But you must stop saying to yourself that there was something you could have done—when there was *nothing* you could have done."

They had returned to the house by then; she turned to him with her brilliant smile. "Now that you have been properly lectured," she said, "let us go in and see what Cook has invented for us today."

Sarsfield felt exhausted by the conversation; and the remainder of the afternoon, and the evening, passed for him like a dream. When he was again alone and settled into his bed, he told himself that he must analyze what had transpired between himself and his cousin,—that he must, surely, decide whether he had overstepped the bounds of propriety by telling her his story, and that he must ascertain what significance *her* story might have for him. But, as he lay back and prepared himself for hours of long, dark thoughts and worries, he fell asleep upon the instant.

Much too soon Sarsfield was again at Harvard. He sat slumped in a corner and watched, with growing annoyance, as Arch, whistling madly, stowed away clothes and sports equipment, arranged his books, and pinned up pennants and pictures. Finally Arch stopped and turned upon his friend a look of solemn regard: "If it's that bad," he said, "why don't you marry her?"

Sarsfield felt a profound inner shock at the words and said nothing for the moment; his mind appeared to be empty of thoughts. "She's my cousin," he heard himself saying. "You can't marry your cousin."

"Don't give me that," Arch said. "You're not first cousins, are you?"

"No, we're once removed."

"I daresay that's removed enough."

"I expect it is, but—" and then Sarsfield found the words to articulate what he had been feeling: "Good God," he exclaimed, "I couldn't marry an heiress!"

One of Harvard's brightest lights, William James, was just on the point of retiring; Sarsfield, eager to study with him, enrolled in a course he would not ordinarily have taken: the Philosophy of Nature. Sarsfield was at home with concrete things—numbers, graphs, measurable phenomena;—and the general, speculative nature of philosophy baffled him; he felt often that he was, indeed, learning something, but he could not have said exactly what. Professor James was a challenging teacher with a wicked sense of humor; Sarsfield felt considerable sympathy with a classmate who interrupted a lecture by exclaiming: "But, doctor, doctor! To be serious for a moment—"

It was not a good year to attempt to comprehend the thought of William James, for Sarsfield would later remember his sophomore year at Harvard as the one he had spent in New York. After the last class of the week, within the hour, he would be on the train; he often missed his Monday classes, and, far too often, his Tuesday classes as well. New York society was notoriously deficient in young men (Sarsfield saw hardly anything of Arthy and Henty; he never did meet Julia's father); and he was welcomed everywhere. He and Julia, chaperoned by Aunt Ida (who liked a good time as well as anyone), attended the theater and the opera, receptions and dinner parties. Then Sarsfield was amazed to receive, in his own right, an invitation to the Astors' annual "crush"— a sure sign that he had made the grade, and rather speedily at that. "Everyone finds you an exemplar of graciousness," Aunt Ida told him "They know you're related to us; and they just adore your photographs of the débutantes.—They can't quite place West Virginia," she added with a laugh; "They know it's down there somewhere; I'm sure they think it's part of the grand, old Confederacy!"

Because of the circles in which he was now moving in New York,— and because of his very indifference to the social life of Boston,—his stock at Harvard was rising rapidly; had he made the least effort, he could have joined any club on campus. But to do so, he would have been forced to spend some time at Harvard.

The summer before, Sarsfield had met, and photographed, most of the girls in Julia's "set"; they all had ridiculous nicknames. (Julia's, he thought, was so apt it was almost pleasant: she was called "Jewel.") Her closest friends were a pair of girls from old New York families; they were pretty enough, and rather sweet, but otherwise unremarkable; Julia styled them (but not to their faces) the rabbits. "Bunny" Van Gort was pale, chatty, plump, and blonde (Sarsfield photographed her in pink tulle); "Mopsie" Smythe was slender, dark, quiet, and smiling (Sarsfield photographed her in blue silk). On snowy winter afternoons when the rabbits came to call, Julia played ragtime on the graphophone; and the girls taught Sarsfield to do the two-step. He grew fond of Julia's friends; and he loved dancing with Julia; he loved holding her tiny, firm waist— the feeling of her "steels" under his hand. When Sarsfield danced with Julia, she pressed into him so tightly they were like two spoons.

And Sarsfield loved the mysterious spell cast by early evening when he would sit talking quietly with Julia and Aunt Ida in the east drawing room. The house had recently been wired for electricity; but Aunt Ida always turned off the electrics and lit candles. Sarsfield drank a single whiskey and soda; the women drank each a tiny glass of sherry. Sarsfield felt calm, quiet, totally at peace in that hour before dinner. Julia had by then slipped easily enough into the rôle of the vivacious society girl: when she was amongst people, she was always in motion—laughing, talking, flirting; but in that quiet hour her face was relaxed. She did not look like an Eberhardt; she had the lean, thoroughbred features of the Revingtons; and Sarsfield could see why she was so often compared to Consuelo Vanderbilt who had married the Duke of Marlborough. She had not Consuelo's height; but she had the same delicacy, air of fragility (which Sarsfield knew, in Julia's case, was deceptive). Julia, so it seemed, had taken the likeness between herself and the Duchess of Marlborough to heart and had developed a worshipful passion for Consuelo not unlike that of a school girl for a beloved actress; although she had never met Consuelo, Julia referred to her by her first name, collected newspaper cuttings and, from Vanderbilts or friends of the Vanderbilts, tid-bits of gossip about her. Looking at Julia's regal profile, Sarsfield prayed that she would not, like Consuelo, allow herself to be transformed into a "baby duchess."

At Christmas, Aunt Ida invited Arch to visit again; and Arch surprised Sarsfield by saying: "Why not? I've got to have my look at high society at least once a year, don't I?" The second day that Arch and Sarsfield were in New York, Julia proposed that she dress as a boy so that they could escort her to all the places she would not ordinarily see. "By Jove, Julia, you can't do that!" was Sarsfield's reaction.

"Why ever not?" she said; and Arch, laughing, echoed her: "Sure; why not? Sounds like great fun to me."

"It just wouldn't be—Well, what if someone saw you?" Sarsfield essayed lamely; he already knew that he had lost the argument.

"Don't be such an old flapdoodle," she replied like the West Virginia girl she had once been; "I'm too old to spank," and went off to search out discarded clothing of her younger brother's.

"She *will* ride that pony!" Arch said.

"Bother you!" Sarsfield said, unable yet to see the humor in any of this.

Julia returned in knickers and boy's boots, her hair hidden by a cap, and posed for the young men. "Strike a wider stance there, Julius," Arch said, chuckling, "or someone will take you for a nancy-boy."

Sarsfield could not say a word; Julia had made herself into a convincing, if overly pretty, twelve-year-old lad. They crept out of the house through a side door, escaped in a breathless rush to Fifth Avenue where they hailed a hansom. Then, within the half-hour, they were, much to Sarsfield's alarm, treading the sidewalks of one of New York's worst slums. The pale, cheerless winter sunlight was rapidly fading; a blustery wind had sprung up with a stinging hint of snow in it; but the streets were teeming with life. The cold had brought a high color to Julia's cheeks; taking long, vigorous strides, she did, indeed, look like a boy. "I miss my skirts about me," she said, giggling; "I feel—almost naked!"

They passed coal-heavers whose blackened hands and clothing proclaimed their occupation, a cluster of working girls trudging wearily homeward, a bent figure pushing a cart loaded with rags and bottles, a little girl with winter sores on her lips hauling a bucket of beer. All along these streets rose ancient three- and four-story tenements with their dim, red paint flaking away; despite the weather, faces hung from open windows; shouting voices were to be heard everywhere. From lines strung on the all but useless iron fire-escapes required by law, laundry depended, frozen stiff.

"Wait; listen!" Julia said. A snatch of gay music drifted from an unseen window. "It's Mozart," she exclaimed, "I can't believe it!" Then, before Sarsfield could stop her, she turned toward a man sitting bundled in a shabby coat on the front steps of one of the dark, crowded buildings: "Excuse me, sir. Who's playing the violin?"

The man looked up at them with tired, red-rimmed eyes; he shook his head shyly, said, in a thickly accented voice, "No English," then called out: "Yankele!"

Upon the instant a small boy appeared from the black hallway within; after a conference with his father conducted in the Jewish tongue, he said: "My pop vants I should ask you gents vat you vant here." Julia repeated her question. "Oh," the urchin said with a broad grin, "dat's Mr. Greenbaum. Ven so tired he gets he can't woik, he plays the feedle."

"What work is he doing?" Julia asked.

"Piecewoik," came the response as though it were obvious; and then, to illustrate, the boy made sewing gestures. "We all do piecewoik."

"You too?"

"Sure."

Sarsfield was becoming overwhelmed by the stench of sewage and cooked cabbage; he gestured for Julia to keep walking, but she ignored him. She continued to ask the little boy questions—which he answered readily enough, grinning at her with inexplicable good humor. He and his family—six people in all—lived in two rooms; no, there was no steam heat or hot water; no, there were no gas lights in the halls. "Who owns this building?" Julia asked.

"Ve pay rent to the padrone—the dago."

"But who *owns* the building?"

"Vy, Mr. Astor owns the building; he owns all the street!"

Then the father spoke a sharp sentence in his own language; the little boy supplied the sense of it: "My pop says Mr. Astor from his mudder's vomb shudda been scraped!"

The festive mood with which the friends had set out had vanished; they walked quickly now along the befouled sidewalks—westward, seeking the end of this impoverished district. "'I lift my lamp beside the golden door,'" Julia quoted bitterly, "what a bad joke that has become!"

"Well, Julius," Arch said, "haven't you been aware that there are poor people living in this fair city with you?"

"You can go to the devil, Mr. Kimbell!" she returned; "being aware of them and seeing them are two different things."

After some further moments of silence, Arch said: "Seems to me we're not about to solve the problems of the underpriviledged tonight, so why don't we have some fun?" With that he plunged through the doors of a workmen's saloon.

A pitcher of beer helped to restore the friends' spirits; and they set out to tour the city. They hired cabs and went where they pleased, driven through the cold night on nothing more substantial than momentary impulse. They walked on the docks, sat in the Bowery Mission for the length of one lugubrious hymn, marveled at the gaudy display of electric lighting in Times Square. Arch took them at last to Chinatown, where he had gone exploring on a previous visit; with his modest experience in the ways of the Flowery Kingdom, he told their waiter to bring them whatever he wished; and, for the next hour, they dined on they knew not what—whether pork, beef, chicken, or, as Julia suggested, alley cat; they could not identify even the vegetables.

At the end of the meal, Julia exclaimed: "Capital!" in a masculine voice; "First-rate!" She was sprawled in their booth with one leg up, expansively smoking a cigarette. In the course of the evening, as Arch had urged her on ("We'll make a man of you yet, Julius!"), she had been mimicking the gestures of her companions; by now, not a trace of the feminine remained. The only thing that Sarsfield saw that might give her away was her manicure: he could not imagine any boy, not even the most foppish, with such perfectly shaped, pointed, and highly buffed nails. Now, by a curious reversal, the nails appeared wrong and everything else right; it was hard for him to imagine that she was *not* a boy.

Sarsfield could not admit to himself how uncomfortable he had been until after they had safely escorted her home. Then, the moment they crept through the small side door for which Julia had secreted a key, she removed her boy's cap, her pins and side-combs, and, in a gesture that was shocking and unexpected, let her long, dark hair come tumbling down. "There!" she said.

"Oh, Julius, Good-by!" Arch exclaimed in mock grief.

"Good-by, sweet gentlemen, and good-night," she replied, all of her feminine gestures at once fully restored, and vanished down the hallway.

That night Sarsfield could not sleep; at dawn he stole out of the house and walked up Fifth Avenue—past the mansions of the rich— aiding his introspection with one of his uncle's cigars. Julia's performance had put him on edge in a way that was both pleasant and unpleasant at once: for one giddy, wholly irrational moment he fancied that his cousin might be free from the constraints that bound ordinary mortals,—that, by an act of sheer will, she could be anything she wished, from school boy to duchess. He felt about Julia that what she was at best was not readily apparent; but he could almost see it—the essential spirit of her—floating just above her shoulder like a tender angel. He knew now what he should have known months—or even years—before: that he was in love with her, that he had always been in love with her.

Sarsfield did not tell Julia what he felt for her,—nor did he tell Arch. He spent every weekend in New York. In Cambridge he brooded, took long solitary walks, and read the poetry of Elizabeth Barrett Browning; he felt as though the poetess had looked into his heart and articulated his innermost thoughts and feelings with a beauty and clarity that he, himself, could never have done: every word of every line of every sonnet was *true*! "A heavy heart, Belovèd, have I borne/ From year to year until I saw thy face," he read, and felt his eyes flood with tears.

Sarsfield barely passed his courses. In the spring Julia and her mother sailed for France and Sarsfield returned to Raysburg. In the stifling heat of long, tiresome afternoons, he escaped from his father by his usual ploy of climbing to the roof of the shop; there he stared at the constant stream of dingy smoke that rose and drifted down the river—the effluence of the mills—and thought of old Karl Eberhardt's motto: "*Streue die Gulden wo sie am besten gedeihen.*" Sarsfield and his cousin were both living on the harvest of the gold that Karl had "sown where it would grow best";—but America, he thought, must not be allowed to continue on this cruel course that made the rich so very rich and the poor so very poor; he was certain that Julia knew that as well as he did. And suddenly it seemed to him right, fitting—almost inevitable—that Karl Eberhardt's granddaughter and great grandson should marry; who could better understand each other than these two? But then, filled with a wordless foreboding, he wondered what dark obstructions yet to be encountered might lie "betwixt the stars and the unaccomplished fate." He went to Newport the last week in July.

The moment Sarsfield saw his cousin, he knew that something was wrong. He had paid his compliments to his aunt who had directed him to Julia in the garden; he walked down the long, straight path and saw Julia in the distance as though on a stage, awaiting him like a figure in a Watteau painting. As he approached, he was struck by the notion that she must have posed herself—perfectly attired in a perfect setting—so that he would discover her there. She was wearing a snow-white frock with an astonishing number of petticoats (her skirt swept the lawn in a circle that must have been a good eight feet around); the bodice was fitted tightly over her sculpted waist—which appeared to have shrunk another inch since he had seen her last. A beribboned hat protected her from the ruddy light of the setting sun; with a tiny pair of silver scissors, she was daintily snipping roses and dropping them into the basket held by her maid who followed silently a few paces behind. Maid and mistress wore identical white kid gloves. Sarsfield felt as though he were walking into a *tableau vivant*. "By Jove, Julia," he exclaimed, "you should have been an actress!"

Instead of laughing or responding with a jocular remark, she kissed him lightly on the cheek. *"Mon cher Cousin,"* she murmured with an enigmatical smile.

For the first time since he had known her, Sarsfield and his cousin did not fall easily into the unconstrained conversation of "old chums." Presently she dismissed the maid and the roses, led him to the conservatory where she had arranged on display the half-dozen pictures she had bought in Paris. He was longing to tell her of his most intimate feelings; but she wanted to talk about recent developments in French painting: "I've decided to become a collector, Sarsfield; what do you think of that?" Her canvases were of the latest "Impressionist" school—glowing, brilliant landscapes; for Sarsfield, the most interesting thing about them was how much they resembled photographs,—how the small dots and dashes of pure color blended in the eye like the grains of silver in a print; but when he tried to articulate his thoughts, she exclaimed: "Oh, do not speak to me of *chemistry*, speak to me of a *symphony* of color—bordering on the obsessive! Speak to me of gold and ochre, scarlet and azure, exhausting themselves in the intense cruelty of light!"

"Oh, Lord!" Sarsfield thought.

In the next few days he soon discovered that Julia had, in Paris, acquired more than petticoats and paintings; there she had been taken up by an alarming pair of New York beauties some years older than herself who were now her inseparable companions; and, upon only short acquaintance with these ladies, Sarsfield longed to have the rabbits back. Sally Tingsley was a tall, slender creature of enormous, doll-like artificiality; her blonde tresses were just faintly brighter than nature could have provided; she was a married woman, but her husband was never in evidence. Gertrude, "Pussy," Sunderland, although well on in her twenties, was still considered a *jeune fille à marier*; in a sibilant voice she pronounced the latest gossip in a manner so gleefully malicious that she fully lived up to her nickname; with her demon-girl's eyes and habit of winding unpleasant beads of glistening jet through her long, threatening fingers, Pussy could have sat for a portrait by a French *decadant*. Julia styled her new friends "amusing," pronouncing the word in a way that Sarsfield found chilling; his Aunt Ida, he discovered, was just as disconcerted by these ladies as he was. "There's some excuse for Mrs. Tingsley," she said, "Her father's a meat packer in Chicago. But there's no excuse for that Sunderland girl at all: her people have been here *forever!*"

Aunt Ida put Sarsfield in a difficult and delicate position; knowing nothing of his feelings toward her daughter, his aunt spoke to him about Julia's prospects as though he were a trusted member of the family—which, after all, he was. It was as apparent to Sarsfield as it was to his aunt that Julia's position in New York society was not so well established that she could afford to take the liberties that her new friends did. Sally, as a married woman, was under the protection of her husband, the powerful J. Endicott Tingsley; and Pussy, no matter what she did, would always be a Sunderland—so some wealthy fool was sure to marry her for the name;—but Julia could, if she did not take care, drift into the outer circles where she would be considered *déclassé*, and, therefore, not be able to get herself a proper husband. "I would so appreciate it, Sarsfield," his Aunt Ida said, "if you could—well, guide her, advise her—try to slow her down just a little. She really is still a child—and she so loves sensation; I can't do a thing with her—never could, for that matter—and there's no talking to her. It isn't as though she has actually *done* anything yet, but—" and here Aunt Ida abandoned words for an eloquent gesture of helplessness.

Sarsfield knew exactly what his aunt meant. To match her new companions, Julia had acquired a surface polish that seemed as hard and glazed as porcelain. In Paris she had sought out the most advanced styles; and, in the stuffy, conservative atmosphere of Newport society where one was not supposed to stand out (ladies often "aged" their new gowns for a year before wearing them), she stood out—like a butterfly amongst moths. Heretofore, she had reserved her most severe tight-lacing for grand evening affairs; now she wore the smallest of corsets from dawn till dusk, and her severely constrained waist no longer seemed a charming anachronism—but rather something more befitting the stage than the drawing room. The most advanced New York ladies had taken to face paint, but it was supposed to be applied so delicately that no one could be certain that it had been used at all; Julia did not observe this rule, and Sarsfield could too often see, even by candlelight, color superimposed upon her lips and occluding the pale clarity of her skin. She wore shoes with the highest French heels, always, and went about in the evenings dripping with diamonds. But worst of all, she now feigned a jejune cynicism, a sophisticated world weariness so unrelieved that Sarsfield felt like spanking her. He could not seem to break through his cousin's newly acquired façade to see if his old chum still lay beneath it. Had she, as he seemed to remember so clearly, really been such a good friend that he had thought he could tell her *anything?* Had he really been in love with her?

"Are we still friends?" he asked one afternoon when he had managed to separate her momentarily from Pussy and Mrs. Tingsley.

"Of course we are!" came the response; "How could you possibly think that we might not be?"; but even as she said it, the manner in which she smiled put a distance between them and the words of brotherly counsel he had been preparing died on his lips.

When Sarsfield was settling in at Harvard that fall, Arch asked: "And how fares the glorious Miss Eberhardt these days?"

"Oh, she's riding her pony at a full gallop," Sarsfield heard himself reply. The young men laughed; and Sarsfield was ashamed: he felt that he had betrayed his cousin. "Oh, she can go to the devil!" he said to himself; but at Christmas, he went to New York.

Pussy Sunderland absolutely *adored* telling him the story of how Julia and Mrs. Tingsley had stopped conversation dead in Delmonico's by walking in with their eyelids painted blue; Julia gleefully told him how she and Pussy had been arrested for smoking in public; he himself was there in the Vanderbilt ballroom, exercising, so it appeared, not the least bit of a restraining influence, when Julia created a scandal by dancing "the hootchy-kootchy." He also accompanied her (he never did understand exactly how she had talked him into it) to the party at Rector's where they dined with an excessively rapid "set" of wealthy gentlemen who brought "actresses" with them; Julia chatted with these brassy, painted, slangy peroxide blondes as freely as if they had been fellow society girls. The host was Bunny Van Gort's uncle Peter—a genial, expansive, florid fellow who gave the lie to the notion that bankers are the soul of rectitude. The aging black sheep of the Van Gort tribe, Peter was known to enjoy his pleasures; he was even considered something of a rake; and he at once took a great fancy to Julia. "Look at her 'figger,' girls," he said to the actresses; "she puts all of you to shame—indeed she does. Why, Miss Eberhardt, you adorable creature, you'd even put Anna Held to shame!"

Sarsfield found these remarks tasteless, to put it mildly (a gentleman does not comment upon a lady's "figger," nor call her "adorable," nor compare her to a naughty French actress reputed to have the smallest waist on Broadway); but Julia only said: "Don't take it so to heart, *mon cher*; he thinks he's paying me a compliment."

Sarsfield and Aunt Ida shared their fears in private: "I can't slow her down one iota," Sarsfield said, "I can barely keep up.—Now she doesn't even take her maid when she goes out; she runs around town without a chaperon—"

"Chaperon!" his aunt exclaimed; "Heavens! She hasn't been properly chaperoned in months. Oh, Sarsfield, she must be married!"

It was bitterly cold that winter and snowed every day; he and Julia skated in Central Park; he loved her splendid black velvet skating costume with its shockingly short skirt (later he photographed her in it—for once in black and white—and made an eleven-by-fourteen gum print that won a prize at the New York City Camera Club). The vigorous outdoor exercise brought a color to her cheeks far more becoming that her Parisian rouge; and the simple, healthy activity restored, at least for the moment, the unaffected, high-spirited girl he remembered. Laughing, they walked back to the Eberhardt mansion arm in arm; like a schoolboy, he carried her skates. "Do they still skate on the back river?" she asked him.

He was startled; he had almost forgotten that she had spent her childhood in Raysburg. "I expect so," he said. "Did we skate together?"

"Of course we did. Don't you remember? There were bonfires on the banks all up and down the river, and we skated from bonfire to bonfire.—I thought we could go on skating forever, for miles and miles, on down to the Mississippi—I thought it was all frozen, you see—and never come back!"

Sarsfield felt a painful stab at his heart; he had planned to say nothing serious to her, but he heard himself exclaim: "Julia, what has happened to you? Lately you've become so—" He didn't know how to complete the sentence.

"Haven't I, though?" she said; and she suddenly burst out with her old intensity: "Oh, Sarsfield, you can't imagine what it's like!—I'm supposed to get myself a proper husband, and I see all these young men looking at me, and there's nothing in their eyes but dollar signs! And I have nothing, nothing, *nothing* to do!—I can do nothing but spend money, and no matter how fast I spend it, there appears always to be more—"; then, giggling, she added: "Yes, I can always count on *cher* Papa to make it faster than I can spend it."

"Well, couldn't you, ah—find some serious activity to occupy your-self, one in which you could—begin to make yourself responsible to society, begin to make a contribution—"

"Oh, Sarsfield, you have no idea what you sound like! Not even Mama can sound so owlishly proper as you—when you climb up into your pulpit. What would you have me do, read poetry to fallen women, join the Epworth League?"

Hurt, he did not reply; she squeezed his arm, said: "Please don't worry about me, *mon cher*; I shall turn out all right in the end."

Sarsfield hoped that this exchange would signal the return of their earlier intimacy; but, by dinner, her distant, glittering façade had been fully restored, and Sarsfield resolved to return at once to Raysburg. As the snowy days passed, however, he continued to find himself in New York; and in the new year he escorted Julia to the Astors'. He danced with the Misses Van Gort and Smythe, and even with Pussy Sunderland (who alarmed him by flirting), and watched the men swarm around Julia; he tried to see them through her eyes: how the devil, he asked himself, *could* one tell which of these smiling, drawling "dummies" was a fortune hunter and which was not? Julia danced three dances with Peter Van Gort.

By the time that he and Julia returned home, it was nearly four in the morning and the house was dark and silent. "Are you sleepy?" she asked him.

"No; not particularly," he said; in fact, he felt fully in the grip of the demon insomnia.

"Good. Allow me—oh, about half an hour—and then come to my rooms—Oh, Sarsfield, you should see your face! You are simply *too* funny! No, *cher Cousin*, I am *not* making an immodest proposal."

With considerable trepidation, Sarsfield did as he had been bidden. He tapped at her door; arrayed in a tea-gown, she ushered him in. Julia's domain, he was not surprised to discover, was Rococo done in white and gold with Louis XV furniture; but he was startled to see that she had framed a number of his photographs and hung them on her walls. No sooner had he settled himself uneasily onto one of the deli-cate chairs than Julia's maid appeared, bearing a tray; with some alarm, Sarsfield sprang to his feet; Julia, laughing, waved at him to sit down. The maid passed by him as though he were invisible.

"Thank you so much, Lucy," Julia said to the girl. "Now you must sleep in tomorrow—promise me you will."

"Oh, I couldn't do that, Miss Julia."

"You shall! I shan't be up before noon, and there's no reason why you should have to be either. No, I don't want to hear another word— now off to bed with you."

"Do you often entertain in your rooms at four in the morning?" Sarsfield asked after the maid had departed.

"You're the first guest of your sex, my dear.—Oh, don't look at me like that. Your mere presence won't compromise me—as if anybody cares anyway!" She lifted the covers from the dishes; he saw that something on the order of a full meal had been prepared. "Tea?" she asked; he shook his head. The midnight supper at the Astors' had been a splendid one, and he was still sated from it; Julia, he recalled now, had eaten nothing.

"Please forgive me," she said, "for I am simply ravenous," and then, glancing up at him, she exclaimed: "Oh, must you perch there like a great bird—quivering with such patent disapproval! Do come here—"; she patted the seat of the couch upon which she was sitting; reluctantly, he joined her.

Sarsfield hid his discomfort by examining the books that lay on the low table before him; they were all in French; he had heard of none of the authors. Julia, by now, had devoured a slice of bread and some half-dozen oysters. Feigning a jauntiness he was far from feeling, he observed that her code of deportment must forbid dining in public. "Oh, no!" she exclaimed with a laugh, "I should have eaten if I could—but in the corsets I was wearing, if I had taken so much as a filbert, I'd have fainted on the spot."

Sarsfield could think of nothing amusing to reply, so he began skimming the pages of the first book at hand. "I've often thought of myself as a sacrificial victim on the altar of beauty," she said, "which, of course, leads one to the question of for whom one is sacrificing—certainly not for any of the idiotic men that come sniffing about one like a pack of hunting dogs.—Do you know what that fatuous old Peter Van Gort said to me?—"

His eyes drifting over the printed words in front of him, Sarsfield listened with only half a mind as Julia rehearsed her flirtations of the evening. He felt a sudden nausea; blood mounted to his face: his command of French was not all that it could be, but it was good enough for him to comprehend the general sense of the immoral and disgusting passage that lay before him. He threw the book down, exclaimed: "Good God, Julia, what a vile load of rubbish! Do you actually read this—?"

"Don't be such a prude!" she responded lightly. "One cannot be corrupted by a book—as Oscar Wilde said—or maybe he said that one could, I can't quite remember—"

"And don't *you* be so damn flippant!" he answered her. He was feeling an unaccountable rage so boundless it frightened him; he did his best to master it.

"Oh," she said after a moment, sighing, "please don't be angry with me, Sarsfield. No one else knows me as well as you do—not even Mama. I'm surrounded by all these men who—There's not one of them who stops, even for a moment, to consider that I might be capable of holding an opinion—on any topic more profound than ribbons and bows. So if I've learned to be flippant, can't you see why? Can't you forgive me?"

"I'm sorry, Julia," he said, mollified. "It's just that—well, lately I haven't been able to tell what you're thinking—about your life, about your future—"

She looked into his eyes a moment he could not interpret her expression. Then she said: "My life and my future? Good heavens, what weighty topics."

She returned to her repast, continued to talk between bites: "When I returned from school in France—that must have been just before you first came to us—I used to lie there on my bed—under that huge canopy—"; and he followed her gesture that invited him to contemplate, through the partially opened door, the high, white-and-gold bed; "and I would think about—'my life and my future.'" She pronounced the words in grave tones that mocked his seriousness. "I would consider my education and wonder what it was that I had been prepared for; I would fancy that I were being made into something, fashioned into something—as Consuelo had been fashioned into a duchess. I would close my eyes and imagine myself sacrificed, immolated.—I would imagine that the least signs of resistance, rebellion, were being ruthlessly crushed out of me—until I were utterly devoid of will. I had no idea to what end I was intended, but I could see—oh, something quite perfect, utterly beautiful and artificial—a painting, a sculpture, a perfect trinket like something made at the whim of the Medici—"

As she continued, she became more animated; her voice took on a gaiety that did not match the import of what she was saying. Sarsfield, who was following the sense of this with the utmost difficulty, felt his head swimming; he understood the surface meaning of her words well enough, but the emotion that impelled them remained incomprehensible to him. "If I allowed myself to enter fully into these fancies," she said, "I would feel as though every fiber of my being had been stripped from me and that all that remained was a tiny spark that might resist— well, no, for I was beyond resistance—that might wish something other than what was being done to me. Then, with the most cruel sensation of anguish—of the most *pleasurable* anguish—I would surrender that last tiny spark of myself—"

Sarsfield waited, not daring to interrupt her train of thought; he was feeling a growing sense of horror that he could not comprehend. "Then, when I returned to France," she said, speaking quickly now, vivaciously, as though she were back at the Astors' ball, "I came upon Saint Julia."

"Saint Julia?" he said. "What the devil—?"

"I was shocked," she said between bites of her glazed pheasant; "I didn't even know there *was* a Saint Julia? Did you?—She was tortured in the most appalling way—and crucified. I came upon her in the Louvre quite by accident. It had never occurred to me that they crucified women; but there she was, hanging upon her cross just like our Lord—with the most lovely expression of mystical resignation on her face—oh, just so utterly ecstatic! I looked down and read: 'Saint Julia,' and a thrill passed through me—a mixture of the most exquisite pleasure and the most profound and terrifying dread.—I returned to her again and again. I wished I were a Catholic so that I could pray to her. Her legend is simply delicious; she was a slave girl, and—"

"Good God, Julia, what are you going on about!"

"Saint Julia of Corsica," she said with her brilliant smile, "my patroness." She tore off a piece of bread and began spreading it thickly with marmalade. "Oh, but I have quite lost track of what I was saying, haven't I?—No, I haven't at all, actually, for it was Saint Julia, seeing Saint Julia—It struck me that—well, if I were being totally annihilated—sacrificed to the ruthless will of another—then whose will was it? Why, my own, of course! *I* was the one who was willing my own destruction, my own recreation.—*I was fashioning myself into my own work of art!*"

Sarsfield's mouth had gone dry. He had by then, along with most of his classmates at Harvard, read Max Nordau; but, until that very moment, he could not have said that he had ever encountered the sickness of profound mental alienation that Nordau; describes. He forced himself to look at his cousin; she was smiling just as though she had been talking of nothing more serious than a new gown. "Julia," he said, "I'm afraid that—By Jove, this is hard to say!—But there's something about you—I mean, about the way you're—I don't know quite—" There appeared to be no way he could avoid it, so he used Nordau's word: "It just seems—*degenerate*."

He saw the shock of the word strike her: a minute quiver passed down the entire length of her body; the color drained from her face. He stared into the brilliant depths of her dark blue eyes as though searching out the meaning of an obscure augury; then he looked away. He was just upon the point of excusing himself, rising and bidding her good-night, when she said in a small, broken voice: "Heavens, Sarsfield, you must think I'm—What would you have me do, seek out an alienist?"

"No," he said, "just stop mooning about and day-dreaming in this morbid fashion and find yourself something *real* to do in the world."

Her countenance, for a moment, wore the look of a child who has been cruelly admonished; he reminded himself that she was only eighteen. After some minutes of painful silence had passed between them, Sarsfield rose and murmured his good-night; she did not respond. He hesitated, then stepped to the door. "Oh, Sarsfield," she called after him, "don't despair of me!"

He could not find it in himself to respond. He smiled, and nodded, and shut the door firmly behind him.

Sarsfield soon discovered that living his life without Julia in it was a task that had been easy enough to plan, but soon proved to be the devil's own work to put into practice. When he had ridden the train to Cambridge, he had felt as grief-stricken as if someone had died,—and also, mysteriously and violently angry; and then his course had appeared clear to him: he must put Julia out of his mind and throw himself vigorously into his studies. But once back in his rooms at Harvard, he sank into a despondent state that seemed to him just as unhealthy as his cousin's; he woke to each new day with all the enthusiasm of a prisoner who has been cast down an *oubliette*. He kept going over the events that had transpired during his stay in New York and trying to make sense of them; for the first time since his childhood, he was not able to master his feelings by a cold, thoughtful analysis. What, after all, had he learned from Julia's revelation?—only that her imaginative faculties were highly developed, that she was capable of acting out any rôle she chose; and neither of these facts should, by now, have taken him by surprise. Why, then, had he been so horrified? She was, after all, still an impressionable girl; and, as such, should she not be allowed her queer flights of fancy?

There was, however, a sense of something gone mysteriously awry. He had felt similarly about his mother, and, in his worst moments, about himself—about the dark, brooding spectres that had haunted his childhood. Perhaps, he thought, there *was* a taint in the blood, but not, as Doc Anderson had suggested, from the Raineys; perhaps it came from the Eberhardts. It had long been the practice upon the birth of any new baby of Rainey blood for the anxious parents to gather periodically at his crib to peer into his face until it could be ascertained whether or not the poor mite had inherited the wandering Rainey eye; perhaps Eberhardt children, Sarsfield thought, should be similarly watched,—but for what? Were there obvious, tell-tale signs of degeneracy? And, oppressed by these morbid thoughts, Sarsfield dragged through his days.

After some weeks of forbearance, Arch shouted at him: "For God's sake, Sarsfield, pull yourself together! If you don't, you'll 'flunk' out of here—and then what'll you do?"

Sarsfield looked up dully; Arch sat down in front of him and said: "Listen, kid, I can guess what must have happened, what you must be feeling—No, no, you don't have to tell me! But now's the time to get down to work, to throw yourself into action.—Turn away from the past; stop dwelling upon it; put it all completely out of your mind. 'The strenuous life,' eh?—That's the ticket. Look to the future. Get on with it. Believe me, kid, good, hard work and the passage of time will cure anything."

Sarsfield was so angry with his friend that he could not speak; but, after some further days had passed, he had to admit to himself that Arch was right. He put aside his brandy and his "Liz" Browning, returned to lectures, sat up till dawn "cramming." He told himself that it was largely Julia's fault that he had fallen so far behind: how could he have been expected to excel in his studies when he had spent so much of his time in New York? By spring he had fought his way back to a position of academic safety; but he knew that a few months in Raysburg (the heat, the mosquitoes, *his father!*) would be the death of him—particularly when he would not be able to console himself with the prospect of escaping to Newport in August; he wrote to his grandparents asking them to continue their support through the summer while he remained in Cambridge; and they did not fail him.

Sarsfield took up boxing seriously again, beat his knuckles bloody on the heavy bag, danced around the light till he was winded, sparred with whoever would "have a go," ran along the Charles at dawn, took showers so cold they made his teeth chatter. He wrote a paper on photographic dyes, sent it to *The Journal of American Photography* where it was at once accepted for publication. He built a new one-shot camera of a lighter, more sophisticated design than his first. And, struck by a sudden, fierce intellectual hunger, he read philosophy, history, political science. He took up again Will James' *Psychology;* he had given only the most cursory attention to the book when he had studied with the great man; but this time he read every word of it. He read Steffens' *The Shame of the Cities* and Ida Tarbell's muck-raking *History of the Standard Oil Company;* "Good Lord," he thought, "what kind of account might be written about the rise of Raysburg Iron and Steel or the financial manipulations of a man like Henry Eberhardt?" For a week or two, filled with rage and indignation, he flirted with Marxian socialism,—until, with soul-satisfying relief, he returned home, his understanding deepened by his sojourn on foreign soil, to the Republican Party of Teddy Roosevelt. When Arch arrived in Cambridge that fall, Sarsfield was ready to argue the notion that the privileged classes "should be hit—and hit hard—with a tax on their incomes."

Arch was delighted to see Sarsfield looking so fit; and Sarsfield had to admit that he was pleased with himself. One gloriously crisp afternoon in October, the young men drank several pitchers of beer and then strolled through Mt. Auburn Cemetery; aware of the many eminent dead beneath their feet, they talked of the great American nation;—they spoke with the gleeful eagerness of good friends who already agree with each other—all the way down to the finest points of the topic under discussion.

"It's clear by now," Sarsfield said, "that Jeffersonian individualism has had its day."

"Absolutely!" Arch agreed.

"Now's the time for sacrifice, for—"

"A measure of discipline," Arch said.

"Yes, that's it!" Sarsfield exclaimed. "Each class has its own task—some, however, need to be severely restrained—"

"The wealthy—"

"Precisely! The least coöperative element in our society—But they *shall* be made to pay their fair share—"

And, speaking of an income tax, an inheritance tax, trust busting, the end of the "boss system," the regulation of interstate commerce, the way Teddy had settled the coal strike ("I represent the third party in this dispute—the public!"), the incorporation of labor unions into the national life, and the absolute necessity of an "imperial democracy," they strode back toward Harvard Square in search of a few more pints of lager to aid them in their frank exchange of opinions;—they found, as well, fine Havana cigars, oysters on the halfshell, and, by nightfall, good steaming bowls of Boston clam chowder.

They sauntered back to their rooms singing "Daisy Bell" and such other old, pleasing tunes as sprang to their minds, tipped their hats to a pair of lovely young girls they passed just outside the gates; and, as Sarsfield stepped into Harvard Yard, looked up and saw the stars shining overhead, he felt his spirit soar to the heavens, thought: "By Jove, *I feel fine!*"

Within the week Sarsfield received a letter from Julia, the first one in months. She had written:

> Mon Cher—
>
> I knew you were angry with me when you did not respond to my letters—but I did not fully understand what I had done until you did not come to me at Newport this summer—I cannot <u>blame</u> you—Oh, how <u>horrible and affected</u> I was! I simply cringe when I remember it—It was like a fever—I caught it—and it had to run its course—can you <u>forgive</u> me?—oh, please, please write to me—and please, please come to me at Christmas—I am still, and always, your chum—
>
> love,
> "Cricket"

Sarsfield did not wait for Christmas but took the next train to New York. Julia was remarkably transformed. Gone were the face paint and the daring French fashions; gone were her flippant, sophisticated manners (she appeared positively demure!); and gone were her two alarming friends. Mrs. Tingsley was sailing in the Mediterranean with an "advanced" crowd (exactly where she ought to be, Aunt Ida said with a sigh of relief; and Pussy Sunderland (at the last possible moment, for she would soon turn thirty) had been married by the heir to an immense Pennsylvania coal fortune and carried off to grace the "top of the heap" in beauteous Scranton. "The rabbits," meantime, had been restored to premier place in Julia's hierarchy of friendship. Mopsie Smythe, who was now to be called "Evelyn," was engaged to the youngest of the Livingston boys (a brilliant match, so it was said); Miss Van Gort, who could still be called "Bunny," had not yet decided amongst the three eminently suitable young men paying her court. "And who," Sarsfield asked his cousin, "is calling upon you?"

"Perhaps," Julia said, responding to his question precisely in the spirit in which he had asked it, "I have taken a vow of chastity."

Sarsfield had expected that he and his cousin would at once fall into an intimate conversation, "have things out," resolve their differences, and resume their old relations; but nothing of the sort occurred. Julia behaved toward him in a distant, nearly formal manner that belied the frankness and warmth of her letter; she had become so proper that her behavior appeared to him a parody of propriety. He asked Aunt Ida what was going on. "I'd be the last to know," came the response; "I'm merely her mother. I just hope someone suitable marries her while she's still in this phase!"

"I know you're still angry with me," Sarsfield said to Julia; "but what on earth are you up to now? Have you decided to become a paragon of maidenly virtue?"

"Perhaps," she replied, "I am atoning for my sins."

"What sins could you have to atone for?"

"They must have been grievous indeed to drive you away from me for ten months."

"Look, Julia, I'm sorry—It was—I've been wanting to—"

"No, don't apologize, Sarsfield," she said; "the fault is all mine."

He fell silent; he could not tell if she were play-acting or not. "After my *degeneracy* had been pointed out to me," she said, still speaking in that carefully modulated, sweetly feminine voice she had adopted (a voice he did not remotely trust); "I resolved to spend two years—exactly to the day—in a state of utter submissiveness to the most minute rules of propriety."

"Oh?"

"At first I thought it best," she continued, "to restrict my reading to the New Testament—there is much in the Old, you know, that is not fit for the eyes of a young lady—but then I thought that I might also allow myself—not often, you understand, no more than once a fortnight—and only as a reward for the most ladylike behavior—a single chapter of *Little Women*. But I realized that with such a regimen I might eventually, and by slow degrees, become accustomed to my punishment—and the pain of it would be diminished; and we wouldn't want that, now would we?—So I hit upon a new plan. For several hours each day I now read the most depraved French literature that can be had—until my passions are aroused and inflamed, my nerves stretched to the breaking point—until, in short, I am utterly beside myself with blazing, unearthly desire—Then, when I force myself to contemplate—"

It had rapidly become clear to Sarsfield that Julia was "ragging" him mercilessly; he had resolved to hold his tongue and give her no satisfaction for her efforts; but now he exploded with: "Oh, for God's sake, Julia, stop that!"

"I'm sorry if my fancies are still too *degenerate* for you, Cousin."

"You little witch!" he yelled at her, "why do you have to be so— insufferably *clever?*"

"And why do you have to be such an—utter ass!" she yelled back.

They had been strolling in the garden; now they turned to face each other. "You prude!" she hurled at him "You—" and she was obviously searching for the most vile epithet she could find: "You *cotillion master!*"

Sarsfield burst out laughing. "Thank you," he said; "Thank you very much."

"Why did you do that to me!" she demanded, still angry.

"You scared the bejesus out of me, that's why."

"I did?"

"Crucified on the altar of beauty—Saint Julia of Corsica—what on earth were you—?"

"I'm sorry! I meant what I said in my letter. I really was horribly horribly affected. I really do apologize, but—"

For a moment both fell silent; they simply looked into each other's eyes. Sarsfield felt a horrible pang of despair; he knew that he was still in love with her. "But I didn't have to do what I did," he said to her earnestly. "I didn't even answer your letters!—Oh, I feel rotten about it,

Julia! A true friend wouldn't have done that. I was just beastly. Will you forgive me? Can we be friends again?"

She sighed. "I shall forgive you—eventually; but I want to make you squirm first."

"I'm squirming."

"No; you're not," she said; but now at least she was smiling. "You're nowhere near abject enough."

"Shall I crawl?"

"Yes; do!—Oh, Sarsfield, I never thought you would desert me like that! It was all just too—You see, it all came to a head within the week. First there was you—then Mopsie and Bunny each took me aside and gave me a stern, sisterly talking to—then Mama! Good heavens, I was causing pain to everyone in the world! I went to Arthy, and—He'd been holding his tongue like a good brother, but he had some plain talk for me too. I just couldn't bear it! What was I doing that was so bad? I was just—well, amusing myself, but you would've thought—But, no; I must've been quite terrible. Everyone was so upset with me!"

She took his hands, gave him a grave look; he had never seen her so stricken. "Yes, I forgive you. Please forgive me too—for whatever it was I was doing. I was just playing a child's game, and—so it appears—I was playing it too fervently. It always seems I play too fervently. Oh, and everyone wants to marry me off, and I suppose I must be married— I shall have no freedom until I am!"

Her eyes filled with tears; she shook her head angrily and blinked them away. "At least Consuelo could blame it all on her mother," she exclaimed. "But no one is *forcing* me—I mean, no one is *really* forcing me—although I do feel forced. Indeed I do. I seem to have—I don't know—reached some cul-de-sac in my heart; and I can't get out of it, twist and turn as I might.—I don't want to be an heiress, Sarsfield! I like having the money—I'd be a hypocrite to pretend that I didn't; but, oh, sweet heaven, I don't want to be an heiress!"

Sarsfield remained several days longer in New York; but, although he and Julia spent much time together and spoke freely enough, they never did overcome a sense of estrangement between them; their friendship now, he thought, was like an image on his ground glass that would not quite come perfectly into focus; his only recourse was to the hope that time might heal the breach. At Christmas, he went home to Raysburg.

It had been a year since he had last been in West Virginia; and he was struck, as usual, by how nothing ever seemed to change there; but something vital in himself must have changed, for he saw everything from a slightly different angle.

"Glad to see the Harvard swell could condescend to visit his folks at Christmas," Jack Middleton said, and then seized Sarsfield's hand and pumped it. "Welcome home, son," he exclaimed with a small, affecting quiver in his voice; "Welcome *home!*"

"He's mad as a hatter," Sarsfield thought, an opinion that he would never before have dared to frame into words,—an opinion that was confirmed later when Jack said in an off-hand manner: "Just wanted to tell you—I'm proud of you, son; guess I've got to admit it.—And you know, you didn't have to go to that old bastard, Thaddeus Eberhardt, for the money. *I* would have sent you to Harvard. Just had to get used to the idea, that's all."

Sarsfield stared at his father. "The truth of the matter means nothing to him," he thought; "He'll say anything that crosses his mind—and convince himself that he means it!"

Sarsfield paid a visit to his grandparents to thank them for their continuing support. "Don't go on so, boy," his grandmother said; "We know you're grateful." She took his arm, escorted him into the drawing room; and Sarsfield realized that he was no longer afraid of her.

Sarsfield's grandfather rose to meet him and boomed out the same fatuous words—they scarcely varied by a syllable—he always said when he first laid eyes upon his grandson: "My boy! How good to see you again. How are you? You look fit, 'pon my soul you do."

"I'm well, Grandfather," Sarsfield replied.

"And how did you find my brother—well, I trust?"

"It might seem odd to you, Grandfather—it seems odd to me—but I've never met Uncle Henry."

Thaddeus produced one of his big, quaking laughs that died off into spluttering bursts of words: "No, no—not all that odd—nose to the grindstone—and all that, eh?—Price one pays; yes, yes, indeed." He mopped his red face on his fine linen handkerchief. "Well, sir, Henry may have amassed more of a personal fortune than his poor older brother, but at what price?—*at what price!* Never at home. Don't know his family. Is it worth it? You tell me, Sarsfield. It's like old John Jacob Astor said—you can live like a rich man on only a million! Ain't that right, Sarsfield? On only a *million*!" And he was lost again in another eruption of laughter.

Smiling dutifully, Sarsfield wondered if this fat fool before him could really be the great Thaddeus Eberhardt,—a man for whom he had always before felt a regard bordering upon awe. But what then, after all, had his grandfather done to arrive at the pinnacle of success? Thaddeus Eberhardt had, through a series of brilliant maneuvers, pitilessly driven from business most of his competitors in the valley; with armies of hired hooligans, he had broken every strike that had ever been attempted at any of his mills; when challenged to justify the low wages he paid, he righteously quoted the social Darwinists; he sent spies to every union meeting within sixty miles so that any Raysburg Iron and Steel employé seen in attendance could be summarily dismissed. And now Sarsfield suddenly saw the man before him as a great, round dog, throwing out his "Woof, woof, woof!" in the hope that no one will notice that he has grown too old to bite; and Sarsfield had to admit that, as much as he might despise his grandfather's business practices, he was quite fond of the old dog.

When Sarsfield was settled with a glass of whiskey and soda, his grandfather said, beaming: "We're so very proud of you, Sarsfield; you're a credit to the family."

"Yes, very proud," his grandmother echoed.

"Your great-grandfather would've been proud of you too! Yes; he would," his grandfather went on; and Sarsfield thought: "Oh, so old, dead Karl has his oar in too!"

"After your graduation, Sarsfield," Thaddeus said, "had you considered joining us at Raysburg Iron and Steel?"

Sarsfield was shocked. "Well, ah—to tell you the truth, Grandfather—"

"Well, give it some thought. We'd be delighted to have you."

"Be a bang-up good start for a young man," his grandmother said, jumping in, "that's right, believe you me.—And the girls in the valley—don't turn up your nose at the girls in the valley, Sarsfield. Some of the new crop of 'debs,' you should just see 'em—sweet and pretty and well turned out—finished back east, you know. New York's got nothing on our 'debs,' Sarsfield."

"I'm sure it doesn't, Grandmother."

"I never cared for New York," Thaddeus said with a sigh, "too big, too dirty, too fast.—Give me the good old West Virginia hills any day!"

Riding back to the Island in the buggy, Sarsfield told himself that his grandparents had never let him down, that they had stood by him when his own father would not, that their support had been far from niggardly. They also obviously regarded him with considerable affection. But, hang it all, if he should decide that he wanted to marry Julia, it was none of their blamed business!

Sarsfield's little brother and sister were strangers to him, and they remained so for the duration of his stay; they stared at him with coal-black eyes like their father's. Olivia was four and prattled ceaselessly; an affectionate child, she sat readily enough on Sarsfield's lap. Kyle was eight and silent; he shook hands like a man and then stood back watchfully. The two lived in the kitchen and the servants' quarters attached to the coach house; they were mothered by Mrs. O'Hara, the housekeeper. Their real mother kept largely to her bed; she took Sarsfield's hands in hers, invited him to sit on the edge of the coverlet, and said, her eyes brimming with pleasure: "Sarsfield, I'm so very proud of you! You've lived up to my highest expectations.—Now you must tell me all about the Astors and the Vanderbilts." He did his best.

"And how is little Julia?" his mother asked; "I gather that she has grown up to be—oh, quite the most clever and beautiful young lady." Sarsfield agreed that Julia was clever and beautiful. "I always loved that girl," his mother said with dreamy smile, "the two of you played so well together as children!"

"Good Lord!" Sarsfield thought, "does the whole world know about me and Julia?" For a moment he was at a loss as to how his mother could have been so well informed; but then he reminded himself that Aunt Ida had always been his mother's dearest friend and that lying abed did not prevent one either from reading letters or from writing them.

"I would imagine," his mother said, interrupting his thoughts, "that your prospects in New York might be so promising that you would be tempted to take up residence there."

"That has occurred to me, Mother."

"You do understand, Sarsfield, that there is little in Raysburg to attract a true gentleman." Sarsfield looked at her closely; for the first time in his life he realized that his mother was even more mysterious and opaque to his comprehension than his father.

Then, just before he left for Boston, Sarsfield was astonished to hear his father ask in a petulant tone: "So, boy, you *are* going to come back here, aren't you?"

"Well, Father, I, ah—think so; yes."

"What d'you mean, you *think* so? What d'you think I worked and slaved my whole life for? Do you want the damned business or no? You want me to give it to Kyle!"

Sarsfield had always been glad to leave Raysburg; but in this particular instance "glad" was too weak a word. Safely shut into his Pullman car, he lay back and watched the snowy fields of Pennsylvania roll by his window. The day of reckoning—his graduation from Harvard—was coming far too fast; he felt a growing sense of panic.

Sarsfield knew that if he did not work like a Trojan, however, his graduation from Harvard was far from a foregone conclusion; he plunged into his studies. Then, in the early spring, as he was allowing himself an hour's leisure in the midst of writing his thesis, he was flipping through *The New York Times* and saw, in the rotogravure section, a picture of his cousin, accompanied by Peter Van Gort, attending a costume ball at the Vanderbilts'; the two were attired in sumptuous costumes based, rather fancifully, upon the age of Louis XVI; the plump banker made the perfect picture of an aging aristocratic roué; Julia was probably the only girl in New York society who could wear the authentic period corset. Sarsfield felt a curious emptying sensation as though all the fluids had instantaneously drained from his body; he threw the paper to the floor. Arch looked up from his medical books, studied his friend a moment, and then asked, concern in his voice: "What's the matter, old man, somebody die?"

It took Arch an evening and three pitchers of beer to get Sarsfield to talk about it. "Don't know why I didn't see it before," Sarsfield said, "but it's a perfect match; I'm sure everybody's going to think so."

"Oh?"

"Well, look, it's obvious she's got to marry somebody with money; and the Van Gorts have money. They're not in the same class with the Astors or the Vanderbilts—or with Uncle Henry, for that matter—but they're no pikers either.—And they're an *old* family, so that's all to the good. The Eberhardts are *new* money, so that ordinarily would count against them; but Peter's the black sheep, and they probably think it's high time he was married,—might settle him down, don'tcherknow? For his part, he probably likes it just fine that Julia's not as stuffy as most of the society girls; he likes a good time, and so does she. And for her part—well, he may be nearly twenty years older than she is, but he's a jolly good fellow, well liked, hasn't got a malicious bone in his body, and Bunny Van Gort's one of Julia's best friends, and—" and Sarsfield trailed off.

"A marriage of convenience," Arch said.

"You bet! Oh, Lord!"

"Are you in love with her?"

Both young men believed absolutely in true love; if Sarsfield answered "yes," then the question would be settled (he knew that as well as Arch did),—and his course would be clear to him: he should have to take the next train to New York and have a serious heart-to-heart with Julia. Now he asked himself—for the millionth time!—if he were, indeed, in love with her. Sometimes he was certain of it; but there were many times when he was far from certain; often he thought he was in love with her but wished that he were not; he could even periodically convince himself that, as a wife, she would only make him miserable. This, surely, was not the single-minded clarity that one should expect from being *in love*. "I don't know," he said.

"Then give it some time."

"That's probably sound advice, but—I'm not sure how much time I've got left."

Sarsfield did nothing; the pressure of his work was too intense. Then, far too quickly, it was all over; Arch had achieved honors (and could now, by God, be called *Doctor* Kimbell!); but Sarsfield had attained that status attendant upon those students whom professors, after the passage of several years, cannot quite recall: neither one of the best nor one of the worst, he had finished firmly in the middle. He had not expected his mother to attend his graduation, but he had thought that his father might; Jack, however, penned a hasty missive that said he was "taking pictures of every damn high school graduate in the whole damn valley, just the sort of thing you would be good at, if you every learned to hump yourself, ha ha, so cannot get away. Congratulations, could not be prouder of you, will I see you in June? Your loving father, J. C. Middleton."

The Kimbells came up to see Arch graduate; and Sarsfield was keenly feeling a lack of family when, to his delight, Aunt Ida and Julia appeared. On a night that would remain fixed in his memory forever, he and Julia strolled around the Yard under hundreds of brilliantly colored Japanese lanterns that had been hung from the elms. Aunt Ida, pleading fatigue, had retired to her hotel; Sarsfield and his cousin were alone. They walked holding hands; and Sarsfield was not unaware of the envious stares of other Harvard men,—for Julia, in a pale-yellow frock blooming with daisies, her hair dressed in the *art nouveau* style, had never looked more charming. The lanterns cast everywhere a variegated array of hues, butterfly-bright amongst pockets of deep shadow; and the campus, now that Sarsfield was upon the point of leaving it, seemed to him the most wondrous and mysterious of realms. Too filled with deep and conflicting emotions to speak more than a word or two, he pointed out President Eliot's house, then led Julia to Johnston Gate, then turned and led her back again to University Hall where gargantuan torches had been lit; the fire bent and hissed with the breeze and the year of Sarsfield's class was also written out there—in small, brave flames: 1905. He turned to say something light and amusing to her; but the words stuck in his throat, and his eyes filled with tears. She flung her arms around him; he clung to her like a drowning man to a life raft; and then, suddenly, they were both forced to laugh, for a number of his classmates, in honor of the embrace, had offered up three loud and lusty cheers.

Sarsfield accompanied Julia and Aunt Ida back to Newport; and there he was surprised (and, he had to admit, deeply pleased) to find a grand party given to commemorate his graduation. Julia's friends and family presented him with odd, small gifts intended to amuse: a volume bound in vellum and stamped in gold that purported to be Aristotle, but, when opened, proved to be a novel by Richard Harding Davis; a foot-high trophy with a reading student on top; a Kodak camera; a "Teddy" bear; a copy of Roosevelt's *The Rough Riders* that Bunny Van Gort (a distant relative of the president's) had succeeded in getting signed by the great man himself. Julia's present drew from him laughter that was somewhat forced: a volume entitled *Our Deportment: or the Manners, Conduct and Dress of the Most Refined Society*, published in 1883, the year that Sarsfield had been born; but, in private, she gave him a set of cuff-links set with diamonds. "I had a few to spare," she said in an off-hand manner, "so I thought you'd like 'em." Then, seeing the expression on his face, she exclaimed: "If you say a word about improper gifts for a young lady to give to a gentleman, I shall simply scream!"—but she had misinterpreted him, for he had been touched.

The late June weather in Newport proved to be everything it ought; Sarsfield and Julia engaged in the activities that usually occupied them at Seacourt: each morning they strolled on the Cliff Walk; they played lawn tennis, attended dinners and balls. But this visit, he thought, might be his last chance to open his heart to her. He did not know how to begin.

Intrigued by the prospect, Sarsfield was sure that he would, at long last, be introduced to Julia's elusive father,—for "The Gray Wolf of Wall Street" was actually in attendance; but, so it seemed, Uncle Henry had serious business matters to discuss with several of the other eminent gentlemen vacationing at Newport, passed most of his time at the Casino, and was never seen at home. Late one night as Sarsfield was walking down the long hallway that led to his bedchamber, he saw, turning a far corner, a tall, lean, elegantly attired gentleman with a magnificent head of silvery hair; "Ah-ha!" he thought, "here's my chance," and set out in pursuit of this figure. By the time he reached the end of the hallway, however, the man had vanished.

Sarsfield knew that he should be well advised to let it go at that; but his curiosity was such that he simply could not do so; he stood listening, heard light footsteps, went in search of them. It took him ten minutes to locate the man again; he saw him through a partially opened door of a small chamber in a distant part of the house. By now Sarsfield was certain that, in following so far, he had well exceeded all limits of gentlemanly behavior; but he did not care. Resolved to brazen it out, he pushed through the door, stepped firmly in, offered his hand, and said in a hearty voice: "Forgive me, Uncle Henry.—I'm Sarsfield Middleton."

The man, who was wearing formal evening dress, rose, straightened himself to his utmost height, stood looking at Sarsfield with a face utterly devoid of expression; he had a lean, refined air about him of such subtlety and distinction that the word "aristocratic" was, for once, absolutely apt. He did not take Sarsfield's hand. Then, just as the tension between them was mounting to the point of becoming ghastly—utterly intolerable— the man said: "I'm sorry, sir. I'm Schindler, the new butler."

The next morning, Sarsfield inquired after his uncle and heard that Henry Eberhardt had departed for New York the previous morning.

The fickle goddess of fashion had decreed a "new figure" that season: the exaggerated curve in the lower back (which Julia had never adopted) was relaxed; the finicky tucks, and folds, and bows, and bits of ribbon that had obscured the waist for some years (which Julia had never worn) had suddenly been whisked away; and a small waist was once again considered highly desirable. These changes had happily taken Julia out of the category of those whose mode was considered "a little too *à la française*" and returned her to the forefront of the fashionable. "You see," she told Sarsfield, "I haven't been behind the times at all; I've been *ahead* of them!"

Julia's figure was still the furthest imaginable from one that could have been described as plump; but the years since she had come "out" had gently smoothed over that fragility which had once made her seem more child than woman; so, surely, Sarsfield thought, she must have gained weight since then; yet, during the same period, the size of her waist had gradually but steadily declined and, as though by stubborn defiance of nature, was now even smaller than it had been when she was sixteen. The best to show off this uncanny achievement, she wore simple frocks with girlish "suspenders" that were like the straps on a child's pinafore, and corsage skirts with high, close-fitted waists; she appeared to Sarsfield both as deliciously demure as a lady in an old photograph—and wonderfully chic.

"All the girls have taken up tight-lacing again," she said with a wicked smile, "poor things—how they must be suffering! But since I began that depraved practice at fourteen and have never abandoned it, I have some years 'jump' on them—and they can't possibly catch me!"

Now that she, herself, had raised the topic, Sarsfield had to admit that he had long been curious why she had taken up the practice in the first place, and, more to the point, why, in the face of changing fashion, she had never abandoned it. He was just on the point of asking her; but then he stopped himself—for such questions a gentleman does not ask a lady.

Days passed, and Sarsfield could not bring himself to the point of saying anything the least bit serious to Julia; he began to feel as though he were about to explode with frustration. It was not as though he had something clear, concise, and urgent he wanted to tell her; if he had, then he should simply have said it; but his feelings were a roiling mass of confusion. Julia was becoming short-tempered, irritable, pettish; and he was getting to be somewhat testy himself. They began to have sharp, spiteful arguments which, when Sarsfield considered them later, appeared to have been about nothing whatsoever.

In late June the weather changed: it became oppressively hot and close with an excruciating pressure in the atmosphere; a storm was predicted. Sarsfield could not sleep; he longed for rain; he felt the constant keening of some fretful, anxious noise inside of him like the ceaseless vibration of a thousand high-pitched tuning forks. One morning he and Julia sat alone at the breakfast table; she was staring fixedly out the window. "The servants say there's a sou'-easter blowing in," she informed him in a small, monotonal voice.

"Oh? I'm glad of it," he replied and watched her. She appeared to be oblivious to her surroundings; she had a butter knife clutched firmly in her right hand and with it was tapping out a steady tattoo on the edge of her plate. For one irrational moment, he fancied that if she did not soon stop it, he should be forced to scream and overturn the table. "They say it's going to be a bad one," she said, still not looking at him; "I hope it's a corker!"

She sprang so suddenly to her feet that he started back and nearly upset his water tumbler. "Come on, Sarsfield," she said abruptly, "let's go for a drive along Ocean Avenue. If there's to be a storm, I want to see it."

"Drive?" he heard himself saying stupidly. "What! In your electric? Good Lord, Julia, you can't take the electric out in a—"

"We'll take one of *cher* Papa's motor-cars."

"I can't drive a motor-car," he replied with some anxiety.

"No? But I can.—If you start one of them, I'll drive it."

"All right," he said, and rose reluctantly; "let me get changed."

"Bother getting changed! Let's just go!" She saw him hesitating, snapped out: "For once in your life, Sarsfield, can't you simply have an idea and then act on it—without considering it from every possible angle first?"

He thought that it would not be wise to remind her that the idea had been hers, not his. "But you should change into something—" he began. She was wearing one of her many light summer frocks—and the daintiest of white kid boots.

"If you don't like how I'm dressed, you can go to the devil!" she hurled at him, turned on her high French heels, and was gone. He sprang up to follow.

By the time he caught up with her, she was already standing in the carriage house, at the end where the automobiles were kept, a slight frown on her face, surveying the lot; and he had the terrible suspicion that, despite what she had said, she was no more experienced at driving any of these motor-cars than he was. To his relief, she did not choose the large, gleaming Mercedes (he had heard it said that this formidable vehicle could achieve eighty miles an hour!) but rather the most modest of the machines—one that looked exactly like a small carriage without a horse. As she climbed into the driver's seat, her father's chauffeur suddenly sprang up, seemingly from nowhere, approached at a speed just short of a run, and, sliding to an abrupt stop, gasped out: "Ah—excuse me, Miss Julia, will you be needing an automobile?"

"I need an automobile, Thompson," she replied without looking at him; "But I'll not be needing *you*." Sarsfield was shocked; he had never heard Julia speak so sharply to a servant; and then, in exactly the same tone she had used upon the luckless Thompson, she said: "Could you please start it, Sarsfield."

Profoundly miffed, Sarsfield walked around to be back of the machine and looked at it. He met Thompson's eyes; and the two exchanged a moment of wordless sympathy. "Excuse me, sir, ah—" Thompson said; "If you wouldn't mind—"

"Oh, no, Thompson," Sarsfield said, "I wouldn't mind at all." The man demonstrated the actions of the spark, the throttle-valve, and the crank; the well-tended motor sprang at once to life. "Capital," Sarsfield said; and then, with some trepidation, he walked around and climbed into the carriage.

"Excuse me, Miss Julia," Thompson said, touching his cap, "would you like me to put the awning down?"

"Bother the awning!" she said and engaged the gear; the automobile sprang forward with a lurch and careened out of the carriage house. "Good grief," she snapped, "you'd think it was *his* motor-car!" Sarsfield looked back and saw Thompson standing rooted to the spot, staring after them, a bemused expression on his face,—as he watched the daughter of the house, wearing nothing but a thin summer costume, drive away with a gentleman, unchaperoned, in one of her father's rare and expensive automobiles with the top up, headed in the direction of what, from the strong wind and the dirty color of the sky, would certainly prove to be a very nasty summer storm indeed.

By the time that Julia had guided the automobile up the road from Seacourt to Bellevue Avenue, Sarsfield saw that, although she was far from being an expert, she must have driven it before—at least enough to know the operations required. Staring straight ahead, clinging grimly to the tiller, she threw in the high-speed; and soon the engine was employed to its fullest capacity, for they were going easily thirty miles an hour. The avenue, which ordinarily at this time of the morning would have been bustling with pedestrians and stylish carriages of every description, was utterly deserted. "Of course," Sarsfield thought, "anybody with a grain of sense is in-doors."

The roar of the wind provided an excellent excuse for not talking. They passed the clipped lawn of the Bailey's Beach Bathing Association; and there was not a soul to be seen anywhere. Even the gold-braided commissionaire assigned to prevent *hoi polloi* from "crashing" this domain of the select wealthy was nowhere in evidence; and seeing the beach and the bath-houses without the customary crowd of matrons, nurse-maids, and laughing children gave Sarsfield a queer, irrational feeling—as though he and his cousin were about to drive off the edge of the known world. "Don't go too far," he yelled over the wind; "That's the last thing we'd want—to get stuck out here with a storm blowing in!" She did not deign to answer him.

They had Ocean Avenue to themselves; Julia guided the small motor-car deftly over the winding road with the overhanging cliffs to one side and the ocean—lashed to spumes of menacing white spray—on the other. The dirty, yellowish light of the sky imparted to the lichen-covered rocks a desolate, even fantastic air; and Sarsfield could not shake an increasing sense of foreboding. The cliffs gave way momentarily to the bleak perspective of a marsh where cat-tails bent and vibrated in fierce gusts of wind; they crossed a small arm of the sea, continued on, winding around crags, passed fields covered with gorse; and then, as the road dipped toward the ocean, Julia slowed the automobile, finally stopped it altogether at a point from which they could look out directly into the face of the oncoming storm. The sea boiled up onto the rocks, rose mightily, and curled back to meet the advancing breakers. Sarsfield could not have imagined a prospect more wild or forbidding.

He clambered out, unfolded the top, lowered it, and latched it firmly into place. Climbing back into the carriage, he saw that Julia was taking advantage of the modicum of shelter he had provided to repair her coiffure; he studied her impassive profile as she resettled her pins and combs. She must have seized a pair of white kids at the last moment; she picked them up from the seat and began to work her hands into them—somewhat late in the game, he thought.

"Well," she demanded in a hard, angry voice pitched loud enough to carry over the mighty roar of the sea, "should I marry Peter Van Gort?"

"How the deuce should I know?" he shouted back at her; and they faced each other like two enemies.

Mastering himself, he said: "I'm sure everyone thinks it's a good match."

"Oh, as matches go, I'm sure it is."

"Why, in God's name, would you want to marry that fatuous idiot?"

Her eyes flashed angrily; but when she spoke, it was apparent that she too was doing her best to keep her emotions in check: "In the first place, he's obviously not a fortune hunter—although I'm sure that *cher* Papa's millions are not exactly a disadvantage—"

"No;" he came back at her, "don't tell me all the obvious advantages; don't tell me what your *mother* would say! Why should *you* want to marry him?"

She took a moment to consider that. "I know what you must think of him, Sarsfield; but he's a kind man for all his faults—and a man of modern opinions. I should have considerable freedom with him—not like some of these other—Well, you know as well as I do, most of the men in society would expect me to be—little more than a 'fashion-baby.'"

"All right, marry him then!"

"Oh, go to hell!" She leapt from the automobile and strode rapidly down toward the sea. The sand ended abruptly at a circling mass of rock—eroded into weird, sinister shapes. Through one enormous fissure, directly below and to the left of them, the ocean, driven by the rapidly approaching storm, rushed and spouted in towering, spasmodic plumes.

He ran after her, caught her arm, and turned her about to face him. The wind was fearsome now; her skirts were rattling in it. "What the devil's the matter with you!" he yelled at her.

"What the devil's the matter with *you!*" she yelled back. His hand was still on her arm; only a few inches separated them. "You are such an utter ass," she told him, her voice quivering with an emotion he could not identify; she sounded just on the edge of tears. She looked out to sea—at the dark and streaming sky; presently she turned back with a queer smile, pressed even closer to him, and said in her most mannered socialite's voice: "Oh, Sarsfield, *do* stop being such a gentleman. You must kiss me before I get a minute older."

He was so angry he did not stop to think but did as he had been bidden,—seized her and pressed his mouth firmly into hers; she clung to him. Then, as though he had entered a new world in which the impossible suddenly has become possible, he felt her lips open.

A profoundly devastating shock passed through his entire body; she was kissing him as a prostitute would!—or so he fancied, for he had never kissed anyone in his life like this, or even remotely like this,— except that he *had*, he suddenly remembered: he and Julia had kissed like this when they had been children and too young to know better. But then they had stopped almost immediately; now they were adults, and they were not stopping. He felt her teeth on his lips, then her tongue on his; and, totally beyond his control, a horrible choking noise like a sob broke from him. This was terrible, sinful surely; he must stop it. He did not want to stop it; he *could not* stop it.—This was not terrible at all; this was paradise! It was as though there had always been a hollow space directly in front of him that she had been specifically designed to fill; it was as though nothing in his life heretofore had the least significance compared to this kiss.

After a time, as though by mutual consent, they stopped, stepped back, regarded each other. The wind howled around them; the sea pounded the rocks below them. The world, he knew, would never be the same again.

A maddening blaze of jealousy suddenly struck him; and he exclaimed: "Have you ever—Oh, Lord, Julia—Have you ever kissed anyone like that before?"

"No, never."

"Tell me the truth, please."

"No, never—damn you! How could you ask me that?"

She caught his hand and dragged him forward; the surf was pounding in as though driven by demons; water surged through the fissure below—rose in a great plume, crested, and fell with a crash. "Yes, I *have* kissed someone like that before," she said, shouting to be heard over the sound of the waves; "I kissed *you* like that before.—Don't you remember?"

"Of course, I remember."

"It was just a child's game to me; I didn't understand—It badly, badly frightened me."

"I'm sorry."

"Don't be an ass. I had no business doing it—like much else in my life." She caught his hand, drew him close—so that she could speak without shouting. "Oh, don't look at me like that, please," she said.

"Like what? How am I—?"

"I seem to be seeing that look from dozens of men now—blinded, as though they had been staring into the sun—and it's *me* they've been looking at! I used to find it flattering, but I don't any longer. It makes me wonder where *I* am—the 'me' that I go to bed with, and get up with, the ordinary old me—it's surely not *that me* they're seeing. If kissing you has made you look at me like that, then I'm sorry I kissed you—I'm just your cousin, Julia—your old chum—"

He stopped her speech by kissing her again. They clung so tightly together that his desire for her—in the most elemental way that a man can desire a woman—must have been entirely apparent to her; yet, far from repelled, she only clung to him the tighter. "God!" she exclaimed after a moment; "Wait! I can't breathe."

He released her; she stood, a look of panic on her face, taking innumerable small, shallow breaths, her shoulders rising with them. "Oh, dear," she cried, "will you catch me if I faint?"

He reached out to steady her; but she pushed his hands away and suddenly ran farther down the beach toward the sea. Disconcerted, he remained stock still. The storm broke over them with a fierce howling of wind and lashing torrents of rain. "Good God!" he said aloud, shook himself free from his trance and ran after her.

An enormous crest had just risen from the demonic fissure and fallen,—had exploded like thunder directly at her feet,—foam thrown coiling and thrashing for yards in every direction.

She stood like a sleep-walker, amazed. Then she stepped forward—one step, then two. The next great, spouting wave would fall directly upon her. He ran like a madman. He saw, high above them, a thick crest rising—gray-green and white-flecked and terrible. He seized her waist to draw her back. "I love you, Cricket," he shouted.

She twisted in his arms, facing him, thwarting his purpose. Her eyes were wild. She shouted something back at him; but he could not hear it. As though by the open hand of an angry giant, they were struck to the sand. He gathered her up bodily, one arm around her shoulders, the other under her legs, and, stumbling, carried her to safety. He heard the next wave break behind them. She was weeping like a child.

He set her on her feet. She turned to him; and they kissed again. Water was streaming from her hair, her face; her sodden skirts slapped in the wind; he tasted sand in her mouth. Then it was she who broke free from the embrace; she pulled him away, back from the sea. "Oh, good God!" she said; and then: "Oh, we've got to get back!"

They stumbled up the beach toward the motor-car; her light frock was soaked through, covered with wet sand; he could see the shape of her soft breasts, the precise lines of her "steels," even her legs beneath the wet skirts. Her fit of crying had ended as quickly as it had begun; she managed a smile, said something to him, but the words were blown away.

"Pardon," he shouted; "I didn't hear you."

"I said—*I love you too!*" she shouted back.

They reached the safety of the automobile, sprang inside. She huddled in the driver's seat, shivering. "I've really done it this time, haven't I?" she exclaimed; "Oh, Sarsfield, what shall I do—if anyone sees me!" She pulled the pins and combs out of her hair; a torrent of water and dark tresses fell down her back. "Give me a moment to collect myself, please," she said.

"Of course."

They sat and looked at each other as the storm beat down upon them. The little awning over the automobile was providing scant protection now, for the hard wind was blowing the rain through the open front and sides of the carriage. "Julia—" he shouted.

She pressed her fingers against his lips. "Oh, please don't make love to me, Sarsfield," she yelled over the storm. "Can you start this damned thing?"

By the time he had succeeded in getting the engine running again, he felt himself shaking in every fiber; there was nothing he wanted so much now as simply to escape from this howling wind and cruel, fiercely driven rain. He leapt back into the carriage; she engaged the gear, turned the automobile around; and they began to flee back the way they had come. Neither attempted to speak again; and Julia drove as though they were being pursued by the Furies.

At Seacourt, they found an obviously worried Thompson waiting for them just inside the carriage house. Despite her soaked costume and long, wet, unpinned hair, Julia put on a regal countenance, and, looking straight ahead, drove into the very spot where the automobile had originally been. She stopped the motor; they sat in silence until the chauffeur discreetly withdrew to attend to business elsewhere.

"Sarsfield," Julia began after a moment, and then hesitated. "Listen, my dear," she said, "I have just turned twenty, and—however much the entire world might wish to marry me off—I am in no hurry to marry."

He stared at her, doing his best to construe her meaning. She extended a hand to him, then, laughing, drew it back, stripped off the soaked glove, and offered it again. "Let us be chums, Sarsfield," she said, "please—for whatever else we might be."

BOOK TWO

[A] new dress doesn't get
you anywhere; it's the life
you're living in the dress,
and the sort of life you had
lived before, and what you
will do in it later.

-Diana Vreeland

There is a reality so subtle
that it becomes more real
than reality. That's what
I'm trying to get down in
photography.

-Alfred Stieglitz

5

Sarsfield slipped the last of his prints into the flowing water; as he watched, the smiling faces of the new graduates, caught in the stream, swirled away, sank out of sight, and then swirled back again—like fleeting images in memory. He stood motionless, as though, in some magical way, his unblinking concentration were required to complete the chemical process. It was unbearably hot in the darkroom; but, for the moment, he could not find the will to move the smallest muscle. He was afraid that he had been back in Raysburg so long by now that he was losing the ability even to *imagine* a life other than the one that he was living; his years at Harvard seemed so far in the past that they might have happened to someone else,—that he might have read the account of them in some dusty old book. Then, suddenly angry at himself—at these recurrent thoughts, he forced himself into action, stepped out of the darkroom, and was momentarily blinded by the dazzling sunlight. As his eyes gradually accommodated themselves to their new environment, he saw that the high, hot sun through the skylight was making the entire studio glow—golden and white. He checked the time. That little Rossiter girl was not due for another hour and a half. He loaded his one-shot camera and carried it up onto the roof. Such a brilliance and purity of atmosphere was rare in Raysburg; and, while he had it, he wanted to take advantage of the light.

Sarsfield looked out over the town and saw little to photograph. The spring day had already grown as intensely hot as mid-summer; and the citizens of Raysburg must have been driven indoors: the cheerful bustle that he had seen earlier had, by now, all but ceased. The streets were shimmering; Sarsfield's vision blurred; his eyes burned and watered; he stretched and yawned.

At this very same moment, on the north end of the Island, Sarsfield's mother was swinging gently on the glider; she raised her eyes from the page before her, saw that the light on the river had become so brilliant that she could no longer look at it; she allowed her novel to slip from her fingers, allowed herself to sink down into a gentle sleep.

Slumped in his chair in the back room at Nolan's, Jack Middleton, meantime, was losing the thread of what the queer Irishman was saying; a number of the denizens of the saloon had gathered around, and the damnable fellow seemed to be telling them some fabulous, tall tale: "—and there they built neither of brick nor of wood,"—the musical Irish voice ran on like the river—"nor of steel nor of iron as in this fair city—" Jack sipped his whiskey; he could barely hold his eyes open. "But they built their high hills and cunning, wondrous towers *of polished glass*—"

On the south end of the Island, little Emma Rossiter suddenly woke up with a start; she had been sitting in the window seat in her room brushing her hair in the glorious sunlight and, so it seemed, must have drifted off for a moment. She knew that she had been dreaming; but, to save her soul, she could not remember what she had dreamed. She picked up her discarded brush, applied it, once again, to its purpose; the sunlight had dried her hair—and heated it; the intense scent of violets was suddenly all around her, and she laughed out loud. She could hear from the kitchen below the sounds of her mother's bustling activity: the banging of pots and pans and then the loud, metallic crash of the oven door.

Just as Alice Middleton had feared, all the "genteel people" had, by that hot spring day of 1908, moved off the Island leaving only the Middletons with any pretensions to being upper-class. The new neighbors on the north end were the families of shop-keepers, mill foremen, a carpenter, a lawyer or two, a baker: good, solid, middle-class folk who were not, by any stretch of the imagination, "society." And on the south end, down below the Rainey properties, were an increasing number of small farms created as the Rainey family, over the years, sold off land as they needed the cash; and there lived people who were (as Sarsfield's mother said) "common as dirt." There the old German, Pete Kaltenbach, raised pigs and made sausages; there the Dutch family of Imhoff raised dairy cattle; and there, on three adjacent plots, lived the large family of the Rossiters. And all that morning seventeen-year-old Emma Rossiter, the youngest of Tom's five children, had been preparing to have her picture taken at the Middleton studio.

The big galvanized bucket the family used for heating bath water had not been good enough; Emma had covered every inch of the stove top with kettles and pans so she could take a really good, hot bath. "Emma, honey," her mother had said, "I guess that photographer's not going to take a picture of your smell." Emma had flushed with annoyance and bitten her tongue. If she had said anything at all, her mother would have repeated, in all seriousness, the ancient maxim "bathing weakens you"; and Emma would have been forced, once again, to give her mother a lecture (straight from what she had read in *The Ladies' Own Beauty Book*) on modern hygiene; and that would have gotten her nowhere at all. Emma often felt between herself and her mother a divide as big as the river at high water. Oh, Emma was not ashamed— would never ever admit to being ashamed—of growing up without indoor plumbing in a cheerful, hard-pressed family that had to scrimp and save to make ends meet; oh, she loved her people and was quick to take offense at anything that appeared to be a slight against them; but one thing was certain: Emma Lee Rossiter was not going to spend the rest of *her* life milking a cow and feeding pigs and chickens and taking baths in the kitchen.

Now, safely hidden behind the firmly shut door of her own gold and white bedroom (she had chosen the wallpaper and painted the woodwork herself; gold and white was what the magazines said society girls had in their bedrooms), Emma found that she was deliriously, blissfully happy. In less than a month she would be graduated from the Raysburg High School—the first of the Rossiters to receive a proper education—and, during her four busy years, she had often doubted that she could do it. Emma was a dutiful girl, but she was not a scholar; and, on top of that, there had never been enough time—what with the chores, and teaching Sunday School, and working Saturdays at Kimbell's dry-goods store, and making all of her own clothes. But, if the truth be known, the hardest part of it had been enduring the taunts and whispers of that gaggle of girls who thought they owned the school—"stuck-up little mushes," Emma thought of them—who never let her forget that her family raised pigs and chickens and her father sold feed and, worst of all, had fought on the wrong side in that stupid old war that everybody should have forgotten about by now, but nobody had. Well, she would show them! She was graduating with the best of them. She had every right to be happy.

After her bath she had sat by the window to let her hair dry in the glorious sunlight. She had buffed her nails until they shone as though they had been shellacked. If her mother had been there to see it, Emma would have heard some comment to the effect that if she buffed them from now till Doomsday, they still wouldn't be bright enough to show through her gloves; but Emma didn't care if they showed or not: *she* would know, and that was what counted. She brushed her hair another hundred strokes, then sat at her vanity table to begin the long and involved process of putting it up into a pompadour. Today she was going to get her graduation picture taken; and she was determined to be dressed, as her mother would have said, "fit to kill and cripple." And if she had her own reasons that no one could have guessed, well, they were nobody's business but hers, were they?

The thunderbolt had hit Emma three years before. Her brother Sam's family sold eggs and butter and frying chickens to most of the families on the north end of the Island. Ordinarily Sam's wife made the deliveries; but on that particular weekend she had been laid up with the croup, and the little one hadn't been too well either, so, even though there were a lot better things she would rather have done on a Saturday morning, Emma agreed to do it. She knew all the people up there anyway; and old Florabelle who pulled the covered cart had made the rounds hundreds of times.

Everything was going just fine until she got to the Middletons. Emma walked around back to the kitchen door and knocked; but instead of the colored lady who cooked for the Middletons, the photographer's son came out. She could see right away that he didn't know who she was; and then, for no good reason, she got terribly tongue-tied. She finally did manage to stammer out her name and her business; and he said, polite as you please: "Why, Emma, you've grown up. I didn't know you. You must know me—I'm Sarsfield."

It couldn't have been any later than seven-thirty or eight in the morning, but he was already dressed just like he was going to dinner— patent leather pumps and all. His shirt front was starched stiff as a board and white as snow and set with pearl studs; unlike most of the young fellows she knew, he didn't wear a moustache; his fair, sandy hair was beautifully trimmed and looked as soft as chicken down. Emma still couldn't find anything to say to him, so she stood, rooted to the spot, and felt her heart beating so loud and fast she was afraid it would jump out of her mouth; then she looked into his eyes to see if he noticed any-thing—to see if he was laughing at her; and they were a pale blue and the kindest, gentlest eyes she had ever seen in a man. He took the basket from her, and she saw that he kept his hands as well as a woman would; she had never seen a man with hands like that. He used scent too; it was strong in the summer air. "How's your family, Emma?" he said. "Everyone well, I trust?"; and she stammered out how everyone was fine even though half of them had the croup.

He must have seen she was upset because he set the basket down on the glider and strolled out with her into the back yard, making conversa-tion the whole way just like they were old friends; and she did not even have the spunk to tell him that she had to have the basket back. She could not quite make out what he was saying because the pain in her chest was so hard and sharp that she had to bite her lip to keep from crying out. He gave her a hand up into the cart and wished her good day. And there she had been, fourteen years old but still in a child's short frock with her skirts way up above her boot tops, and her limbs bare, and her old brown boots caked with mud, and her hair in braids, and her apron filthy, and all of her so soaked with perspiration she prob-ably looked like she had been swimming in the back river. So she said, "get up," to old Flora; and the horse slowly lifted her head and dutifully plodded along to the next house and stopped on her own. And Emma climbed into the back of the cart where nobody could see her; and right there, amongst the butter and eggs and the stink of the chickens, she bawled her eyes out.

Sarsfield hardly remembered that incident which had so impressed itself upon Emma's mind. He had not risen and dressed early that par-ticular morning for any mysterious formal occasion; he simply had not been to bed. The night before, he had dined with Arch at their club. "OK, kid," Arch had said over the soup, "are you going to make me worm it out of you, as usual?"

"Lord help me," Sarsfield had replied, "I don't even know where to begin." Sarsfield had, only a few days before, returned from Newport; he was remaining in town to work for his father; Arch was leaving the next afternoon for Boston to begin serving as an intern at Massachusetts General. The friends had set aside that night for a good, long talk—the last, perhaps, that they would have for quite some time to come.

"Well, did you ask her to marry you?" Arch asked. "You could start by telling me that."

"Not exactly."

"Oh, bother you! Come on, give!"

"I told her I loved her," Sarsfield said with an eloquent shrug.

"Oh? Well, there's a start.—And what did she say to that?"

"She said she loved me too."

"Why the devil are you so gloomy then? I should have thought that would have settled it!"

"With any other girl, it should have settled it," Sarsfield replied; "With Julia—Lord knows! She said she was in no hurry to marry."

The champagne loosened Sarsfield's tongue; and he told his friend as much of the story as he thought fit for discussion. Arch produced a sardonic expression accompanied by a raised eyebrow and said: "So she asks you if she should marry that Van Gort fellow, and then she kisses you in the midst of a hurricane,—and then, to top it all off, she says she's in no hurry to marry. I swear, kid, I've given up trying to understand the behavior of the rich. You can have 'em!"

"I don't claim to understand her either," Sarsfield admitted. "Sometimes I think I should forget her, let her marry that fatuous idiot if that's what she wants."

"That's the ticket. Find yourself a nice girl here. Your flighty cousin's had your tail tied in knots for years—I wouldn't put up with it any longer. Good lord, kid, the world's full of girls—"

"True enough. And there's something to be said for Raysburg. The old man keeps telling me he's going to turn the business over to me one of these days; and maybe he'll actually do it. I'd have plenty of time to work on my color process—It's just that—Well, the society girls in Raysburg don't have much to recommend them."

"Why do you have to marry a society girl?" Arch asked innocently.

Sarsfield found the question deeply aggravating; he was astonished at his friend's obtuseness. "Because I'd be a damned fool not to," he answered shortly.

"Come on," Arch said, laughing, "you can't be that much of a snob.—Besides, who gives a hang in Raysburg anyway? It's not like New York."

"Lots of people give a hang," Sarsfield retorted with some heat; but then he had the presence of mind to pause and ask himself why he should be so angry. "Snobbery has nothing to do with it. Marriage is a blending of souls—or that's what it should be—and without an immediate, deeply intuitive understanding—shared ideals—" He heard himself running down like a cylinder on a talking machine that needs winding. "I wouldn't want to marry a girl who wasn't fashionable," he concluded.

"Ah, now there's the rub!" Arch exclaimed with a grin. "You're like Dick Davis. Somebody asked him once what he admired most in women, and he said, 'clean gloves.'"

Sarsfield laughed at that. "Oh, I'm not as bad as you'd make me out, but—Well, of course I like clean gloves, if you're going to take that as your metaphor."

"And Paris gowns," Arch said with a wink, "and a good pair of quality corsets laced up to beat the band—Oh, yes, old man, I know what you like in women: a girl you can photograph!—And a certain charm, and wit, and sophistication—and a sensibility that only comes from having all the advantages. So what's wrong with that? If that's what you like, find somebody who fits the bill and marry her. It isn't as though it's Julia Eberhardt or nobody."

"Sometimes I think maybe it *is* Julia or nobody—If I stay here—I don't know, Arch; I think maybe she's spoiled me for other girls. The girls here are—well, compared to Julia, they're empty-headed, silly—"

"*All* of them? You've looked over the entire herd, I take it?"

Sarsfield shrugged. "They're all my cousins."

"You give me a pain, kid!" Arch exclaimed with a laugh. "Come on, we've got to 'duck' or we'll miss the opening," and he jollied Sarsfield along, out the door and into the buggy, and over to the theater where a musical troupe had condescended to entertain for the night—on its way through to Columbus and St. Louis.

Raysburg was a town that loved its entertainment; the citizenry supported five theaters; of them, "The Virginia" was the most expensive, as it offered "class acts" only and catered to the entire non-colored population:—from the wooden benches high in the back where mill-workers took their families for a big night out on the town, all the way to the boxes, rented by the season, that overhung the stage. Sarsfield and Arch strolled through the lobby; heard—and ignored—the local louts who said, "Jesus, look at them jane-dandies, will you?"; climbed into the Eberhardt box where they were greeted—if the word were not too strong for the languid, simpering performance—by Sarsfield's cousins, Bedelia Eberhardt and Lenore Staub. If Raysburg had society beauties, these were they; and Sarsfield gave Arch a look that said: "See what I mean?"

Bedelia and Lenore had received every inch of the proper education required by Raysburg "debs": they had passed their early years at Miss Crawford's and then had attended a stylish academy in Baltimore; under the tutelage of Aunt Lou Eberhardt, they had "done" Europe where they had "come out" together at a grand ball given by some ancient, obscure Parisian duchess (and they made sure that no one in Raysburg ever forgot it). Since returning home, "finished," they had comported themselves in a manner considered either enchanting or asinine depending upon the eye of the beholder: they rode about in an old-fashioned landau driven by a colored boy in livery; they took pink tea with their gloves on and fanned themselves with jeweled, miniature fans; they strolled through town under the most diaphanous of pastel parasols, occasionally accompanied by a tiny, beribboned poodle whose name appeared to be "Sweetums." They were dressed that night in Paris gowns that were positively Byzantine in their complications—plaits, ruchings, shirrings, and lace; their coiffures were piled high as haystacks; and (Sarsfield could not imagine where they might have acquired this particular tid-bit of naughty affectation) both girls wore rings over their evening gloves.

Bedelia Eberhardt was Sarsfield's first cousin, and so not a possible match for him (not to mention that he'd always regarded her as only slightly superior to a moron); but Lenore, who was Sarsfield's *third* cousin (Karl Eberhardt's wife had been Hedwig Staub), certainly was—a fact that did not appear to be lost upon her. "Why, Sarsfield Middleton, how perfectly enchanting to see you again," she said in a voice dripping with innuendo, and turned upon him the full impact of her great, gleaming eyes that were obviously supposed to strike him dead; Sarsfield returned a few fatuous words and then glanced down at the seats below where a great throng of sensible, ordinary West Virginia souls was staring up into the Eberhardt box as though at some particularly entertaining specimens escaped from a zoo. Thus welcomed back to his home town, Sarsfield settled down for a lovely evening of coon songs.

The show opened with a good, hot rendition of "All Coons Look Alike to Me," after which—perhaps, Sarsfield thought, to prove the point—two white men in blackface jumped up for their first turn:

"Say dere, Rastus, dis here Raysburg sure am a unique town."

"You-neek? What do dat mean, you-neek?"

"Well, ya see, dat come from de Latin. 'Unus' meaning 'one' and 'equus' meaning 'horse.'"

The drummer hit a press roll followed by a good loud thump; and Sarsfield saw that his cousins had misplaced their sophisticated manners and were giggling like a pair of schoolgirls. The band kicked into "Little Alabama Coon," and Sarsfield's mood was getting more sour by the minute; he found himself remembering the wonderful weekends in New York. He and Julia had seen plays as serious as "The Doll's House," as light as "The Girl from Kay's"; they had seen the notorious Mme. Réjane in "Sappho"; of course they had seen "Florodora" with its chorus line of stunning beauties; they had seen Lillian Russell, Otis Skinner, Sarah Bernhart, and the Barrymores; they had heard everything in the way of music from high opera to the wonderful "Sultan of Sulu"; and now, here he was, back in good old Raysburg, listening to "Rastus on Parade."

At the interval, Sarsfield told Arch that he could not face another minute: "Let's get out of here," he said; "Let's buy a bucket of beer and drive up to Billy Rainey's place."

They did exactly that. Arch drew up the buggy in what should have been the turn-around; then, carrying the bucket of beer, the two young men climbed the front steps, passed through the open space where the front door should have been, strolled across the long, leaf-strewn platform to what should have been the rear of the house, and came to a standstill in what should have been Billy Rainey's drawing room. The huge expanse of cement flooring and the tall, bare chimneys created the impression of some mysteriously romantic ruin left behind by an obscure, earlier race; and Sarsfield said: "Isn't this typical of Raysburg? Can you imagine anything more ridiculous, more half-assed than this?"

That hilltop—the highest point overlooking Raysburg—had always been owned by the Rainey family; old Malachai, long dead, had planned his whole life to build a mansion there so that the Raineys could, as was proper to them, look down upon the city they had founded, but, with one thing and another, he had never got around to it; his son, Daniel, had gone as far as clearing the land, but then had passed along the property to his son, Ezra, as a wedding present; Ezra had laid the foundation, but, when he had considered the cost of piping up water, had concluded that the custom of making the land a gift to the eldest Rainey boy upon the occasion of his marriage was a sound and decorous one; Jed Rainey had widened the road, added the two chimneys, and then had decided that the bother and expense could better be incurred by a younger, more vigorous person; so he had deeded the place to his son, Billy, who, at the moment, was two years old.

Arch and Sarsfield had come up there for the view. Looking toward the left, they could see as far as the Staub Glass Works in South Raysburg, and then, on up the river, old Tom Schneider's brewery and several of the foundries—the Washington Iron Works, the Eagle Mill, the Revington Nail Works—that had been, over the years, gathered into the fold of Thaddeus Eberhardt's Raysburg Iron and Steel; directly in front of them, Rainey Street led down the hill through the center of town to the wharf; just off to the right was the imposing McClain Hotel with most of its windows lit; the electrics of the down-town glittered brilliantly. They could see as far north as the Top Mill; in the distance, to the west, beyond the long, soft expanse of the river, lay the wooded Island with gas street-lamps glowing softly as candles; and beyond that, Bridgeport on the Ohio side. Cows were lowing on Ez Rainey's farm just below; they were so high that the smoke from the mills hardly reached them; and, overhead, the stars were splendid.

Arch poured beer into the mugs brought for that purpose; the friends toasted each other and drank. "The moving finger writes, and having writ—" Arch quoted.

"Moves on," Sarsfield finished the line.

"You know, kid," Arch said, surveying the scene, "I don't hate this place the way you do.—It's my home town, and I'm actually kind of fond of it. I'll be ready enough to come back here and hang up my shingle."

"You'd be content to be a Raysburg doctor, would you?"

"Sure. Why not?"

Sarsfield sighed. "I wish I could be content to be a Raysburg photographer, but—" He did not know what to say; no matter how much he thought about it, he still remained confused. "You saw Lenore and Bedelia, didn't you? You see what I mean? They're like society girls in the funny papers—a cartoonist's impression! But the horrible thing is that if I stay here long enough, Lenore Staub will start to look like Helen of Troy—"

"All right, go to New York."

"But I don't know what Julia's—"

"What the devil's Julia got to do with it? You've got to make your own damn life, Sarsfield! You've told me a million times how you're all set up to be a New York society photographer."

"That's true. I could be making good money in no time. It's just that—Well, in New York nobody takes a man seriously unless he works down-town—you know, in a bank or something, so I'd turn into one of those 'women's pet' sort of fellows—like that damn foppish painter, what's-his-name—tolerated because he amuses one's wife—"

"Oh, I give up!"

The friends talked until dawn; by the time the first light of the sun appeared and cast long, dramatic shadows from Billy Rainey's chimneys, Sarsfield had vacillated between Raysburg and New York a dozen times. "You think too much for your own bloody good!" Arch exclaimed; "You've got to make a move—do something even if it's wrong." He drew from his pocket the old half-eagle he carried as a good-luck piece. "Going to New York—call it!"

"Tails I go."

Arch sent the coin spinning high into the air, caught it, slapped it down onto the back of his wrist. Sarsfield held his breath. Arch lifted his hand away; the gold twinkled in the ruddy light of the rising sun; it had fallen tails. Arch looked at Sarsfield with a grin: "Will you do it?"

"Yes!"

But now, three years later, despite what he had said to Arch, Sarsfield was still in Raysburg, still muddling along in his father's business, still marking time. He should have decided upon the course of his life by now—or at least upon the course of his life's work—but he had not done so. He had improved his color process, had entered photographs in contests and won a number of prizes, had written articles for *The American Photographer*. He had received letters from around the world asking his opinion as though he were an authority on color work. He had dutifully taken out patents on all of his inventions—his one-shot camera, his latest, color-corrected emulsion, the various gadgets he'd built to make transfer printing easier—but, so far, none of these efforts had earned him much money. Jack Middleton appeared to regard his Harvard-educated son who could make a color photograph much the way he might regard a circus bear who has been trained to play "The Star Spangled Banner" on a glockenspiel;—and Jack might well have been right: in three years, Sarsfield had sold exactly four color pictures, all of them to Eberhardts—the only people in town who could afford to pay what Sarsfield had to charge if he wanted to get even a minimal return on his labor.

Now, on the roof, as Sarsfield was setting up his camera to make yet another pointless color photograph, he felt,—even after all this time, and quite "out of the blue,"—a wave of longing for his cousin Julia; it was so intense, he felt sickened by it.

Emma's hair was up; on the third try she had got her pompadour right; now she powdered her nose just enough to take the shine off, then fluffed the powder away until no one could have known she had used any at all. Hidden at the back of her underwear drawer (along with the latest Laura Jean Libbey novel) was a tube of rouge; but Emma would never have dared to wear any, except in the privacy of her room, just "to see how it looked"; and she never—rouged or unrouged—sat like this in front of the glass, contemplating her hair and her complexion and her beautifully buffed nails, without remembering the story in the *McGuffey's Reader* about the vain little girl who was struck dead while beautifying herself. ("Never have I seen so loathsome a sight as a corpse dressed for a ball!") Oh, Emma knew that true beauty comes from within; but she was a practical girl, and so she also knew that, in spite of what spinster school teachers might have to say, if a girl wants to get ahead in this world, careful attention to what shows on the outside does not hurt one little bit either.

As yet she had put on no clothing beyond her best chemise and drawers; now she lifted her new mail-order corset from its tissue paper. Emma took the fashion notes she read in the ladies' magazines with a grain of salt; what was done in Raysburg was far more important to her than what was done in London, New York, or Paris; and it was a truism to her, as it would have been to any small-town American girl, that when dressed for the finest and fanciest of occasions, she must have the neatest waist she can manage,—so Emma had ordered "The Smart Set" because the advertisement in the back pages of *The Designer* had not once mentioned anything about "comfort or hygiene" but had rather guaranteed that the garment would "instantly create the daintiest and most stylish of figures." The corset had cost her the staggering sum of five dollars; it was made of the finest white coutil, trimmed in the most delicate of lace and ribbons, but—with an astonishing number and thickness of steels and a multitude of heavily reinforced bias seams— had appeared so intimidating that Emma had yet to work up her courage to try it on. Now she spread it out on the bed and threaded it with the long lace, being most careful to maintain a good wide gap open down the entire length; then, standing before her glass, she gathered it around her and attempted to fasten the exceptionally long steel busk that closed the front; even with as much extra room as she had left in the lacing, she had to fight with the fasteners; and, by the time she had forced the busk closed, she was all in a lather. She looked to see the effect she had achieved; and she had to admit that she was pleased as punch. "Now," she thought, "if I can only get the blessed thing laced up—" She turned, looked over her shoulder, and saw, just as she had so carefully left it, that good wide gap of open lacing. Her heart sank.

Like most of her friends, Emma, because she could get herself laced part-way into an eighteen-inch corset when occasion demanded it, claimed to have an eighteen-inch waist; but she also preferred that occasion not demand such sacrifices of her very often (she would have been astonished to know of the years of protracted and painstaking effort a girl like Julia Eberhardt had expended to achieve her dramatic figure). Now Emma was trapped by her own vanity: the waist of her graduation dress was a perfect twenty inches (she ought to know; she had sewn every stitch of it herself); given the thickness of the coutil and the heaviness of the stays in "The Smart Set," the difference between the inside and the outside measurements must be a good two inches; the simplest of mathematics, therefore, told her that if she did not get this contraption fully closed, she would not be able to get her dress done up. The steels encircling her already felt like railroad ties; and she longed to have her good old ninety-five cent Acme back; but there are times, she thought, when a girl must simply look her best;—so, resigning herself to her fate, she took the last deep breath she was likely to enjoy for the next few hours, reached behind her, and attempted to catch hold of the topmost laces. After some minutes of furious struggle, it became apparent to her that she could not possibly draw the garment closed without assistance; then, to make matters worse, she looked at the clock and discovered that she was nearly out of time; she felt her lip quivering—a certain sign that she was about to burst into tears—and cried out: "Mama—Oh, Mama, please come and help me!"

In a moment Emma's mother pushed through the door; and Emma caught the scent of her mother's baking—which reminded her that she had eaten nothing since supper the night before. "Lord, honey," her mother said, "you're laced up like a Sunday chicken."

"Mama, *do* dry your hands," Emma wailed.

Mrs. Rossiter dried her large red hands on her apron. Emma turned and presented her mother with her back. "Honey, you don't want this thing any *tighter*, do you?" her mother asked and pulled cautiously on the laces. "You'll faint dead away."

"Oh, please, Mama, hurry. It's got to be closed up or I shan't be able to get my dress on!" Emma braced herself against the wall and shut her eyes.

Doing her best to prevent the laces from slipping, Mrs. Rossiter began to work her way down her daughter's back; with each sharp tug that drew the edges of the garment firmly together, she offered a comment: "Lord, Emma Lee!—You ain't used to this.—First you'll get—a sick headache.—Then you'll get—nauseated.—And then—in an hour—all the blood—will drain out of your brain—and you'll just fall over—in a dead faint—and lay there—like a catfish."

By the time that her mother had completed this exercise and tied off the laces, Emma was certain that she knew now exactly how the little girl in the *McGuffey's Reader* had come to be struck dead.

For a moment, Emma had to fight off the nearly overwhelming desire to beg her mother to reverse all of her hard labor and remove "The Smart Set" at once; but then she lowered her arms, opened her eyes, and studied the effect in the mirror. She hardly knew herself: she looked like a fashion drawing ("neat as a little doll!" she thought); her figure, in fact, had never in her life looked as good as this. But she essayed the few steps to her bed and discovered that something as simple as walking had now been rendered difficult; and, attempting to put on the first pair of real silk stockings she had ever owned in her life, she discovered that sitting down was not something to be recommended either.

"Here!" her mother said sharply; "You just stay still." Mrs. Rossiter assisted her daughter in drawing on the stockings and fastening them to the hose supporters. She slipped the corset cover over Emma's head and tied the draw string; "How were you proposing to get to town?" she asked mildly.

"Isn't Daddy going to take me?"

"Honey, your father's had his lunch and gone." ·

"Why didn't you tell me?"

"All I hear all morning is, 'Mama, leave me alone,' and then you shut yourself up in here like Mrs. Astor—"

"Ohhh!" Emma exclaimed in exasperation.

Supporting herself on her mother's shoulder, Emma worked her feet into her brand new white slippers with their lovely tapered Cuban heels. She powdered her hands and arms and began to work them slowly into the tight, white twenty-four button glacé kid gloves; her mother, with a tiny hook, began fastening the buttons.

Mrs. Rossiter could see that Emma had "got herself into a state," so she restrained herself from any further of the comments that were springing rapidly to mind; and when she spoke, it was in the most soothing tone she could muster: "Honey, it's been a couple hours since your father's come and gone. I'll ask Pete to carry you over in the trap."

Before she could stop herself, Emma burst out with: "I won't ride to town in the Kaltenbachs' old trap!"

"Well," Mrs. Rossiter said—and she could pack a mountain of meaning into that single word—"should I send word to those Wright boys to come up and fly you over?"

Mother and daughter looked into each other's eyes; then Mrs. Rossiter began to laugh. After a moment, Emma joined her; she didn't feel much like laughing, but sometimes it was the only thing to do. "Oh, Mama, please hurry," she said. "I'm going to be late."

Her mother slipped the spanking new white taffeta petticoat over Emma's head and settled it in place; and now was the time for the graduation dress itself. Emma had spent months poring over *The Designer* magazine before choosing the pattern; then she had spent weeks making it: a classic princess design in snow-white silk Sublime set with Valenciennes lace, it had a straight, plaited skirt and a demure, high-boned collar. While her mother fumbled with the multitude of tiny hooks in the back, Emma studied herself in the mirror. She had never been so thoroughly dressed up in her life; and she wasn't at all sure she had ever made the acquaintance of the elegantly attired young lady looking back. Emma's mother took the hat from its box—one of the newest "Merry Widow" sailors in a white fancy straw trimmed with a broad satin ribbon and an enormous splashing rosette bow—and fastened it to Emma's hair with steel hat pins. "Well," Mrs. Rossiter said dryly, "I guess you'll do."

While Emma's mother hurried over to the Kaltenbachs', Emma made her way slowly down the stairs. She was not totally immobilized by her costume, but nearly so; and she wondered how fashionable ladies ever got anything done—beyond getting dressed. Passing by the pantry, seeing the six new pies on the shelf, smelling them—apple, peach, pecan!—she felt her mouth water and thought she might faint; she was as empty as a blown egg. She stepped out onto the porch; and the sunlight struck her like the blast from an iron-foundry. She reached out to steady herself on the porch railing, but then drew back, not wanting to mark her glove. Unseen by the outside world, a rivulet of perspiration ran down her neck inside her collar; immediately others joined it; she was afraid that soon her underwear—Smart Set and all—would be soaked through. "Oh, Mama, please come back," she thought; "I don't feel very well."

But, as she waited, the sick, queasy sensation gradually left her; and she began to experience the sensation of floating—like a water skipper on a pond. She closed her eyes, and a hundred patches of golden light continued to dance behind her lids; she heard the stolid clomp clomp clomp of Pete Kaltenbach's dray horse, looked and saw the old farmer in his slouch hat, his red, unshaven face flowing with perspiration. "Mein Gott, Emma," he said, "you look chust like a pikchure." He climbed down to offer her a hand; but then, seeing the brilliant whiteness of her dress and gloves, he withdrew the offer, turned to Emma's mother with a look of helpless frustration. Mrs. Rossiter ran to get a quilt, covered the seat of the trap with it, helped Emma climb up. "Oh," Emma said, "I feel so queer."

"Let me get you a cup of buttermilk."

"No, thank you. No, Mama, please." Then she saw that her mother had begun to cry. "Mama, what *is* the matter?"

"Lord, honey, it seems like only yesterday—You were such a fat baby, and *so* good!"

Pete had swiveled around on the seat to make sure that Emma was settled; Emma met his eyes. He nodded, gave the horse a slap with the reins. "You come right back," her mother called, mopping her face with her apron; "Don't you walk around down-town in that rig!"

"Not much chance of that," Emma said under her breath, but sang out brightly: "I shan't, Mama." The old gray began plodding toward the bridge; and now that they were moving, Emma felt simply

wonderful, as though she were floating like a wisp of white Valenciennes lace a mile above the Island,—high up in the mazy heights of
the lovely azure-blue sky.

On the roof of the studio, the focusing cloth over his head, Sarsfield
watched, on his ground glass, the activity below. He had measured the
light; it was even brighter than he had guessed. And then, suddenly, he
heard his father's roaring voice: "Good Lord! What are you doing up
there, you puppy?" His father's image, upside down, appeared suddenly
at the edge of the glass, wove its way unsteadily toward the center. The
tall man in the odd green suit Sarsfield had seen earlier in the day was
assisting Jack in remaining upright; Jack—it was painfully obvious for
anyone to see—was one hundred percent saturated.

Sarsfield stepped out from under his cloth, heard his father say,
"That damned fool up there with the camera—that's my boy, Sarsfield."

"Sarsfield, is it?" Jack's companion said. "Ah, there's a name to
conjure with." Grinning up like a lean tomcat, the tall man called out:
"Be of stout heart, Sarsfield! Like your namesake, your troubles are
none of your own."

"Pardon me, sir," Sarsfield said, stepping to the edge of the roof.
"What did you say?"

"I said, be of stout heart, *mo mhic*. You're one of God's own gentlemen." He gave Sarsfield a wave and a wink and walked on with his
arm around Jack's shoulders. Sarsfield sprang to his camera; he thrust
the blue record plate home behind the lens; he drew back the three
dark slides; he was ready to go. He held the bulb in his hand; but then
he knew he couldn't do it—take a full-color picture of his father
stumbling around in the middle of the afternoon dead drunk with
some outlandish, incomprehensible Irishman. He stared after the two
men as they turned down at the end of Short Market Street and
headed toward the river.

Sarsfield wished—fervently!—that his father might fall off the end
of the Suspension Bridge and drown himself. He waited until the
movement in the street below arranged itself, at haphazards, into a
pleasing pattern; he made his exposure. He stood there afterward, angry
and baffled; businessman, inventor, portrait photographer, color
printer, photo-chemist, perhaps—God knows!—artist: he was all of
these things and none of them. It would take the strength of ten men

to follow every course he imagined for himself; and, even if he were to accomplish everything he desired in photography, he was afraid it would not be enough. What he wanted—most truly—was the simple, ordinary human happiness any young man has the right to ask from life.

Last September Sarsfield had, after a long silence, finally heard from Julia; unlike her usual letters, this one appeared to have been penned slowly and with considerable care:

> My dear Sarsfield,
>   By the time you receive this, I will be engaged to Peter Van Gort. As difficult as it is for me to write this to you, I know that I must do so, for I want you to hear it from me rather than from someone else. I have given the matter endless thought and soul-searching; and I know that it is the right thing for me. I assure you, and hope you will believe, that my engagement, and, when it takes place, my marriage, will in no wise diminish either the nature or the depth of feelings I have for you. I pray to God that we shall always be "chums."
>
>   Julia

Upon reading Julia's words, Sarsfield felt a rage so intense that it frightened him; he tore the letter to shreds and strode out of the house. By the time that he was able to think clearly again, he had walked all the way over Raysburg Hill and was on his way down the far side. He wandered off into the woods near Goosetown, sank to the ground, pressed his back against a tree, and stared up into the twilight sky. It was the time of year he ordinarily loved best in West Virginia: the heat of summer was over; the leaves were beginning to turn; the crisp air stirred one's blood. But now, as the autumnal darkness closed around him, he felt as though he were sinking into a melancholy so profound that he should soon be robbed of all volition,—that, like the victim of "La Belle Dame Sans Merci," he might be found in this very spot sometime next year "alone and palely loitering." He asked himself—not for the first time in his life—why the intensity of his emotions should always take him by surprise; it was as though the self that considered human affairs with the detached clarity of a scientist were his friend and constant companion—while the self that felt and suffered remained a stranger. By the time he had mastered his emotions, night had fallen; he rose and wearily plodded his way back over the hill. What had he expected, that Julia would wait forever? He had not seen her since that fateful Newport season when they had kissed in the storm.

Several days later Sarsfield's mother received a long, chatty letter from Aunt Ida, so he heard the remainder of the story: Julia and Peter were to be married early in the new year; they would honeymoon in Europe until the following summer when they would return to Newport.

For several nights running, Sarsfield could not sleep. How had the two years passed? Never in all that time had he been able to think things through to a stable point within himself; he had never been able to answer the crucial question: "Am I in love with her?" Just as he had learned to do at Harvard, he had thrown himself into his work.

Now he had to admit to himself that he had longed for a rapid and spectacular success so that he could have gone to her and said: "You see, I'm not such a useless fellow after all." But the world, so it seemed, was not ready for color photography;—and he was still no more than an unpaid assistant in a modest family business in a dull, backwater town. It would have been different too, he thought, if Julia's family had been merely wealthy; but the monstrous size of Uncle Henry's fortune had kept Sarsfield at bay like the thorn hedge around the princess. Julia had written to him, now and then, from New York or Newport or Paris; he had replied—now and then. Upon those occasions when he could have gone to see her, he had not done so.

His mind told him again, as it had so often in the past, that Julia Eberhardt would have made him a terrible wife; his heart, as it had so often in the past, told him something entirely different. Eventually he concluded that, painful as it might be, it was all for the best that he had not married Julia;—but he could not shake the conviction that Julia should not marry Peter Van Gort either—and that it was his responsibility to talk her out of it. He considered going into the 'phone company and trying out the remarkable long-distance telephone that now stretched all the way from New York to Omaha; but he could not imagine what he could convey the least bit convincing while shouting over a "line" to New York. He sent her a telegram proposing that he visit; she replied immediately with three words: "Oh do come."

Sarsfield had not been to New York since he had been graduated from Harvard, and he found the city remarkably changed. Automobiles were everywhere; the good old horse-drawn *coupé* appeared to be losing the battle with the new French taximeter cab; Sarsfield hired one of these electric vehicles; and, as soon as he settled in with the rug over his legs to watch the panorama of the greatest, most energetic city in the world unroll beside him, he had the chilling thought that perhaps the longer one lived in a backwater, the less one was able to remember that it *was* a backwater. "I've got to get out of Raysburg," Sarsfield thought. "I'll sink in that backwater—I'll vanish without a trace."

He arrived at the Eberhardts' feeling melancholy but surprisingly calm. It was not until he looked up and saw Julia rushing down to meet him, her long, ice-blue gown foaming behind her on the staircase, that he knew he was not adequately prepared—that there was nothing he could have done to be adequately prepared. Her hair was up in a Psyche-knot—which showed to excellent advantage the white sweep of her neck and shoulders. His memory had not exaggerated the brilliance of her sea-blue eyes; but he had forgotten the exact, thrilling timbre of her voice: "Oh, Sarsfield," she said, "how lovely!" Struck speechless, he allowed her to embrace him; he turned to kiss her; and she averted her head slightly so that his lips struck her cheek. "Do come along now," she said, taking him by the hand. "It's been too long, *mon cher*—and you are quite the hopeless correspondent. Oh, you must tell me everything!"

He had hoped to see her alone, but there, in the east drawing room, was Aunt Ida who greeted him warmly; "Mother sends her love," he said to her, and bent to kiss her cheek. And there was Peter Van Gort himself: "Hallo! Well, if it ain't Sarsfield Middleton in the flesh!" The banker, in evening dress, rose to his feet, extended a hand, which Sarsfield took,—and was enveloped, for the moment, in the refined scent of the man's talcum powder and facial tonic. Seen thus closely, Van Gort was a round, pink, gleaming man—nearly bald—exquisitely finished all the way to his buffed fingernails. "I say, you're looking splendid, old chap.—Julia, my sweet, get this poor man a drink; he looks positively parched. How good to see you, my dear fellow.—Sit down, sit down! You must be quite done up after that beastly Pullman all the way from Virginia—"

"*West* Virginia," Sarsfield said automatically. He accepted the small bourbon whiskey with soda that Julia had poured for him; their eyes met, and he silently thanked her for remembering what—and how little—he drank. Van Gort, meantime, quite as much as if he were in his own home and not his fiancée's, continued to play the genial host: "Oh, I'm sure he'll want to see something—won't you, Middleton? How about that Shaw thing with Ellen Terry in it? Is it still running? Or how about something light—'The Parisian Model' or, ah—now I've hit it! 'Peter Pan!' Eh? Eh?"

"Don't be silly," Julia said to Van Gort; "*You're* the Peter Pan," and then to Sarsfield: "We're going waltzing, waltzing!" As though to prove it, she spun about the room, her skirts swirling, while her mother watched with a pleased and indulgent air. "Aunt Ida certainly looks happy enough," Sarsfield thought, "with the prospect of fat, old Van Gort as a son-in-law."

So there she was, his lovely cousin, not quite as Sarsfield had remembered her over the intervening years—oh, the flashing eyes, heart-stopping smile, irrepressible energy were the same; but a last vestige of a delicate, elusive quality nearly boyish had dropped away; and it had been precisely that quality which had made people compare her to Consuelo Vanderbilt, he saw now, for the resemblance had largely vanished. Julia's shoulders were sleek and smooth; her bosom was fuller; every line of her now proclaimed her a full-grown woman; yet her waist was certainly as small—or perhaps even smaller—than it had ever been. The comparison Van Gort had made years ago at Rector's had now been fulfilled, Sarsfield thought darkly: she *was* very like that saucy soubrette, Anna Held. Perhaps Van Gort encouraged her to be like that—to be so theatrically tight-laced, to wear as much paint as she was at the moment, to look so thoroughly like—well, there was no other word for it—an *actress*. And then, at the same time that he was condemning the changes he saw in her, Sarsfield caught himself: "Sour grapes!" he thought. He knew that he desired her more than ever. He put down his bourbon at a gulp. "I should not be here," he thought. "No, I should not be here. I *absolutely* should not be here."

But they went waltzing. "The Merry Widow" was all the rage; and Sarsfield tried to sleep that night with Lehar's unforgettable melodies pounding in his brain. Sailing around a dance floor had not been conducive to the intense, heart-to-heart conversation he had been planning. "Maybe tomorrow," he thought.

Since Sarsfield had seen her last, Julia had been to Paris twice; she had brought back with her half a dozen new, small, brilliant pictures—and a maid called Marie. The young girl, it seemed, spoke not one word of English and was, to Sarsfield's taste, far too pretty for her position (he was used to large, plain maids). Marie was also the most elegantly turned out domestic employée he had ever seen. Julia kept her maid as trimly corseted as if she were a débutante and dressed her in fancy black taffeta uniforms so exquisitely designed and fitted they must have originated with Julia's own dress-maker; the flounces and lace on Marie's immaculate white aprons were so finicky they could have adorned a ball gown. The maid giggled and chatted freely in French with her employer; Julia called the girl "*ma chérie*" and "*ma petite*"—terms that struck Sarsfield as highly inappropriate. When Julia set out upon afternoon errands, Marie often accompanied her; and, upon these occasions, Julia dressed her maid to complement herself—with pins or scarves or gloves identical to her own. There was something about seeing Julia with Marie that set Sarsfield's teeth on edge.

The days passed, and Sarsfield could not manage to see Julia alone. There was either the vivacious maid fussing about in the background (Sarsfield had never fully acquired the knack of regarding servants as though they did not exist) or Peter Van Gort blowing away like an Atlantic gale. Sarsfield was sure he'd come on a fool's errand; the best thing for him to do was depart gracefully, return to his backwater and make the best of it; but he could not quite screw himself to the point of leaving. If he could only talk to Julia *once*, he told himself—if he could have even an hour alone with her to try to find again his old chum so he could speak to her from the heart, then he would be satisfied—or so he thought. He was doing his best to convince himself that his motives were of the most purely altruistic nature, that he was an entirely disinterested party; but alone in his bed at night he remembered, in excruciating detail, the passionate kisses they had exchanged in the storm at Newport; and he writhed in an agony of longing and jealousy.

The opportunity Sarsfield sought finally arrived when he asked if he could photograph her in the autumnal setting of Central Park. He had brought only a small, roll-film camera with him; he set it up on a portable tripod and arranged her before a cluster of trees half-stripped of their leaves; the sky was thickening with rain. "No; do not smile," he said; and she turned to him a large-eyed regard.

"Julia," he said, "are you happy?—No, no; don't answer automatically. Are you sure?"

"As sure as one ever is," she said. "Must we discuss this, Sarsfield? I know your opinion of Peter. You've told me before, remember? I didn't fancy you'd changed your mind." Her expression was sombre; he made his exposure.

"Now turn and look toward the sky," he directed her. "Yes, of course I remember;—but when we talked about this before—well, you hardly knew the man—I would have thought—I was hoping—"

Sarsfield was finding this attempt at restoring their old intimacy painfully difficult; he wanted to raise certain delicate questions about Peter Van Gort, but he did not know quite how to go about doing so. When Sarsfield had first become acquainted with the ways of New York society, he had heard that Van Gort, like many men of his class, kept a mistress. Oh, it was done discreetly and quietly enough; the man, after all, was a banker. But was she *still* there—that faceless chorus girl— waiting in the wings for Peter, once the annoying matter of marriage was concluded, to resume their relations?

"I would have hoped that—upon further acquaintance—you might have found him a bit too much of an old-fashioned New York bachelor to make an ideal husband," Sarsfield said, hoping Julia would guess at what he was implying.

"Oh," she answered—and she must have "caught his drift" immediately—"if Peter could have had *what* he wanted, *when* he wanted it— well, then, I daresay we wouldn't be getting married at all—which is all quite amusing enough, but, yes, you are right, rather *comme il faut, n'est-ce pas?*"

Sarsfield's heart sank; if she were going to take that tone, he might as well stop before he began. He made several more exposures, saw that she was growing impatient. "Are you finished?" she asked him, and, before hearing his reply, walked away. He seized his camera and followed. He astonished himself by calling after her: "Don't marry him!"

"Why ever not?" she said, turning about with an angry snap of her skirts.

He caught up to her; they stood, staring at each other; and Sarsfield had a horrible feeling that he had experienced the present moment in its entirety before. It began to rain; and the weird mental sensation of a repeated event persisted even more intensely.

"Oh, Sarsfield," she said in a softened tone, "Peter would be the last to interfere with my friendships." She spoke these words with considerable force.

This conversation by innuendo was driving him mad; but he could not see any way out of it. "You'll have a marriage—much like that of your parents," he said.

"I expect that I shall—Oh, must we continue this conversation out of doors?"

They did not speak again until he had followed her into her rooms. "Leave us," she said to her maid. Marie, so it seemed, must have been able to understood at least that much English; she dropped a curtsey, and, with a *"Oui, Madame,"* was gone in an instant.

Laying aside her hat and gloves, Julia said: "You don't understand, Sarsfield. I have very little choice in all of this."

"You!" he said, incredulous.

"You idealize me." Her voice sounded bitter and unpleasant. Then, with an attempt at a laugh, she said: "Oh, can't you simply wish me well?— I was hoping that's why you had come. Can't we do something amusing? Oh, please, Sarsfield, let us go for a drive. We could go to Delmonico's—"

She studied his face for a moment, walked deliberately up to him and took his hands; her fingers were moist and cold like something dragged out of the Ohio River. "I didn't notice that poor Consuelo had much choice in whom she married," she said quietly; "Why should it come as a surprise that I don't have much choice either?"

More angry than he would have thought possible, Sarsfield drew away from her. "Poor Consuelo, indeed! Am I supposed to feel sorry for Consuelo Vanderbilt?—And Peter Van Gort is not exactly the Duke of Marlborough—"

"No; but the Van Gorts are as old and solid as you could ask for;— their connections are excellent; and in financial circles, no one is better placed than Peter—and his brother's in the Senate—"

The long constraint had told on both of them; now they flung words back and forth with abandon. "Oh, *in the Senate*, is he?" Sarsfield exclaimed. "His *brother*! Oh, indeed. Should I applaud?—Don't you see what's happening to you? You're being sacrificed for the sake of Henry Eberhardt's business interests—"

"No; not merely for my father—for all of us, the entire family— which, please remember, *mon cher Cousin*, also includes you."

"Oh, so *my* life is going to be enriched if you marry Peter Van Gort?"

"Yes; it will."

"My God, Julia, I don't see—"

"You're Thaddeus Eberhardt's grandson!—You could get on rippingly here. You could be *the* society photographer in New York.—Why, with the family behind you, there's nothing you couldn't do—"

"Nothing, it seems, except marry you!"

She looked as though he had struck her. Sarsfield felt his heart beating—furiously, like a steam engine. "That's torn it!" he thought.

They regarded each other in a silence that threatened to go on so long he feared he might break it by shouting;—what words he would shout, he was not sure. He listened to the rain beating against the windows. He watched her remove the jacket of her elegant suit, throw it aside onto a chair where, he assumed, her maid would find it and hang it up. The innumerable perforations in her shirt-waist formed patterns of roses; through them he could see the flushed pink of her skin. Finally she spoke in a low, expressionless voice: "There are so many other people involved.—We can't hurt them."

His heart leapt up in a wild rush; for a moment he could not trust that he had heard her correctly. He rehearsed half-a-dozen replies before he said: "If they loved you truly—they wouldn't want to hurt *you*."

"Sarsfield, please! Listen to reason. Why in heaven's name would you want to marry me? For all my indiscretions, I am quite the cowardly little thing. I just couldn't—Oh—"

Sarsfield knew that if he spoke now, he would regret it; he breathed deeply to calm himself.

She spread her hands open in mute appeal. "We're from Raysburg, West Virginia!" she said. "We're going from an Ohio River mill town to the absolute top of the heap in one jump; *and I'm the only girl*. Of course it matters who Arthy and Henty marry, but it's not the same thing;— they can't just languish about and spend Papa's money. They have to get on;—this is, after all, the twentieth century. But I *must* marry well. Don't you see? Oh, my dear, you *must* see!"

Sarsfield was losing all mastery of himself. "I don't give a hang for any of that!" he exploded.

"Oh, you damnable fellow," she exclaimed, her voice quivering, "I hate you!"

Sarsfield felt his traitorous eyes flood with tears. Julia looked at him in astonishment; then she leapt across the few feet that separated them and threw her arms around him. "Oh, darling, darling," she cried; "Oh, please don't! I couldn't bear it!"

As they waited for the car to come around to take Sarsfield to the station, it was in that painful moment of twilight when the intensity of blue defies description; in the rain, the electric lights of Fifth Avenue shone on the sidewalks in poignant yellow pools. Sarsfield's mind was, by then, totally emptied; he could not find a single polite triviality. The car approached, pulled up at the curb. For a moment Sarsfield felt again that eerie sense of timelessness: it was as though he had been here with Julia before and would go on being here with her, forever and forever, his heart breaking through all eternity. Then, in spite of the eyes of the driver and the passers-by on the street, Julia held him close and kissed him a last time—as passionately as if they were alone and had been lovers forever.

In his Pullman compartment Sarsfield sat up all night and stared out into the black, rolling countryside of Pennsylvania. Small farm houses, their lights mere yellow dots, drifted by in a sea of darkness; the clatter of the wheels on the tracks was hypnotic. And Sarsfield could no longer hold back the tears. He wept for Julia; but he also wept for the quality of light in the dark,—for the people he would never know who lived in those farm houses, for the vast reaches of America filled with people he would never know, for each of those people with a life as complicated and mysterious as his own. He wept because he knew now that he could never take a photograph that would capture everything that was in his heart.

Sweating profusely, blinking against the phenomenal sunlight, Jack Middleton was making his way, not without some considerable difficulty, along what appeared to be Main Street. "Ah, yes, indeed, of course," he thought; "by God, it's got to be Main Street!" All was well then: if he kept on going, he would reach the end of the bridge and everything would be capital; he would merely have to follow his feet, one after the other, and he would end up, eventually, back in his own dear bed where he could rest and recover from—well, it must be the uncustomary heat and light that had done him in. He had almost forgotten the Irishman until he heard the voice in his left ear: "'Tis a fine walking stick you have there, Captain. I myself like a good stick that balances well to a man's hand."

"Do you now?" Jack said; and something had been bothering him ever since he had run across this eccentric fellow: "Forgive me, Sean Quinn, but I'm no captain. Just plain Jack Middleton."

"Ah, and it must be misinformed I am for I did mistake you for the man called John Cowper Middleton of County Wicklow."

Jack turned and stared. "You've got my name right," he said. "I was born and raised in Wicklow."

"And there was in Wicklow—as I recall—a man of that very name who was commissioned in the Royal Irish Light Cavalry and known to all as Captain Jack. D'you mean to tell me that fine gentleman is not yourself?"

"That's been a good many years ago," Jack said.

"Yes, Captain, but we Irish have long memories," and the man winked at him.

Jack felt suddenly as though he had stepped into an ice house. But Quinn, smiling affably, had taken his arm and was guiding him toward the sign on Nolan's that read: FREE LUNCH. "Brush a dog any way you will, he'll still go after the rabbit," the Irishman said in a fruity, mellifluous tone; "Forgive me for making the presumption, Captain Jack, but I do believe that some nourishment would not go amiss with you."

Jack pulled away; he had to get home. Then he heard whistles, catcalls, shouting voices, the stolid thump of a big-hooved horse. Without the Irishman's steadying hand, he felt adrift; he stumbled, his knees as slack as a marionette's,—came to rest with his shoulder against a lamp post and his feet at the edge of a curb. He looked up and saw old Pete Kaltenbach's trap rattling along the street, a good half dozen lads trotting beside it, yelling and waving. In the trap, like a sudden revelation—sitting bolt upright under a huge beribboned hat, slender as a sapling, white as a sunlit cloud—was an absolutely splendid girl. "Hail Columbia!" Jack murmured, and bowed deeply at the waist.

Then Jack said: "Ah, the ladies," like a prayer.

The voice in his ear was soft as an angel's: "The ladies, is it? Tell me then, Captain Jack, of the hatred you felt in your heart for the women who lay beneath you to get you your children."

Staring at the Irishman, Jack couldn't be sure that the man had said anything at all like that.

"Good Lord," Emma Rossiter thought, "there's Sarsfield Middleton's father in the street drunk as a weasel in the middle of the afternoon!" Some queer fellow in a messy green suit had caught the old rip just before he should have fallen over and was leading him in the direction of Nolan's saloon.

Emma composed herself and looked straight ahead again. Most of the hateful little boys who had been following the trap fell behind to jeer at the drunken old photographer and his lanky companion (who ragged them back and threw them a few pennies); the journey was— thank heaven!—nearly over. Emma was sure that she was going to perish from the sun and sheer mortification: since they had arrived in town, they had been dogged up the street like a circus display. Now the trap was banging along toward the market; Emma saw workmen stop their hammering at a new store-front; they turned and stared at her; one of them thrust two grimy fingers into his mouth and produced an ear-splitting whistle. "Oh, Lord," she thought, "haven't they ever seen a lady in a dress before?"

Pete made noises in German to his horse: "*Ach, Putzi, Putzi, ja, ja,*" which must have meant "whoa" because the mare shambled to a stand-still and dropped her head as much to say: "Well, that's done it!" Emma saw that she was directly across from the photographer's studio; now how was she going to manage to get out of the trap and across the street? As though she had all the time in the world, Emma surveyed the situation in the most ladylike manner she could muster; she was not sure what made her look up, but when she did, she saw that Sarsfield Middleton was staring at her from the roof of the building. She felt her face blazing and immediately looked down at her tight, shiny, perfectly white slippers resting side by side as though they belonged to someone else. "Emma, *liebling,* vot you vant I should do now?" Pete said.

"Wait," Emma said.

After what seemed an eternity (but was probably less than a minute), Sarsfield Middleton appeared at the side of the trap. "Why, Emma, I didn't know you!" he said; and she thought: "That's what he always says to me."

She forced herself to look at him; she fancied that if he were to touch her face with his bare fingertips, they would come away scorched. His eyes were just as blue and gentle as she remembered; and she could see that he was flustered. After a moment, he said: "How absolutely perfect you look for your picture, Miss Rossiter."

"Thank you, Mr. Middleton," she replied.

Then he regained his composure, took Pete's horse by her bridle strap, and—chatting away to Pete just as though he were a farmer him-self ("How's the planting going? Have you got your corn in yet?")—he walked the trap to the end of the street where there was room enough, turned it around, walked it back, and up onto the sidewalk so that, when she got out, she would have only a few steps to the door. The traffic, she thought, could not have melted away before him any more quickly if he had been President Roosevelt. He offered her his hand.

Sarsfield felt, under his fingers, the hard, hot, shiny surface of the lacquered leather and thought: "Oh, why didn't someone tell that poor girl not to wear glacé kid gloves on a day like this?" She swung her feet around, hesitated; if she had still been the child in pigtails he remembered—and it couldn't have been that long ago either—he would simply have put his arm around her and lifted her down; she was still such a little thing, it would have been easy enough. Instead he took her other hand, allowed her to shift her weight onto him as she slipped to the sidewalk. Once she was safely established, he offered his arm. He felt as though someone, somewhere, should have been applauding.

"Thank you so much, Mr. Kaltenbach," she said to the old farmer (who could not hold back his surprise at the manner in which he had been addressed). "There's no need to wait. Dad can carry me home." She took Sarsfield's arm; and he led her into the shop and up the stairs.

Emma hesitated inside the entrance to the studio proper; and Sarsfield imagined that it must look to her like a furniture emporium improbably located in a greenhouse.

The entire west wall of the large room on the second floor comprised windows which rose in an increasing diagonal to become a vast sky-light above and then continued down the far wall on the east side; from the moment the sun cleared Howell's Livery Stable across the alley at the back of the shop until it was lost behind the buildings on Short Market Street, it shone into some portion of the studio. Each section of glass was affixed with spring-loaded rollers from which layers of white muslin or thick, opaque canvas could be drawn so that the light in any area could be diffused to whatever degree was required, or blocked entirely. This arrangement was all Jack's doing; Sarsfield had grown up with it and had long been skillful in its operation. And, over the years, Jack had collected furnishings for use in photographic settings, so the studio was cluttered with chairs and stools and tables,—and an ornate davenport, and sideboards, and dressers, and a lady's vanity with a mirror, and various ferns and palm trees. There were also a number of backgrounds; these were paintings on wheels that were placed behind the sitter; each had its own proper name; the most popular were: "The Sylvan Scene," "The Halcyon Skies," "The Columned Portico," "The

View from the Tower," "The Autumnal Garden," "The Medici Palace," "The Grand Old Tree," "The Beribboned Bower," "The Vast Heavens," and "The Fading Light." There was, finally, a small selection of painted window frames that could be interposed between the sitter and a background. The customers generally chose their own settings; and Sarsfield remembered one ancient lady who had been photographed reading the Bible in a fake Louis XVI chair flanked by an enormous elephant fern in front of the window of a Dutch farmhouse through which could be seen, in dazzling moonlight, the distant lineaments of the Parthenon.

The new graduates who responded to Jack's offer of a bargain price were to be run through the studio as quickly as possible, like so many sheep over a stile. "The Halcyon Skies" had been chosen as the proper background for these hopeful young people embarking upon life's adventures; all that was required of them was that they stand in front of it and face the camera. They were lit by sunlight diffused through a single layer of muslin which struck them at a forty-five degree angle and was augmented by light bounced from a large reflector on the other side; each was allowed only one exposure. From the moment Sarsfield had seen Emma in the trap, however, he had known that her family might be paying the bargain price, but they were going to get, nonetheless, a quality portrait—the very best work he could do. He deposited her for safe keeping on the davenport and went to rearrange the setting. She would, he was sure, want to look exactly like a drawing in a fashion magazine; he wheeled away "The Halcyon Skies" and replaced it with a background of a plain gray.

He had learned long ago that a photographer must talk to the sitters—constantly; what you said didn't matter so long as it was friendly and reassuring; if you didn't talk to them, they would turn to pillars of salt in front of your lens. "This must be an exciting time for you, Miss Rossiter," he said.

"Oh, yes!" she said, lowered her eyes and blushed again. "By Jove," he thought, "that girl's got beautiful color!"

He pushed up a fake window seat, angled it away from the direct sunlight, and invited her to sit on it. She crossed the floor with small, careful steps, sat down gingerly on the very edge, and arranged her skirts around her. He placed a footstool for her so that she could show the tip of one white slipper. She allowed one hand to rest on the cushion at her side, the other on her skirt, and looked up at him shyly. "Marvelous," he thought. The light was falling over her right shoulder now; and he placed a reflector quite near to her to illuminate her face, another one behind her to separate her from the background; then, in a moment of inspiration, he drew back the muslin diffusion screen and let the full light of the sun fall upon her.

Emma was immediately ringed with an aureole of molten gold; the reflector before her blazed back a lavish outpouring of pure white light. Her appearance had, up until then, struck Sarsfield as the brave, hard work of a naïve Raysburg girl striving to imitate the mannered elegance she could have seen nowhere else but in the ladies' magazines; now, suddenly, she was perfection; even the glacé kid gloves worked to her advantage, for her dainty arms and hands glowed brilliantly, edged with gold. She appeared inwardly lit. He stared at her, his heart racing: if he could make the photograph he saw in his mind's eye, she would no longer be little Emma Rossiter from the south end of the Island; she would become the very personification of all the delicate, hopeful, striving beauty of every wonderful young girl in America.

Sarsfield measured the light, quickly exposed two black and white plates just to get that part of the job over with, then set up his one-shot color camera. Emma, waiting patiently with the sun burning down on the back of her neck, responding automatically to Sarsfield's inquiries about her mother and father and brothers, was not even aware that her picture had been taken. "Oh, why can't he hurry!" she thought. Her high collar had begun to chafe her neck; her "Smart Set" corset (although she was, by now, depending on its stays to hold her firmly upright) felt as though it were compressing her like the skin on a boiled sausage; she could not have felt any worse inside her gloves if she had plunged her arms in hot water up to the shoulders before she had put them on. But, oddly enough, she also felt as giddy as a Junebug—drunk on the sunlight—and, if anyone had asked her, would have claimed she was having a thoroughly wonderful time, thank you.

"We're almost ready, Miss Rossiter," he said. "Could you please arch your hands slightly? Yes; that's right. And—slowly, very slowly, please turn toward the light. Yes; that's it. Now please hold that pose."

Sarsfield wanted to make her blush. "That shouldn't be hard," he thought, and said: "Of all the girl graduates in the valley, I'm sure you are, by far, the loveliest."

Color flooded her cheeks for the duration of the exposure. "Thank you," he said.

"Is it over?"

"Yes. It's over."

"Oh!" She rose to her feet. He found himself stepping up to her as though he were about to ask her to dance; but they were, of course, not on a dance floor. He had been so taken up by the photographic work, he had been unable to reflect upon what he had been feeling; and now that he was standing close to her, holding her gloved hand, he did not know what to do with it—or with her. He heard himself saying what he had not, by any stretch of the imagination, planned to say: "May I call upon you, Miss Rossiter?"

"Oh, yes!" she said.

After an hour's rest in Nolan's (and the free lunch—boiled potatoes and sausages—washed down with a pint of lager), Jack felt entirely himself again, so much so that he risked a small whiskey to speed him on his way. The day—he saw as he stepped outside—had just kept right on coming: it was even bigger, brighter, hotter than before. By God, it could be July! And the damnably boring Irishman was still with him; he just didn't seem able to shake the fellow. "Where are you bound for, Quinn?" he said.

"Well, I'll tell you, Captain, it's my intention to stroll on to the west a bit, across that fair island of yours and into the great state of Ohio, where I've never been. I've a fancy to take a drink in the state of Ohio."

"Come on then," Jack said, swinging his walking stick.

As they strode onto the Suspension Bridge, the Irishman began to sing, softly, under his breath: "Ride through the world in my sulky, oh Lord, just listen to my rubber tires roll—" It was a tune Jack had heard the darkies singing down on the pier: "and it's not the grave that's chilling my blood, but the fate of my wandering soul."

"That's not the way I've heard it sung," Jack said sourly. He felt again that queer confusion that had afflicted him earlier.

"We Irish are great ones for changing the words," Quinn said.

They walked on, and Jack struggled to make sense of the afternoon snatches of the earlier conversation were coming back to haunt him. Lord, but he wanted to be home and out of the sun!

Quinn hummed a bit of the tune, then said: "Your father, that grand old man who taught you to make pictures with a camera, is dead and gone now these fifteen years, God rest him; but your old mother is hale and hearty, nearing ninety though she is—"

"What?" Jack said. He stopped walking, searched the other's face. The deep blue eyes looked sparkling and gay.

"For a man of his class, he was not the worst—nowhere near the worst—your father; and your old mother is beloved by all, I'm pleased to tell you that, Captain. And sorry they were, and sorry she is, never to have heard a word from the youngest son," Quinn said, "the one who spread his wings and flew away without so much as a sad farewell—"

Jack could no longer contain himself. "What the hell are you talking about, Quinn?"

"Ah, there's more than just the long and the short of it, Jack Middleton. There's many a way to tell a story, as you yourself should well know, being Irish born. Stay awhile, sir, and you shall hear all of it— Now your brother George is head of the house these days, and a hard man he is, Jack, but he's not long for this world, God be good to him and give him rest. And his own dear son, who is also called George, is a strong, sturdy man who, most say, will do better. Now the tenantry, sir, coming around to them—"

"What the devil d'you want with me?" Jack shouted. "Money?"

"Oh, no, Captain," the man said with a laugh. "I've little use for that. I'm here to bring you word of the Middletons of Wicklow and to tell you how fares—and how will fare—the house of Middleton. Now the tenantry, as I began to tell you, is no worse off than anywhere else in that good green island, and they're better off than most, for you Middletons are not the worst of your damned rotten class—no, sir, and I'll have to admit it. Now your blow-by, Jack, coming around to him—well, sir, he's grown into a fine upright man, your bastard boy; indeed he has, Captain Jack, and he's hale and hearty with a grin for the whole world."

Jack stared at the grinning Irishman, then stepped back and raised his walking stick.

"Try it on, you Sassenach bastard," Quinn said slowly, drawing the words out, "and you'll be after hauling your arse out of the Ohio River."

"You go to hell," Jack said and swung his stick straight at the lean face that he saw, suddenly, was so much like his own.

The Irishman sprang back quick as a tomcat; Jack's stick swished harmlessly past his ear. Jack nearly lost his footing. "Ha, that's it,

Captain Jack!" the man called out; "Mad Jack, Jack the Divil, they called you. Go to it, Jack. Hit me with that big stick of yours. Come on, man, come on!"

Blind with fury, the photographer struck time after time—and never connected with anything more substantial than the air. "So, jump up, Jack," Quinn sang out. "Jack be lively. Jack be quick. Ah ha, oh ho, there you go, Captain Jack!" And Jack felt his walking stick torn from his grasp, saw it fly away, spin, brilliantly in the sunlight, and fall with a splash into the river.

"Oh, yes;" Quinn said, "you'll whistle your own tune and dance to it too, before it's all over, Captain Jack."

Jack rushed upon the damnable man, bent upon killing him with his bare hands; but once again Quinn eluded him, skipped a quick jig to the side and then gave Jack a good boot up the arse that sent him sprawling. Totally blown, blood pounding in his ears like kettledrums, gasping, fighting for air, Jack lay flat on his face on the wooden flooring of the bridge; he could see, far below him, the sun burning in the Ohio river. He humped himself up like a caterpillar, made it to his elbows, looked up at his tormentor. The Irishman, the blinding sun at his back, was like a lean shadow.

"My curse, my curse, my curse upon you, John Middleton," the Irishman said. "My curse upon you and your house. So will all your roads go crooked and all your plans awry. You will build nothing good and keep nothing you get; and the lot of the Middletons will be sorrow and sorrow and sorrow; and nothing will go right with them, ever and ever and ever, till God gives them rest."

Sarsfield walked briskly onto the Suspension Bridge; he loved the elegance of the thick steel wires that supported the span, looked up at them spreading out like an ink-drawn web against the startling sunset (the improbable color of strawberry jam), and felt happier than he had in months. He had strolled with little Emma from the shop down to her father's feed and grain store on Main Street. She had, by then, overcome her blushing shyness, and holding his arm, had chatted gaily. She was to read a poem of her own composition at her graduation and would be so pleased, she said, if he ("Mr. Middleton," as she was calling him) were to come and hear it. Sarsfield smiled and walked more quickly; freed from the constraint of her tiny steps, he was revelling in the sensation of his legs striding along and his lungs working hard. He had, he was certain, made an absolutely splendid color picture of her.

Waiting for him at the end of the bridge was the children's dog, Shep. The name could not have been more inappropriate for the short-haired, flop-eared mongrel who had nothing of Shepherd in him; but Olivia had insisted, and so Shep he was; now, stopped by the bridge (he was afraid of it), he was barking frantically and chasing his tail in circles. Olivia, just as frantically, was running hard toward the bridge. "Sarsfield, Sarsfield," she called out, "come quick!" She was so agitated, she ran right out from under her sailor hat; she doubled back to get it, snatched it up, and came straight at him again. "Hurry, Sarsfield, Kyle's getting a licking!" Alarmed, Sarsfield let her seize his hand and pull him forward. "Daddy's drunk as a lord!" she shouted in a voice that must have carried all the way to Belle Isle.

"Shhh!" Sarsfield cautioned her.

The dog yapping at their heels, they rushed down the walk-way toward the river. From the carriage house, Jack Middleton was hollering like a stevedore: "*Mine*, you hear me? Mine, mine, mine!"; and Kyle's treble voice answered with an inarticulate howl. Sarsfield got a glimpse of his white-faced mother by the back porch, her hands waving in the air; and then he saw Mick O'Hara, the hired man, standing like a statue with his huge fists hanging at his sides; "It's not me place!" the man shouted, "Can't be interfering—"

Sarsfield let go of Olivia's hand and broke into a run. Jack's sulky was out in the drive and ready to go; the mare, her ears pricked up, was staring with intense curiosity in the direction of the ruckus. Sarsfield ran past the sulky and into the carriage house. Jack had Kyle by the collar, was doing his best to lambaste him with a harness strap. Kyle—his knickerbockers and drawers down around his ankles—was screaming, squirming, and kicking. Jack aimed a mighty blow; Kyle twisted away like a cat, and Jack landed the strap on his own leg with a resounding *thwack!*; he yelped with pain and screamed: "You're mine, you rotten little bastard! Mine, do you hear me, *mine!*" It would have been, Sarsfield thought, a scene from a vaudeville comedy—except that his father had connected at least once: there was an angry red welt across the little boy's bare backside.

Jack raised the strap again, and Sarsfield caught his father's arm: "That's enough of that."

Surprised, Jack let go of Kyle's collar; the boy made an enormous jump that carried him well out of his father's reach, hauled up his clothing, and vanished. Sarsfield saw that his father was staring at him with a total lack of recognition; Sarsfield grabbed the harness strap, yanked it free, and threw it aside. "You son of a bitch," Jack said. "You rotter. You bastard."

Sarsfield was breathing hard. "Father," he said, "whom do you think you're addressing?"

He saw Jack return to his senses,—or as close to them as he was likely to get with all the whiskey in him. "I'm surrounded by vipers," Jack shouted out, "ungrateful venomous serpents! You're all against me, every one of you. Traitors! Cowards! Miserable, wretched, lying, sneaking, conniving—"; and he stopped, his mouth hanging open.

Sarsfield knew that his father was not finished; he was only casting about in his mind to prepare a truly magnificent torrent of abuse. But, while this moment of silence was available to him, Sarsfield thought he should take advantage of it. "Father," he said, "never touch him again. Do you hear me? Never."

"Or you'll do what?" Jack said gleefully, and looked to the right, and then to the left, appealing to the invisible audience that always appeared for him at these moments.

Jack laughed a big, hearty laugh for the sake of the throng of ghostly spectators, said: "You? You mollycoddle? You milksop?" and gave Sarsfield a strong push that set him back on his heels.

Before he could stop himself, Sarsfield pushed back. His father nearly lost his footing.

Jack recovered, began to posture like John L. Sullivan, his fists waving, and shouted: "Hit me. Come on, you priss, hit me if you dare."

Kyle shouted, "Hit him, Sarsfield, hit him!" and immediately Olivia took up the cry. Sarsfield turned around and saw the children, standing just inside the door, jumping up and down and chanting in unison: "Hit him, Sarsfield, hit him!" The dog thought this game to be great fun and added his barking to the contumely.

"You kids get out of here," Sarsfield yelled at them, turned back toward his father, and caught one of Jack's fists full in the mouth. It had been a light blow; but it had stung.

Sarsfield had never been so angry in his life; at the same time, something in him went cold as death. If anybody should have remembered that Sarsfield was a "southpaw," it was his father; but Jack obviously had forgotten: Sarsfield feinted twice with his right, and then, when Jack was wide open, fired a solid left-cross directly onto the point of Jack's chin.

Jack's head snapped back in an entirely satisfactory manner, and then his body followed his head: his arms waving like windmills, he stumbled backward, doing his best to maintain his footing. The children were screaming with delight; and back and yet farther back their father went, his arms waving in increasing circles. Sarsfield was astonished that his father was still on his feet. On back Jack went, his feet scrambling in a frantic dance. Then, at last, he arrived at the far wall, rebounded from it, collapsed against it, and slid to the dirt. Jack was out cold. It had been one of the most purely comical sights Sarsfield had ever seen; and he bent double, laughing.

Jack was out only a second or two; then he began to moan: "Christ; oh, Christ; oh, Christ; oh, Christ."

"Hurray for Sarsfield!" Kyle yelled, and Olivia echoed him. The dog joined in.

"Shut up," Sarsfield managed to yell between spasms of laughter, "for God's sake, be quiet!"

Jack sprang suddenly to his feet, and, with horrible racking sobs, ran pell-mell for his sulky. "Stop him!" Sarsfield's mother called; the notion was so absurd that Sarsfield did not even consider it.

Jack whipped up the mare, and—his eyes rolling in his head, looking for all the world like a demon from hell—galloped madly off. In a moment a great shout went up from the end of the bridge where Jack had nearly collided with a buggy; and then there followed the frantic sound of hooves on the wooden flooring. Eventually the sounds of Jack's departure died out. Sarsfield's mother turned on her heel and, without a word, walked into the house. Sarsfield saw that the children were looking up at him, their eyes wide; Mick O'Hara was grinning sheepishly. Shep sat down abruptly and scratched himself. It had become, at last, so quiet that Sarsfield could hear crickets and frogs, and, somewhere far above, a nighthawk.

It was a lovely evening. The sky over the river had become a delicate gray-blue; and, behind the house, there was an iridescent glow the gentle color of an apple that has just turned pink. Sarsfield breathed deeply. He could smell daffodils, new grass coming in. There was a wonderful sense of peace everywhere.

"Are you all right?" Sarsfield asked his little brother.

"Shucks," Kyle said, "he didn't hurt me a bit." And then he said, awe in his voice: "You licked him, Sarsfield. Danged if you didn't lick him good."

"Danged if you didn't," Olivia echoed.

Sarsfield put one hand on Kyle's shoulder, took Olivia by the other, and walked the children toward the house. It was a shame what was happening to them: they were running totally wild. After all his mother's talk, in his own childhood, about what genteel people did and did not do (after dressing him in skirts until he was six!), she hardly seemed to care what happened to these two; except for giving them occasional extravagant presents, she might as well have forgotten they existed. She had her frail health as an excuse, he supposed; but he often thought that she could overcome her infirmity by an exercise of the will—that she should at least *try* to overcome it for the sake of the children. They were gone from dawn till dusk every day, and, except for their hours in school, Lord knows what they were doing; they roamed freely from one end of the Island to the other. It was Mrs. O'Hara who fed them and and put them to bed and taught them whatever few manners they managed to acquire. Here they were—like two little ragamuffins, talking like—well, he might as well admit it—like the Rossiters. (Poor Emma!)

"I want you kids to dress for dinner," he said.

"What d'you mean?" Kyle asked as though the concept were totally foreign to him, "like for church?"

"That's right," Sarsfield said, "like for church. And wash your face and hands. You too, Olivia. And *use soap*."

In the kitchen, Minnie, the cook, greeted them with: "'Scuse me, Mister Sarsfield, but Miz Middleton say she ain't coming down to dinner."

"Yes; she is," Sarsfield said, "and the children will dine with us."

"Really?" Kyle said.

"Yes; really." Sarsfield saw Minnie's face go slack with astonishment.

Sarsfield went to his room, wiped the blood from his lip, and changed into evening wear. Kyle appeared briefly in his doorway to ask: "Like for church?"

"Kyle," Sarsfield told him, "the very best you've got."

Sarsfield knocked on his mother's door, received no answer, knocked again. Her muffled voice said: "I'll be down later, dear."

"No, mother," he said, "now."

In a moment she opened the door. He saw, from the size of her pupils, that she had sipped a substantial quantity of the tonic that old Doc Anderson (that quack) prescribed for her neurasthenia. He took her gently by the arm and led her downstairs. "Come on, mother," he said, "it's a lovely time of evening."

When they entered the drawing room, she began to speak in a light, distant voice: "It is a lovely time of evening, is it not, Sarsfield? Wouldn't you say that it was a lovely time of evening?"

"Yes," he said, "I would."

He lit the gas, turned the lamps low so that their light would blend gently into the twilight at the windows. He lit the candles on the table, stood back and surveyed the scene. He loved the light at that hour; he loved the moment that often arrives just before dinner—when night seems to pause, and hover breathlessly, before advancing; he always expected some enormous secret to be revealed in that moment. He poured his mother and himself a glass of sherry. "Will you serve dinner?" he asked her, speaking softly, "or shall Mrs. O'Hara do it?"

"Why—I will," she said with a brilliant smile. He brought up a bottle of his father's best French wine from the basement and opened it to air.

The children came in more quietly than Sarsfield could have imagined. Olivia, who loved dressing up, was grinning like an imp; she had put on her best flounced frock—a white lawn with pale blue ribbons. But it was Kyle who Sarsfield found extraordinary: the boy had actually put on a blue cheviot serge suit with an Eton collar that Sarsfield had never seen before, and white kid shoes with black enamel leather foxings that Sarsfield certainly *had* seen because Kyle had claimed he would rather die than wear them. Kyle had wet his hair and combed it; water was still dripping down his forehead. Both children were clean. In a breathless silence, Sarsfield led them to the table and seated them. He poured Kyle a glass of water, added a few drops of wine to it, and said: "Kyle, my boy, you're going to learn to drink a little wine with your dinner—like a gentleman."

Sarsfield sat in his father's place at the head of the table. The quiet in the room was so delicate that, for a moment, he hesitated to speak. Then he said—very softly: "Mother, will you please serve the soup."

6

Sarsfield spent several days making a print of Emma Rossiter. The powerful feeling that had swept over him when he had seen, on his ground glass, that vision of tender girlhood brushed with gold, had carried through to this physical, man-made object and imbued it with an inexplicable vitality all its own. The girl sat, poised; and every line of her—the oval of her hat, the sweep of her sun-drenched neck and arms, the firm curve of her waist, the brilliant fall of her gown, the small, brilliant point of the toe of one slipper—led the eye to every other line, forming a pleasing, harmonious whole. The most delicate of pinks was mounting to her cheeks; her blue eyes were glowing with expectation; her warmly colored lips were slightly parted as though she had been caught in the act of drawing a tender breath. Light, golden light, radiated from her; and the girl quivered on the very edge of womanhood—and life. He could have shown his print to any photographer in the world as a scientific demonstration of the finest quality yet achieved in color; he could have hung it beside the most majestic examples of the painter's art with full confidence that it would not suffer by comparison. "Stunning, beautiful, perfection itself—," Sarsfield thought from time to time; but, throughout his long hours in the darkroom and at the work bench, it never occurred to him that he had quite forgotten the real, flesh and blood Emma Rossiter in favor of the exquisite image that was gradually appearing before him.

Emma, however, had not forgotten Sarsfield. At first she had been certain that he would call upon her as soon as he could—on Sunday, the day after he had taken her picture. She kept remembering the way he had looked at her, the way he had offered her his hand. Then, when she had risen to her feet (so close to him!), he had not stepped back; "May I call upon you, Miss Rossiter?" he had said. On Sunday, she dressed in her daintiest white lawn and tied a pretty blue ribbon in her hair and wore her white slippers all day long; it was her fancy that, having seen her in her most formal, ladylike, and grown-up attire, he should see her also as a pretty country girl with her hair down. By the time that twilight was settling over the Island, she knew that he was not coming; she tore off the ribbon, and changed her shoes, and walked down to the river so that no one could see her tears. In her mind, she called him conceited and cruel. But then she thought that perhaps he did not wish to appear too eager; perhaps he had fallen horribly in love with her—at first sight! That could be it: the very moment he had seen her in Pete Kaltenbach's trap, he had been struck to the heart with the knowledge that suddenly, appearing like a vision before him, was the girl he must make his wife. If that was the way he felt, then he should have to *force* himself to stay away; she could imagine him giving himself a good talking to, saying: "Well, old man, you must allow a decent interval to pass—" She kept hearing his voice in her memory—so ardent and sincere: "May I call upon you, Miss Rossiter?"

Each night, after school, Emma expected him. By the end of the week, she could think about nothing but the events of the Saturday before; she reviewed them repeatedly in her mind. How could she have been so silly as to think, even for a moment, that he might have fallen in love with her? She knew by now that she must have done something wrong. "May I call upon you, Miss Rossiter?" he had said; and she had said: "Oh, yes!"; and that must have been a mistake. Yes, that was it: she should not have agreed so readily. She should have been coy and bright and clever and said: "Oh, Mr. Middleton, I am just so busy—" But, no, that wasn't clever—"just so busy"—that wasn't clever at all; that was dumb as a post. What would one of those out-the-pike girls have said, one of those Eberhardt girls? But try as she might, she could not imagine what one of those girls would say, because she had never talked to one of those girls in her life. But she was certain by now that saying "Oh, yes!" like that had been too forward. Men didn't like girls who were forward; and someone like Sarsfield Middleton would certainly notice even just a tiny little speck of forwardness—but, no, she was being foolish: how could saying "Oh, yes!" be considered forward? Maybe it was Pete Kaltenbach's trap? But, no, he had seen her in the trap, and *still* he had said: "May I call upon you, Miss Rossiter?" Maybe she had said something wrong when he had walked her down to her father's store. What on earth could it have been? Oh, she had invited him to her graduation; that must be it. Why, of course that was it: that was far too forward! And she blushed, remembering it.

By the next weekend, Emma was in agony. She waited for him all day Saturday. Working at the dry-goods store, she was waiting; doing her chores around home, she was waiting. She waited all through dinner; and she waited until the sun set; then she went to bed and cried herself to sleep. She woke up Sunday morning so early the sun had not even come up yet; and she gave herself a good talking to and told herself she was behaving like a silly little girl in a novel and she should stop it and get on with her life; but she waited for him all through church, and all day Sunday, and all Sunday evening. By then, both her mother and father (and even her brother who never noticed anything!) were asking her what was wrong; and every ten minutes or so, it seemed, she was bursting into tears and running off to her room. Sunday night she was too "done up" even to cry; and Monday, when she got up to go to school, she prayed to the Lord to give her strength to get through the next few weeks. And she thought: "Well, maybe I'll go to normal school and be a school teacher. I shall never marry; I shall be an old maid school teacher, and dedicate my life to teaching, and people will say, 'What a noble woman! She must have been stunningly beautiful in her youth; why d'you suppose she never married? Perhaps there is some deep sorrow in her life'—"

Sarsfield, meanwhile, had been making a second print of Emma. No sooner had he finished the first than he had seen a slight error in the balance and intensity of his colors that could easily be corrected. He completed the second print late on a Wednesday afternoon, carried both into the studio and arranged them under the skylight so that he could compare them; anyone other than the photographer would have been hard-pressed to distinguish one print from the other, but Sarsfield could distinguish them; and he saw that his second print was as close to perfection as he could achieve. He was satisfied.

Since his days at Harvard, Sarsfield had cultivated the ability to withdraw deeply into his scientific and photographic work; whenever he completed a project and was forced to pay attention, once again, to the commonplace activities he had been ignoring, he always felt as he was feeling now: exhausted, somewhat gloomy, astonished that the ordinary world still remained much as he had left it. He climbed up to the roof to give himself a moment to reflect. On that particular Wednesday, Raysburg looked the way it usually did: like a dim gum print in shades of gray. There was no wind to speak of; and the smoke from the Top Mill rolled steadily upward, spread, and drifted down the river. It was a cold day for spring, as though the calendar had been turned back to March; Sarsfield felt chilled to the marrow. "The old bastard's got to come back some time," he thought as he stared out into the dirty haze that obscured the river.

Although neither had mentioned it, both Sarsfield and his mother had expected Jack to return home within two or three days; anything longer than that meant a real "bender." It had been now—and Sarsfield counted it up—eighteen days; Jack had never been gone that long. "There's going to be all hell to pay," Sarsfield thought grimly. Every time he remembered knocking his father down, he felt a sinking sensation in the pit of his stomach.

As soon as Sarsfield thought of his absent father, he found himself thinking of myriad other things he had been neglecting. His negatives of Emma may have been splendid; but his negatives of the street scene below were so thin that there was barely an image upon them at all— which meant that his prediction of the response of his emulsion had been off by a mile, and he would have to make a series of tests. Then he remembered that he had turned away customers, telling them to wait for Jack to return, when he could have easily done the work himself; then he remembered that he had somehow not managed to finish printing the portraits of the new graduates; then he remembered that he still had not decided whether to stay in Raysburg or remove to New York; and then, at last, he remembered Emma: "Did I ask if I could call on her? Good heavens, it seems to me I did."

By that Wednesday, Emma had decided that she didn't give a tinker's dam for Sarsfield Middleton. She wore her navy blue suit to school and took some considerable satisfaction in how smart and grown-up she looked in it; and even stuck-up Sarah Williamson said something to her in the hall about how nice she looked, and Emma cut her dead and was glad she did it. Then, after school, Emma stopped in to McKeen's and flirted disgracefully with Sid Smith who jerked soda in there; he was supposed to be "fast," and she knew he had a soft spot for her; and she said a lot of outrageous things that ordinarily would have embarrassed her half to death, but she didn't care. It was a chilly, nasty day; and she was walking quickly to get home when she saw their cow—dumb old Sally—standing down on the river bank by the Imhoffs' landing road. "Sally, you get up here!" Emma called;

Sally gave her a look that said: "Do I know you?" and then turned her mournful gaze back toward the Ohio River. Emma wondered if that was a punishment God had sent her for cutting Sarah Williamson.

Emma hurried home; and her mother greeted her with: "Emma, honey, the cow's got out."

"I know, Mama," Emma answered back. "Who left the gate open?" It was unwritten law that whoever left the gate open had to get the cow.

"I'm afraid I did," her mother responded with an apologetic laugh.

Emma, standing there in her trim, spotless "butterfly" cut-away with matching kid gloves and dainty, high-heeled oxfords done in navy and white, looked at her mother who had five pots cooking away on the stove and her arms deep in soap suds. "I'm going to run away from home," Emma said; "I'm going West."

"Be sure to send us a postcard," her mother replied.

Emma changed into an old, brown mother hubbard she used to do chores in, and her old boots, and grabbed up a jacket of her brother's and went after the cow. There had been high water earlier in the spring; and the long flat slope behind the Imhoff place was covered in mud two feet thick. Sally seemed to have been drawn to the river by some fateful attraction; and now she was truly stuck. Emma pushed the cow, and twisted her ears, and broke off a branch from a tree and switched her with it, but to no avail; Sally lowed in a dismal, heartbroken tone and stood stock still. "You hateful thing!" Emma said. It had begun to rain.

Emma was so angry she was determined to move the cow if it killed her, so she slogged around behind her, grabbed her tail and twisted with all her might; Sally bellowed and took several steps forward. Progressing in this slow fashion, Emma managed to turn the cow around and propel her back to where she belonged; the process took so long that by the time Emma returned to the house, everyone was waiting dinner for her. "Emma, Emma, Emma!" her mother shrieked, "take your boots off! Good Lord, was you born in a barn?" Emma saw the tracks of mud she'd left on her mother's freshly washed floor.

"Yes, Mama," Emma said, retreating to the porch, "I was born in a barn; and I grew up in a hog wallow. You may's well bring the chickens in and let them roost in my room."

"That's enough of that, you spiteful girl!" her mother yelled back at her. Emma pulled her boots off and flung them down. She was muddy to her knees. She pulled her stockings off and threw them after the boots; she entered the kitchen barefoot.

"Don't say a word to her," Tom Rossiter said to his wife.

"I wasn't going to say a thing," Mrs. Rossiter said.

"You and me grew up eating our dinner barefoot, so don't you say a thing to her," he said.

"I *wasn't*," snapped Mrs. Rossiter who was now truly angry.

"Emma, what are you *doing*?" her father demanded.

"Washing the mud off my hands, Daddy," she said and mercifully stopped her tongue before it got her into any more trouble.

Emma sat down at the table across from her brother, Clayborn; the sight of his sparkling white shirt and pomaded hair parted in the middle as neatly as if he'd done it with a paring knife—and of his pink, self-satisfied, grinning face—made her want to scream; and she asked: "Where were *you* when the cow got out?"

"Down in the basement eating sauerkraut," he replied with a laugh.

"Well, Mr. Smarty-pants," she came back at him, "when are you going to get a job?"

"That's enough!" Tom Rossiter said. He glared at everyone at the table and folded his hands.

Emma sighed and closed her eyes. "For the gifts we are about to receive, dear Lord," her father prayed, "make us truly thankful. Remind us how tough times can get, oh Lord, and how we got it pretty good these days. Calm these troubled waters with the spirit of thy love, oh Lord, so we can eat our dinner in peace. Amen."

Emma looked up and saw that her father was looking at her. "Amen," she said.

The fried chicken had just gone around when there was a knock on the front door. "Now who can that be?" Mrs. Rossiter asked and looked up and down the table as though expecting someone to tell her. Mr. Rossiter rose reluctantly to his feet and walked into the front of the house. Emma heard a man's voice, felt the blood rush to her face and then drain completely away. If she leapt up without even a second's hesitation, she could run down the hall; if they were walking back through the parlor, they wouldn't see her; she could run up the stairs to her room at the same time they were entering the kitchen. But she sat, rooted to the spot, and her opportunity was lost. Yes, it was Sarsfield Middleton, dressed, as he always was, like a dummy in the window of a haberdashery store.

"Mrs. Rossiter, good evening," Sarsfield said.

"You know my boy, Clayborn, don't you, Mr. Middleton?" Tom said.

"Hi there, Sarsfield," Clay said, rising and extending his hand. "Calling him by his first name," Emma thought, "that fresh thing!"

Then, at last turning to Emma, Sarsfield said: "How nice to see you again, Miss Rossiter. I brought your picture."

"Well, how d'you like that?" Mrs. Rossiter said with an embarrassed laugh, "a home delivery. Sit down, Mr. Middleton, and take something with us."

"Oh, no, thank you," Sarsfield said. "I'm expected at home."

"Well, you can kindly set a moment, can't you?" Mrs. Rossiter asked him.

"I'm sorry—this is an inconvenient time," Sarsfield said. "Do please continue with your dinner." What he did not realize was that what he had asked was an impossibility: the Rossiters would no more have dined in front of a guest in their home who was not dining with them than they would have taken off their clothes and danced around the kitchen naked.

Sarsfield sat down on the chair offered him, looked at their strained faces regarding him with fixed smiles, and thought: "Hang it all, I should have known they'd eat at five-thirty." There was nothing to do now but give them the pictures and leave as gracefully—and quickly— as possible. He drew the black-and-white photograph out of his package and handed it to Emma's father.

Tom studied the picture carefully, nodded several times, passed it on to his wife. "Well, well, well," he said, "quite something. Emma, you look pretty as can be—don't she?"

"Oh, yes," his wife said. "Just like a grown up lady. Well, yes. She's always taken a good picture," and she passed the photograph on to the subject.

Emma, to her own surprise, was so angry by now that she could have cheerfully ripped the picture up into a thousand pieces; without taking more than a glance at it, she handed it over to her brother. She had slipped around to the far side of the table to hide her bare feet; but nothing could hide her disgraceful, muddy old mother hubbard. "*Now* he comes," she thought, "after all this time, and bringing his business with him.—Well, see if he gets one word out of me!"

"That's good work, Mr. Middleton," Tom said. "What do we owe you for it?"

"Oh," Sarsfield said, "we can settle the account any time."

Sarsfield had decided to give Emma his second best color print of her; he had thought that it might make up for his having forgotten to call on her; he had even taken the trouble to frame it. But now he suspected that his plan had been a foolish one indeed; he was out of his depth here, unsure of the customs and manners of a class of people that was not his own. He felt, however, compelled, as if by some mindless inertia, to continue: "Miss Rossiter," he said, "I brought you a graduation present."

Emma looked down at the rapidly cooling fried chicken in front of her and remained silent. "Emma!" her mother admonished her sharply.

"That's lovely, I'm sure," Emma said in a dim voice without looking up.

Sarsfield unwrapped the framed print and stood it on the table where all could see it. Mrs. Rossiter gasped; and then a heavy, strained, interminable silence settled over the family. Even Clay Rossiter, that voluble young man, had nothing to say and appeared to be looking to his father for guidance; but Tom continued to sit there unspeaking, rigid and perplexed.

"Lord almighty!" Mrs. Rossiter said eventually, "it's an oil painting."

"I'm sorry, ma'm, no," Sarsfield said; "It's a photograph."

"No! Really? How did you get it colored?"

"It's a photographic process, Mrs. Rossiter."

"Lord save us," she said, "I've never seen the like of it. Don't that beat all, Emma? It's colored! It's just real as life. My, my, my. Look at that, Emma. You look just like the girl on the soap package."

Emma could cheerfully have strangled her mother just to shut her up; the picture was one of the most beautiful things she had ever seen in her life, and it almost made her want to forgive him.

Tom cleared his throat, said in a deep, formal voice: "Mr. Middleton, could I have a word with you, please?"

Sarsfield, puzzled and apprehensive, followed Tom out onto the back porch. "Now's my chance," Emma thought, "at least I've got to get some shoes on," but then she saw that Sarsfield had stopped just outside the door and could still see into the kitchen, so she was forced to remain where she was.

Tom Rossiter was a spare man, even taller and thinner than Jack Middleton (whose height Sarsfield matched); and Sarsfield had the unaccustomed experience of having to look up to someone who was addressing him. "That color picture—" the older man began, and then stopped, as though some profound indignation had choked off his speech. Sarsfield could not imagine what was transpiring.

Tom Rossiter was an angular man, made up of knobs and straight hard lines; his body, contracted into an oddly coiled posture, seen against the rainy evening sky, seemed to Sarsfield like a piston arrested in mid-stroke. "I didn't order no color picture," the man said, "but you tell me what the cost of that color picture is, and I'll pay it."

"I never intended for you to pay for that picture, sir," replied Sarsfield in his mildest voice; "I meant it as a gift for Emma."

"No, sir! With all due respect for you, Mr. Middleton—I thank you for the thought. But I shall pay you what that picture's worth. You tell me what you charge for them pictures, sir, and I'll pay it."

The last time Sarsfield had sold a color photograph it had been to his cousin Bedelia; he had charged seventy-five dollars and considered the price a bargain. He would be surprised if Tom Rossiter's little feed store made that much money in a month. He could, he knew, lie about the figure; but some mysteriously firm streak to his character wouldn't let him do that: the man would pay full value or nothing. Sarsfield was surprised at himself,—at his own vehemence concerning a matter, upon which, only a few seconds before, he had not even been aware that he held any opinion whatsoever. To calm himself, he looked out toward the river. The other alternative, of course, was that he would simply take the picture home with him.

"Mr. Rossiter," Sarsfield said, "I grew up on the Island. My family and your family have been neighbors for years now. Why, I'll never forget that time when—oh, I couldn't have been more than four or five—when you took me up behind the oxen and gave me a ride around your field—"

Sarsfield saw that the old Southerner was looking at him intently. "And I'll never forget the 'ninety-eight flood when you and your family rowed around the whole Island delivering bread and eggs to everyone who needed them."

"Oh, well, Mr. Middleton, that was just what anybody would of—"

"Please, sir, call me Sarsfield.—And what I'm trying to say, the point I'm trying to make—is that good neighbors should value, should respect, should appreciate one another. It is a great accomplishment, a great day, when one's daughter graduates from the high school; and I was hoping that your family would accept this little, ah—token from my family to commemorate that memorable occasion."

That was the best Sarsfield could do; he felt mentally exhausted by the effort.

Tom Rossiter stared at him a moment longer and appeared to be weighing the matter in his mind; then he gestured for Sarsfield to follow back into the kitchen.

"Well, now," Tom said, "it's a mighty neighborly thing that Mr. Mid—that Sarsfield here has done. Don't you think you ought to thank him for that gift he's made to you, Emma?"

"Thank you, Mr. Middleton," she said and hated the demure, girlish sound of her voice. She saw that he wanted to leave; he was murmuring polite phrases and backing toward the kitchen door. Now someone had to see him out, and neither of her parents showed the least inclination to do so. Suddenly Emma felt a wave of cold, violent, resentful anger and thought: "It's no disgrace to work. Goodness knows, that's the last thing in the world that's a disgrace." She stood, drew herself up to her full height, stepped out from behind the table, and walked past him,—leaving him no alternative but to follow. She saw him glance down at her bare feet and then look quickly away; she sailed on through the parlor, her chin in the air. When she was out of earshot of her family, she said: "Please forgive my appearance, Mr. Middleton, but the cow got out."

Sarsfield was touched by her simplicity. "The cow got out?" he said and couldn't help a smile. After a moment, she smiled back, ruefully; and he knew—from visceral intuition rather than from any ratiocination—that he had hurt her. He tried for a simplicity to match hers: "I'm sorry I haven't come to see you before now. I've been appallingly busy. May I call tomorrow night?"

Now was Emma's chance to say: "Well, I'm pretty busy too, Mr. Middleton." Instead she said: "Yes. When may I expect you?"

She closed the door behind him. She felt all the force of her anger flow out of her; her knees threatened to buckle, and she had to lean against the closed door for support. "Oh, Lord," she prayed, "please give me a second chance."

"Good people," Sarsfield thought, walking fast up Front Street, "the salt of the earth," but he was as relieved to be out of the Rossiters' kitchen as if he had been serving a penitentiary term at hard labor and had just been told that he could go home. He could not understand now why he had landed himself into such a "pickle" in the first place; as touching as he had found the image of the fiercely proud, barefoot little girl in her mud-spattered dress, the differences between himself and Emma Rossiter—in background, class, age, social standing, temperament, and aspiration—were obviously insurmountable. He would call upon her again because he had said he would, and that would be the end of it; by the time he got home, he had put the Rossiters quite out of his mind.

The children had already eaten and vanished again into the rainy evening; but his mother had waited dinner for him. They dined quietly, spoke little; Sarsfield listened to the hiss of the gas lamps and discovered, to his total astonishment, that he missed his father. Without Jack's force, energy, and vast exuberance, the house had begun to feel oppressive, overly quiet—even sad. His mother must have also been thinking about her absent husband: "I'm worried," she said. "Do you suppose you could, ah—make enquiries?"

"I suppose I could."

"Perhaps he has come to some misadventure—"

"I'll talk to the Sheriff tomorrow."

Then he saw from the expression on his mother's face that she was having difficulty speaking,—was profoundly embarrassed. At first he thought that she must be steeling herself to make some allusion to Mrs. Smith's establishment; but, as it turned out, that was not the topic that was giving her such trouble. "Sarsfield," she said, "it is beginning to become a matter of—well, of some urgency. The accounts are—somewhat in arrears."

In polite society, at least as it was understood by Alice Middleton (nee Eberhardt), money could never be discussed; to mention a figure, name the actual price of anything, remark, for instance, that the butcher needed to be paid, would have been unthinkable: one could not say the word "dollar" any more than one could say the word "syphilis." Once a month Mrs. Middleton presented the household accounts to her husband; and he presented her with—but here Sarsfield had to pause, because he did not have an inkling how the transaction was concluded. Did she get cash? Did Jack write drafts against his bank account? The ritual was always conducted behind closed doors; and Jack and his wife might as well have been engaged in the intimacies of their conjugal relations for all the information that was available to their children. The words she had just spoken were the closest she would ever come to saying that the household was in financial difficulty.

Sarsfield did not know what the devil he was supposed to do about it. He had his own savings accrued from the sale of photographs in New York; but he had no intention of touching it. The shop had taken in hardly anything since Jack had left, so there was no help to be had from that direction; Sarsfield, in fact, had been worrying about how he was supposed to pay Miss Calendene's modest salary. "How, ah—do the O'Haras stand?" he asked.

"Not well, I'm afraid, dear," she said. "Hang it all," Sarsfield thought, "they have to be paid too. Damn the old bastard!"

Mrs. Middleton retired; and Sarsfield continued to sit in the drawing room, staring out the window as the night deepened. Mrs. O'Hara interrupted his introspection: "Excuse me, Mr. Middleton—" He had to suppress his annoyance at hearing himself thus addressed; until his father had left, she had always called him by his first name.

"Master Kyle hasn't come home," she said. "He *never* comes home—I do the best I can for those two, Mr. Middleton, and I don't mean to be complaining to you, sir, but, by the sweet Mother of God, an easy task it is not. Now if you was to ask me, sir —"

"I know where he is," Olivia piped in, surprising both adults who were not aware that she had followed Mrs. O'Hara into the room.

"Let's go get him," Sarsfield replied, took his little sister's hand and allowed her to lead him out of the house and up toward Belle Isle.

Olivia, as a baby, had adored people; she had howled bitterly when left alone even for a moment, but, in company, had been content so long as she could fix someone—anyone would do—with her big, dark eyes that were exactly like her father's. Only a few months after she had been born, she had decided that she could talk and had spent entire days staring at whoever was handy and saying, "Wow wow wow wow wow wow wow!" in a tone so convincingly like adult speech that visitors were often deluded into believing that the tiny girl who had yet to learn to crawl had said something intelligible to them. Except for those hours when she slept, she had been talking steadily ever since.

"D'you think Daddy's going to come back?" Olivia asked but did not wait for a reply; she never waited for a reply. "I don't think he's going to come back," she said, "but Kyle thinks he will come back, but Kyle wishes he *wouldn't* come back. Where'd he go, anyway? Mother says he's gone on business, but Kyle says he's at a house of ill repute. What's a house of ill repute? I asked Kyle how he heard that, and he said he heard it from some of the older boys, and I asked Mrs. O'Hara, and she said little girls shouldn't use words like 'house of ill repute,' and if she ever heard me say that again she'd wash my mouth out with soap, and just see if she wouldn't. Do people really do that to naughty children? I guess they do because Amy Arthur said she said a bad word—I can't tell you what it was because it's *bad*, or maybe I can, just to tell you what it was, anyway, so you'll know; she said 'damn it all to hell'—Oh, sugar, now I've gone and said it! That's really bad, isn't it? But she said it and had to stand in the corner with a bar of soap in her mouth for hours and hours and hours, d'you think she really had to do that? And she said it made her throw up, and I told Mrs. O'Hara that, and she said little girls shouldn't say 'throw up'; they should say 'be sick,' but 'be sick' doesn't mean the same thing as 'throw up,' does it?—There he is."

The sight that greeted Sarsfield's eyes as he followed Olivia's pointing finger was so poignant, so melancholy, that he felt a painful constriction in his heart. Perched high in the bare branches of a tree, Kyle made a small, motionless silhouette in the rain; the little boy was looking out over the river. Sarsfield had to call several times to get his brother's attention; then Kyle came down readily enough. "What were you doing up there?" Sarsfield asked him.

"Nothing."

Back at home, Sarsfield turned Olivia over to Mrs. O'Hara and accompanied Kyle to his room. He gave the boy a pat on the head and was on his way out when Kyle, with no preamble, asked: "Sarsfield?— Who are we?"

Sarsfield was taken aback. "What d'you mean, Kyle?"

"You know, our family."

"Come on, Kyle, you know who our family is. There's your grandfather, Thaddeus Eberhardt, and your great-grandfather, old Dan Rainey—"

"No, not *Mother's* family—I mean the Middletons. Who are the Middletons?"

"Well, you know what Dad always says—'land given by Queen Elizabeth—'"

"I know that!" the boy exclaimed. "I know what he says. But Dad's a liar."

If Sarsfield had been doing his duty to the ideals of home and family in which both he and his mother firmly believed (even if Jack Middleton might not), he would have said: "Don't talk about your father that way." Instead he found himself saying: "Oh. What makes you think that?"

"I've caught him at it. Haven't you?"

Sarsfield could not suppress a smile. "Yes; I guess I have."

"D'you suppose we was kings in Ireland—?"

"Were," Sarsfield said firmly, "suppose we *were*—By george, Kyle, you're going to have to learn some grammar one of these days!—No, I don't think it's very likely we were kings in Ireland."

"Mrs. O'Hara says there were kings in Ireland in the old days," Kyle replied in a stubborn voice, "and queens too. She says there were kings and queens in Ireland when the English were still running around naked like savages."

"There might very well have been kings and queens in Ireland; but the chances of us being related to them are kind of slim, don't you think?" By now Sarsfield had become fascinated by his little brother's thoughts; he sat down on the end of Kyle's bed so he could hear more of them.

"Maybe we're not his," Kyle said. "Maybe our father's somebody else."

As a child, Sarsfield had entertained the same notion; he would often have preferred to have sprung from any other father than Jack Middleton. Sarsfield was fair, blue-eyed, and rosy complexioned like both the Eberhardts and the Raineys, and there had always been much argument about which of these families he favored the more; but one thing was certain: except for his height and slenderness, he did not resemble his father in the least. The two little ones, however, appeared to have received a full dose of Jack: both Kyle and Olivia had skin white as parchment, hair and eyes black as jet.

"That won't wash, Kyle," Sarsfield said. "Just look in the mirror."

Kyle made a wry face. "Yep," he responded, "I favor him, don't I? And you know what he always says—'Black Irish through and through,' that's what he says. OK, so I asked my teacher, and she said that Queen Elizabeth was an English queen, and if she gave land to somebody in Ireland, they had to be English. And she says she guesses that Middleton is an English name—that it don't sound Irish to her. So if the Middletons are English, why do Ollie and me look like black Irish?"

"Good grief, Kyle, you've sure been thinking about it, haven't you."

"I wrote them a letter," Kyle said solemnly, "but I haven't sent it yet. You want to see it?"

"Wrote? Who'd you write?"

"The Middletons of Wicklow," Kyle replied as though it were obvious. He rummaged around in his toy box, produced a dog-eared piece of paper, and handed it over.

"Dear Middletons of Wicklow," Sarsfield read, "my name is Kyle Rainey Middleton and my father is John Cowper Middleton and we live in Raysburg, West Virginia, in The United States of America, and he says that the Middletons of Wicklow had there land give to them by Queen Elizbeth, is that true? Please rite and tell me who you are. I am your devoted sarvant, Kyle Rainey Middleton."

Sarsfield was astonished. His first reaction was to laugh; but then, looking into Kyle's intensely serious eyes, he knew that he must do no such thing. "I'll write it for you," he promised. "Now you go to sleep."

Sarsfield retired to his room, lit the student lamp, sat in the chair by the window overlooking the river, and wondered what to do next. He did not feel the least bit sleepy; he got up and began to pace. "From the mouths of babes," he thought, "good Lord!" It was so profoundly simple that it had never occurred to him; no, it had taken a twelve-year-old to think of it: if the Middletons were, indeed, a prominent family in Ireland, a letter addressed to them in County Wicklow should, in all likelihood, reach them. He took out pen and stationery and wrote to the mysterious Middletons on Kyle's behalf; by the time he finished, he realized that he was just as curious about them as was his little brother.

Sarsfield yawned and stretched; he fervently hoped that this was not going to be one of those terrible nights in which sleep eluded him until dawn. He felt as though he were caught in Raysburg like a catfish in a net; but what, he wondered, comprised the net? The strands of it, he supposed, were made up of knowing every twist and turn of every street in the city, of knowing the name of every member of every old family, of knowing who was related to whom back three generations,— of being able to close his eyes and see, as in a dream, the Ohio River born at Pittsburgh and flowing down to the Mississippi, the fat hills of

Pennsylvania rolling away to the east and the soft farmland of Ohio to the west;—and all of it, the whole geography of the United States, circling around that small, gray, smoky point of Raysburg, West Virginia. And the strands were also the lives of his little brother and sister. He could, just as he had done for so many years now, go on regarding his mother and father as strangers with whom he had been forced by random circumstances to share a house and a business; he was certain, however, that if he allowed himself to know them much better, a day would come when he would not be able to leave his little brother and sister. "Now's the time," he told himself; "It's now or never."

Paper and pen still lay ready for use on the desk in front of him. "My Dear Julia," he wrote, looked at the words at the top of the page, balled up the paper and threw it into the waste basket. "Dear Julia," he began, then sat musing over the next line: "I hope you and Peter had yourself a capital honeymoon—"; "I trust that your sojourn in Europe—" He trimmed and lit a cigar, wrote: "My warmest regards to Peter. I expect that—" He crumpled up that sheet and threw it away. "Lord," he thought, "this is absurd!"

"Dear Julia," he wrote on the next sheet, "I must apologize for the long silence, but my business affairs—"

He gave up, walked down to the river and along the bank. The rain had broken the chill in the air; and it felt like spring again. As he always did when he was in such an introspective mood, he let his eyes drift over the lights of down-town reflected in the satiny sheen of the water—just as the thoughts drifted by in his mind. He missed Arch who was still in Boston, who was now one of the resident surgeons at Mass General; he knew that if Arch had been in town to give him a good swift kick when he needed it, he might not have fallen into such a hopeless muddle. He lit a cigar and listened to the symphony rising up from the weeds; Sarsfield had always fancied that the existence of frogs proved that the good Lord had a sense of humor;—and if the good Lord had a sense of humor, he thought, then he should do well to maintain his own.

He threw his cigar into the river, walked quickly back to his room, sat down and wrote:

> Dear Aunt Ida,
>   I trust this letter finds you and your family well. I shall be coming to New York later in the summer to establish a photographic business there; and I hope that it will not be inconvenient for you to

extend to me, yet again, the kind and generous hospitality which
you have proffered so freely and graciously in the past. Please give
my warmest regards to Uncle Henry, Henry Jr., Arthur, and Julia.

The next day Sarsfield went to see the Sheriff. From the dense cloud of
cigar smoke that hung over the offices and the presence of an astonishing
number of spittoons, Sarsfield surmised that considerable smoking and
chewing were done on the premises; it was difficult to see what other
business was concluded: the five men employed by the county were
lounging about the Sheriff's desk at the back, swapping stories. Sheriff
Emmory himself, a man built along the lines of Big Bill Taft, rose to greet
Sarsfield effusively and offer him a seat. The position of County Sheriff
was an elected one; Emmory had just survived the primaries in which a
young fire-brand Republican, yelling of graft and corruption, had tried to
"knock him off"; in November, he would have to face the voters again;
the Sheriff turned upon Sarsfield a sympathetic, smiling countenance
that positively radiated helpfulness and civic accountability.

Sarsfield said that his father had been missing for nineteen days.

"Missing or just—gone?" the Sheriff asked with a wink; he was a
contemporary of Jack Middleton's and, in his time, had been known to
take a drink or two in Jack's company.

"Ordinarily," Sarsfield said, "we'd have thought he was spending
some time, ah—just over the county line."

Sheriff Emmory was suddenly regarding Sarsfield with wary, speculative eyes glinting out from beneath hooded lids; it was exactly like looking
into the face of a snapping turtle, and Sarsfield was glad that he had (so far
as he knew) committed neither a crime nor a misdemeanor in the County
of Ohio, State of West Virginia. "Cigar?" the Sheriff said, offering a box of
his best coronas; Sarsfield helped himself. "I'd say, son, that you probably
guessed her just about right. That's unofficial, of course."

"Of course. But is there any way we could find out for certain?"

"That place you're referring to—if you was to be referring to some
particular place—well, I guess that'd lie outside my jurisdiction."

"I'm aware of that, Sheriff; but is there any way you could, ah—
Completely unofficially, of course—" Sarsfield knew that Sheriff
Emmory, from time to time, availed himself of Mrs. Smith's services; he
also knew that the Sheriff knew that he knew it.

"You leave it with me a couple days, son," came the response, "and
I'll see what I can do for you."

That night Sarsfield called upon Emma Rossiter. She wore a beautifully tailored cutaway suit; and they sat on the glider on the back porch, swinging and drinking lemonade. The other members of her family were surprisingly absent. His fickle emotions did a turn-about; and, looking at the lovely cameo of her profile, Sarsfield remembered how she had charmed him the day he had photographed her. Yes, he mused, she was quite fetching—quite a lovely, winsome little thing. He did not quite understand what he was doing there; but, in the meantime, he resolved to enjoy the company of someone so pretty, so profoundly different from himself;—although, if the truth be known, he longed for her mother to appear and wondered why the devil he and Emma had been left unchaperoned.

Of course Sarsfield had learned by now that different classes have different courting habits. Arch had kissed the "bachelor girls" of Boston without it meaning anything more than a bit of naughty flirtation; and Sarsfield understood that at least some New York socialites kissed without the least sense of being compromised thereby. The two occasions upon which he had kissed his cousin Julia, he would not have considered "courting" at all, but rather mysterious and anomalous events wholly beyond any ordinary rules of deportment. The society girls in Raysburg, he had heard, were known to kiss; and he was sure that he could, should he wish, kiss a girl like Lenore Staub without expecting any serious repercussions. The middle-classes in Raysburg, however, were another matter: to kiss a bank clerk's daughter was to propose marriage to her; but it was unlikely that one could declare one's intentions in such a fashion, for one would never be left alone with her. Emma Rossiter, he knew, did not fit into any of these categories; he was not well enough acquainted with her class of people to be able to guess the rules under which she conducted herself; he had decided, therefore, to err on the side of caution; and so he was on his very best behavior as though calling upon an ancient maiden aunt. He would have been astonished, however, had he known the full extent of the freedom Emma enjoyed.

The rules of the Shenandoah Valley which the Rossiters had brought with them to Raysburg were based upon absolute trust of daughters. Once it was ascertained that a gentleman caller was "suitable," a girl would be left alone with him; and it was expected—boys being boys and girls being girls—that a certain amount of kissing would take place. It was even expected that the kissing might turn into "spooning." Some clothing might even be displaced (there were, of course, specific limits to this, and they were well known by all); the young people might even become quite agitated; loud breathing and perhaps even the occasional stifled moan might be heard. But if the boy were seen leaving with his body bent at an odd angle, his eyes glazed, rendered incapable of speech and unfit for human company; and if the girl became irritable and moody, given to sudden outbursts of weeping; if she paced the house like a trapped and suffering animal,—then the parents exchanged knowing smiles and remembered their own courting days when exactly the same thing had happened to them. They would never, of course, discuss this matter openly; but it was understood that if the desire of the girl for the boy and the boy for the girl became urgent, forceful, painful, *cruel* enough,—then they would marry.

It was also understood that the courting process could trickle out, go nowhere; and nothing in particular was made of that; it was considered only natural that sometimes it just did not "take." So Emma had certainly been kissed; what girl these days, Emma would have said, much after her fourteenth birthday, has not? She would have been astonished to learn that many of her contemporaries at the high school—particularly some of those she envied for their lovely clothes and fine manners—had yet to be kissed; she would have been even more astonished to know that this sophisticated older man sitting on her glider was less experienced in these commonplace matters than she. They spoke in the most airy generalizations—of the future of America and themselves; they avoided the forbidden topics of politics and religion. Emma said that the highest ideal of womanhood was to be a good wife and mother; Sarsfield said he agreed with that and left at nine-thirty.

Emma did not know whether the evening had been a success or not. She took off her suit and hung it up carefully; then, teary-eyed, she threw herself onto her bed. With Sid Smith or Billy Imhoff, she would have known if the evening had been a success; with Sarsfield Middleton, she simply had no way of knowing—but that wasn't right; there *was* one way of knowing: if he came back again. For the first time since she had decided she was in love with him three years before, she asked herself if it was worth it. "I don't understand him," she thought. "I'm not sure I ever could."

. Sarsfield was similarly inconclusive about the success of the evening; and he could not decide whether he wanted to see Emma again. Talking to her could not have been any more difficult if she had been a Hottentot; but, at the same time, there was something about her—something more than her obvious physical charms—that he found enormously appealing.

Sarsfield knew himself well enough by now to know that he generally preferred (with Arch Kimbell as the one great exception) the company of women to the company of men; it was this preference that could make him a first-rate society photographer: he liked and admired women; they sensed his regard and responded to it. But in Raysburg this quality in him, should it be widely known, would mark him as peculiar, not to be trusted; and so, during the first two years after he had returned to Raysburg, Sarsfield had gone about his business (or his father's business, he thought wryly) and had largely neglected the ladies. Looking back now, he knew that he must also have been "mooning" over Julia, for once it had become clear that he had lost her irrevocably, he had begun to attend all the social functions to which he was invited and, dutifully, had made himself pleasant to any of Raysburg's "debs" who had crossed his path. Lenore Staub had not, as he had predicted to Arch, begun to look like Helen of Troy; but he would have been blind not to have admired the fine thoroughbred beauty that shone through the silliness of her mannered façade. Sarsfield also knew that he would like to be married. In theory, Lenore Staub was precisely the sort of girl who should appeal to him; but she did not appeal to him, and little Emma Rossiter did. But could he marry a girl like Emma Rossiter? No, there were a thousand excellent reasons why he could never marry a girl like that.

Early next week the Sheriff stopped into the shop. It was a measure of the respect with which he regarded the Middletons—as solid citizens and good Republicans—that he made the call himself. "Stop worrying," he told Sarsfield, "your father's exactly where we guessed he was."

Throughout the day, Sarsfield boiled with indignation: his father was spending hundreds—yes, hundreds!—of dollars in a fancy whore house while he was left holding down the besieged fort. There was not enough money to pay Miss Calendene let alone the O'Haras or any of the bills to which his mother had vaguely alluded. As soon as the old bastard came back, Sarsfield was going to New York; and that was all there was to it.

Sarsfield spent the remainder of the week chasing down and collecting outstanding accounts; on Friday he was able to pay Miss Calendene what was owed her, but there was nothing left over for anything else. On Saturday evening he called on Emma again; spring was in full bloom by now, and she wore a lovely muslin dress in pale blue. This time he held her hand and stayed until ten.

Early Monday morning, Sarsfield opened the shop and went over the books for the past few years. He was trying to understand how on earth his father had ever made any money. Business, he saw, had been booming; but that fact was not exactly news;—since he had been working in the shop, he could not remember a time when the business was as dead as it was at the moment. Why should that be? The answer was simple: because Jack Middleton was not wandering amiably around town—from the saloon to the race track to the Kyle Rainey Club and back to the saloon—ready with a wink and a grin and a tall tale and a handful of cash for the next round, ready at just the proper moment to say: "Now listen here, old man, isn't it about time you brought that lovely daughter of yours in for a picture?" And suddenly Sarsfield understood what should have been obvious to him by now but never had been: his father might well be an indifferent photographer, but as a businessman, he was a genius.

The first Saturday in June was the occasion of Emma's graduation from high school. The day was as hot and sunny as if it were midsummer; and Emma, dressed as she had been when Sarsfield had photographed her, was becomingly flushed with heat and excitement. Sarsfield was not yet sure how he "stood with" the Rossiters; but Emma's parents and brothers chatted with him pleasantly enough. Each of the graduates presented a poem, speech, or recitation; Emma, in her clear, high voice (with only an occasional quiver to betray her nervousness) read her poem, which began:

> Oh, Raysburg High School, fare thee well!
> For must thy children bid adieu,
> With wat'ry eye and saddened brow,
> Depart for byways strange and new.
> But though we wander far from thee,
> Our hearts shall always hold thee dear,

Nor faded shall our memories be
Of dearest friends of yesteryear.

She continued on for nineteen stanzas, and her meter never failed her; Sarsfield thought her quite the clever seventeen-year-old. She blushed sweetly when she received her diploma; and, afterward, they took cakes and tea on the school lawn.

The following Thursday evening when Sarsfield called on her, he found Emma in a peculiar mood that was entirely unfamiliar to him. She suggested that they take a stroll around the Island and had prepared for the outing in a virtuously white shirt-waist and a short, smart walking skirt. They struck out from the Rossiter house down to the river bank; and he was hard pressed to keep up with her. She proceeded fearlessly right to the edge of the water and leapt easily from one dry patch of land to another, her little patent leather oxfords twinkling in the light of the setting sun, as Sarsfield scrambled along behind her the whiles and muddied his feet. He began to feel as though his companion were a tomboyish twelve-year-old rather than the proper young lady she had been at such pains to show him heretofore; and his memories of her as a child in pigtails came vividly back. "Miss Rossiter," he called after her, "if you don't mind—could we please walk on higher ground?" She came to him with a small, self-satisfied grin like a wicked cat's, and,—just as though it were *she* who had been experiencing difficulty negotiating the river bank, allowed him to take her hand and help her up onto a firmer footing. They walked rapidly toward the north end of the Island; he was sure she was trying to outwalk him. "What a little romp she must have been," he thought; to slow her down, he offered her his arm and asked her if she felt any different now that she was a high school graduate.

"Oh, I'm pleased as punch to be out of the high school," she responded.

"I would have thought, from the sentiments you expressed in your verse, something quite the contrary—" he began, intended to take his revenge by teasing her.

"The sentiments I expressed in my verse," she said, deliberately imitating his tone, "were just what was expected of me, now weren't they, Mr. Middleton?"

He was astonished and said nothing. Then she added: "Oh, there was truth to it, too, but—It was no easy road for me to get through there. Some of those girls made it really hard on me."

"What girls?" he asked her.

"Oh, Annie Phillips and Sarah Williamson and that crowd."

Sarsfield spoke before he had taken sufficient time to consider his words: "Why, they're just shop-keepers' daughters." He immediately felt the blood rush to his face; he would have given anything to recall that ruinous sentence.

She turned and looked at him with a small smile. "Like me?" she said.

He cleared his throat. "What I meant was—"

"I know what you meant. They're not society like your cousins. Well, there's no society at Raysburg High. The la-dee-da girls go out the pike to Miss Crawford's—which you know darned well, Mr. Middleton. So there!"; and she stuck out her tongue at him.

He laughed so hard he had to stop walking; she laughed too. "Well, they might have been just shop-keepers' daughters," she said, "but they sure lorded it around Raysburg High School, all right." He heard something severe and not altogether pleasant in her voice; and he thought: "She's not ever going to forgive them for it either."

They walked on to the tempo of her rustling skirt which swung along bravely just at her ankle bone; and he thought that this was the first time that they had ever engaged in genuine conversation. "You know, Miss Rossiter," he said, "being out in the world is a wholly different proposition from the high school—"

"Oh, do call me by my name!" she interrupted him.

"Emma," he said.

They stopped walking and looked at each other. He dared to take her hand; she allowed him to do so. Through the soft kid leather of her glove, he could feel her warmth. He wanted to say something to her; but he had trouble finding an adequate means of expression. "Society in Raysburg is not—" he began. He looked up into the evening sky where nighthawks were flying in jagged, unpredictable patterns. "If society has any genuine meaning, it's in a graciousness, a kindness, a *responsibility*—" ("There," he thought; "Mother would be proud of me!") "Without that," he finished, "it's an empty show."

He felt a tension in her small hand; and when he looked back down at her, he saw that her eyes were shining. Without planning to do so, he bent and kissed her lightly on her pretty lips. After that, they stood motionless while he wondered what her reaction would be to his action that had irrevocably altered the relation between them.

After some time, she said quietly: "Come on, Sarsfield, I should get back before dark."

They walked north until they hit sidewalk. "You've got mud on your pretty shoes," he told her.

"Oh, heavens. They'll wipe clean."

They passed the lamp lighter, old Hank Schmidt, who said, "evening," to them, and tipped his slouch hat. They walked on, around Belle Isle, turned, and started south again; now they were passing Sarsfield's home again. "Would you care to come in for a moment?" he asked her. "We could have tea."

"No," she replied. "Not tonight. Thank you. Another night." He looked at her closely to assess her mood, but he could not do so.

When they reached the end of the Suspension Bridge, they stopped to enjoy the sight of the incandescent lights of the down-town stores. She was standing quite close to him, and it seemed to him the most natural thing in the world to put his arm around her waist; he heard her sigh.

"I got whipped in the high school once," she said.

"Oh? Did you?" He was startled; he could not imagine what she might be thinking about. "What on earth did you do to warrant that?"

"I wouldn't read the lesson."

"Now why on earth did I bring that up?" Emma thought,—particularly when all she had wanted had been to stand quietly in the lovely twilight and feel how wonderful it was to have his arm around her,—particularly when her plan of being a tease and a bit contrary seemed to have been working. Not ten seconds ago she had been thinking that with a man like Sarsfield Middleton, she would never have to be afraid of that crowd of stuck-up girls ever again, that she could go anywhere, do anything,—with a man like Sarsfield Middleton, why, she could even go to a party or a dance out at the Eberhardt mansion! And then that dumb thing about being whipped in the high school had just popped into her head—out of nowhere—and then out of her mouth; and now she guessed she would have to say something more about it. "It was a history lesson," she told him.

It was the worst thing that had ever happened to her in her life; and Emma knew that she would never forget it if she lived to be a hundred. Emma had been fourteen, had just started in at the high school, and she had not yet found a friend there; it had been in the fall, and still hot—Indian summer; and the children had been taking turns reading the lesson. Emma had always been a good reader; and so she had been reading ahead when her eyes had lit on something down at the bottom of the right-hand page:

> The members of Congress from the rebellious States would listen to no words of conciliation, but, gloating in their treason against their lawful government, resigned their seats, fled from Washington, and returned to their homes, there to foment further sedition. Robert E. Lee turned his back on the nation that had honored him, the nation that he had sworn to defend, and, as a traitor to his country, took command of the armed forces of the State of Virginia.

When Emma read those words, her heart went sick inside of her, and she prayed: "Dear Lord, please don't let her give me that to read."

The teacher was Miss Klausen, and Miss Klausen was a spinster lady. Emma knew from somewhere—she must have heard it said somewhere—that the reason Miss Klausen was a spinster lady was because the boy she was going to marry had died at Gettysburg. The room was too hot, and Emma's head was buzzing as though it had bees inside of it, and each of the children read a paragraph, and still she had not been called upon. It was getting closer to those terrible words, and she wished with all her heart that she could just stand up like the other children and read aloud what was in front of her, but she knew that she could not. "Please, Lord," she prayed, "let her give it to one of the others."

It was as though Miss Klausen could read Emma's mind like the history book open in front of her; they were down at the bottom of the page, and Miss Klausen said, sharp: "Miss Rossiter."

Emma stood up with the hateful book in her hands; and she wanted to die. She could not say anything at all.

"Have you a tongue, Miss Rossiter?"

"Yes, ma'm."

"Do you know the place, Miss Rossiter?"

"Yes, ma'm."

"Well, then, proceed."

Emma's eyes filled with tears; and she heard the other children moving around, shuffling their feet, and those nasty girls in the front, giggling. "Excuse me, Miss Klausen, I can't read it."

"What did you say, child?"

"I said, excuse me, Miss Klausen, I can't read it."

"Why ever not?"

Maybe it was blasphemy, but all she could think of was the Lord Jesus in the Garden of Gethsemane praying: "let this cup pass from me," and she thought she could say, "I lost my place," but that wouldn't get her anywhere; and she couldn't think of anything else to say, but she knew what the Lord wanted her to say; so she closed her eyes and said it: "Excuse me, Miss Klausen, I can't read it because it says that Robert E. Lee was a traitor, and he wasn't a traitor."

You could have heard a pin drop. Emma opened her eyes and saw that Miss Klausen looked mad as a hornet. "Let me see if I understand you correctly, Miss Rossiter. You are putting yourself in judgment over the history book provided to you by the Ohio County Board of Education; and, in your infinite wisdom, you have concluded that what is written in that history book is incorrect. Is that your understanding of the matter, Miss Rossiter?"

Emma could not say a single word.

"Answer me, child!"

"I don't know, ma'm."

"She does not know," Miss Klausen said, looking at the other children who, all of them, had become silent and still as statues. "She *does not know*. That is the absolute truth, Miss Rossiter, *you know nothing at all*. Now, you ignorant little girl, *read that passage*."

"Excuse me, ma'm, I can't read it."

"You mean you will not. Miss Rossiter, please fetch me the cane from the back of the room."

There was a tittering from some of the children, but Miss Klausen glared at them and they shut up fast. Emma was so sick at heart and scared that she couldn't think of a thing—there was *nothing* in her head at all—and she just put the book down on her desk and turned and walked to the back, with all the other children looking at her, and took the cane down from the wall, and turned and walked back, with all the children looking at her, and handed the cane to her teacher. "Thank you," Miss Klausen said.

"You're welcome, ma'm," Emma said.

"This is your last chance, Miss Rossiter. Will you read that passage?"

"No, ma'm."

"Then bend over the desk, please."

Emma had thought that she was going to get her hands switched. She'd had her hands switched plenty at Jefferson Grade School; all the children there had their hands switched, boys *and* girls; but this was the high school, and it was humiliating enough to get her hands switched in the high school, but on the backside?—in front of everybody? Emma just couldn't believe she was going to get it on her backside. That was too cruel. Nothing like that could happen to a good girl, and she was a good girl, and this simply could not be happening to her. She was sure that the teacher was just going to scare her. "Please reach all the way across and grasp the edge, Miss Rossiter."

Emma did what she was told. "Do not let go, Miss Rossiter. And do not move, Miss Rossiter. *Do you hear me?*"

"Yes, ma'm."

Then Miss Klausen lit into her like fury. Emma pressed her cheek into the hard wood of the desk top, and she hung onto the edge so tight she thought she'd cut her hands clean in half, and she'd had some foolish thought that she'd be brave and not cry, but that notion was gone quick enough, and she heard herself bawling her head off. Three times Miss Klausen asked her if she was ready to read the passage, and three times Emma said: "No, ma'm," and each time she got it worse than the time before.

Then Miss Klausen let her stand up, and she turned her around so she had to face the class, and she said: "I know your kind, Miss Rossiter. You require the most severe discipline. Each day I will offer you the opportunity to read that passage. Each day that you do not read it, I will whip you. And if you do not read it, I will whip you every day until school is out next June. Do you understand me, Miss Rossiter?"

"Yes, ma'm."

"Now you just stand there so the other children can see what a disobedient, ignorant little girl looks like."

Miss Klausen went about the rest of the history lesson; and Emma had to stand there on the platform facing the other children, and there were all the boys on the boys' side; and they had seen it all. Annie Phillips and Sarah Williamson were right in the front with their pretty new dresses; they grinned up at Emma, and smirked and giggled and made faces. Miss Klausen must have seen them, but she did not reprimand them or even look in their direction; so they grew even bolder and started rubbing their backsides and making a pantomime as though they were crying, and making gestures like the cane coming down,—and they giggled, and giggled, and giggled. Emma would have given anything if she could have stopped crying, because the more she cried, the better those girls liked it; and she knew the boys were still looking at her too, but she couldn't stop. She could hear Miss Klausen going on with her lesson—about *rebellion*, and *treason*, and *sedition*, and *dishonor*; and all of a sudden she understood, exactly, why none of her four brothers had ever made it through the high school.

"Good Lord!" Sarsfield said, "what did you do?"

Emma had just given him a brief account of the story, leaving out those details about which she would have been too embarrassed to speak. "I didn't know what to do," Emma said. "I wasn't going to go to school and get whipped every day till next June, that was for certain. And I wasn't going to read it either."

"Did you tell your parents?"

"No; I didn't. I was of a mind to, but the more I thought of it, the more I couldn't see any good coming of it. It'd just make a big row, and—Well, there aren't that many Southern people in Raysburg, you know—"

Without being quite aware that she was doing so, she pressed herself more closely into him; his arm around her felt so good. She had hoped she could talk to him straight out like this; it felt so good to be able to talk to a boy straight out like this—Oh, but he was *a man*, wasn't he? That's right, and Billy Imhoff and Sid Smith and those others were *boys*. Oh, Sarsfield Middleton stood with her just about right, and that was the truth of it. It was dark already; she knew her mother would be mad at her for staying out so late, but she didn't care. He had kissed her like such a gentleman.

"I went to school the next day," she said, "and she didn't whip me in front of the class, but she kept me after and whipped me then. Just the two of us in the room. And then she said, 'Miss Rossiter, I will not allow you to shame me in front of my class.' After what she'd done to me! I'd never been so humiliated in my life as what she'd done to me, and I didn't know what to say back to her.

"But then something—I don't know what—I got up my courage and told her I had no desire to shame her in front of her class. And I

could see she was ready to listen to me, Lord knows why, and so I told
her that I was named for Robert E. Lee. And I told her that my daddy
had fought all the way through the war, and he never would talk of it.
But the only story he'd ever told me was about how he was there at
Appomattox, on that last day, and all he wanted to do was touch Lee's
horse. And Lee came by, slow, with the tears flowing down his face, and
all the men were weeping too, and they all just wanted to touch Lee, or
touch Lee's horse, and my daddy reached up and touched Lee's horse,
and he said, 'General, we love you still,' and he always told me that the
finest man he'd ever known in his life was Robert E. Lee. And I just
could not stand up there and read it out that Robert E. Lee was a traitor
to his country.

"Well, she didn't say anything back to me. And she thought about
it. And she thought about it and thought about it. And then she said,
'Miss Rossiter, tomorrow you shall pick any passage you wish from that
history book—one that does not offend your conscience—and you
shall read it to the class. And you shall apologize to me in front of the
class for your disobedience. And that will be the end of the matter.' So
I did what she wanted—I read out about how Lincoln had said 'with
charity toward all and malice toward none,' and I apologized to her,
and she never bothered me again."

"How splendid of you!" Sarsfield said. "Oh, how very splendid of
you!" They began to walk back to the south end of the Island.

They walked holding hands; and Sarsfield told her how brave she
was and how noble she was and what a fine thing she had done; and it
was music to her ears because she had never told that story to anyone
before—she had always been too embarrassed by it—and she had
always wanted someone to listen to her and tell her that she was noble
and brave. They got home; and she was going to ask him to stay a
while, but she got a look from her mother, so she didn't; but she did ask
him to come to dinner on Sunday, and he said he would. He squeezed
her hand and said good-night to her, and to her mother, in the most
polite way. It was dark by then, and the lightning bugs were up, and she
watched until she saw his shadow go around the side of the house, and
she thought: "What a fine man. What a fine, lovely man!"

Mrs. Rossiter was still working at the kitchen; she liked it to be spic-
and-span before she went to bed. Emma came in, walking on clouds,

and sat down at the table just as though there was nothing left to do. "Emma," her mother said, "I'd deeply appreciate it if you was to make yourself useful as well as decorative."

Emma rose like someone half asleep and began putting things away—one plate and one saucer at a time. "Was it all right to invite him to Sunday dinner, Mama?"

"Now that it's over and done with, she asks me," Mrs. Rossiter thought; but she saw the smile on Emma's face—just like a pussy cat that's had too much cream—and so she said: "Sure it was, honey."

Then they heard Tom's footsteps, coming up the path, and then up the back steps. Mrs. Rossiter could tell just by the way he walked that her husband was dog tired. He came in and sat down at the table; he let his body sag like a sack of potatoes. "I done your chores for you, Emma," he said.

"Thank you, Daddy."

There was a heavy silence in the kitchen. Ordinarily, Mrs. Rossiter would have started talking to fill it up; but she could see from Tom's face that whatever was on his mind was serious, so she kept her mouth shut. "Was that the Middleton boy?" he said.

"Of course it was," Emma said. "Who d'you think it was?"

"Emma, don't you dare take that tone with your father," Mrs. Rossiter said. The silence in the kitchen got worse.

"Could you give me a glass of water, please," Tom said. Emma poured it and handed it to him.

"That Middleton boy—" Tom said. Then he stopped and rubbed the bones in his face. "He's—I don't know—he's what a real gentleman ought to be and most of them ain't. But—" He sighed deeply, looked directly at his daughter, and said: "Emma, you ain't agoina marry him."

"Daddy! I just took a walk with him, that's all."

"But I know what you're thinking, honey, and you ain't agoina marry him, and that's the long and the short of it."

Emma burst into tears and ran from the room.

Mrs. Rossiter turned on her husband, angry, and said: "Tom, now why the devil did you have to go and do that?"

"Somebody's got to tell her," he said, "and sooner's better than later."

"Well, I never!" Mrs. Rossiter said, dried her hands on her apron, and hurried upstairs to Emma's room. The poor girl was lying on her bed sobbing her heart out.

"Emma, your father means well—" Mrs. Rossiter tried.

"It's that war!" the girl wailed. "That war, that darned war! That war he won't even talk about! Nobody cares any more. Everything's different now."

"Emma, honey, you sit up and listen to me. It's not just the war, it's—Lord, Emma, he's old man Eberhardt's grandson!"

"I know who he is," Emma said; she sat up and glared at her mother. "Isn't this America? Isn't that what they taught us in school? 'All men are created equal'—"

"Good Lord, girl, don't you start quoting the Declaration of Independence at me! You're talking like a foolish child, that's all. Good Lord, that's what I'd expect a ten-year-old to say, not somebody who's pretending to be a grown woman. There ain't a whole hell of a lot in this big, broad country that's equal for nobody, and you know that as well as anybody does—all the complaining you done about the hard time you had over at the high school! Lord, Emma, what on earth are you thinking about?"

"What d'you think he is? An earl or something? He's a shop-keeper same as daddy is."

"Shop-keeper? Good gracious, girl—" Mrs. Rossiter ran out of words; if her daughter was going to be that foolish, she didn't even know what to say to her. She sat down on the edge of the bed and started in again, taking a reasonable tone the way she would with somebody who was out of his head and raving: "Emma, sweetheart, I know you know who the Eberhardts are, and I know you know who the Raineys are—"

"Oh, Mama, go 'way and leave me alone!"

Talking to her daughter had put Mrs. Rossiter totally out of sorts, and she wanted to talk to Tom about it, but he'd already gone to bed, so she went out onto the back porch and set on the glider and looked out at the river. Still lots to do, and she was dog tired the way she always was by that time of night, but, Lord, she'd been up since five-thirty, the way she always was, cooking and cleaning and working in the garden the whole day, the way she done most days, so didn't she deserve to set there a minute and collect her thoughts? It was a good life but a hard one, and she'd been glad enough when the Lord had seen fit to stop sending her children, and years had gone by without another one, and so she'd thought: "Well, there's no more in me, then, is there? Good." But at the same time she'd felt sad for the little girl she'd never had, the little girl who'd always been called Emma Lee. And then, at the last minute, there'd been a child in her—forty years old!—and she'd said, "All right, Lord, you fooled me, but is *this* my baby girl?"; and the Lord smiled upon her and gave her little Emma. After four rambunctious boys tearing the house down, Emma was such a joy—such a sweet, fat, affectionate little thing. But let them get into their teen years, it was a different story. "Seventeen years old," she thought, "give me a boy any day. Give me ten boys. A seventeen-year-old girl is like one of them plagues of Egypt!"

Emma was spoiled. That's right, spoiled rotten. Emma didn't have the first notion of what life was all about, that was her problem. Emma thought she had it rough—because she had to milk the cow and feed the chickens and the pigs,—because, if she wanted to buy foolish things like twenty-four button gloves, she had to work Saturdays at the dry-goods store to get them. That's right, and Thomas told her straight out, "Emma, honey, I'm sorry, but with some of them luxuries you want, you're going to have to pay for them yourself," and so, naturally, Emma couldn't just accept that but had to talk right back to him and argue about what was and what wasn't a luxury. And lots of girls brought home their pay envelope unopened to their people, but Emma never did—no, it never crossed her mind, and they never saw a red penny of it—she spent it all on herself, and when she was out of the high school and had a regular job, she'd probably go on spending every bit of it on herself. White glacé gloves, Lord preserve us!

And now she's got her heart set on that Middleton boy—a polite, well-spoken boy sure enough—but poor Emma didn't know what she was getting into with that one. She was sure getting in over her head with that one. What did she think—that old Thaddeus Eberhardt's grandson was going to marry her? Good Lord, them society boys will trifle with a nice girl and ruin her and won't think twice about it and just go on their merry way. Maybe Tom was right to tell her that straight out; yes, well, maybe he was. But Mrs. Rossiter knew exactly what her daughter was thinking—that if she married that Middleton boy, she wouldn't have no more to do with cows and chickens and pigs, and fancy gloves wouldn't be a *luxury* but a *necessity*—same as fancy dresses, and fancy shoes and hats—and she'd get to go to them high muckety-muck affairs and put on the dog with the best of them. Created equal? What did she think? Did she think them skinny, la-dee-da out-the-pike girls was going to accept her as one of their own? Good Lord!

"I don't know what the world's coming to," Mrs. Rossiter thought; "and why the girls nowadays want to be thin as dragon flies, I'll never know." And it weren't just the out-the-pike girls, but *all* the girls. That's right, it seemed like all the girls nowadays wanted to look like society girls and look like they hadn't had a decent meal in a year, and it was just plain unnatural. "And back then," she thought, "all we ever wanted was to be plump and pink and look like women." And when she thought of "back then," Mrs. Rossiter was going all the way back to 'sixty-four when she'd been little Abbie Quarie, and that's exactly what they'd called her, *little* Abbie, and it had been a good name for her because you could have threaded her through a needle. And even now, on a fall day when they was burning up the leaves on the Island, the smell of it could twist her heart up like a knife in it, because even after all the years of trying to forget, she never could forget, and she'd smell them leaves burning and she'd go all sick inside.

Emma would never know what it was like to wake up hungry, go to bed hungry, spend every waking hour hungry, thinking only about one thing, which was how to get something to eat. Emma and her mail order corsets, Lord! Country girls back then didn't wear corsets at all till they was of courting age, and sometimes not even then. And she'd got an old belt of her brother Seth's and put it around her middle and cinched it in till she could feel it cut into her good, and it weren't for vanity of it, (Lord knows, there was no young men around to notice) but to cut against pain in her that come from having nothing in there, not a bit of pork, not a grain of corn— Lord, they boiled up tree bark and drank the tea from it. Lord, she ate grass and was sick on it. Lord, she'd never forget old Grandpaw Quarie, standing up straight and tall, seventy-four years old, standing up to that Federal officer on his big horse—yes, a clean and shiny, well-fed man sitting on that big, well-fed horse in the fire light from the barn burning down. The Federals took the horses and the mules. They took every cow, every pig, every chicken. They took the flour, and the corn meal, and the salt pork. What they couldn't take, they burnt up. They burnt the feed. (Lord knows what for, there was nothing left to feed it to; did they expect the folks to eat it? Well, maybe the folks would have et it.) They burnt the seed grain so the folks couldn't even plant. And that Federal officer found the food hid in the house, the little bit of salt pork and corn meal and molasses. And Grandpaw Quarie stood up there straight and tall and as angry as a man could get and he said, "What the devil d'you expect us to eat?"

And the Federal officer said right back to him: "You should of thought of that before you rose up in rebellion against your lawful government." And the Federal officer had his men make sure there was nobody left in the house, and he burnt the house down, and Grandpaw Quarie said, "The Lord will call you to judgment for this," and the Federal officer said, "Listen to me, you old reb, don't you invoke the Lord's name to me. It's the Lord's wrath you're feeling at this very minute. If I had the time to do it, I'd sow salt into your fields," and he tipped his hat and rode off.

They wouldn't even let the folks go back in to get their clothes, and all she had left was the dress on her back and that one pair of boots. And there was no shelter from the rain, and none of the neighbors was any better off, and black smoke hung over the whole Shenandoah Valley from one end to the other of it (that valley that was like paradise back before the war), and some folks they left their houses stand, and some folks they burnt their houses down with only the chimneys sticking up all black like something dead, but they left no food nowhere, and no seed grain nowhere, and later on the folks heard what the man said who'd done it—that if a crow was to fly over the whole Shenandoah Valley, he'd have to carry his own supplies—and the man's name who done it was Phil Sheridan. And the folks by the hundreds had to walk down the valley to Winchester because there was nothing else to do, and by the time they got to Winchester, her boots was worn through and her feet was bleeding with every step and Grandpaw Quarie was dead and buried halfway down the valley, and, Lord, when they got down to Winchester, they had to beg for charity just to live another day, and live another the day after that. And Emma had a hard life, did she? Lord, but that foolish girl didn't know the first thing about it.

As Sarsfield strode up Front Street, all he could think was: "What a spunky girl! By God, she is—a lovely spunky girl!" He walked around to the back of the house looking for his father's sulky, was met by Shep, tail wagging, who came for a pat; and there was still no sign of Jack. Inside, the house was quiet; all he could hear were murmuring voices from the back that told him that Mrs. O'Hara must be putting the children to bed.

Alice Middleton, as her son knew from long experience, would have retired by now. She would be reclining on half a dozen flounced pillows, her latest novel open before her; on the coverlet next to her right hand would be the menthol pencil she used to anoint her temples whenever her neurasthenia became particularly vexatious; a crystal decanter of water would be resting innocently on her bed table along with a tea cup and saucer; in the tea cup would be a cloudy, sweet-smelling mixture of the water and her nerve tonic—a powerful compound of opium tinctured in alcohol that she kept hidden in the table drawer. On nights when Sarsfield entered her room early enough so that she would not yet have imbibed too deeply of this Lethean draught, they often engaged in long, meandering, dreamy conversations which both mother and son found quite agreeable. He was, he thought, in the mood for precisely this manner of diversion and was just on the point of climbing the stairs to his mother's room when he spied a letter waiting for him on the table by the landing; the envelope was stamped with the Van Gort crest.

Sarsfield picked up the fine vellum envelope and felt a sudden "wallop" inside of him as though his heart just delivered a hard blow to his rib-cage; if this were a reply to the missive he had written to Aunt Ida, Julia must have responded the moment his letter had arrived in New York;—what could she have to say that was so urgent? He retreated to the privacy of his own room to read it. He had not received a direct communication from his cousin since she had married; she had sent him a formal invitation to her wedding (unaccompanied by any personal note); he had replied with his regrets and a gift of fine Staub crystal; now here, he saw, was a letter just like those he used to receive at Harvard. Julia had always possessed the uncanny ability (for such a thing is easier to conceive than to accomplish) to write exactly the way she talked; and, reading her words over a second and then a third time, Sarsfield felt that she might just as well have been standing a few feet away delivering her comments in person.

Mon Cher Cousin,
I thought of you often in Paris—you would simply <u>adore</u> the new "directoire" gowns that fit tight tight tight—and even tighter than that!—so not even un petit peu de mouvement is possible—and the rustle of petticoats shall no longer be heard in the land—and, mon cher, I was simply adored by all at the Paris races and could only walk in tiny tiny tiny <u>tiny</u> little steps like une vrai chinoise!—which

renders Monsieur so very very solicitous—Oh, you would love Paris, Sarsfield, you <u>must</u> go to Paris, Sarsfield, just to see les jeune filles— Tout le monde improves upon nature with rouge and paint, so delicate, so tasteful, not like New York where everyone is <u>so afraid of looking artificial</u>—and the hats, and the gloves, and the veils, and the pumps with such perfectly shaped little heels!—only the French understand these things—you would simply perish with delight!—I simply perished with delight!—I bought some new pictures too which are simply smashing and absolutely <u>swimming in light</u>! you must see them—and then we went to England and <u>I met Consuelo</u>! My cup runneth over!—I was in no way disenchanted, she is just as fine and good and beautiful as I expected—and even more than I expected—She is separated from Marlborough who was a terrible beastly man, I gather, and she is so brave, and I admire her just enormously, she was so lovely to me, and so understanding, and made me quite ashamed of myself—and <u>I have resolved to be good</u>!—Dear Maman received your letter today and grumbled why couldn't the sweet boy wait till fall and asked me to write you—Maman and the boys will be at Newport—why didn't you remember, you silly thing?—after all the times you have come to us—but the house will be kept open so Arthy and Henty can dash back at a moment's notice <u>and attend to business, what a bore</u>!—so of course you may stay there as long as you wish—you may stay <u>forever</u>!—I am <u>so happy</u> you want to come to New York—do stay forever—and please do come to Newport, oh, do not even stop to change your clothes, leave your things at the house and leap on the train and come straightway to us at Newport—Three young ladies of my acquaintance—beautiful as trois petites fleurs all in a row—are simply <u>dying</u> to have their portraits done in your glowing colors!—and all are of marriageable age et terriblement chic—Oh do come, Sarsfield, I should so adore to see you again—

All my love,
Julia

Sarsfield folded her letter and replaced it in its envelope. He was furious. It was not lost upon him that she had not (unless one could count the curiously impersonal word, "Monsieur") mentioned her husband once; he mulled that lacuna over for some minutes, but what it might signify still remained a mystery to him; and he could not understand how she could have written him such a gushing, inane piece of trivial nonsense. The last time they had been together was enshrined in Sarsfield's memory as the most painful—and beautiful—moment of his life; he had told no one about it and intended never to tell anyone about it;

he thought of it in terms something akin to a mystical revelation; but could she have felt nothing?—or so little? How the devil could she write to him about gowns and shoes and face-paint and Consuelo Marlborough and *trois petites fleurs* of marriageable age?—good Lord, as though he could marry any petted, fashionable society girl to come down the pike!

Sarsfield stormed out of the house, walked up and down the river bank until he had mastered the blazing anger that had rendered him incapable of rational thought; then he threw himself down on the grass, put a lucifer to a good cigar, stared across the front river at the crepuscular twilight sky, and fell into a "brown study" such as afflicts the heroes of British novels. He sat thus until he had lost complete track of time; every advantage and disadvantage of Raysburg, as compared to New York, once again passed through his mind. He was thoroughly sick of spending so much of his time mulling over things that should, by now, be absolutely clear to him. At last he felt a grim peace descend: "I'm going to stay right here in this God-forsaken town and make a go of it," he thought. "Julia and her *trois petites fleurs* can all go hang!"

7

Forty days after he had galloped away into the night, Jack Middleton came home. Something was "up," Sarsfield knew, by the way the dog greeted him: Shep could barely contain himself—running forward to make sure that whatever was so interesting was still in place, then running back to make sure that Sarsfield was indeed coming to see it: the sulky. It was spattered with mud; and one of the rubber-tired wheels was dangerously askew. The mare, however, looked fit enough; she stared at Sarsfield with an expression that said, "Well, what are you going to do about it?" He approached cautiously and peered inside. He saw a dark, immobile form, huddled up more like a pile of rags than a man, and was struck at once with the notion that his father was dead; then he looked more closely and, with a terrible thrill of dread, fancied that his father might be *long* dead: the caved-in white face with closed eyes, perched bizarrely above a black shape folded in upon itself like a bat, looked like nothing so much as a disinterred mummy Sarsfield had seen once in a disturbing and unforgettable photograph.

Sarsfield heard, at his elbow, a sound like a cough; he sprang back from the sulky as though he'd been caught staring at something obscene. Turning, he saw Mick O'Hara. "Excuse me, Mr. Middleton," the man said, touching his hat brim, "he won't let me move him."

Then, from inside the sulky, came a small, fragile cry: "Son? Son?" Sarsfield approached again, saw that the corpse was breathing. "Son," Jack said, "can you help me into my bed?"

Sarsfield unfolded his father from the seat; Jack was trembling with severe ague; as soon as he attempted to walk, Jack began to sweat profusely—great washes flowing down his pinched, convulsing face. By now Sarsfield's mother had rushed out; between the two of them, they assisted Jack into the house and up the stairs to his bedroom. Sarsfield, still uncertain how to respond to all of this, stood back while his mother and Mrs. O'Hara stripped Jack down to his long underwear and piled him over with blankets.

"Alice," Jack croaked. Mrs. Middleton bent down to the prostrate man; Sarsfield could just make out his father's words: "Have you any laudanum, Alice?"

Sarsfield saw his mother hesitate. Of course she had laudanum; of one thing one could always be certain: Alice Middleton would always have laudanum. But would she admit it? It appeared that she would: she fetched the brown bottle, poured out a dose that would have staggered a strong man in a circus, mixed it with water, and assisted her husband in drinking it. Jack sucked the cloudy fluid up like a man dying of thirst, gestured for another. Mrs. Middleton poured out a second dose just as big as the first; Jack drank that one down, fell back onto the pillow with a sigh, pulled his wife close, and whispered something to her.

Mrs. Middleton stepped back from the bed and then, with uncharacteristic abruptness, said to Sarsfield and Mrs. O'Hara: "Leave him."

Sarsfield followed his mother out, stopped her with a hand on her elbow. "What did he say?" he asked her.

She looked at him a moment; and he was not at all certain that she was going to reply. When she did, it was in an expressionless voice: "He said he should never have left Ireland."

Profoundly agitated, Sarsfield paced up and down the drawing room. Within the hour his mother appeared; he saw from her eyes that she had also taken recourse to the brown bottle. She drifted through the room and settled into the chair by the window. "Is he all right?" Sarsfield asked her.

"How the devil should I know?" she answered him. He was shocked; he had never heard his mother speak like that.

She also appeared to have shocked herself. She attempted several times to speak again, but did not succeed. Sarsfield sat opposite her and waited. "Please, my dear," she said eventually, "could you bring me a small glass of brandy?"

He did as she had requested; she looked up at him with a wan smile. "Sarsfield," she said, "when you consider marriage, do so only after long and careful deliberation. Marriage is for life."

"Well, Mother," he said lightly, "I am in no hurry to marry."

"How soon our time on earth is run," she said, looking out the window. "I have always been so glad that you inherited so little of his blood."

Her remark left Sarsfield speechless. Having denied herself religion, politics, money, and her own personal feelings as topics of conversation, his mother had always appeared to him, when she was engaged in discourse, as a being intangible as smoke. Now she had just said something of substance,—or at least he thought that she had,—and he did not know what to make of it. While he was considering an appropriate reply, she surprised him again: "I gather," she said, "that you have been calling upon the Rossiter girl."

"Yes. I have."

He, of course, expected to hear some comment upon Emma or the Rossiters; but, instead, perhaps following a circuitous path induced by her drug, she said: "I should never have married your father."

"Oh," was the only response he could find. He was suddenly, and inexplicably, angry with her. "Forgive me then, Mother, if you don't mind my asking,—why did you?"

She spoke immediately, as though she had, over the years, prepared an answer for just that question: "My head was easily turned. He was a gentleman—obviously a gentleman;—and he had the air about him of the drawing rooms of Europe. I knew nothing of life, you understand— you *must* understand. Oh, Sarsfield, I have so wanted to speak to you about this—"

"Yes, Mother?"

"Your grandmother ruled me with a rod of iron. The freedom that girls have now—oh, it was simply impossible. When I think the girls now, your cousin Julia—Oh, but it has become such a different world—!"

"Julia has far less freedom than you would think, Mother," Sarsfield said, interrupting her.

His mother did not appear to have heard him. "But you must understand, my dear," she continued, "that if I were to have even a modicum of independence, I must marry.—Your father was a handsome man, yes, the devil's own handsome man;—and in those days—to succeed in business in those days, why, it was unheard of. Mother thought it a good match; yes, to my amazement, she did.—I was born just before the war. I am not certain how that would have affected our affairs, but I know that it did. Surely it did—"

"Yes?" he prompted her again. "Mother?"

"I was five when the war ended. I did not know my father. I had hardly seen him. Oh, Sarsfield, I feel as though I am getting lost! What was I talking about?—I am so afraid, Sarsfield, for the little ones. They are so like him. Be careful of a young girl's honor, Sarsfield.—Oh, I do not have to say that to you. I know I do not." She began to weep.

He gently removed the glass from her fingers (she had not drunk any of it), offered his hand; she took it and rose gracefully to her feet. She did not appear to be aware of her flowing tears. "Thank you, my dear. I must lie down now. Do not wait dinner for me.—No; please, do not."

She began to walk from the room, then suddenly stopped and turned back toward him. "Go to New York, Sarsfield," she said in an entirely different voice—that of someone in full command of her faculties.

He stood, rooted to the spot, and listened to her footsteps ascending the stairs. Why, Sarsfield asked himself, did he have the feeling that life had been, upon the instant of his father's return, transformed into an old melodrama? "That's it," he thought, "it might as well be some ancient, shop-worn thing like Under the Gaslight with the heroine tied to the railroad tracks." He stood a while longer listening to the silence in the house. "He won't let Mick touch him," he thought; "No; he's got to wait for me to come back so he can croak out 'son, son' in that pathetic fashion; and then Mother, out of nowhere, decides to talk of God knows what—being ruled with a rod of iron, and marrying the wrong man, and a young girl's honor.—Do I know these people? Good God!" He walked out of the house, headed south to pay a visit to the Rossiters.

Jack remained in bed for the better part of the next week. Old Doc Anderson called, left behind a gill of bitter Vega-cura nerve tonic and a pint of tinctured opium; he cautioned the family that Jack was entirely vitiated, that he needed quiet above all; so a painful hush fell over the household, and everyone tip-toed and whispered. Mrs. O'Hara reported on Jack's progress: on the second day, he was able to take a little clear broth; on the day after, several slices of milk toast; by Thursday, he managed to keep down a bowl of thin gruel. Sarsfield made a point of staying well away from the invalid's bedroom. On Friday morning, as he was on the point of leaving for the shop, Sarsfield received the message that his father wished to see him; feeling a mixture of anger and dread, Sarsfield mounted the stairs. Jack—white-faced, half-dressed, and shaking—was fumbling with a collar stud. "Can you help me, son?" he said in a feeble voice; "I'm none too steady."

Sarsfield fastened the collar, saw that the bitter tonic had been scarcely touched but the opiated solution had been well used. "Oh, Christ," Jack said in a melancholy tone, "my bowels are all backed up. I'm going to need a high enema just to get them flowing again."

Sarsfield did not reply; he assisted his father in putting on his suit jacket. "Oh, Christ, my gland," Jack said; "It's swollen up like a hot pigeon's egg. Oh, God, I can hardly void my urine—"

Sarsfield felt a wave of nausea sweep over him. "I'm sorry to hear that, father," he said instead of what he was thinking: "After six weeks in a whore house, what the hell d'you expect?"

Jack required a ride to town; Sarsfield got out the buggy. Even though the temperature was close to eighty, Jack shivered and complained of a chill. Sarsfield knew from long experience that the only thing that would restore Jack Middleton to himself was a large whiskey; but Jack asked to be dropped at his bank. "Is he going to try to stay sober?" Sarsfield wondered. "God help us!"

In an hour Jack crept into the shop,—white and shaking,—and called for a glass of water. "Sarsfield," he said, "I've been lying there, day after day, and—and in my lucid moments—on those rare occasions when I have been, at least partially, *free from pain*—I have been considering the future course of my life, of all of our lives—"

"Oh?" Sarsfield said and sat down.

"I can't go on much longer," Jack said, his voice quivering. "I'll do my best to get my affairs in order—*if I have the strength*. But I swear to God, son, I don't know how I can—Oh Lord, how I can—even manage—to *continue* in this weary round from day to day, out to the last syllable—Ah, younger hands than mine must take the helm; braver hearts than mine must leap to grasp the reins. I've fought the good fight—alone!—for so long. Ah, so long! So many cruel years. Such a long, bitter road!" And, although he and his son were alone in the studio, Jack looked right, and Jack looked left: the invisible spectators were applauding. "I've got to slow down," Jack said. "I need my rest. Don't I deserve my rest, Son? Don't I? Oh, Lord, Sarsfield, I'm an old man!"

Jack Middleton, his son knew perfectly well, was fifty-seven.

Sarsfield brought the buggy around, drove Jack home again, and assisted him in returning to his bed. Jack did not reappear for another two days; Mrs. O'Hara reported to the expectant family that Jack was now able to take solids. Monday morning, when Sarsfield entered the dining room, he saw that his father was there ahead of him,—fully dressed, clean shaven, smelling of hair tonic; Jack was wolfing down eggs and country ham and mopping up the plate with biscuit. Sarsfield helped himself from the sideboard and sat down across from his father. Jack was white as fresh Solio paper, but steady, and, the best Sarsfield could tell, sober as a stone. "Son," Jack said in a firm voice, "have you a dollar?"

The question was such a strange one that Sarsfield did not reply for a full minute; then he said: "Yes, Father; of course I have a dollar."

"Good," Jack said. "I'll sell you the business for a dollar."

"What?"

"The building, the equipment, the merchandise—the whole shooting match—lock, stock, and barrel,—and the good will, of course—which is incalculable, which is invaluable.—What d'you say, boy?" Sarsfield hesitated; and Jack, fixing him with his black eyes (glinting this morning like a hawk's), said: "It's a damned sight more than I had when I started."

Still Sarsfield hesitated. "Well, you think about it," Jack said, sprang to his feet, seized a walking stick from the hallway, and strode out of the house.

Jack Middleton was sober. Jack Middleton intended to stay sober (at least that was the impression he gave to all those who inquired after his health and to many who did not). He was seen drinking a large glass of lemonade at Nolan's; he was heard extemporizing to a crowd of his cronies down at the racetrack on the certain path to ruination that was sure to follow a lad's first drink of spirits. The entire citizenry of Raysburg was deeply astonished when Jack appeared at the Wednesday night temperance meeting and spoke for two hours—so eloquently that many were moved to tears. Among the small, hard knot of Republicans who, as Thaddeus Eberhardt's vassals, controlled the commonplace life of the city, bets were placed upon how long Jack's conversion to teetotalism would last. At one extreme was old Jim Greer, the mayor, who had known Jack intimately for thirty-five years; his money was riding on "another five days at the most." At the other extreme was Sheriff Emmory, who cited his experience of Jack Middleton's "sheer blamed cussedness"; his bet was: "'till the real good dog-days hit in August." And then, after all the wagers were duly noted, the boys fell to telling, yet again, of how Jack—the dirty old bugger!—had raced up and down the stairs at Mrs. Smith's wearing nothing but his long johns, a beer stein filled with straight bourbon clenched in his fist, yelling out that he'd ram every girl there in all three of her orifices if he had to stay till fall to do it. "Jesus, I can just see him!" Councilman McHenry said, laughing until the tears ran down his moustache.

"Lord, it was a rare sight," Chief of Police Kavanaugh said; "Poor old Mrs. Smith was going to call her boys out to simmer him down, but I told her to leave off—'We're all enjoying the hell out of the show,' I said, 'let's just see how far he'll take it.' By Christ, he was done up right proper, I'll tell you; and then you know what he did?—"

And the boys bent close like football players in a huddle.

"He didn't? Right there in front of everybody?"

"You bet your sweet ass he did—!"

"Not *your* sweet ass, that poor little whore's sweet ass!"

"Oh, Lord Jesus on the B 'n' O!"

"Right there up the—In front of God and everybody?"

"You're goddamned right, he did; he was cutting the corn like a McCormick reaper!—Patrick, you old villain, bring us another round!"

Then, Raysburg being what it was, the stories got back to Sarsfield; he was sickened by them;—and, like everyone else, he was wondering how long his father would stay "on the wagon." There was to this current period of his father's sobriety however, a quality markedly different from the dry periods of the past: a queer reasonableness had fallen over Jack. If he recalled being knocked down by his son, he did not mention it. "I need to devote myself entirely to my investments," he told Sarsfield; "I'm going to sell the business off by fall; and if you don't want it, there's plenty that will—and for a pretty penny, believe you me.—But take your time, boy, take your time."

And, Raysburg being what it was, Jack, of course, heard that Sarsfield had been calling on little Emma Rossiter. "I don't give a damn who you marry, Sarsfield," he said, "but there's a few things you should—"

"Hold on, Father, who said anything about marriage?"

Jack made an eloquent shrugging gesture. "Well, you know, one thing follows another.—As far as I'm concerned, you can marry anybody. You can marry some plucked chicken from some clapped-up crib in South Raysburg, for all I—oh, don't look at me like that. Don't be so much like your mother; you're a man, aren't you? Don't act like such a damned nancy-boy—"

"Father, there is no point in continuing this conversation."

"All I'm trying to say to you, Son, is this: if you're going to live in this town, you've got to take some cognizance of what's what and who's who—*as you damned well know by now*. The opinions of the Raineys don't count for all that much any more;—they've kind of run to seed,—but they do count for something, and they're not going to be pleased to see you mixing their blood up with Southern trash—"

"Father, I will not listen to any more—"

"Now, Sarsfield, just shut your face and let me finish! This is man to man, all right? I'm sorry if I don't put things gracefully enough to suit you; but we're calling a spade a spade here, and I just want you to hear me out. And if you marry that Rossiter girl, that's the end of you as far as Thaddeus Eberhardt is concerned; and if the Eberhardts aren't with you, then you've got one long, rocky road ahead of you in this wretched town, and you know that's the truth as well as I do!"

"How about the long, rocky road," Sarsfield thought, "with Jack Middleton for a father?"

When he had "cooled down," however, Sarsfield had to admit that there was a solid kernel of common sense to what his father had said: Grandfather Eberhardt's hand was felt everywhere in the valley;—there was no escaping it. Thaddeus Eberhardt had certainly smoothed the way for Jack Middleton; without Thaddeus Eberhardt, Jack Middleton would be nothing more, by now, than a drunken, dirty old fool with a camera. And it had always been common knowledge that Sarsfield stood high in his grandfather's favor,—almost as high as if his name had been Eberhardt; it had also become apparent over the past few years that his grandmother, for all her blunt, irascible Rainey ways, had a soft spot for him as well. So the hard question was: how much did Sarsfield care about his grandparents' opinion? The hard answer, found after much soul searching, was that he cared very much. He owed his Harvard education to them, and he was not about to forget that; and he, moreover, had grown genuinely fond of the queer old couple.

But he felt that he could not make a move without the Eberhardts looking over his shoulder. Should he remove to New York, he would be living under the auspices of Eberhardts *there*; he could (God help him!) even avail himself of Julia's Van Gort connections! But he, like many another young man, wanted to live his life to suit himself; and he could see no way to do it untrammeled by obligations; the only way he could escape these blood ties would be to pack up his camera and flee to a distant city—San Francisco might be far enough—where the name Eberhardt meant nothing;—and Sarsfield felt like a moral coward, for he knew that he could not set out alone in such a pioneering fashion. If he wanted to enjoy the advantages of his position, however, he must hold himself responsible to his obligations; and, clearly, the Eberhardts would wish him to make a proper marriage.

These sorry speculations made him question his motivations in regard to Emma. It had never occurred to him that he wanted to marry her; but if he did not want to marry her, why was he calling upon her three or four nights a week? It was only natural that people—his father, his mother, his grandparents, Emma herself!—would begin to think that he was courting her; so, if he were *not* courting her, he had better stop seeing her. He knew that he did not want to stop seeing her; but he did not know why. There was something about the girl—even something about her family—that he found hugely appealing. But could it be that by picking someone whom his mother would describe as "common as dirt," he was only trying to prove to his family that he could do what he damned well pleased?

"Where the devil's Arch when I need him?" Sarsfield asked rhetorically. Since he had been thirteen, Sarsfield had depended upon Arch for advice, encouragement,—that good swift kick! But, good Lord, he was twenty-five; and he should by now be able to make decisions without his friend at his side to point him in the right direction, should he not? But it seemed as though, no sooner had Sarsfield found a course of action that was right and manly, than suddenly,—just by thinking about it!—everything was turned upside down, and his clear direction of a moment before was revealed as the height of folly. For the first time Sarsfield understood how Julia could have found herself forced into a position (a "cul-de-sac in the heart" she had called it) where, seemingly of her own volition, she had married Peter Van Gort; and he felt that he, too, could become so worn down that he might do what everyone expected him to do just to get it over with—or that he might do *just the opposite* for exactly the same reason.

Emma, however, had firmly "set her hat" on Sarsfield: it was clear to her that if a young man came calling as often as he did, then he must have marriage on his mind; and she knew that *she* wanted to marry *him* (it would not have occurred to her to ask herself why). When she lay abed and mulled things over, she knew that she still did not understand Sarsfield Middleton—that the way his mind worked seemed just as mysterious now as upon the first night when they had sat on the glider and talked a lot of nonsense. But Emma reminded herself that she was only seventeen, that many a girl marries a man whose innermost thoughts she does not fully comprehend, that marriage, God willing, provides a couple with a lifetime in which to become better acquainted. She also knew—and this she had known forever—that if you want something, you can't be "lolly-gagging" about, you have got to go out and go after it! And thus she had laid the last of her inner doubts to rest and was now proceeding full speed ahead.

It was inconceivable to Emma that she could marry without her parents' consent; all she had to do, then, was convince them. She set about her work in the manner with which she had won all of her previous battles—by slow attrition. Her father, as was his custom, had withdrawn from the fray into a dignified and somewhat pained silence that forbade the raising of contentious issues; but about her mother one thing was as certain as the sun's rise: no matter how dangerous the topic, her mother would always discuss it. The question of marriage was still a long way down the pike, so the flank upon which Emma attacked was that of Sarsfield Middleton's general "suitability."

"Why d'you and daddy always say 'Thaddeus Eberhardt's grandson'?" Emma asked with an air of sweet, girlish innocence.

Mrs. Rossiter was not fooled and gave her daughter a withering stare. "Because that's what he is, that's why."

"Why doesn't anybody ever talk about that disgraceful old Jack Middleton? Why doesn't anybody ever say, 'He's the son of one of the biggest rips in the city of Raysburg'?"

"What are you going on about, Emma? Of course he's that old drunk's son. D'you think that makes him any more—?"

"You don't seem to hold that against him, Mama. And why don't you ever talk about his brother and sister running wild from one end of the Island to the other like a couple little Indians?"

Mrs. Rossiter realized that if she tried to continue the conversation with only half a mind, she would find herself led down the garden path, so she turned away from the stove to look directly at her daughter. "I guess you've got some point to make," she said; "Let's hear it."

"His people aren't all that high and mighty," Emma replied.

"Get on with you!"

"They're not. His great-grandpaw, old Dan Rainey, buys his feed from Daddy's store. They're just like us—"

"Like us! Lord preserve you from such foolishness, Emma Lee! The Raineys have been around longer than Adam's off ox. Why, you can't spit in this town without you hit some Rainey property—"

"So what? Old Dan Rainey's been here to dinner—"

"Yes, he has. He's a good man and a good neighbor. But d'you see Ez Rainey coming down here and taking dinner—?"

"Ez Rainey can't stay sober long enough to take dinner with anybody!"

"Emma, you are a scandal," Mrs. Rossiter said; but she was laughing.

"You see what I'm saying, Mama? It always comes back around to Old Man Eberhardt. Well, what are the Eberhardts anyway? They're just a bunch of Germans—not any different from the Kaltenbachs, except they made a whole pile of money."

Mrs. Rossiter took a moment to reflect on that. Her daughter had a point—except that "a whole pile of money" made a whole pile of difference. "Emma, honey," she said, "the Lord works in mysterious ways, and only He knows what's what—all the way down to who's saved and who ain't. And if He wants something to be, then it's going to be, and I'd be the last to try to stand in His way. But I just want to tell you one thing plain and clear so's you'll have it in your mind and you can't come back at me and say I never told you:—if you think your father's going to let you marry Thaddeus Eberhardt's grandson, then you've got another good think coming!"

Emma nodded gravely; but inwardly she was pleased as punch. Her mother, she was sure now, would not oppose her. The only obstacle that remained was her obdurate father. She knew that a direct assault would lead to disaster, so she resolved to bide her time, study him as carefully as a farmer studies the evening sky, await his subtle signs and signals. Buoyed up by the natural optimism of her youth, she was sure that he could eventually be persuaded to her point of view.

Tom Rossiter, for his part, was perfectly aware of what was going on; and Emma would have been thrown into utter dejection had she known that her father's point of view was *already* close to her own. Tom had decided that Sarsfield Middleton was an excellent fellow—a polite, respectful, hard-working, responsible young gentleman with good prospects—in short everything that anyone who was not a total fool would want in a son-in-law; but the fact that he held a high opinion of the boy only made things worse. Tom had taken to spending long hours walking up and down the banks of the river when he should have been in bed asleep, thinking the same gloomy thoughts over and over again. Most other men when faced with the question of a daughter's marriage would have begun with a consideration of the daughter, and then of the family, and then of the suitor and *his* family,—moving outward from that personal center to the broader world. Tom Rossiter, however, was not like most other men; he always began by considering the good of the nation.

It was plain as the nose on your face (he thought): the only thing that could have saved this country from sure ruination was the free coinage of silver, and the only man who could have brought that about was William Jennings Bryan, and it was people like Thaddeus Eberhardt who stopped him—that fat, old kraut standing up there on his platform all draped over with flags like he owned the whole damned country, lock, stock, and barrel (and, the way things was going, maybe he did), making his speeches and twisting everything so what was true and simple got all turned around and come out looking false and crooked—and good, honest working people like Tom Rossiter got skinned and slapped up on that old cross of gold same as they always did, same as they would forever if people like Thaddeus Eberhardt had their way.—Yes, and Lord willing, Bryan would get the nod from the Democratic Party; and if he did, Old Man Eberhardt would be up there on his platform talking against him again, and going on about "*what we fought for*"—Well, what Thaddeus Eberhardt had fought for and what Tom Rossiter had fought for hadn't been exactly the same thing, but Tom had done his best to forget the war, but men like Thaddeus Eberhardt sure hadn't forgot the war, not for a minute, and didn't want anybody else to forget it either, and brought it up every chance they got, waving their bloody rag: "Did we fight and bleed and die for—!" Well, the devil take the lot of those damned Republicans!

Except now that fat, evil, old Republican's grandson was coming around to call on poor little Emma who was a silly, sweet girl who didn't know what was what,—who wasn't even dry behind the ears yet —and who thought she wanted to marry him.

"Maybe we never should of stayed on in Raysburg," Tom thought. "Maybe we should have gone back home to the Shenandoah—" But it had been hard enough, the way things was in the years after the war, to scratch a living out of the dirt; and Tom's little brother, Seth, was doing his best at it, and taking care of their old mother; and they'd needed the cash money Tom had sent back to them. So Tom had stayed on working for the Dutchman, old Stoetwegen, in this Northern town where some folks wouldn't even give him a "Hello, how are you?" on the street. "Look at that damned reb," that's what they said, "who does he think he is? He fought against our country, and he owned slaves back before the war, so what's he doing up here?" And it didn't do any good to keep saying over and over again how nobody much in the Shenandoah Valley had owned slaves, how the Rossiters and his wife's people, the Quaries, had never owned no slaves, how the folks in the valley hadn't been much for secession and would've loved to stay in the Union if there was any way they could've done it—with honor—but, Lord, when Old Virginia went to war, why, there was nothing to do but go with her. No, it didn't do any good to say any of that, because nobody ever paid the least bit of mind to any of that; and Tom had grown old in Raysburg, and now they called him "that old Southerner."

"If a darky comes in my store and wants to buy his seed grain from me, or his feed, do I tell him to go buy them somewhere else?" Tom thought. "Do I have a sign in my window says NO COLOREDS! No, Sir, I don't. If a darky comes in, I serve him just as polite as can be. Ain't his money as good as a white man's? In fact, if the truth be known, the coloreds is more likely to get a fair shake out of me than out of some of them folks that grew up around here and are so damned proud of the fact they fought for the Union—hypocrites!" It was men like Thaddeus Eberhardt who got up there, making their speeches about Abraham Lincoln to get the poor darkies to vote the Republican ticket,—and the poor, ignorant fools don't even know what it is they was voting for. Well, if Thaddeus Eberhardt loved the coloreds so much, why didn't he pay them what he paid a white man? But Thaddeus Eberhardt was a great man, yes sir, he fought for the Union!

Fighting in it had been plenty enough war for Tom; and he had done his level best to forget it and put it behind him; but now this whole thing was making him think about it all over again. He remembered marching back into the valley with Jubal Early—which weren't the proper name for him; he should of been called "Late"—and getting their behinds kicked good and proper, and the hardest thing Tom ever done in his life was to march back out of the valley with old Jubalee, and even to this day, Tom thought maybe he should've stayed behind to look after his people there,—maybe his Daddy would've had a few more years. "Lord," he thought, "the Shenandoah Valley after the war was as desolate a place you'd ever see in your life. Months since the Federals been through there, but everything still smelled burnt—"

Tom got into bed with his wife, and she was sound asleep. He lay there and listened to her snore—that good woman who was his wife, who'd cleaved to him, flesh to his flesh, and bore him five live children—and thought: "Dog tired, that poor old woman, working the whole day," and thought how strange the years was that brought them to this place. Standing at the point where the Great Kanawha meets the Ohio, and the only way that made sense was *west*—on out the big Ohio— maybe just keep on going, overland to Texas. But then that paddle-wheeler come by short-handed, going the wrong way: "Hey, Reb, can you hump freight?" And Tom answered straight back, "You bet, Cap!" so there he'd been headed *north*, which didn't make a lick of sense; and then he was in Raysburg, West Virginia, and that didn't make a lick of sense either. Yankeeland! And then old Stoetwegen give him that job, the old Dutchman dead and gone now all these years—who'd left him the store just like Tom was his own son. And then going back home to see how his brother was doing, to see his mother one last time, and little Abbie Quarie was all growed up, and here she was asleep in their bed—all the years rolling by—that good old woman who was his wife.

Oh, it weren't that he didn't see the hand of the Lord in lots of things—everywhere he looked he seen the hand of the Lord, but—Yes, that Middleton boy was a nice boy. A fine boy. But when you marry someone, you cleave to them, your flesh to their flesh, and you become one flesh, and, Lord willing, there's many a year goes by with that wife who's your one flesh. "Emma, honey, I wisht you was older and knowed more about life," Tom thought. And there was no getting around it: nice as he was, that boy was still Thaddeus Eberhardt's grandson.

One sunny morning near the end of June, a messenger appeared in the shop with a note from Grandmother Eberhardt requesting that Sarsfield dine with his grandparents on Saturday night. He wrote a reply saying that he would be delighted to do so and then wondered if there might be some hidden significance to the invitation. He had always been summoned from time to time in exactly this fashion, so it might mean nothing at all out of the ordinary; but, nonetheless, he had an ominous feeling about it.

The moment Sarsfield saw the other guests—or rather the lack of them—he knew that his grandparents knew about Emma. Sarsfield alighted from his buggy, turned over the reins to one of the stable boys, and paused to consider the two automobiles drawn up in front of the carriage house; there were so few of these vehicles in Raysburg that Sarsfield knew at once to whom they belonged: the Mercedes Simplex was owned by Charlie Staub, the brand-new, magnificent "Silver Ghost" by Uncle Maynard Eberhardt;—and, indeed, as Sarsfield approached, these two gentlemen were immediately revealed, standing back out of the afternoon sunlight, deeply engrossed in conversation with each other; from their expansive gestures and the glow of pride radiating from them, it was apparent that they were discussing the merits of their respective cars,—while their wives dutifully awaited the termination of this essential, but, from the distaff point of view, tedious exchange. Of the vast number of possible Eberhardts, Raineys, Ebelings, Revingtons, or Staubs, these two families had been invited, quite obviously, because of their daughters,—for, walking toward Sarsfield was Bedelia Eberhardt, accompanied, as always, by Lenore Staub. Both girls had brothers—who were not in attendance. "I'm in for it now," Sarsfield thought.

If the girls had arrived wind-blown from their automobile rides, they must have found the time to repair themselves, for they appeared as unruffled as if they were crossing a drawing room. They wore hats adorned with splashes of gauzey fabric nearly three feet across, and glistening crêpe gowns that appeared, as new fashions often do, dramatic and shocking: the skirts were fitted so tightly—from the waist, down over the hips, practically to the knees—that the entire womanliness of the figure was revealed with little left to the imagination; and the girls were forced to mince along in tiny, bird-like steps. Each girl held a parasol in her free hand; Bedelia's was raised to ward off the sun; Lenore's was closed, and she carried it at a jaunty angle as though it were a walking stick.

In the past year Sarsfield's path had crossed that of Bedelia and Lenore quite often; and he knew their ways by now. Although both had turned twenty-one, they enjoyed cultivating a show of petted, per-fervid girlishness: when they met, they squealed, rushed upon each other, embraced, and kissed as they had learned to do at their Balti-more finishing school; they giggled and leaned close to whisper secrets; they held hands, fed each other candies; they simpered, smirked, flounced, pranced, preened, fluttered, and flirted; and then, without warning, they would assume demeanors that were so ironic, cynical, and world-weary that any boy who could have been such a fool as to take their performance seriously was reduced instantly to utter shame-faced ignominy. As they approached now across the clipped, smooth lawn, each with her free arm wrapped around the other's admirably small waist, they appeared as irrevocably united as Siamese twins. "Dare I believe my eyes?" Lenore said, falling into the stage-play speech she affected; "Could it be that Middleton boy about whom I have been hearing so much?"

"Why, I do believe it is," Bedelia replied. "He certainly has the air about him of that Middleton boy. What have you been hearing about him, you naughty little eaves-dropper?"

"Oh—only that he is so utterly indifferent to the charms of our sex that he has left behind him many a tender heart—bleeding at his feet," and, with that, Lenore gave Sarsfield a long look from under her flut-tering lashes; her huge, opalesque eyes were one of her best features.

"Our sweet cos, Sarsfield Middleton? Oh, you must be mistaken," Bedelia continued the banter. "I have never heard of him bespoken as anything other than a thorough gentleman."

"Did I say that he was anything other than a thorough gentleman?" Lenore asked, her voice purring and resonant and suggestive of other, far more interesting, matters.

In spite of his annoyance at what must surely be his grandmother's ploy (for his grandfather limited his manipulations to the iron and steel business), Sarsfield had to laugh. "Good evening, ladies," he said, play-ing his part, "I have never seen either of you looking more lovely—like two denizens of fairyland." He kissed Bedelia's hand, took up Lenore's to do the same.

Lenore, for a brief moment—one that stopped just short of scan-dalous—would not let her hand fall, but pressed the smooth, tight kid leather of her fingertips firmly into Sarsfield's lips. "Now," she said, "I shall never take off my glove."

Sarsfield quite enjoyed this performance; he gathered up the girls, one on each arm, and led them toward their parents. "It's really a shame," he thought, "that I haven't got a camera with me."

The company exchanged pleasantries and then followed Black George down into the garden where Sarsfield's grandparents were taking "a little something" before dinner—his grandmother sherry and his grandfather the tiny glasses of fiery schnaps he loved and drank by the half-dozen. "Ah, the ladies!" Grandfather Eberhardt called out in the booming voice he used to disguise the fact that he was, at heart, a shy and reserved man; and his wife rose from her lawn-chair to accept the greetings that were offered her; she took Sarsfield's hand and did not let go of it. "My boy! How good to see you," Thaddeus was braying at him; "How are you? You look fit, indeed you do."

"I'm well, Grandfather," Sarsfield said.

His grandfather, however, looked far from well; Thaddeus had always been a large man, but, since turning seventy, he had been growing heavier at a truly astonishing rate. Formally dressed for evening, he perspired profusely; in the hot light of the setting sun, steady rivulets poured down the vast folds of his pink chins; even his hands were gleaming with moisture. He paused, wheezing, as though the exertion of welcoming his guests had been too much for him; for a moment, he looked befuddled and old. But then Thaddeus drew himself up, assumed his evening's smile; and, once again, his loud, round, public voice could be heard as he turned his attention to Charlie and Maynard.

Grandmother Eberhardt stared at the girls, shook her head. "So that's the latest from Paris, is it?" she said under her breath to Sarsfield. "If you ask me, you can send those dresses straight back to France on the next boat." She still had not released her grip on him; and Sarsfield found himself neatly cut away from the others, herded off, and led on a stroll past the show-piece rose bushes; his grandmother's corpulence did not appear to bother her in the least, and she strode along with surprising vigor. "What you young people are coming to, I'll never know," she said. "Imagine! Appearing in public like that—Why, look at them; they can't even walk. If we'd worn dresses like that in my day, we may's well have been carrying red lanterns;—but I don't guess you mind a bit, do you, Sarsfield?"

"No, Grandmother," he replied. From the slightest suggestion of a smile, he saw that she was not nearly as scandalized as she let on. In her

day (if he could believe the story she had told him dozens of times), her
waist had been a perfect sixteen inches; and she had been forced to ride
kneeling on a pillow because otherwise she would not have been able
to fit her hoopskirts into the carriage.

She stopped walking abruptly, drew away from him to look directly
up into his face. "We've been hearing reports of you, Sarsfield," she said
in her blunt Rainey fashion, "that have given us quite a turn."

"Oh?" He looked back and saw that the others were well out of
earshot.

"You know damn well what I mean," she said, staring at him with
one of her eyes.

"I am not—at least at the moment I am not—planning on marrying anyone," Sarsfield told her, controlling his temper.

"See that you don't," she responded, and then, softening, took his
arm. "Your grandfather is very fond of you," she said, "and so am I—
although I don't expect you to believe that. Be careful, Sarsfield. Do
not ruin your life before it is well begun."

Dinner at the Eberhardts' was the high point of the day. Thaddeus,
as he had done his entire life, still rose at five-thirty and was found
behind his desk hard at work by six; but, in the last few years, he had
begun to require a nap in the afternoon. His custom, of late, was to
abandon work altogether at three and sleep until just before dinner; in
that fashion, he could rise, refreshed and eager, to enjoy what had
become his primary pleasure in life. Grandmother Eberhardt had never
been converted to the new-fangled practice of serving dinner in courses
à la Russe, but rather kept to the good, old country custom of the
Raineys and presented all the food at once; guests were expected to help
themselves,—and the devil take the hindmost. So, approaching the
table, Sarsfield saw that the Eberhardts' estimable German cook and his
five assistants had been hard at work: hot corn bread, beaten biscuits,
strawberry short-cake, and apple tart; raspberries, strawberries, New York
apples, and the first Georgia peaches; corn on the cob, pole beans, broad
beans, new peas, mixed pickles, and sliced tomatoes and cucumbers;
scalloped potatoes, deviled crabs, creamed turkey, an entire ham set
with cloves, and scrambled eggs on rusk; scallops and hake rushed in on
ice from the coast, now lightly braised and brushed with butter; a good
hare cooked German style with sauerkraut on the side; corned beef
hash, wilted lettuce salad, and forty or so of Pete Kaltenbach's best

sausages (Thaddeus loved the heavy German cooking of his childhood); slips, ices, and jellies; stacks of small German pancakes with jugs of Vermont maple syrup; and all of this, of course, accompanied by eight varieties of relish, six of mustard, huge mounds of fresh butter, and four silver pitchers of heavy cream bedewed from the ice. The roast had just arrived, crackling from the oven; five bottles of German wine waited ready at hand.

Sarsfield, just as he knew he would be, had been seated next to Lenore; he resolved to do his best with the rôle assigned to him, so, as she began tugging at the finger tips of her glove, he said: "Oh, Miss Staub, I am deeply hurt;—You assured me that you would leave it on forever."

"Would that please you, Mr. Middleton?" she purred back at him, and, with a theatrical gesture, drew the white kid firmly back up again. As Black George carried dishes from guest to guest, Sarsfield was forced to enjoin Lenore repeatedly to remove her gloves, while she demurred. With the silent efficiency perfected in years of service, George was so good at his work that anything one wished was presented—as though by some miracle of mind-reading—upon the instant one wished it; Sarsfield had yet to raise his hand, yet his plate already held heaping mounds of scalloped potatoes and creamed turkey. "Please begin—that's right, while it's still hot," Grandmother Eberhardt commanded; her husband reacted to these words like a horse to the starter's pistol; and his wife fell in not far behind him. Lenore at last, wringing every possible ounce of drama from the performance, removed her gloves,—revealing her slender, soft, perfectly white arms that had never seen the sun. She began to cut up a cucumber slice into tiny morsels, while, on the far side of the table, her mother was saying something about "the defilement of society."

Bedelia's   mother   (Sarsfield's   "Aunt   Lou")   concurred   with: "Absolutely! If we allow the criminal classes to propagate their vile species at this rate—why, in ten years, we shall be utterly swamped."

"What're you going to do to stop 'em, shoot 'em?" Charlie Staub demanded, grinning, and then laughed loudly as he peered up and down the table to make sure that his witticism had been duly appreciated.

"Don't see a blamed thing funny about that, Charlie. You think it's funny?" Maynard snapped out. "Uncle Mayne," the eldest of Thaddeus Eberhardt's sons, could not have been less like his father if his Maker had set out to create him as a polar opposite; old Dan Rainey's blood was apparent in Maynard's physiognomy:—he was spare and bird-like,

with darting, dark eyes; but, unlike either the Raineys or the Eberhardts, he seemed to have been born with no sense of humor whatsoever. He scowled at the company and muttered: "Things have got too
far, if you ask me.—Yes, indeed, much too far!"

"What's gone too far?" Sarsfield wondered; "What criminal classes?
What on earth *are* they talking about?" But he could not follow the
conversation, for Lenore had just asked him something about Wagner.

"When it comes to German music, I tend to prefer a good, rousing
chorus of 'Down Where the Wurzburger Flows,'" he told her, only half
joking. "Oh, Mr. Middleton," Lenore said and produced a light tinkling
laugh as though he had just uttered words of vast subtlety;—but she
would, he thought, talk about Art; now she was leading the conversation in the direction of poetry—the work of Swinburne, to be exact.

"Read somewhere that Swinburne's one of Teddy Roosevelt's
favorite poets," Sarsfield said, but couldn't help adding: "Never could
understand why."

"The last thing we need is any more danged immigrants!" Charlie
Staub was saying.

"Hear, hear!" Uncle Mayne intoned.

Thaddeus Eberhardt enjoyed hearing conversation as he dined, so
guests were always invited; but he, himself, spoke not a word; and the
only sounds to be heard from him were the inexorable clinking of his
silverware and the steady rhythm of chewing and swallowing. But now
he looked up and gave his eldest son a stare that could have withered a
maple tree; Thaddeus was proud of being German-American and would
hear no talk of "danged immigrants."

His father's warning appeared to be lost upon Maynard, for he
plunged doggedly on about "the dregs of Europe."

"How the devil did they get from criminal classes to immigrants?"
Sarsfield wondered; but once again he was distracted from the conversation opposite, for Lenore suddenly began to chant: "The heavy white
limbs, and the cruel—red mouth like a venomous flower—"

"Oh, Lord," he thought, "now she's quoting Swinburne!"

"I fear that we're making our last stand," Aunt Lou said; "What's at
stake are the very ideals and values of our Christian civilization—"

"That's right, Mother," Bedelia pronounced with considerable
fervor; "and we don't have to look at the degeneracy of Europe;—we can
see it happening right here in the Valley!"

"O mystic and sombre Dolores, Our Lady of Pain!" Lenore concluded with a smug smile.

The conversation on the far side of the table circled about the
weighty matters of blood, breeding, immigration, the criminal classes,
the evils of labor unions, and the threat to our Christian civilization;
while, on Sarsfield's side, the topics of poetry, chamber music, Pre-
Raphaelite painting, and the cathedrals of France were thoroughly considered. Sarsfield watched, in fascination, as Lenore, severely corseted to
fit her "sheath" gown, pushed food around in decorative patterns on her
plate, giving the illusion of eating when, in fact, she was partaking of
hardly anything at all; and he was, of course, reminded of Julia. He was
afraid that any society girl he ever met (whether of this silly Raysburg
variety or of the more elegant New York species) would always remind
him of Julia,—would seem only a flawed and distant and misshapen
copy of Julia, leaving him with an intensified longing for the original.

After dinner, the men withdrew to the library for cigars and brandy.
Sarsfield was so groggy from the heavy meal that he could scarcely
frame a sentence, but his grandfather was now at the top of his form;
Thaddeus, well fed, was the very picture of a jolly fat man,—as close to
benign as the world would ever see him. It soon became apparent (even
to Sarsfield in his dazed state) that his grandmother must have been
assigned the job of delivering the direct, crushing body blow; now the
men were to follow up with innumerable light feints and jabs designed
to finish Sarsfield off.

"I want you to know, my boy," Thaddeus said: "that we shall always
have a position for you at Raysburg Iron and Steel."

"Oh—well, that's really white of you, Grandfather, but—"

"No, no. Don't say a word. It's there if you ever want it. Why, a
Harvard man—we can always find room for a Harvard man. Wouldn't
you say that, Maynard?"

"Absolutely!" came the immediate response; and Uncle Mayne's
opinion, Sarsfield knew perfectly well, carried considerable weight:
Maynard had long been his father's good right hand; of late he had
been assuming an increasing weight of responsibility; upon his father's
death, he would be left in control of the vast and complex business
empire of the Raysburg Eberhardts. "Times are changing," Maynard
said; "It's not enough any more just to be a gentleman—although, Lord
knows, we could use of few more of them—but what's needed now are

fellows with a proper education. We can always find you a good position, Sarsfield. Something at the top, you understand—"

And somewhat later Charlie Staub said: "Don't be such a stranger,
Sarsfield. You've gotta come see us. Come for dinner—come after
church some Sunday, spend the day. Lenore's always complainin' about
how there ain't any fellows can talk about all the arty stuff; she'd be just
tickled pink. Yep, come any time—How about next weekend? I'll fix it
up with the wife."

And, while Charlie and Maynard were absorbed in conversation,
Thaddeus took Sarsfield aside to say: "Been wanting to tell you, boy,
how much I admire those colored pictures you make. They're bully
things, simply bully! And should you ever require capital to expand
your photography business—*yours*, you understand—well, I'm certain
that it could be arranged."

And over the second brandy Thaddeus said: "Well, son, I gather
from Henry that you've been considering establishing yourself in New
York. I'm a selfish old man, and I would prefer for you to remain in the
valley, but, ah—a man must follow his destiny, eh?"

"Oh, but there's lots of opportunity in the valley," Maynard interjected; "I'd think long and hard before I left the valley."

"Me too!" Charlie Staub chimed in; "This is a real go-getter
town—good, old Raysburg. You just wait and see, Sarsfield; we're goina
be on the map!"

And, as they stepped through the French doors to take a turn in the
garden in the lovely, cool twilight where the long, blue shadows were
punctuated with fire-flies, Charlie and Uncle Mayne, strangely enough,
went one way while Sarsfield and his grandfather went the other. "Just
want you to know," Thaddeus said, "that if there's *any* way in which we
can assist you here—even perhaps a long-term loan at low interest—"

"Oh, Grandfather, that's just—"

"No, don't say a word, Sarsfield. You're part of the family!"

And, a few moments later, Thaddeus said: "Nothing would please
your grandmother and I more than seeing you properly married, Sarsfield. I am not as young as I used to be, and I—well, I wish to see my
heirs properly provided for;—and if you were to marry a—well, let us
say, a girl of your own class, a good high-strung, fine-bred northern
girl—a proper mother for your children, *for our great-grandchildren*—
why, we would be so happy and proud!"

There was no denying it: the evening was exquisite, particularly when seen from the Eberhardt gardens looking down over the hundred acres of the Eberhardt estate built high above the river where the mosquitoes seldom flew and even the smoke from the mills rarely drifted; and Sarsfield had nothing against million-dollar estates and dining well and gentlemanly postprandial strolls over lawns clipped and watered to the consistency of an Oriental carpet—smoking the finest of handmade Havana cigars and watching the diamond points of Orion glitter in the clear, dark sky. There was also no use denying that Lenore Staub was a beautiful girl; prized loose from Bedelia and given a few years to mature, she might even prove to be an amusing and intelligent one. She had an excellent sense of style (she knew when to stop, which Bedelia did not); and her fine-boned figure would age well. At the moment, at twenty-one, she was playing the fool under the mistaken notion that her performance made her irresistible; but she would not be twenty-one forever. She was not a Julia Eberhardt; she was a blessed long way from being a Julia Eberhardt; but there was, after all, only one Julia Eberhardt. Yes, and, finally, there was the matter of the Staub glass-works which had made Lenore's father a millionaire. For only a moment—but a moment of blinding intensity—Sarsfield was so angry at Thaddeus Eberhardt that he could have cheerfully thrown the fat old criminal down the steps of the gazebo and throttled him on the spot.

The Rossiters always had a big picnic on the Fourth of July; and Emma asked her mother if she could invite the Middletons. "Why don't you just invite the Eberhardts while you're at it?" her mother said; but Tom told his wife to go ahead and let Emma do it: "They ain't agoina come. You can bet your bottom dollar on that," he said.

The invitation—which Emma wrote with white ink on pigeon-blood stationery—sent Sarsfield's mother to bed early. Sarsfield replied—on plain white vellum—that Sarsfield, Kyle, and Olivia Middleton would be pleased to attend but that Mr. and Mrs. Middleton were regretfully engaged elsewhere—and signed his mother's name. Emma, who had never before in her life sent a formal invitation and received an answer back, took it as a favorable omen that Mrs. Middleton had replied—and glued Sarsfield's efforts into her keepsake book. "Well, at least we shan't have that old rip falling down in our back yard," she said to her mother.

"Nor his la-dee-dah wife giving herself airs, either," Mrs. Rossiter said.

Sarsfield asked Emma if she would like the occasion commemorated with photographs; she said that would be lovely, but he had better let her father pay for them. Olivia wanted to wear gloves and carry a parasol, but Sarsfield told her that she had better save that for the Eberhardts' lawn party later in the summer; Kyle wanted to go barefoot, but Sarsfield told him to at least *start out* with shoes on.

Emma and her mother and her brothers' wives had been cooking for days so there would be enough food for everybody. The Fourth of July was the occasion when all the Rossiters within traveling distance got together; this year, Uncle Seth and his people were coming up from Virginia, and Emma's oldest brother, Mat, who was "on the river," was going to try to make it. If everything worked out all right, it would be the biggest picnic in years.

As soon as the sun was directly overhead, Emma began looking for Sarsfield. The men had carried the kitchen table out onto the lawn, and the women were loading it up with potato salad, cole slaw, ham, tongue, fried chicken, pickles, lemonade, cakes, and pies. Emma stood under the elm tree, distracted, with a platter in her hands. "What on earth's got into you?" her mother asked, taking the platter. "You practicing up to be a marble statue?"

"Oh, Mama, where *is* he?"

"Well, what did you write on that fool invitation you sent?"

"I wrote 'afternoon'—"

"Lord save you, Emma Lee, them society people think 'afternoon' means late in the day."

"How could they think that? It's as clear as a bell. 'Noon' means noon and 'after' means after. What could be clearer than that?"

"You just mark my words, honey. You ain't agoina be seeing him for an hour or two yet.—Why, them society people always come late anyway. That's what they think's polite. If you wanted him here at noon, you should of writ 'eleven.'"

Emma sighed at her mother's foolishness; but Mrs. Rossiter was not far off the mark. Sarsfield had construed "afternoon" as two o'clock, which is when he arrived. As soon as she saw his buggy in the distance, Emma, who, up until that point had not done much of anything but stand about in people's way while she stared intently toward the north end of the island, threw herself into a great flurry of activity and had to be summoned twice before she could manage to free herself from her burdensome duties.

Tom Rossiter, to make up for all his hard thoughts (true as they might be) about Thaddeus Eberhardt, greeted Sarsfield with a great effusion of welcome—"Nice to see you, boy! So glad you could make it down!"—called upon Clayborn to tend to the horse, patted Kyle on the back, helped Sarsfield unload his camera, said to the little Middleton girl who was staring at him with big, black eyes: "What's the matter, honey, cat got your tongue?"

Olivia was amazed. No one had ever said that to her in her entire life. As they had been driving down Front Street, Sarsfield had shouted at her: "Olivia, can you please be quiet for five minutes? Your voice is like having a magpie in my brain!" and Olivia had resolved to be so silent that her brother would feel bad about saying such a mean thing to her; but now her resolve vanished in an instant, and, without pausing for breath, she said: "No, sir, the cat's never got my tongue and she never shall, thank you. Are you Mr. Rossiter? I thought so; I must have met you before, and I'm so pleased to meet you again, happy Fourth of July!—Oh, look at all the people, isn't it splendid! There's just masses and masses of people—and look at all the food, Sarsfield, look at all the cakes and pies! Aren't the ladies just fine in their white dresses? Are these people all Rossiters? Good heavens, I didn't know there were so many Rossiters in the whole world, is there going to be fireworks? Oh, I do hope so!—and look down there! Yes, right down there in the rocking chair by the river bank—isn't that my great grandfather? Oh, yes it is! Oh, look, Sarsfield, it's old Grandpaw Rainey. What's he doing here? Is he related to the Rossiters?"

"Shhh," Sarsfield said automatically; and, following the line of Olivia's pointing finger, he was surprised to see that indeed it was Daniel Rainey resting under the shade of a tree. "Don't point," he said to Olivia, "It's not polite." The spare, bald man, rocking slowly and staring out at the river, looked as old as Methuselah.

Emma arrived at just this moment. Daniel Rainey's presence was her doing, and she had meant it to be a surprise for Sarsfield; but Olivia had "stolen her thunder." Hiding her irritation, she greeted Sarsfield, held out her hand to the child, and said: "Oh, you must be Olivia. I'm Emma Rossiter. How are you today, dear?"

Olivia began to tell her exactly how she was;—she began to tell her in great detail and at great length. "Go say hello to your great-grandfather,"

Emma said to Sarsfield. He saw a small, triumphant smile on her face and thought, "How did she manage that one?" He walked across the lawn toward the rocking chair. The ancient figure appeared to be entranced by the view of the river.

"How are you today, Grandfather?" Sarsfield said.

Dan gave him a quizzical look but did not answer; the old man returned his gaze to the slowly moving water and went back to his steady rocking. It had been some months since Sarsfield had seen his great-grandfather; old Dan Rainey was known to be "sharp as a tack"— although his mind did, from time to time, wander. Sarsfield hoped that the old man's mind had not, by now, wandered away entirely. "Couldn't ask for a better Fourth," he tried.

The old man looked at him again, his head tilted to one side. "Fourth is it?" Dan asked.

"That's right, Grandfather."

"Fourth of July, is it?"

"That's right."

"Good, good—Now who the hell are you?"

"Your great-grandson, Sarsfield."

"Middleton?"

"That's right, Grandfather."

Dan rocked and thought that over; then, suddenly, he exploded into speech: "Goddamn British, trying to burn our White House down—We oughta go up and invade 'em. Whole goddamned continent's ours, ain't it? President said so. My half-witted grand-daughter married one of them damned British fellers. Never could abide them British—"

"Irish," Sarsfield said.

"What's that you say, Ezra?"

"I'm *Sarsfield*, Grandfather." Sarsfield stepped closer to the old man and raised his voice. "I said the Middletons are *Irish*!"

"Hell. Same thing, ain't it? Foreign—Oh! Sarsfield! Is that you? Well, sir, for a minute there, I thought you was Ezra, but, hell, you ain't Ezra. You don't look a thing like him. Why don't you ever come down and see me, Sarsfield? Hell, you just live up there on the north end, what d'ya think, I'm goina live forever?—They ain't ashippin' on the river the way they done in the old days—Lord, everybody and their dog was agoin' west in them days, and they all floated right on by here, and I seen 'em comin', and I seen 'em goin'. Lord, seems only yesterday my daddy was holding my hand and he points out there and he says, 'Lookie thar, boy, thar comes old President Monroe.' Yep, and he come floatin' on by here—fired off cannons for him all up and down the river. Yep, that was the time o'life, all right, and things ain't been right since. 'Bout the only thing you can count on, Sarsfield, is that river rolling by—You figuring on marrying that little Rossiter girl?"

Sarsfield laughed: he was delighted to discover that there was, as usual, nothing wrong with Daniel Rainey's mind. "I don't know, Grandfather. I might."

"Let me tell you a thing or two, Sarsfield—You know, my daughter Amanda, she done married that rich Dutchman's son, lives out there on her by-Jesus hundred acres, and that rich Dutchman had to buy every one of them hundred acres from me—though they don't seem to want to recollect that fact much these days. Yes, sir, well, little Emma done walked over and invited me, just as pretty as you please, so I says to Amanda, 'I'm too old to be riding all the way out the pike, and I guess right here on my own island is where I'll take my Fourth, thank you.'—She's a sweet little Island girl, and you could do a damned sight worse than little Emma Rossiter, and don't you pay no mind to what my wall-eyed daughter says to you on it."

Sarsfield was struck speechless. Emma had "squared away" Dan Rainey; Sarsfield's opinion of her common sense rose by several large degrees. He looked back and saw that Emma and Olivia were meandering in his direction, Olivia clinging tightly to Emma's hand. Dan followed Sarsfield's eyes, said: "Yep, there she is. Lovely girl. You go over there with her now, and with all her people, and you make yourself liked."

"I'll do my best, Grandfather," Sarsfield replied.

Emma was dying of curiosity to hear what Sarsfield and old Dan Rainey were saying to each other, but Olivia was slowing her down; and, even though she was well in earshot by now, she couldn't hear a thing because the little pest wouldn't shut up. The sound of that child's voice was like being bitten by a blue bottle fly. "What's the difference between lawn and organdie?" Olivia was saying, "I should really know the difference, but I'm not sure I can tell. Organdie's finer, I guess, and more expensive—is that dress of yours lawn or—"

"Lord, child, will you please be quiet!" Emma exclaimed.

Olivia was hurt to the quick; she had thought that Emma liked her;—and Olivia was always getting in trouble for talking too much. At

school she was always having to stand in the corner or stand in the
cloakroom or stand in the hall. She'd had her hands switched; she'd
been threatened with the strap; once she'd had to go around all day
long with a sign around her neck that said CHATTERBOX. She tried
really hard in school—grownups didn't understand how hard she tried,
she really did, she tried her best—but school was out, it was the Fourth
of July, the sun was shining to beat the band, and it just wasn't fair—
first it was Sarsfield, and now it was this nasty woman, and she just
wasn't going to put up with it from any Southern shop-keeper's daughter—even if she was a grown-up lady and her brother's sweetheart. "I'll
talk if I want to talk," she said.

Emma stopped dead still. She felt her heart pounding. She had a
temper like the Quaries, and she'd grown up hearing that she should
always count to ten; but she was not about to be addressed that way
by any child—not even Sarsfield Middleton's little sister. "You hold
your tongue, you spiteful little thing," Emma snapped out before she
could stop herself.

"I won't," Olivia answered back, "and you can't make me."

"You shall, or I'll slap you silly," Emma said.

Olivia's eyes stung with tears. She drew herself up to her full height,
looked up at Emma with a gaze filled with fury, and said: "I'll tell my
brother on you—nasty, mean, hateful, stuck up!" Then the little girl
turned and marched away with an air that would have done justice to
any of her older relatives in Raysburg's high society. "Oh, Lord, what
have I done now?" Emma thought; but here was Sarsfield, saying to her:
"How nice of you to invite old Dan."

She put on her best smile and said, "Well, he probably gets lonely
sitting over at his place all day long—"

Then they heard Dan Rainey shouting after them in a surprisingly
firm voice: "Sarsfield, Sarsfield! You're agoina get some land from me
no matter who the hell you marry!"

Sarsfield suppressed the laughter that was bubbling up inside him;
he waved at his great-grandfather, took Emma's hand. She looked at
him quickly, then away. "I didn't know you knew him that well," he
said.

"Oh," she replied sweetly, "we've always been neighbors."

All afternoon people continued to pour into the Rossiters' back
yard. Although he was introduced to everyone, Sarsfield couldn't begin

to keep track of who was who: aunts, uncles, cousins, in-laws—friends of aunts, uncles, cousins, in-laws. They brought yet more ham and tongue and potato salad, yet more jars of jams and relish, yet more loaves of fresh-baked bread and white "Sally Lums" with blood-red berries, yet more thick fruit pies, and sticky shoo fly pies and brown betties, yet more fried chicken—piles and heaps and mounds and mountains of golden fried chicken. The women embraced each other with tears in their eyes; the men grinned and strolled up and down, side by side, going nowhere in particular;—they kicked at the dirt, hunkered down to exchange views on the crops or the river or the B and O or the state of the nation. The word must have gone around that he was Emma's sweetheart: the entire company cast upon him a bright-eyed regard that was curious, inquisitive, but also strangely tender. Uncle Seth and the other Virginia Rossiters from the Shenandoah spoke in slow, mellifluous southern voices; the West Virginia panhandle Rossiters had acquired the pinched, nasal twang of the mountains; they all talked at once, and even Olivia, going non-stop, could not outdo these garrulous folk. Sarsfield felt overwhelmed by these voices, drowned in them. Kyle, who appeared oddly bemused, glued himself to Sarsfield's side. The little boy stared at the company for a long time and then asked in an awe-struck tone: "Lord, Sarsfield, is they all Democrats?"

Sarsfield set up his camera facing the rear of the house; Mrs. Rossiter gathered up the aunts, uncles, cousins, and in-laws; and Sarsfield took several of the large, formal, family arrangements he knew they would like. This serious business concluded, he turned his camera around the other way, faced toward the river. Beneath the focusing cloth, he swung the camera side to side until he found the most pleasing "frame"—the laden table before him, his great-grandfather in his rocker to the far left, the river behind all—and then screwed the camera firmly into place and loaded it with a plate prepared with his fastest black-and-white emulsion, one that would, in this brilliant light, receive a full, deep exposure in only a second or two. Then, looking outward, he waited for he knew not what; something told him that the picture he sought had yet to compose itself before him.

Late in the afternoon, Emma's brother Mat appeared, walking up the path from the river, walking between the knee-high stands of tasseled corn. Sarsfield had heard that Mat was "on the river"; but no one had explained to him exactly what it was that Mat did there; no sign was visible of how Mat might have arrived so suddenly; and, for a moment, Sarsfield fancied that the man must have walked directly out of the muddy Ohio itself. Mrs. Rossiter wept at the sight of her eldest son. "Now, Mama, it's me in the flesh and no ghost," he said, kindly, with a wink, "so you can just hold back on the waterworks."

Mat was a spare man like his father; he was dressed in a wrinkled black suit and, against the trend of current fashion, wore a beard that gave him an antique look like a figure from one of Jack Middleton's photographs from the seventies. He was nearly twenty years older than Emma, which made him Sarsfield's senior by a good ten years. When the introductions were out of the way, he said to Sarsfield: "Would you care to take a little walk with me, Mr. Middleton?"

Startled, Sarsfield complied. He wondered if the man were going to "quiz" him as to his intentions concerning Emma; but, once they were out of earshot of the others, Mat Rossiter said: "Will you take a drink of old yeller moon with me, Mr. Middleton?"

Sarsfield had learned enough of the ways of these people by now to know that there was only one possible answer he could make to that question: "Yes, indeed. Thank you," and he added, "Please call me Sarsfield."

"And you call me Mat, sir, or Matthew, for one's just as good as t'other—" Mat Rossiter knelt, poked beneath a broad rhubarb leaf, fetched out the demijohn that was hidden there, stood and held it in his big hands with such gentleness and reverence that it might as well have been a new born babe; he spoke with a deeply resonant voice of such a compelling nature that Sarsfield thought he could listen to it forever—no matter what the man was saying—and what the man was saying at the moment was: "Well, now, Sarsfield, this ain't none of your new white moon, this here's the real thing—yep, your old yeller moon. Don't see it around much, but I know the boys that make it—'way on down in McDowell County. Yep, 'way on down below Mr. Mason and Mr. Dixon's line—and they make it just the way their people made it back three hundred years before them—so they tell me, so they tell me. Ah, and she's well thumped out and twisted back and aged in hickory, Lord, save us with Thy righteous ways!"

Sarsfield was not a connoisseur of hard liquor, but he had sampled Henry Eberhardt's imported whiskeys; at the first sip he took from the proffered demijohn, he thought that this indigenous West Virginia beverage, as Mat himself might have said, "beat them all hollow." He had never tasted a whiskey as clear, and sweet, and smooth, and easy. A second later, however, a roar of flame shot through the back of his head; and it was as if molten steel flowed down his throat. Mat was still talking; and Sarsfield dimly heard the words, as though from a great distance: "—still tell the stories of how they was run out of Pennsylvania by King Washington hisself. You know that old fellow was a king, they say, because didn't he go and have that city named after him?" Sarsfield steadied himself on Mat Rossiter's outstretched arm and began to walk back up the hill. When he had coughed and cleared his head and blinked away the tears, Sarsfield saw that Mat was winking at him. "Some folks take it with branch water," Mat said in a flat voice with a tickle of a laugh under it. Up and down the river, fireworks boomed out.

Then, under the hot, fat sun of the late afternoon, the Rossiters began to sing. Urged on by half a dozen men who pushed him and pummeled him and joshed him along, an uncle, his face red with embarrassment, launched into "Oh, Don't You Remember Sweet Alice, Ben Bolt?" He had been chosen for his barbershop baritone; the company joined him; supported by their rising voices, he carried them along, deep into the melody. No sooner was the song finished than an ancient lady who could not have been a day younger than eighty sang out in a thin quaver: "Shall We Gather by the River?" Immediately everyone joined her; Sarsfield was astonished to hear the voices divide easily into the weird, thrilling harmony of the Southern mountains—four parts, then five parts—"the byoo-tiful, byoo-tiful river!" Kyle, who had never heard music remotely like that before, stared up at Sarsfield with his mouth agape. Once begun on hymns, the company moved right along into "Bringing in the Sheaves," and "Throw Out the Lifeline," and "Nearer My God to Thee," and "Rock of Ages."

There was a pause in which the next song had not yet risen spontaneously to anyone's lips. Sarsfield had positioned himself by his camera, the bulb in his hand; he almost opened the shutter then, but a voice in his mind said: "Not yet."

"Say, Paw, why don't you sing that old song from the war?" Mat Rossiter said to his father. "You know, the one about the poor rebel soldier."

"Well, I don't know," Tom said. He looked around with a baffled, melancholy expression.

"Oh, Daddy, do sing it," Emma said; and her mother said, "Go ahead, Thomas, it's such a pretty song."

A hush suddenly fell over the assembly. Sarsfield clearly remembered how the scene before him had been framed upon his ground glass; Tom Rossiter was standing just inside the boundary, to the far right of it, faced toward the camera; old Dan Rainey, in his rocker, sat in the background at the far left, turned toward the company, his face clearly visible; various of the people were arranged between these two poles; all were looking at Tom; behind everything, the river ran on. Tom cleared his throat, and then, hesitantly, began to sing: "I'm a poor rebel soldier, I'm a long way from home—" The entire company was struck immediately into a grave silence; the people stood as motionless as stones. Tom sang about marching north, into the land where the snows fall. Sarsfield almost made his exposure, but something said again: "Not yet."

"You tell 'em, Pop!" Clayborn Rossiter exclaimed; and his brother Mat slapped him on the back of the head so hard his teeth rattled.

Tom Rossiter closed his eyes, his face tilted back with the sun full on it; he looked as though he had forgotten where, and, perhaps, even *who* he was. He was singing out now in a voice powerful and true: "I'm a poor boy in trouble. I'm a long way from home."

Tom pressed his hand over his closed eyes and sang that last verse again. Sarsfield, his head spinning from the whiskey, felt the big day all around him, felt the eternal sun blazing on him; he closed his eyes so he could better hear the words: "Oh, the winds they do whistle—and the waters do moan. I'm a poor boy in trouble. I'm a long way from home."

Sarsfield opened his eyes, saw Kyle staring up at him in wonderment. Tom had fallen silent; he was looking down at his boots.

Mrs. Rossiter said, "Yes. Yes. Well," and mopped her face with her apron. It was so quiet that Sarsfield heard the wind in the trees. He looked out at the people. There was beautiful young Emma, her face flushed; there were all the uncles, aunts, cousins, and in-laws standing as though in prayer. There was his great-grandfather quietly rocking. Beyond them all, the river rolled by, slow and steady, on its way south. A sense of absolute rightness, of completion, of perfection welled up in Sarsfield; and, without conscious thought, he found that he had opened his shutter. He counted two seconds and allowed the shutter to close.

Someone began to sing: "God Be With You Till We Meet Again"; gratefully the company took it up.

Sarsfield was not drunk, but he felt the whiskey deeply; a hidden passageway in his mind seemed to have opened along with his shutter, and he felt America all around him. His own family now seemed effete and isolated and crazy; he hated the privilege that he had always taken as his natural birthright. He longed to walk through the fat fields of Pennsylvania, to float down the long, slow river, to vanish into the southern mountains or ride the rushing trains that tied the continent together,—to walk all the roads of the nation and see the yellow light of sad farm windows spilling out into an inky blue night. He imagined the graves of the Union and Confederate dead and felt the loss of those boys in a way that had never struck him before; the war that had killed them still seemed senseless to him, but the fact of their death was enormous. And now the life of a miner, a farmer, a man on the river seemed, somehow, preferable to his own—yet he knew he was bound to his own. And even as he felt all of this, so strongly and deeply, he knew that it was also false; that the America he longed for was one of his dreams—something deep in his heart, something yet to be born, something that had to be called into being—and that his only way to approach it was through his camera. He took Emma by the hand and walked with her to the river bank. He suddenly understood why he had been coming to see her night after night. He was filled with tears and did not trust himself. He spoke without planning it: "Emma, will you marry me?"

He looked down at her, astonished. For the last several hours he had hardly been aware of her at all. He had, up until this moment, almost forgotten her. Now, once the words were out of his mouth, he knew that he could not recall them; he did not even know if he would wish to recall them if he could.

They walked together; Emma did not speak. It had gone twilight. Looking back, Sarsfield saw the figure of his great-grandfather as a small silhouette, absolutely featureless—the figures of the others, of his little brother and sister, and Mat and Tom and Mrs. Rossiter, and the aunts and uncles and cousins and in-laws—as small silhouettes, absolutely featureless. He heard crickets and frogs. Up and down the river, the fireworks continued; the boom and crash proclaimed the birth of a nation that Sarsfield found sad and mysterious, maddening and beautiful, his own—and yet totally beyond reason, beyond understanding.

"Sarsfield," Emma said. "I am deeply touched and honored." She spoke slowly, her voice as formal as if she were already saying her wedding vows. "I will marry you—if my father will give us his blessing."

On the Fifth of July, Sarsfield woke before dawn with a fearsome hangover and a heart filled with misgivings. Except for the formidable resonance of his father's snoring, the house was silent. Sarsfield shaved and dressed and took a strong dose of headache powder; he walked down Front Street toward Emma's. With every step, he damned Mat Rossiter and his "old yeller moon": Sarsfield had been back to the demijohn far too often. "Middletons should never drink," he told himself grimly once again.

The sun, just risen, promised another hot morning; the low rays struck the rear of the Rossiter house, cut through to the sidewalk on either side. The clarity of the light was so intense that Sarsfield drew in a sharp breath and stopped to stare. He was amazed at how each drop of dew—of the infinity of drops that bejeweled the grass stems, the cob webs, even the wicker-work of a chair left out all night—was a perfect globe that gave back the wonder of pure white light. Strange as it seemed, this household of early risers appeared to be slumbering as profoundly as if an enchantment had been cast over it; and Sarsfield could not, for the life of him, understand why he had come at that hour; then, following an impulse he knew to be wholly irrational, he walked around the side of the house directly into the brilliance of the new day. A multitude of tiny, corruscate gnats rose at his step and sailed away like fairy dust. Emma, barefoot, wearing a white cotton gown elaborately smocked at the throat, her hair still braided for sleeping, turned toward him, her eyes large with the sun behind her. She was feeding the chickens. "Oh, Sarsfield," she said in a voice just above a whisper, "you've caught me again." In spite of her words, she did not appear surprised to see him. "Let me go get dressed," she said, but made no move to do so.

"It doesn't matter," he said, speaking just as quietly as she had. He felt awkward, unsure of himself in this hushed, glowing world that should have been entirely familiar—but was, instead, a secretive and magical kingdom. Afraid of breaking the spell, he stepped slowly forward and deliberately kissed her on the forehead. She looked up shyly, then away. Something had changed between them—something subtle yet profound; they both felt it. "I couldn't sleep," he said.

"Neither could I," she said; and then, with a single, exuberant motion, she flung the last of the corn from her shallow basket; pecking chickens immediately converged at her feet. He had held her in his arms before, but never uncorseted; and he could not help but feel the yielding softness of her supple young body; deep within him, the life force responded powerfully; and he released her immediately. She regarded him with astonished eyes; a deep flush rose to her cheeks. "Oh, Sarsfield," she said, "I am only seventeen!"

"We don't have to get married right away," he said.

Emma looked out at the river where the sun was burning off the mist. She had known that he would appear when he did and walk toward her with the sun full on his face. If she could have done so, she would have married him that very day; but she required her father's permission. She did not want to speak to her father—to make the serious, formal request—until she was certain he would say yes; she knew that once he said no, he could never be induced to change his mind. "Let us not rush into things," she said.

"No, we wouldn't want to rush into things," he said.

She took his hand and led him away from the view of the back windows. Her little feet, he saw, were white and slender with elegantly high arches. "Stay for church with us," she said, whispering.

"I can't, really, I'm sorry. I always take Mother and the children out to the First Presbyterian—Why don't you come with us?"

She was just on the point of exclaiming how nice that would be when she remembered his horrid little sister. "Oh, Lord," she thought, "why can't everything stay like this,—perfect like this, forever?" Soon she would have to try to square things with that hateful child. "They're counting on me today," she said. And then, suddenly, they both felt the danger of their situation. "Mama never sleeps in," she exclaimed, "never!"

"Shall I come back tonight?" he asked.

"Not tonight—wait for a day or two. Please?"

"Yes, of course." He kissed her quickly and fled.

He was already walking quickly up Front Street when he heard her urgent voice behind him: "Sarsfield!" He turned and saw her standing near the front of the house; the sunlight blazing at her back turned her into a hazy, brilliant figure of gold and white. "I swear, Sarsfield," she called to him, "I'll make you a good wife!"

8

Sarsfield woke and fought for his life;—he fought to beat his way free of this horrible, nameless thing that was pressing him down, smothering him, choking the breath out of him. The sensation was as though a hundred thick, hot, wet blankets had been spread over his face and chest,—as though some monstrous, infinitely heavy living being had thrown itself on top, determined to hang on, to press down, to crush out not merely life but even the last vestige of immortal soul. Sarsfield flung the covers away, sprang from the bed, and thrust his head through the open window. It was not yet dawn; but the peeping of a multitude of birds told him that the first light was not far off; he breathed deeply of the warm summer air. Being damned to hell would have been preferable to what he had just experienced, for he had felt as though he were being pressed into nothingness.

Sarsfield dressed and walked, as he had so often before, along the river. This had been the worst nightmare he had experienced since he had been a small boy; and, in some mysterious fashion, it appeared to have opened a flood-gate in his mind through which poured memories that he would have done anything in his power to circumvent. Whenever Sarsfield met any of those happy souls who pronounced childhood a blessed state, he was thrown into puzzlement, for, to him, childhood was a time of life that he had wished, even as a child, to leave rapidly and firmly behind him,—a time that, once he had left it, he preferred never to recall. But now he remembered, with an uncanny clarity, the feeling of his father's hands as they seized him under his arms and lifted him high into the air;—*he is wearing a plaited skirt and it swishes up with the motion; he arrives on the bar in Nolan's saloon; he can feel the polished wood under his thighs; he can see the men staring at him—big, rough workmen; he can see their smiles. His father's voice booms out: "Well, gentlemen, here's my boy; what the devil d'you think of him?" He cannot stand all the eyes looking at him; he stares down at his patent leather boots; but he can still hear their voices: "Fine boy, Jack! Yes, sir, a fine boy!" The men are not laughing; but he knows that he's a laughing-stock nonetheless. Then he is lying in his bed, the covers pulled over him, as he hears terrible grunting noises torn from his father's guts, hears his mother screaming. Then he is with Julia again, not as she had been in New York or Newport, but standing by Rainey's Creek; her huge deep-blue eyes are turned toward him as she says: "Let's play at kissing like grown-ups."*

These memories were accompanied by a feeling of profound morbidity, an unmistakable sense of something terribly wrong; Sarsfield knew that he must not dwell upon these memories, that he must put them forcibly from him, but he did not know how; he kept walking, urging himself on to an ever increasing tempo. Remembering his childhood trick of doing mathematical problems to calm himself, he imagined a young student before him who knew nothing of photography, imagined that he had at his disposal a vast blackboard; then, in a detailed mental rehearsal, he took up chalk, drew the camera, the lens, the lines of the light as they were refracted and focused on the plate; and thus, explaining the entire process from the exposure to the print, he walked over Raysburg Hill, turned and walked back. By the time that he was recrossing the Suspension Bridge, the vivid memories—along with the irrational, unhealthy feeling that had accompanied them—had left him. He did not know what had caused the morbid state to arise; but he knew that the only cure for it was precisely what had always worked in the past: the most strenuous of activity, the full reliance on his rational faculties, and the careful avoidance of unhealthy thoughts.

When he walked into the house, Sarsfield saw that his father was eating breakfast. Sarsfield took out a single dollar greenback and laid it firmly down onto the table. Jack looked up with a sudden, brilliant grin: "You'll have to hump yourself, boy," he said.

"I am well aware of that, Father," Sarsfield replied.

Jack had already had the papers drawn up; they signed them the next afternoon. Sarsfield decided to leave his father's ostentatious sign (J. C. MIDDLETON AND SONS, PHOTOGRAPHERS, EST. 1873); but he ordered a smaller one to hang beneath it: SARSFIELD MIDDLETON, SOLE PROPRIETOR, PHOTOGRAPHS IN FULL COLOR.

Since the Rossiters' picnic, a full week had passed before Sarsfield turned his attention once again to Emma; he had concluded by then that he was in no more hurry to marry than she appeared to be,—and, as further time went by, that they might decide not to marry after all. They hardly knew each other; and the profound differences between their backgrounds and social positions should not be discounted. One thing was certain: they should not rush matters. But he felt, despite all of his thorough ratiocination, an irrational sense of misgiving as he approached the Rossiter house. Emma appeared delighted to see him, however; and his spirits lifted at once.

They sat on the glider and drank lemonade. "Have you talked to your father yet?" he asked her, hoping that she had not.

She looked away toward the river, her expression unreadable. "No," she replied after a moment; "not yet." Then, turning toward him, she said: "Please don't press me, Sarsfield. Things have to take their own time."

"That's right," he said reassuringly; "We have all the time in the world."

She smiled in obvious relief, settled into the crook of his arm; then, by unspoken mutual consent, they kissed. "Everything's going to work out just fine," he told himself.

Sarsfield might not have felt so optimistic, however, if he had known what Emma was thinking: that she wanted to marry as soon as she could, and that the only thing stopping her was her father.

The summer wore on; and Emma watched Tom Rossiter as diligently as a hound watches a rabbit hole. The day he heard the news that the A. F. of L. had come out for Bryan, Tom Rossiter held forth at the dinner table for nearly an hour. The American people must surely see the handwriting on the wall by now, he said; big Bill Taft was a decent man, but there was no getting around it: he was still a Republican (Sarsfield was not dining with them that evening), and the Republicans could talk all they wanted to about busting trusts and being "progressive," but everybody knew they was in the pocket of big business. The country wanted a change, that much was certain; and the Democrats was the ones who really cared about the little guy; and the country desperately needed Bryan, and this time around, he had him a danged good chance at it— why, with the unions behind him, and the farmers behind him—*and the good old solid South behind him!*—then, Lord willing, maybe the honest working man would get him a welcome break in November. And Emma saw her father so full of hope and high-spirits that she almost asked him then; but a voice of caution told her to wait.

Then she picked up *The Raysburg Times* and read that Thaddeus Eberhardt, just the night before, had delivered a fiery speech for Taft to the members of the Kyle Rainey Club; amongst his many remarks, "Major" Eberhardt (as, according to the paper, his most intimate friends fondly called him) had said that if any honest working man were to cast his mind back to the bread lines of the Cleveland administration, he would, at once, be freed from the lunatic notion that voting for a Democrat could ever lead to anything other than the total and instantaneous devastation of the entire American economy; later in his speech, he reminded his listeners that the Republican Party was not only the party of Teddy Roosevelt, it was the party of Abraham Lincoln, and told them that a vote for Taft was a vote for "the shining ideals for which so many of us fought, and bled, and died." Emma threw the paper back down on the glider and thought: "No; tonight's not the night."

Sarsfield was content for things to continue in much the way they had before he had proposed and Emma had accepted; he knew that if he wished to back away from the prospect of marriage, however, now was the time to do it; all it would take would be to stop calling, and Emma would quickly get the message. Yet, instead of doing that, he now spent most of his evenings with the Rossiters. Emma's family, so far as he knew, liked him well enough; but something in the careful, distant formality with which Tom Rossiter proffered his amiabilities, suggested that the old Southerner was not entirely delighted with the prospect of Sarsfield Middleton as a son-in-law. In the meantime, Sarsfield and Emma were still getting to know each other (so he told himself);—and they still could, at any time, decide that they had been premature, foolish;—but also there was no good reason why they should not continue to enjoy their long, tender kisses in the summer moonlight.

Sarsfield had, just as he had planned, thrown himself into vigorous activity; but now he appeared to be running out of steam. His days were taken up with worries about the business that he had so suddenly and unexpectedly acquired. He knew that soon he must again pay Miss Calendene, and there were not sufficient funds to do so. Sarsfield studied the books and saw (his father had taken no pains whatsoever to hide it) that Jack had skimmed off every loose penny and left behind no operating capital whatsoever. Each morning Sarsfield arrived at the shop promptly at eight and found Miss Calendene there ahead of him,—doing what she always did when she had nothing to do: cleaning the reception area. He had long ago finished up all the left-over photographic work; now he sat musing at the roll-top desk where the accounts were kept, or he poked around in dusty corners wondering if he should throw out the junk his father had accumulated over the years,—while Miss Calendene dusted or swept or polished the front window; the squeak of her vinegar-soaked rag was enough to drive him mad, but he could not find it in himself to tell her to stop. She had nothing to do—and *he* had nothing to do—because no one was walking through the door asking for a photograph.

Sarsfield now owned the whole building and everything in it; eventually he decided that it was incumbent upon him to see exactly what it was he owned. He began with the huge, cluttered storage area at the back of the shop. There he found a half-dozen old broken cameras that Jack had been planning to repair and sell—the same cameras that Sarsfield had seen when he had last visited this neglected store-room some nearly twenty years before. He found an ancient Voitlander shaped like a fat telescope, an instrument that must already have been antiquated when Jack had arrived in seventy-three; it was a museum piece, and he decided to display it in the front window. He found dozens of boxes stuffed with hundreds of glass negatives—probably of every photograph his father had ever taken; there was nothing to do with these but leave them in storage. He found all the equipment and supplies necessary to make tintypes and wet plates (more museum pieces!); and several hundred tubes of oil paint, all of them dried to the consistency of granite (these he threw away). He found stacks of badly faded commercial portraits of Lillian Russell, President Lincoln, and President Grant; ancient "dodgers" advertising a special, once-in-a-lifetime price on *Portraits of The Whole Family Colored by Hand!*;—and none of these mementoes of his father's business could he bear to part with. And then, while poking about amongst these useless artifacts, Sarsfield found, buried under pictures of the Suspension Bridge, the photograph of the whore.

The word was not one that Sarsfield ordinarily used, certainly not in speech, and not even in his thoughts; but the moment he laid eyes upon the picture, the word sprang unbidden into his mind: *whore*—for that was, quite obviously, what the young girl was. There were some dozen prints; Jack must have sold them,—but to whom, Sarsfield wondered, and for how much? And he had the sudden conviction that old Jim Greer, the mayor, and the Sheriff, and the Chief of Police,—and, in fact, every one of the good, old Republican boys of Jack's age had, most likely, each his own copy of this photograph secreted away for his private delectation.

The setting, Sarsfield suspected, must be one of the rooms in Mrs. Smith's notorious house; the girl wore the short, curve-front corset of the seventies laced cruelly tight, and long ribbed stockings, and pumps with high French heels, and a loose gown hanging open, and nothing else beyond her face-paint. She had taken her weight upon one plump leg, raised the other, her knees pressed together, in a coy pose turned just slightly away from the camera; her expression was not in the least lascivious, but rather one that might have been worn by any pretty girl still in her teens who was about to break out into a fit of the giggles. For once Jack Middleton's name had not been stamped in gold on the bottom of the photograph,—although everything about it—from the stiff pose of the subject, to the dazzle from the flash powder reflected on the wall, to the indifferent printing—proclaimed it as Jack's work. And, indeed, Jack's blurred hand could be seen at the far left side of the pic-ture,—thrust out as he had counted off the exposure on his fingers: a ridiculous mistake that far too often marred the work of the great J. C. Middleton, photographer.

"Maybe Julia was right about me," Sarsfield thought; "maybe I am a prude." Staring at the picture, he had actually broken out into a sweat. The most shocking thing was not the young prostitute's state of disha-bille—although that was shocking enough—but rather the thoroughgo-ing work of depilation that had been done on the small, tender triangle that was the most private portion of the poor girl's anatomy. "Merciful heaven," Sarsfield thought, "the old man would sell *anything*!"

Then, later, after Sarsfield had absorbed the shock of his discovery, he thought wryly that if the Eberhardts had a motto and it was: "Sow your gold where it will best grow," then the Middletons should have one too, which could be: "Make your buck any way you can."

Sarsfield had put his nightmare of earlier in the summer firmly out of his mind. He knew that the scientific understanding of the chemical and electrical states of the human brain was still rudimentary; but he was certain that his terrifying experience must have been the result of a momentary aberration arising from purely physical causes,—for, since he had instituted a regimen of long, brisk walks, simple food, and cheerful, optimistic thoughts, his sleep had been healthy and sound. But now he had another nightmare—much like the first: he was being smothered, crushed. This time the sensations were less intense; and he fought his way free of them more quickly. When his rational faculties returned and he could examine his mental state with a cool detachment, he was surprised to find himself inexplicably angry at the situation in which he found himself.

"I'm an educated man," he thought; "Good Lord, I've got a Harvard degree! And I'm one of the best photographers in America. There's only a handful of people in the world who know as much about color photography as I do. Why the devil should I have to chase my tail around town like a patent medicine salesman?" But, after an hour of such self-justifying ruminations, another voice in his mind suddenly interrupted him: "Hey!" it said; "That won't wash, kid. Get on with it."

He returned home, bathed, and dressed carefully. He stopped for a "singe" at the barber shop at the end of the bridge, bought a *boutonnière* at the florist's, had the shoe-shine boy on Short Market slap a good coat of gleaming polish onto his boots, purchased half a dozen of the finest Eberhardt coronas. He burst into the shop by nine-thirty and, to the thoroughly startled Miss Calendene, said: "Look, we haven't got any up-to-date catalogues from Eastman. Send 'em a telegram. Get 'em to ship everything they got out to us today—C.O.D."

Having delivered that message, Sarsfield went rapidly on his way to see Jimmy Schenk, the sign-painter; he ordered a huge board for the side of the Middleton building listing all the services to be newly offered to the amateur photographer; then he strode over to *The Times* and commissioned a series of advertisements to run in the Sunday papers for the next six months. His final stop of the morning was at the printing company of Hollowell and Frankhauser; he insisted upon seeing old Tim Hollowell in person. "Your color work—" Sarsfield burst out before the old printer could get the ink wiped from his hands, "who makes your plates?"

"Why—I do 'em myself," came the amazed response.

"So let's say you got something you want to do up right, a pretty water color painting, say—how many printings would it take you?"

The old man stared at Sarsfield over his spectacles, a look of puzzlement on his face. "I don't know," he said; "Depends on the job—four if you're real lucky, sometimes five, six—"

"If I made color-selection negatives for you, you'd get it in three every time," Sarsfield said.

The look on the printer's face changed from bemusement to annoyance; he summarized his reaction in one word: "Bullshit." Then, in deference to the fact that he was addressing Thaddeus Eberhardt's grandson, he added: "Look here, Sarsfield, I know you been to Harvard and all, but I was mixing colors before you was born, and believe me, you can't get her on three. That old three-color theory just doesn't hold up when you try to put her in practice.—Why, shit, you can't even get a decent black!"

Sarsfield could not suppress a grin. "Forgive me, sir," he replied, "if I differ with you on that. I can mix you a black you won't be able to tell from lamp-black."

The blood mounted to the printer's face; and, for a moment, Sarsfield was afraid that he was about to be thrown bodily from the shop; but then Hollowell must have decided that the only proper reaction to such lunacy was derisive amusement; he shook his head and laughed. "Five bucks says you can't."

"You're on. Show me your inks."

Sarsfield selected a transparent yellow, a peacock blue, and a crimson lake. "Hell, son," the printer said in disgust, "you ain't even got your primaries right. You need a cobalt blue and a real scarlet—"

"I'm sorry to differ with you again, sir," Sarsfield said in his most gentle and persuasive tone, "but science says you need *minus* red and *minus* green, and that's what I'm giving you." As he mixed his inks, he went on to explain the subtractive theory of color mixing; he explained it in considerable detail. Then he moved on to a thorough discussion of dollars and cents, pointing out to the printer the great savings possible when the guess work—the tedious trial and error method—was eliminated from the printing process and replaced by the reliability of science. He clinched his argument by suggesting that a portion of the savings could be passed on to the customer, thus enabling the firm of Hollowell and Frankhauser to beat the price of any other printer in the Ohio Valley.

To complete the demonstration, Sarsfield had proofs pulled from carbon black as well as his own black. The proofs were passed around the shop; and not a single employé could tell the one from the other. "I'll be damned," Hollowell exclaimed, produced a five-dollar bill and passed it over. "Look here, Middleton," he said, "I ain't going to guarantee you anything, but the next fancy color job I get, I'll give you a crack at it."

"That's all I'm asking for," Sarsfield said with a smile.

That day Sarsfield took his lunch at the Kyle Rainey Club—along with merchants and businessmen and the better class of salesmen; with bankers, brokers, and at least one financier; with managers from the mills; with doctors, lawyers, accountants, real estate agents, and the editor of *The Raysburg Times*; with the Sheriff of Ohio County and Raysburg's Chief of Police—in short, with the good, solid Republicans who made the city the energetic, booming metropolis it was. Looking for a likely prospect, Sarsfield walked around the vast, gloomy dining room; he managed a smile and a cheery word for everyone he knew (and he knew everyone),—and found that it was not anywhere near as odious a task as he had expected. He saw, at a corner table, several councilmen and Jim Greer, the corrupt old mayor—a man Sarsfield had always despised. "Gentlemen, gentlemen, good day," Sarsfield said as he joined them. "Any recommendations for the fare?"

The expression on the mayor's face said, clearly: "Now what the devil do you want?"; but, after a moment, he suggested that Sarsfield might try the veal.

At a lull in the conversation, Sarsfield said in the most hale-and-hearty voice he could muster: "Mr. Mayor, isn't it about time that a man in your position had a fine, new portrait made?"

The Mayor gave Sarsfield a dubious look. "Your father done one up for me a few years back," he replied.

Sarsfield reminded himself that the only reason Jim Greer was the Mayor of Raysburg was because the Republican "machine" owned him—and that the largest single contributor to the Republican Party in Raysburg was Thaddeus Eberhardt. "I'm sure he made a first-rate picture for you, Mr. Mayor," Sarsfield said, smiling, "but I'll bet you anything it's not in full, natural color."

In August, Mrs. Rossiter received a formal invitation from Mrs. Thaddeus Eberhardt: the presence of Mr. and Mrs. Rossiter and their daughter, Emma Lee, was requested at the Eberhardts' annual lawn party on the second Saturday in September, R. S. V. P. "Lord save us, what am I supposed to do with this?" she wailed, waving the white card in the air.

"Not for a million dollars would I set foot on that man's property," Tom said.

Emma was too astonished to say anything; she was not naïve enough to believe that the Eberhardts had decided to welcome her into their family with open arms. She asked Sarsfield what it meant. Sarsfield did not know what it meant; but he did not care for the sound of it. He asked his father what it meant.

Time hung heavy on Jack Middleton's hands now that he had joined the saintly proponents of sobriety; pleased at the prospect of distraction, he threw down the newspaper. Father and son trimmed cigars and, smoking them, took a turn around Belle Isle. "Could they be softening up on their position?" Sarsfield asked.

"Not a chance in hell of that," Jack said. "Look here, boy, let me tell you what's what. Your mother goes out there and unburdens herself to your grandmother every week or two, so old Amanda knows damn well you're still seeing the Rossiter girl."

"Oh," Sarsfield thought, "of course." And he reminded himself that there had also been all those invitations to the Staubs' that he had refused—some three or four of them—sending some lame excuse or other; so his grandmother must know by now that her plan of matching him to Lenore was not working.

"All right," Sarsfield said to his father, "so they don't want me to see Emma—so why on earth did they invite her and her family—?"

"To show everybody just how unsuitable it is," Jack replied.

"Unsuitable?"

"You're goddamned right. Listen, you've been going to those damn lawn parties for years, Sarsfield; you know what they're like. All the Eberhardts—and the Revingtons and the Staubs and every other benighted soul in this two-bit town who thinks his shit don't stink— as the plain folk around here put it—and everybody standing around with hundreds of dollars worth of clothes on their backs, trying to think of something sophisticated to say, while a bunch of dressed-up niggers pass around 'horses' doovers' on silver trays—So how d'you suppose Tom Rossiter's going to fit in with that? Suppose he owns a monkey suit for a 'do' like that? Figure he'll go out and buy one? And how about little Emma? Think she'll know what to say to people like your sappy cousins? No, the whole point of it is to make it plain as day that you should never marry the girl."

"Good lord," Sarsfield said. He knew that his father was right. "What on earth should I do?"

There was a long pause in which both father and son considered the singular fact that this was the first time in his adult life when Sarsfield had ever solicited his father's advice on any matter whatsoever. "You going to marry her?" Jack asked.

"I don't know," Sarsfield answered honestly; "I might."

"Well, if you think you might, then, you tell that old Southerner to put on his best Sunday-go-to-meetin' suit, and his wife to put on her best bonnet, and you take that girl out there, and you just brazen it out,—and Thaddeus and Amanda can choke on it!"

Sarsfield thought over his father's advice; he saw no need to subject Tom and his wife to the humiliation the Eberhardts had planned for them; but, if it turned out that he did marry Emma, then, by God, the Eberhardts were going to have to get used to the idea. "Be careful," he cautioned her. "They mean you no good will by this. It will require a thick skin."

Inwardly Emma blanched; but bravely she said: "Oh, I got plenty of practice for that at Raysburg High." She thought over Sarsfield's advice and told her mother that she would prefer that her parents stay home. In bed, Mrs. Rossiter said to her husband: "She's afixing to go with the Middleton boy to that muckety-muck thing. Should I tell her not to?"

"No," Tom said. "Let her go. Let her see for herself how she'll never fit in with them people."

"She doesn't want us to go with her."

"Oh, she don't, huh?" Tom was furious; all the minor aggravations of the last year or so—the twenty-four button gloves, and the mail-order corset, and the ungodly expensive fabrics Emma used to run off her dresses, and the five pairs of shoes when one would do, and the times he'd caught the foolish girl giving herself airs—all suddenly added up to one big aggravation. "Ashamed of us, is she? Well, you just tell her we're going. We're as good as anybody, and we're a damned sight better than that fat old kraut for all his millions."

Jack's assessment of the situation had been quite accurate; what he did not know, however, was that Thaddeus Eberhardt was firmly opposed to the scheme. "I have never, since the war," Thaddeus said to his wife, "knowingly sat at the same table with a Democrat."

"You won't have to sit with him," Amanda said. "You'll just have to stand with him—and I guess you can manage that all right."

"Well, Mother. I don't like this. I don't like it at all."

Thaddeus sat and fumed; but he knew that it was not going to do him any good whatsoever. He was not in the best of spirits to start with because his stomach was bothering him again; he had experienced considerable difficulty with it of late; and tonight, once again, something was not digesting properly. He could feel the pain spreading all the way through the left side of his body,—all the way up into his left shoulder. He wanted to press his hand firmly under his ribs where the pain was the worst; but he restrained himself from doing so because he did not want to worry his wife.

Thaddeus and Amanda were hidden away behind closed doors in the library, doing what they generally did when alone: Amanda was steadily knitting, a habit she had acquired in her Rainey girlhood and maintained ever after—no matter how unsuitable such a practice might be to Mrs. Thaddeus Eberhardt; and Thaddeus had settled down to his reading; although still fully dressed even to his jacket, he had removed his boots and stockings and was resting his tiny, aching, flat, bare feet on a hassock. He looked over at his wife and wished, as he had often over the years, that Amanda had found for herself a pastime somewhat less like that of Madame Defarge (she bore too much of a resemblance to that fictional personage as it was). Throughout the war, Amanda had provided him an endless supply of Union-blue socks; no matter where he had served—from Missouri to Washington—the packages of socks always caught up with him; his fellow officers had ragged him half to death about them; he had, he guessed, a few pairs of those socks still.

"No, I don't like it," Thaddeus said to his wife again, more firmly this time. "What am I supposed to say to him?"

"It doesn't matter a damn what you say to him. The point ain't to entertain that damned family of hill-billies, the point is for everybody to see how plain foolish—"

"I know, I know. But I can't invite someone to my home and not act the host—"

"Act any way you please," Amanda said abruptly, closing the conversation.

The main reason why the Eberhardts had maintained for fifty years what they both believed to be an excellent marriage was that they had, from the beginning, firmly divided their responsibilities: Thaddeus was in charge of business affairs, Amanda of domestic. Not only was his opinion on the matter of the lawn party of no import; he had stepped far out of bounds even to voice it at all. He sighed. "I suppose I could talk to him about the war," he said; she did not deign to answer.

The war still fascinated and perplexed Thaddeus Eberhardt; he spent most of his meager spare time reading about it; even now, every few months or so, he still awoke from terrible dreams in which he was back in the army. His business associates sometimes called him "Major"—which genuinely embarrassed him. He had admitted it to no one, not even to his wife, but the greatest sorrow of his life was that he had not been able to do more for the Union cause.

Thaddeus had been twenty-four when the war broke out; by then he had assumed most of the duties of managing his father's iron works; and, when he talked of joining the army, his father would hear none of it. Thaddeus argued for honor and justice and the righteousness of the Union cause; Karl Eberhardt replied by reminding Thaddeus that he had two small children at home and suggesting that he could best serve the Union cause by seeing to it that the production of good wrought-iron plate did not slacken. Neither could convince the other. One could gauge how angry Karl was by the percentage of German in his speech; father and son had been at it the better part of the evening when the old man finally shouted out his last word on the matter: *"Du sollst nicht!"*

"Ich kann nicht anders!" Thaddeus shouted back (and didn't realize until he was alone in his bed that night that he had inadvertently quoted Martin Luther).

As Raysburg's iron king, Karl Eberhardt had long strings that led to Washington; and, if he could not keep his son out of the war, he could at least make certain that his son survived it. Despite the fact that he had no military training whatsoever, Thaddeus found himself commissioned Second Lieutenant and, because he could speak good German, assigned as aide-de-camp to the befuddled General Sigel. He did not like General Sigel; and the general did not like him and gave him nothing whatsoever to do. At Wilson's Creek in Missouri, he watched, amazed, as Sigel mistook Confederate troops for Federal, became enfiladed and then routed. Thaddeus, home on leave, suggested to his father that the famous Dutchmen's slogan "I fights mit Sigel" should be amended to "I runs mit Sigel." He begged his father to get him transferred.

To his son's astonishment, Karl complied; having done nothing noticeable to advance the Union cause, Thaddeus then found himself a First Lieutenant in the largely German-speaking XI corps (although his own men, Ohio farm boys, spoke not one word of German). Thaddeus discovered soon enough that the XI Corps was reputed to be unsound and so was generally kept in reserve and not expected to see action. When their captain went home to do the spring planting, Thaddeus replaced him just in time to command his company at Chancellorsville when the XI Corps was flanked, overrun, and routed by Stonewall Jackson. Karl, alarmed that his son had actually been fired upon, pulled another string; and Thaddeus spent the remainder of the war in Washington with the Commissary General of Subsistence where, with a speed that was as rapid as it was mysterious, he rose to the rank of Major.

"I wonder who he fought with—" Thaddeus said.

"Who?" Amanda said. "That old Southerner? What earthly difference could it make who he fought with?"

Thaddeus knew that he could not possibly explain such matters to his wife, so he did not bother to try;—and thinking about the war, and his father, reminded him of dreaming about the war, which reminded him that he had recently dreamed about his father. Thaddeus had been wandering around the house in the middle of the night; it had been so real that, if someone had stopped him in the midst of his perambulations to inquire, he would have firmly held to the opinion that he was not dreaming at all, but fully awake and in command of his faculties— this in spite of the fact that he *never* wandered around the house in the middle of the night.

He had entered the drawing room and known at once that someone was sitting in the high, wing-backed chair; because the chair had been turned away from the center of the room and faced outward toward the window, the identity of this person had not been readily apparent. Thaddeus, suppressing an irrational and unmanly sense of dread, had walked around the chair to say a sharp word to this intruder who had been so bold as to reverse the proper direction of the chair— and had discovered his father.

In real life, Karl Eberhardt had been a short man, barely five-feet-four, although of such a powerful physique, with such a thick neck and broad bull-like shoulders, that people always supposed him to be taller than he was; in the dream, Karl looked much as he had in the last few years before he died,—except that he had inexplicably become even shorter: he was, in fact, so little that his feet did not reach the floor. He looked up at his son with an expression that bespoke both sorrow and anger, and made his characteristic noise of disapproval: "Tsk, tsk, tsk."

Thaddeus was astonished; he had been certain that his father was dead; he stopped stock-still and gazed at the old man in some perplexity. "Ach, Thaddeus, was hast Du getan?" Karl Eberhardt asked; and Thaddeus woke up.

"What d'you mean, what have I done?" Thaddeus now mentally addressed his dead father. "All I've ever done my whole life is exactly what you taught me to do: 'Streue die Gulden wo sie am besten gedeihen!'—and I've made a packet, believe you me! We own fifty times more than when you were alive—Lord, no, a hundred times! I can't help it that Henry made more money than I did. Henry also took damned sight bigger risks than I would ever have taken; dozens of times he could have lost it all—" Then Thaddeus stopped, for he sensed, he was not sure how, that his father was not impressed.

There was more that Thaddeus wanted to say to his dead father, but he was not certain exactly what it was. No one ever pronounced his name in German these days; but he could hear his father's voice: "Ach, Tah-dé-us—" He looked over at his wife; she looked up and met his eyes. "You eat too much, Teddy," she said; and he discovered that his hand had betrayed him; unbeknownst to him, it had crept up to press the spot where the fiery pain was at its worst. "You know what Doc Anderson told you," Amanda said severely; Thaddeus saw the fear in his wife's eyes.

"I know, Mother; I'll do better," he said and forced his hand back into his lap. "Nothing but custards and bread-puddings for a few days," he said; "That should do it."

There was no sound in the room now but the click of Amanda's knitting needles. "The children are well provided for," Thaddeus told his dead father, "and the grandchildren too. The house is in order;—Schlaf gut, mein Vater, alles ist in Ordnung."

Sarsfield had almost become accustomed to seeing Jack sober; he had almost decided that, mirabile dictu, he might possibly grow to like the man;—but, from time to time, he wondered how long it could last.

Could the old bastard manage to stay sober forever? But then something like the old "black mood" began to descend upon Jack. "Did ya see 'em there!" Jack shouted out, seizing Sarsfield by his arm.

"Who, Father?" He turned to look in the direction Jack was pointing: down the alleyway behind the shop, toward Howell's livery stable. Sarsfield saw nothing whatsoever out of the ordinary.

"That Irishman!" Jack shouted; his black eyes darting from side to side; "That damned skinny Irishman. He was right there, leaning on the side of the building!"

All Sarsfield could see on the side of the building was the shadow cast by the afternoon sun. "You must have imagined it, Father," he said. "There's nobody there."

"He was there—just a second ago, damn it! What the hell's he doing there spying on me—the son-of-a-bitch! Well, I'll get him. He can't get away with it. This is America, by God!—The damn Fenian shall find that out quick enough." And with that, Jack strode off down the alley at a frantic pace, his walking stick swinging, leaving his son to stare after him.

The problem, Sarsfield thought, was that his father had nothing to do. Jack still talked vaguely of his "investments"; he rose just as early as he had his entire working life, dressed just as carefully, and walked to town; he appeared to be passing his time in either the Kyle Rainey Club or at the Raysburg Stock Exchange; but he had given up his business, and he had given up drinking; what, after all, was left? One evening Sarsfield came home to discover that his father was hiding in the basement. "What the devil you doing down here, Father?"

Jack was huddled in a corner, his arms wrapped around his knees; he stared up with terrified eyes. "They're plotting against me," he muttered in a hoarse voice; "You've got to do something, Son. It's those goddamned black Irish—I want 'em off my land!"

It took Sarsfield some time to extract his father's meaning from the torrent of incoherent words. Jack had spent some days watching the O'Haras; he had seen them, so he said, talking to "that damned skinny Irishman"; he was convinced that they were about "to have another rising and burn the house down and murder us all in our beds." Sarsfield urged his father to his feet and led him out of the basement; he reminded Jack that the O'Haras had worked for the Middletons for twenty years and had never displayed anything but the utmost loyalty.

"That's the way they are," Jack whispered, "devious as snakes." Then, suddenly, he shouted out: "Did ya hear that!"

"Hear what?" Sarsfield asked in some exasperation.

"The whistle. The damn Irishman's whistle!"

"Now you listen to me, Father. What you heard was the train on the B 'n' O line all the way over in Center Raysburg."

Then, in late August, in that period of oppressive heat known as "the dog-days"; on a terrible afternoon when there was not left on the deserted streets even a desperate memory of a breeze; at precisely the moment when the blistering, fiery sun was directly overhead so that he did not cast a shadow; Jack Middleton was seen ducking quickly into Nolan's saloon. He did not, as he ordinarily would have, stride forcefully through the swinging doors with a ready jibe for all; he slipped in so surreptitiously that the boys were immediately alerted, and, out of the corners of their eyes, followed Jack's furtive progress. They noted that, instead of taking up his usual position at the very center of the bar from whence he could survey the entire scene and project his torrent of words to every corner, Jack withdrew to a table in the dim, hot recesses far in the back; and there, silently, he removed his jacket. This was a phenomenon so rare that the boys gave up all pretense of disinterest and turned to stare; afterward, many said that they had never before seen Jack Middleton in his shirt-sleeves. "'Tis a terrible hot day," the bartender observed. "Will you take a lemonade, Mr. Middleton?"

The boys in the bar held their collective breath as Jack pondered this suggestion. "I do believe, Patrick," he said slowly, quietly, "the day being what it is—that I will take a small glass of beer."

The first Sarsfield knew of his father's fall from grace was when he was walking home that night from Emma's and heard the frantic pounding of hooves on the Suspension Bridge. Jack's huge voice, rendered hoarse from hours of screaming, brayed out: "Ta-ra-ra, boom-de-ay!" Sarsfield stopped at the corner of Front and Rainey, watched as the sulky tore by as though his father were emulating the chariot race in Ben Hur. Jack was bent forward, his face cracked open into a murderous, lunatic grin, as he urged on his mare with a buggy whip. "Ta-ra-ra, BOOM-de-ay!" Jack howled.

Sarsfield kept on walking until he reached his own home, waited on the sidewalk to see if his father would reappear. In a moment, he heard the hoofbeats coming back; Jack must have galloped in a circle around Belle Isle. "Ta-ra-ra-ra, ra-ra RAH," Jack shouted, "boom-de boom-de BOOM-DE-AY!" He reined up abruptly, sprang from the sulky, and strode toward Sarsfield without giving a single thought to his lathered and blown mare. "There he is," Jack yelled out, "that wretched sneak-thief who calls himself my son."

Jack gestured grandly to the invisible multitude of appreciative shades who must instantly have sprung up. "But 'thief' is too fair a word for such as he," Jack hissed, "this miserable, wretched, lying, conniving little snake who did insinuate himself into my good graces, who did lie and dissemble—yes, who did lie in his teeth, his very teeth!—Who took advantage of my most grievous moment of doubt and weakness and despair, and who then, without a moment's hesitation, did jew me out of thirty-five years of hard, back-breaking, slavish labor!"

"Father, for God's sake," Sarsfield said.

"Father! He dares to call me 'Father'! Good God in heaven, what a travesty! The blackguard who struck his father full in the face—Such a black and cowardly deed has scarce been recorded in all the annals of perfidy—why, Brutus, Benedict Arnold, Judas Iscariot himself could scarce have stooped so low—why, the lowest scum that creeps in the rotting slime of the lowest bowels of the earth could scarce have—" and here Jack took a deep breath as a happy new thought struck him: "No son of mine, by God! *No son of mine!* A Jew must have fathered him, a crooked old Jew peddler—"

"Father, you disgust me," Sarsfield said, turned on heel and walked into the house.

"Judas got his thirty pieces of silver," Jack shouted after him, "but you did your foul deed for a dollar, a single foul and bloody dollar." Sarsfield did not look back; but he heard his father break into a shambling run to catch up. "All that I built and slaved for ripped from me in a trice," Jack bellowed. "For a dollar, a single dollar! Oh, Lord, how could this be? No son of mine, I tell you. An old pox-ridden Jew crept in when I was hard at work and fathered this monstrous freak of nature!"

Sarsfield took the stairs two at a time, his father hard at his heels. "Your jewed me out of the business, you miserable little prick!" his father shrieked.

Sarsfield slammed his bedroom door in his father's face and locked it. Out in the hallway, Jack leapt up and down like a little boy; he hammered the door with his walking stick and bawled out in a voice gleefully pleased with itself: "A kike! A kike! A hook-nosed sheenie!"

Sarsfield knew that if he unlocked the door and stepped out into the hallway, he would beat his father senseless. "You evil old bastard," he thought. "I will never trust you again. Never."

Jack stayed roaring drunk for several days; and then life returned to the old pattern: Jack was himself again; Jack was drinking again—in the old steady, daily, predictable way. On Monday morning, Sarsfield faced his father over the breakfast table; he was resolved to speak not a single word. Jack helped himself to an enormous mound of home fries, said: "Well, boy, how d'you like being a businessman—are you humping yourself?" When he heard no response, he looked up with a hard stare, said: "What the hell's the matter with you, son, got a burr up your arse?"

"He doesn't remember," Sarsfield thought in amazement. "Every single despicable word he said to me—it's all gone from his mind."

"Meant to tell you," Jack said, "you better get in to see the Sheriff. Back in April he was talking about some photographs for his campaign; and if you want his business, you'd best remind him."

"What's the use?" Sarsfield thought. "I will, father," he said. "Thank you."

Then, one Friday afternoon in early September, Sarsfield was astonished to discover an envelope with an Irish postage stamp lying unobtrusively on the table by the landing; it was addressed to Master Kyle Rainey Middleton. "By Jove," he thought, "it's from the Middletons of Wicklow!" He picked up the envelope, turned it over, and saw the Middleton crest; a sudden wave of irrational, idiotic, childish elation burst over him, and he thought: "It's true, by God! *We're aristocracy!*"

He set off immediately to find his little brother, located him on the river bank, settled down with him under the shade of a tree, and opened the letter. It was written in a difficult, looping, old-fashioned hand on the most immaculate of white bond paper. "Can you read it to me, Sars?" Kyle asked, "I can't quite make it out."

"Dear Master Middleton," Sarsfield read, "I am writing on behalf of your grandmother, and of the entire family, to convey to you how terribly pleased we were to receive your letter. You asked for an account of us, and I shall attempt to render one—albeit, in brief. Your father, although he has been absent from Ireland for many years now, is still well remembered—and remembered as a man with a great fondness for a jest—" and here Sarsfield began to snicker; but, when he saw the look on his brother's face, he resumed reading in his most serious manner: "a great fondness for a jest, which, perhaps, accounts for his having told you that the Middletons received their land in grant from Queen Elizabeth. The truth of the matter is that the first Middleton in Ireland, George, was a soldier with Oliver Cromwell and received his land—"

Sarsfield could not go on; it was too deliciously, ridiculously funny; he howled with laughter. "What?" Kyle demanded, "What's funny?"

With difficulty, Sarsfield controlled himself. "Well, you see," he explained, "Oliver Cromwell was just about as Protestant as you can get—and so what does Father name me, his first-born son?—Sarsfield. And Patrick Sarsfield was just about as Catholic as you can get; he fought against Protestant King William—"

He looked into his brother's dark eyes and saw no comprehension whatsoever. "Is that funny?" Kyle asked.

"Well, I suppose if you didn't laugh, you'd cry," Sarsfield replied and returned to reading the letter: "—received his land in County Wicklow in 1653 as payment for service—land which is still held by the Middleton family. The Middleton men have always been soldiers, and in every generation since the original George, at least one Middleton has served the Crown with distinction. You might find it of some interest to know that your father is not the first Middleton to cross the seas to America. Sir John Apley Middleton served with distinction with Sir William Howe in the American colonies in 1776—"

Again Sarsfield had to stop reading; he was laughing so hard he had to wipe his eyes; and again Kyle demanded an explanation: "What's funny? Tell me what's funny."

"Oh, one of our ancestors fought against the American Revolution, that's all."

"Is that funny?"

"No; I don't suppose it is, Kyle," Sarsfield replied; but he couldn't suppress another gale of whooping delight.

"Sarsfield!" Kyle exclaimed with growing annoyance.

Sarsfield took a deep breath and continued: "The Middleton men have traditionally been named either John or George, a fact which causes some considerable confusion even to those well versed in family history. My husband, your uncle, is George Middleton; his father was called George Middleton, and our eldest son is also called George Middleton—"

Sarsfield felt the letter slip from his fingers as he fell back against the tree. He clutched his sides, he doubled up, he rolled on the ground. Convulsed with laughter, he screamed and moaned. "What, what, what?" Kyle demanded; but Kyle's bewilderment only made Sarsfield laugh harder. "George," he managed to gasp out weakly, "they're all named George!" and that set him off again: "Oh, nooooo! They're all named Ge-ooorge!" He was sure if he couldn't stop laughing soon, something essential in his belly would snap clean in half.

Eventually Sarsfield sat up, mopped his streaming face with his handkerchief. He saw that his little brother was deeply offended. He picked up the letter, and, in the most serious tone he could manage, read the remainder of it which gave an account of the current Middleton family.

"Now," Kyle said, "you've got to tell me what was so funny."

"The hardest thing in the world," Sarsfield said, "is trying to explain what's funny to somebody who doesn't think it's funny.—Come on, we've got to get back for dinner."

They walked in silence as Kyle kicked at stones; then the little boy said: "Shucks, Sarsfield, you gotta as least *try* to tell me."

Sarsfield considered that request—and considered his father. The more he thought about it, the less humorous it seemed; he felt his old anger returning like a freshly-stoked fire. "Remember when you called him a liar?" he asked his little brother. "Well, you were right. And I guess that was what was so funny—to see it in black and white like that and—to know that he *is* a liar."

Sarsfield stopped on the street, turned his brother toward him, gripped the boy's shoulders, and looked him straight in the eyes. "Listen to me, Kyle," he said. "Don't pay any attention to blood and family trees and who's related to whom and all that.—It's just a load of guff. Don't worry about the family—Mother or Father or the Eberhardts or any of them. It doesn't matter a damn what they expect of you. Make your own way in the world. Find what you want to do and go after it. And if anybody starts telling you that you can't do this or that because of the Middleton or the Eberhardt or the Rainey blood in your veins, you just tell 'em to go to hell!"

Sarsfield was, by now, making money;—and, not merely staying one jump ahead of Miss Calendene's salary and the bills, he was turning a profit. He had instinctively known that, if his business were to survive, it could no longer rely primarily upon portrait work; he had, just as instinctively, sought new income where it could best be made: in services for the amateur, and commercial work in the printing trade. Once they knew that they could get their prints back in a few days, that they could buy chemicals and equipment to do the printing themselves, that they could buy cameras and all the allied paraphernalia; Raysburg's "snap-shooters" began pouring through the door;— and the first payment Sarsfield received from Hollowell and Frankhauser put him well into the "black." Sarsfield was overjoyed; he had always secretly doubted his ability to make money; and now, with every dollar that came into the shop, his spirits rose. That he was working twelve or fourteen hours a day, six days a week, did not bother him in the least: such vigorous activity was precisely what he needed. The nightmares that had troubled him only a short time before now seemed so far in the past that they might have happened to someone else. It was clear that if he kept going at this rate, he would be a success; and he began to ask himself why he should not have a wife and a family.

Sarsfield had often heard it said that a man finds himself truly in love only once in his life; he had heretofore doubted that old "chestnut," but now he suspected that it might be true,—if not for every man, at least for himself; and it followed (if one were thinking things through in a clear, dispassionate way) that, from the moment he had lost Julia, it had ceased to matter all that much whom he married. He should choose a girl, then, for practical reasons—assessing her as a potential wife, mother, and home-maker—and forget all the romantic nonsense about "blending of souls." After due consideration, he concluded that he might do far worse than Emma Rossiter—and he might look long and hard before he could do better.

Emma was as pretty and sweet a girl as one could wish; and she was obviously in love with him. He also knew, from certain of her timid, hesitant questions, that, in respect to style and deportment, she was eager for guidance, that he could dress her quite as he pleased and polish off the rough edges from her country manners;—and thus refurbished, she would make a wife of which he could be rightly proud. He also was fully aware by now that she "knew her own mind," that there was to her a spirit as stubborn as a bulldog's; and such a fiercely unbending will was all to the good: Emma would stand by her husband "come hell or high water"; she would make a good mother—loving but firm. She believed in precisely the things in which a woman ought to believe: in marriage, and the home, and the good, old-fashioned laws of Christian morality; her people were the salt of the earth; yes, indeed, there was something solid and substantial and utterly reliable about Emma (and she fit so sweetly into his arms when she sat on his lap on the glider and kissed him). And with these thoughts in his mind, Sarsfield did a full "turn around" and decided that he wanted to marry her after all; but, despite the sound advice he had given to his little brother (and he had believed every word of it—at least as it applied to Kyle), he was still worrying about the Eberhardts. He decided to consult with his mother.

The oppressive "dog-days" had by then imperceptibly dove-tailed into a long, pleasant Indian summer. One weekday, late in an afternoon when a cool, persistent breeze had already begun to disperse the diurnal heat, Sarsfield looked through the window at Nolan's, saw his father in there, firmly ensconced, engaged in lively colloquy, his elbow on the brass rail and his fist wrapped around his beer glass with the air of a man who will not happily stir for any reason short of a fire-ball rolling directly toward him down the polished bar;—and that was exactly where Sarsfield wanted him. He walked quickly home, found his mother, too, exactly where he wanted her: sitting on the glider on the back porch, her novel open upon her lap. He joined her. "You're home early, dear," she said; and he saw from the immediacy with which she had looked up and greeted him that, if she had been sipping her nerve tonic (and it would have been a rare day when she had not been), she had not yet sipped enough of it to be transported to that distant land from whence she could offer communication with only the utmost difficulty. Alice Middleton passed many of her days in her tea-gown; that she was fully dressed upon this particular occasion indicated that she must be feeling, as she would have put it, "stronger." Everything was as he had hoped; now all Sarsfield had to do was find some way to introduce his chosen topic into conversation. "What're you reading, Mother?" he asked.

Smiling, she passed him the book; it was the new Mary Roberts Rinehart. "Any good?"

"Oh, yes, dear," she replied; "It's quite absorbing."

They swung gently on the glider; he could hear the raspy voices of nighthawks that signaled the coming of evening. "The lawn party—" he began, "perhaps you have, ah—been talking to Grandmother about it?"

After some moments, she surprised him by saying: "Yes, Sarsfield, your grandmother is quite angry with you."

"Oh?" he said; "and what is your opinion, Mother?"

"My opinion?—Since I was old enough to think that I had one, my opinion was never sought;—I have long ago given up the practice of having an opinion."

He was puzzled by her response; it appeared to preclude further conversation.

"This year I will not attend," she said.

"What do you mean, Mother?"

"Why, the lawn party."

He was astonished. That annual affair was one of the few events at which Alice Middleton felt duty bound to put in an appearance no matter whether she was feeling up to it or not. "But this year, I will not go," she said. "No; I will not be drawn into my mother's schemes—not this time." She turned to look at him. "You do know what I'm talking about, don't you, Sarsfield?"

"Yes, Mother, I do.—Look, I don't like the thought of the Eberhardts being angry with me. Is there anything I could, ah—"

"No. Nothing. Sarsfield, do not try to live your life to please your grandparents. It is a hopeless cause. Believe me, I know."

"They accepted your sister's marriage—" he tried.

"Yes; they did—eventually. But Mathilda and George will inherit *nothing*! And the Ebelings are far from the Rossiters."

They sat side by side looking at the river. "I had so hoped you would marry your cousin Julia," she said.

"There were many times when I had hoped so too," he replied.

"I find it inconceivable," she said, looking away from him, down the sloping lawn, "that you should have picked a girl—a girl, well—common as dirt."

With that, he was suddenly violently angry; controlling himself, he said: "Perhaps 'common as dirt' is what I want, Mother. She's a good, strong, healthy girl with lots of *common* sense—"

"I expect that she is.—Oh, dear, Sarsfield, nothing has turned out as I had hoped!"

"What *had* you hoped?"

"That you would leave this God-forsaken—this crude, this ugly—this *foul* mill town!"

"I often thought that I should."

Again some time passed as he tried to imagine what she was thinking. "No matter what you do, Sarsfield," she said, "you have my blessing."

"Well, thank you, Mother. I take it then, that you don't, ah—approve of what Grandmother is planning—what she's—"

"Approve!" she exclaimed with the strength of her emotion apparent in her voice; "How could I approve of that? How could you think for a moment I would approve of that?—To shame people, not for anything they have done, but for who they are—for their blood and their birth—things that can't be helped! How *could* I approve of that? To do such a thing is not proper behavior, it's not gracious—it's not *right*—"

She had taken up her fan to cool herself; now she threw it from her, rose to her feet, walked to the edge of the porch, and, grasping the railing, stared fixedly out toward the river.

Sarsfield rose hesitantly to his feet; but, the moment he heard the restrained intensity of his mother's overwrought voice—quivering with profound feeling yet held firmly in check, he stopped stock-still; she spoke with her back to him: "Oh, Sarsfield, what you must think of me!—And whatever you think of me, do not think—not for a moment—you must never, never think—that there is some weakness, some flaw, some taint in my character—in our blood!—*What I am is what was made of me.*

"I was never allowed a life of my own, a moment to myself, a thought of my own—never was permitted—even the most innocent, most innocuous of pleasures. The will to disobey was broken in me long ago, Sarsfield; and it is far too late to hope that—I should ever again—recover it. I have often thought that Our Lord must weep to see a little child used so!—and I weep for other little children used so. And then I married your father; merciful heavens, what an irony! Judgment is the Lord's; and His judgment will be sure—and certain—Oh, I know that if there's a Lord in heaven, His judgment will be certain!—You're a good man, Sarsfield, a kind man; you must always be kind. Pray to Our Lord to guide you; and whatever course you choose will be the right one—"

She broke off and bent forward, gripping the railing; he fancied that she might fall. He thought that she was weeping; but then he saw that she was not.

Sarsfield knew by sudden, unbidden intuition that he had heretofore heard so little of any account his mother might make of herself for the simple reason that he had not wanted to hear it and had never sought it; he was filled now with a terrible pity for her—and a shame-ridden embarrassment at the strength and irrational incoherence of her emotions;—at the same time he knew that the innermost feelings of his heart were just as strong and irrational as hers. If he could, at that moment, have struck down the world that had so long, and cruelly, imprisoned her, he should have done so—yes, even if by so doing he should have destroyed the very foundation under his feet. He stood, rooted to the spot, while he attempted to understand, and master, his inner turmoil,—while he attempted to find some simple, consoling thing to say to her; but then his mother straightened up, returned to the glider. He, too, returned to the glider; they sat again side by side, swinging and looking out at the river. After a time, she said: "The nights are becoming cooler now."

"Yes, they are," he answered her.

"I'm glad of it," she said and took up her novel.

On the morning of the Eberhardts' lawn party, the sun rose like a fat, blood-red ball—like a big, nasty peony filled with ants, Emma thought—and lit the river with a blazing, unpleasant light. The slow Indian summer had turned hot again; days had passed without rain, without much of a breeze. The smoke from the mills made the air hazy and heavy; and, in every tree on the Island, the locusts rasped out their steady, pulsing complaint. Emma hated the locusts that day; they sounded like a million old women muttering to themselves; the night before, as she had been falling asleep, the locusts had begun to sing to her: "It's no use, it's no use, it's no use." She had been awake since dawn, listening to the hateful locusts since dawn; she had bathed in the tub in the kitchen while her father had stamped up and down on the back porch and fumed. He had been up since dawn too. "Dear Lord, help me to get through this," Emma prayed as she brushed her hair. "Don't let me disgrace myself."

By mid-morning, Tom Rossiter had talked himself into staying home and took his wife aside to tell her the news. "Lord, Thomas," she said, "you can't do that. We writ and said you was acomin'."

"You just tell 'em I come down with something at the last minute. I ain't agoin' out there and be insulted by the likes of that fat, old kraut. I don't know what the devil I was thinking about to say I would," and he stormed off to poke around in the garden and not accomplish much of anything there that his wife could see.

At noon Mrs. Rossiter found her husband leaning across the kitchen sink toward the mirror on the wall, his lean jaws covered with a good soapy lather and his razor in his hand. "What on earth are you doing, Thomas?" she exclaimed.

"Gone blind, have you, woman?"

"But if you're not going, why are you—?"

"I'm going."

"Oh." She knew better than to ask him why he had changed his mind. "Well, you be civil."

"Civil," he said with a bitter laugh. "Civil? Oh, Lord in heaven, *civil!*"

Sarsfield, meantime, had hired a large, stately landau to transport himself and the Rossiters out the pike; one of the boys from Howell's had driven it up to the back of the shop; and Sarsfield was, at this very moment, loading his photography outfit onto it.

If Raysburg could be said to have a Mrs. Astor—a single, powerful personage who set the standard of social life—then Sarsfield's grand-mother, Mrs. Thaddeus Eberhardt nee Amanda Rainey, clearly was she; if there was a single event, like the Astors' annual "crush," at which anyone who was firmly established—or ever hoped to be firmly estab-lished—as a member of Raysburg's most elite genteel society was required to be seen, then the annual Eberhardt lawn party was it; and this monumental occasion had been commemorated with photographs for as long as Sarsfield could remember. The practice had begun, in fact, when Jack Middleton had married Alice Eberhardt; and by now it had become an inexorable tradition. The prospect of being captured forever by the cruelly honest grains of silver in a photographic plate provided even more reason (although any such further urging was hardly required) for the wives and daughters of the great Raysburg fami-lies to array themselves in their finest; so, if one wished to see the most fashionable ladies in the valley fully "rigged," then the Eberhardt lawn party was the place to do it. When Sarsfield had returned from Har-vard, he had been dismayed to discover that Jack intended to turn over to him the weighty responsibility for these indispensable photographs:

"For twenty years I've been stuck behind that damn camera;—now it's your turn." Sarsfield took his duties quite seriously indeed; now he checked to make sure that he had everything—all his lenses, enough plates, and even a second camera,—for he knew that if the pictures were not "up to snuff" no one would ever forgive him.

When, shortly before one in the afternoon, he arrived at home, Sarsfield was surprised to find his mother dressed and waiting for him. "Mother?" he said.

"Your father and the children have gone on ahead," she told him.

"Yes; that was what we'd—But, *you're* not going, are you?"

"I am. The Rossiters are our guests this afternoon, Sarsfield; and it is only common courtesy that I escort them." This was delivered in a firm, proper voice totally devoid of any sign of emotion.

"Oh," was the only response Sarsfield could think to make. He assisted his mother in entering the landau, helped her settle into the right of the seat facing the horses—the proper position for the hostess she had so suddenly and incomprehensibly decided to become. He tucked a light blanket about her to protect her dress from the dust, handed her parasol and fan, and stood a moment, regarding her. "Do you want the top down, Mother?" he asked; he knew that she found driving a trial, that a long ride in the sun often occasioned a severe "bout" of her neurasthenia.

"Heavens, no," she answered; "I shall raise my parasol if need be."

He hesitated a moment, then said: "Grandmother will never forgive you."

"I expect she won't," his mother replied, looking straight ahead.

Sarsfield stepped up into the driver's seat, took up the reins. The landau had been brought into the twentieth century by the addition of rubber wheels; so, with hardly a sound at all but the steady clomp of the horses, they proceeded south along Front Street to Emma's. They found the Rossiters dressed and waiting,—sitting silently in a row on the front porch wearing expressions that would have been suitable had they been prepared to attend the funeral of a dearly beloved relative suddenly taken in the prime of life. Sarsfield greeted them in his heartiest voice: "A beautiful day for a lawn party!"

"A perfect day for it, I'm sure," Tom replied grimly.

"Why, it's Mrs. Middleton!" Emma's mother exclaimed, her surprise and consternation written clearly on her face; "Good heavens. How are you, Mrs. Middleton?"

Sarsfield could not recall whether the two women had ever met; he had yet to bring Emma home;—but, before he could attempt an introduction, he heard his mother saying, just as though she and Emma's mother were old friends: "How nice to see you again, Mrs. Rossiter; oh, do please sit here by me."

As he escorted Emma down the front steps, she asked urgently under her breath: "What's your mother doing here?"

"She's quite graciously assumed the rôle of hostess," Sarsfield replied just as quietly; then, when he saw her expression of bewilderment, he added: "Don't worry about anything, Emma. It's all going to come out just fine."

"Do I look all right? Lord, I didn't know what to wear!"

"You look splendid; you're perfection itself."

She blushed at that; she had chosen her graduation dress—and the glacé kid gloves that were no more appropriate on this hot Indian summer afternoon than they had been on the day he had photographed her. His heart went out to her; and he gave her his most reassuring smile as he helped her into the seat with her father.

Sarsfield took his place as the driver of this curious *entourage*; and soon they were rolling across the Suspension Bridge; he looked out and saw the sun brilliantly reflected in the waters of the Ohio; and, for no good reason that he could find, his spirits rose. Everybody kept saying it; but it was true nonetheless: it *was* a splendid day. And once they cleared the top of Raysburg Hill and began to leave the smoke of the mills behind them, even the Rossiters, in spite of themselves, began to enjoy the drive. Tom allowed as how they hardly ever got out of town these days; and it certainly was pleasant to sit back and relax and have a look at the scenery. "Yes," his wife said, "it's just nice as can be." Then, to his amazement, Sarsfield heard his mother remark how much she simply adored a good drive on a pretty day. He turned in his seat to look back at Emma, who, for the first time, returned his smile; speaking so quietly only he could hear her, she told him: "Don't you worry about me, Sarsfield. I'm going to act just as proper as a girl in a novel."

He gave the horses their head; and they stepped out at a good, lively pace. As they passed the turn-off to Goosetown, a welcome breeze sprang up, abating somewhat the heat of the late summer sun. Sarsfield heard his mother and the Rossiters fall into precisely the kind of pleasant, inconsequential conversation at which his mother excelled; he relaxed and watched the glorious prospect of the West Virginia hills drift by him, thought that, indeed, this was a beautiful part of the country; thought that, perhaps, he could do worse than spend the remainder of his life in this familiar, yet mysterious, locale; and then he felt a puzzling and subtle happiness arise in him. He found himself curiously distanced from the unfolding events—as though a great burden had rolled from his back. No matter how fiercely he had wrestled with the problem, he had not been able to discern a course of action that would satisfy both himself and his grandparents; so he had decided to do exactly what he had told Kyle to do: please himself. If the worse came to the worst and this afternoon were to be the last he ever saw of Thaddeus and Amanda Eberhardt, then so be it.

As the horses began to labor up the steep, twisting road leading onto what (as Sarsfield remembered, smiling to himself) Dan Rainey had called the Eberhardts' "by-Jesus hundred acres," Maynard Eberhardt's "Silver Ghost" overtook them. "Good lord!" Mrs. Rossiter exclaimed; "Why, just look at that thing, Thomas! I never seen the like of it."

"Easy, easy," Sarsfield called to the horses; Uncle Mayne had slowed so as not to frighten them. Sarsfield saw his Aunt Lou wave as the car passed. Bedelia and Lenore were sitting in the back; but they did not deign to notice him.

Then, coming around the next steep curve, Sarsfield heard yet another automobile overtaking; this time it was, of course, Charlie Staub in his Mercedes. The Rossiters had fallen silent. The car roared by without slowing; and Sarsfield had to draw up the horses to a dead stop before the poor, agitated beasts were calm enough to continue.

Finally they emerged from the last steep turn at the top of the hill; and they could see, through the clear September air (in which was left not a trace of the smoke produced by the manufacturing of iron and steel), the white, monumental Eberhardt mansion, freshly painted every summer, with its Corinthian columns and multitude of twinkling windows, all of them polished, just that morning, as clean as spectacle lenses. Sarsfield heard an involuntary gasp escape Emma's lips; from her parents, he heard not a sound. He urged the horses into a trot; he would, by God, arrive in style.

In the turn-around, a colored boy in livery leapt forward to take the reins; Sarsfield assisted his mother in alighting,—and assisted Emma and offered his arm; like a sleepwalker, she took it—but remained a moment, rooted to the spot, fiddling with her parasol (glancing back, Sarsfield saw that his mother had opened *her* parasol and that Emma was doing her best to follow suit). Mrs. Rossiter was huddled against her husband with an expression on her face like a whipped child's; then Tom drew himself up like the soldier he had been and urged her forward. Black George had already arrived unobtrusively to say, in a deep, round voice that was perfection itself: "Mr. Middleton, suh, if you would step this way, please, suh—"

"Could you have one of the boys bring my camera 'round?" Sarsfield said; and George instantly raised a finger, which Sarsfield knew from long experience would cause the deed to be done.

Sarsfield had timed their arrival perfectly: they preceded the majority of the guests, but neither were they the first. Thaddeus and Amanda were receiving under a vast canopy at the rear of the mansion. The rest of the Middletons were already there (Jack had probably galloped the whole way—with the children shouting him on); Sarsfield saw Jack respond to the arrival of his wife with surprise followed by a broad, malicious grin. Then his father's amused eyes met his own,—as Jack, radiant with joy, took a long pull from a goblet of Thaddeus Eberhardt's famous mint and bourbon punch.

"What a lovely day, Mother," Alice Middleton said in her most musical and beautifully modulated voice; "Please allow me to present Mr. and Mrs. Thomas Rossiter.—My mother, Mrs. Thaddeus Eberhardt."

Amanda's mouth dropped open in total astonishment; the expression she turned upon her daughter was one of blazing, unbridled fury; but then—and it could have been from no other force but that of years of habit—she seized control of her notorious Rainey temper and muttered: "Pleased to know you, I'm sure."

"My father, Thaddeus Eberhardt," Alice continued.

"So pleased; indeed, indeed," Thaddeus boomed out. Tom Rossiter and Thaddeus Eberhardt managed a handshake so abbreviated—executed at such high speed and with such painful discomfort on both sides—that Sarsfield could not recall ever having seen anything quite like it; once the two had accomplished this necessary but obviously repellent act, they stepped away from each other as though fearing that mere proximity would cause further contamination. Thaddeus cast his eyes about wildly, fervently longing for another guest to claim his attention, but there was no one to hand. Behind him, Sarsfield heard his father snicker, then manage to turn the sound into a discreet cough.

Mrs. Middleton urged Emma forward and introduced her; and Sarsfield was delighted to see that Emma, once she had executed a deep, perfect, old-fashioned curtsey, was looking his grandmother straight in the face; Amanda stared back with one eye, for the other, as it so often did when she was distressed, had wandered away to regard the distant hills.

"Well, well, well!" Thaddeus brayed on, his voice so loud that Sarsfield knew that his grandfather must be profoundly ill at ease; "So pleased to meet a young lady as charming as yourself.—And how are *you*, my boy? You're looking splendid, simply splendid!" Then, his pink, sweating face stretched into a strained smile, he turned back to Emma's parents, obviously searching his mind for his next fatuous remark; Amanda pushed past him and withdrew—in a display of discourtesy so obvious that Sarsfield was, in spite of himself, shocked by it.

His timing perfect, the boy arrived with the camera: "'Scuse me, suh. Where you want I should put this, suh?"

"Forgive me, Grandfather," Sarsfield said. "While things are still fairly quiet, we should take a photograph or two—"

"Photograph?" Thaddeus asked as though the term were entirely new to him.

"Yes;" Sarsfield replied, "we should get most of them over with before the party is fully underway.—I thought up there on the verandah. D'you see how beautiful the light is—shaded, clear and bright, but with no shadows—"

Thaddeus looked toward the rear of the house. "Yes, yes," he said; "well—"

"We should begin with some family groupings," Sarsfield said. "It won't take a minute." He had learned from his father just how powerful the rôle of photographer can be: at the proper time and place, the photographer can command presidents and kings—and, it seemed, even one's grandfather, for Thaddeus now went to retrieve his wife and direct her toward the verandah. Amanda, however, appeared to require considerable urging; she sent Sarsfield a look of profound annoyance that she did not bother to disguise. "It won't take a minute," Sarsfield repeated for her benefit and urged on the others. The company began to straggle toward the verandah. "D'you want us *all* to go up there?" Emma asked.

"Yes, please," Sarsfield replied. "Go up with your parents." Then, seeing the expression on her face, he assured her: "Everything's going to go off just fine. Really it is—just fine."

Emma was so frightened that she felt as if her brains were not working properly; and she did not trust herself to speak again. She was laced into her "Smart Set" so firmly that she could not take a deep breath to save her soul; her gloves were too tight and hot; the inside of her mouth was as dry as an ant-hill; and the last thing in the world she wanted to do was walk up onto that verandah. She glanced toward the drive and saw arriving— of all things—a brougham drawn by two snow-white horses; "Lord almighty," she thought, "somebody thinks he's the King of England!" Following behind this picture-book vehicle came yet another vast and gleaming automobile; "Oh my," she thought, "this is like a bad dream!" Then, afraid of being left behind entirely, she finally urged herself into action, gathered her skirts clear of the grass, and hurried to catch up with the others. Seemingly out of nowhere, she heard Olivia Middleton's affected giggle behind her,—followed at once by the child's voice fluting away in a lofty tone: "Why, just look at that trash give herself airs! She looks just like somebody's kitchen help got up in that funny home-made dress."

Emma spun around just in time to see the child send her a sassy, triumphant grin; then Olivia lifted her nose into the air, and, with a flounce of her petticoats, walked away, hand in white-gloved hand with another little society girl, cutting Emma dead. "Oh, you'll get your turn, all right," Emma thought. "You horrid little snake, you just wait!"

Tom had paused at the top of the stairs to look back down at the rolling lawn. "Lord save us," he whispered to his wife, "he's got more darkies than he's got guests!"

She shushed him. "Thomas, please—"

"I ain't agoina say—"

And Emma arrived, nearly running, her eyes stinging with tears and her cheeks blazing with anger and resentment. "Good heavens, child—" her mother began.

"Oh, Mama, do be quiet!"

The Rossiters stepped onto the verandah where the Eberhardts were waiting for them. Thaddeus looked at his wife, saw that he could expect no help from that quarter; it had been a major accomplishment just to get her to agree to the damn fool photograph; and so, just as he had feared, he now found himself in a position in which he would have to attempt a conversation with this damnable old reb;—and, just as he had planned against such a contingency, Thaddeus opened with the only topic he had been able to imagine: "Well, Rossiter, I gather that you and I are both veterans of that late, great conflict between the states.—Well, well, yes. Seems a long time ago, does it not?"

Tom could not believe his ears: the old bastard wanted to talk about the war! "Yes, sir," he said, "surely does seem a long time ago— over and done with, I mostly think of it—"

Thaddeus looked down onto the lawn to determine how the photograph might be progressing and saw that Sarsfield had not even got the camera unpacked yet;—he had not even chosen the location for it. "Yes, well," he said, cleared his throat, and doggedly turned back to his unwanted guest. "So then—what was your regiment?"

"The Twenty-seventh Virginia," Tom said reluctantly.

"By Jove, Rossiter, you were with Stonewall!"

Tom didn't know what to say to that; he would have walked ten miles barefoot if it would have got him out of talking about the war with this man; but he did not want to seem impolite either. "Yes, sir, I was with Jackson," he said. "But we mostly called him 'Old Blue Light'—but not to his face."

Tom saw the fat, old Republican bend slightly toward him with an inquiring look; and so, he supposed, now he was required to elaborate. "Well, you know, sir, Jackson had blue eyes," Tom said; "and he used to get a real wild, crazy look in them—"

At that, Thaddeus Eberhardt laughed much too heartily. "'Blue Light!' Did you hear that, Mother? Jackson got a crazy look in his blue eyes, so they called him 'Blue Light.' That's choice, Rossiter. Yes, indeed. Capital!"

Amanda, hearing herself thus addressed, withdrew to the rear of the verandah so as to avoid being drawn into the conversation. "For God's sake, fetch us some chairs!" she hissed at George.

Thaddeus and Tom stood rooted side by side, staring out across the rolling hills of the Eberhardt hundred acres as though both were hoping for a speedy rescue to arrive from that direction. "So," Thaddeus boomed out after a moment of painful silence, "what kind of a man *was* Jackson? Was he as hard as they say?"

"There he goes!" Amanda thought; "As if things ain't bad enough, now we're going to get the war for the next half hour." And she resolved to sit there as silently as a stone for just as long as this charade required her to do so.

"Guess there's no avoiding it," Tom thought and braced himself to do his duty at keeping the conversation going. "Was old Jackson hard?" he said; "Lord God almighty, that ain't the half of it. In the first valley campaign, we was so fed up with him, we was agoina quit on him and go home.—He allowed as how if we tried that, he'd have us all shot."

"Oh, yes, yes. Were you in the Stonewall Brigade the whole war?"

"I expect so, Mr. Eberhardt."

"Oh, so then we've met before, Rossiter."

"Can't say as I recollect—"

"At Chancellorsville," Thaddeus Eberhardt proclaimed in a round and portentous voice.

Tom was seriously aggravated; but he said, mildly: "Oh. You was there, was you, sir?"

"I certainly did not distinguish myself that day," Thaddeus informed Tom—and the others, for he was keenly aware of them—with what he had calculated to be appropriate modesty; "but, yes, Rossiter, indeed, I was there."

"Well, at least he ain't abraggin' on himself," Tom thought; and Tom could have said that, as well as at Chancellorsville, he had also been at Bull Run (twice), with Jackson in the Shenandoah Valley, at Gaines's Mill, Cedar Mountain, Antietam, Fredricksburg, the Wilderness, Spotsylvania, Gettysburg, with Early back in the Valley, and at Appomattox,—but he didn't.

"It was real hard for you'ens to distinguish yourselves much that day," Tom said, "what with Jackson and Lee on the field." He had meant that to sound friendly; but, reflecting on it, he was afraid that it might not have come out that way.

"Yes, yes; I'd have to agree with you there, Rossiter," Thaddeus said. "The generalship was all on your side. We were saddled with Hooker."

Tom had never seen Raysburg's iron and steel king up close before; and, now that he had a chance to study the man, he could see that the old kraut's health was failing him. "Poor feller," Tom thought, "he ain't long for this world." Thaddeus, for his part, had concluded that Tom Rossiter wished to avoid any unpleasantness quite as much as he did. "Mannerly old boy, I'll give him that," he thought.

Sarsfield, meantime, had chosen a location close enough to the verandah so that he could hear the conversation; now he selected his shortest lens and began to set up his camera. "What the hell are you up to, you damn puppy?" his father asked quietly, his eyes glinting with amusement.

"I'm going to take a picture, father," Sarsfield replied blandly.

"A picture—horseshit!" Jack whispered and, with a laugh, strode up onto the verandah so that he could get a ringside seat.

A darky arrived with a chair for Tom, and he sat in it. "And they told us they was fighting to end slavery," he thought, "the hypocrites!"

Alice Middleton—oblivious to the looks of fury directed at her by her mother—had engaged Mrs. Rossiter in conversation; Mrs. Middleton remarked upon how lovely Emma looked, how lovely the day had turned out, and how lovely it was that they could all be in attendance. Thaddeus settled into the chair that had arrived for him and, once again, found himself confronting Tom Rossiter. "Well, yes," he said; "General Hooker—'Fighting Joe Hooker' they called him, good Lord, what a travesty that was! He lost his nerve at Chancellorsville, that's for sure!"

Tom searched his mind for a response. "We, ah—never put much stock in your General Hooker," he tried.

"No? To tell you the truth, Rossiter, neither did I. No; I never cared for the man. He always looked far too pleased with himself to suit me," and then Thaddeus looked down again to see how his damnably slow grandson was coming.

"Not much longer, Grandfather," Sarsfield called out. "Be patient." Kyle, self-conscious and unhappy in a fawn-colored Eton suit and white kid boots, shambled up to watch Sarsfield load the camera. "Go find your sister, and get up there and get in the picture," Sarsfield told him.

On the verandah, Thaddeus continued, manfully, to bear his burden. "I'll never forget it," he said, "Along about noon General Hooker himself rode through to inspect the lines.—Well, there he was, sitting up on that big, high-stepping white horse of his, beautifully turned out, all pink-faced and smiling just as though he were posing for his portrait—although if my grandson had been taking it, he'd probably be waiting still!—Yes; and looking at him, you would've thought there wasn't a reb for a hundred miles. And the whole time our right was resting on nothing at all—"

Tom, who had not thought about the battle of Chancellorsville in years, now found himself remembering that day: how the devil had old

Stonewall known that the Federal right had been resting on nothing at all? Lord knows, but that's what made him a great general. And Tom couldn't resist a chuckle. "We'd been marching hard since dawn to get there," he said, "marching right in front of your whole damn army— excuse the language, ladies. Course we didn't know that at the time. We was just wishing we had a drink of water; Lord, we was spitting cotton, all right! Them thick woods was between us and you'ens; and old Stonewall never told nobody what he might of had in his mind, not even his officers—"

Tom paused and wondered why he was talking so much; he was surprised that he remembered it all as clear as he did. He looked up and saw old man Eberhardt's eyes on him, waiting to hear the rest of it. "Guess it can't hurt," he thought, and launched in again: "Well, long about—oh, I guess two or three in the afternoon—I seen old Stonewall riding by. You talk about your Joe Hooker looking like a fine man that day, all smoothed up and all,—well, Stonewall looked—hard to describe, but I seen him like that before. Riding his horse like he'd forgot he was on it, and his arms flapping up and down like he was a scarecrow, and his lips moving like he was saying his prayers, but no sound coming out, and his eyes burning in his head, but him not seeing nothing with 'em, and I thought, 'God help the Yanks.'"

"God help us, indeed!" Thaddeus said with a laugh. Listening to the old reb talk was bringing it all back to him as though it had happened last week.

"Mama," Emma whispered, "he's talking about the war!" In her entire life, Emma had never heard her father talk about the war.

"You just hush up now and let him talk," her mother whispered back, but she was just as astonished as her daughter was; hearing Tom talk about the war like that hurt her heart, and she was afraid if she tried to say anything more to Emma, she'd bust out crying right there in front of everybody.

Sarsfield threw the focusing cloth over his head and brought the image into sharp clarity on his ground glass. The two older men were sitting facing each other in the foreground. Without being aware that they were doing so, Emma and her mother and Sarsfield's mother had fallen into a pleasing pattern in the background; each in her own way had taken up an expectant, listening stance that led the eye back to Tom Rossiter and Thaddeus Eberhardt. Far to the rear of the picture, like remote personages brought to witness the event, were Sarsfield's grandmother and father, the one sitting enormously, the other leaning at a rakish angle against the wall, both exactly where they ought to be—out of the way. The light was splendid, exquisite—flat and shadowless, but brilliant; Sarsfield should have measured it, but he knew that he could guess the exposure well enough. Then, as he watched, he saw his brother and sister arrive, completing the scene. Sarsfield stepped out from under the cloth, looked directly at the company; he felt overwhelmed by the light.

"I remember my men were chatting and smoking—even playing cards," Thaddeus was saying in a slow, musing voice. "Their muskets were stacked. Some beeves were being butchered up; and we were all looking forward to a good supper. And then, late in the day, one of our scouts came back—I'll never forget this. His horse was all lathered, and he had the most distressed expression I've ever seen on a man, and he said, 'For God's sake, Captain, prepare for an attack!'—"

Although Thaddeus hated to be engaged in conversation, he loved addressing an audience; looking around now, he saw that he had a ready-made one. All other conversation had ceased; the entire company appeared to be hanging upon his every word; wonder of wonders, even his wife appeared to be listening to him.

"No," Thaddeus said, raising his voice so that all could hear clearly; "I shall never forget it!—'Prepare for an attack!' he said, and I asked if those were orders; and he said: 'Orders be damned. The rebs have come up on our right. I've seen them myself.' I stood there amazed and just stared at him. He said: 'I've just been with the Colonel to see General Devens, and you know what the General said? He said: 'There is no danger, sir. You westerners are simply frightened. Lee is in full retreat to save his trains. Go back to your men and do not trouble me again with these phantasies.'—And the whole time our right flank was just hanging out in the air."

Thaddeus grew animated as he warmed to his story: "And no sooner had he spoken those words than game began to come out of the woods directly from that damnable open flank—first pheasants went up with that kind of *boom!* they make, and then deer and rabbits, scurrying along pell mell. The men thought this was a capital joke and began laughing and cheering; but I knew we were in for it. I opened my mouth to shout out the order to form; but there was a terrible whistle, and a shell burst over our heads. Then came the rebs, firing— with that blood-curdling yell. How on earth did you boys do that yell?"

"Couldn't rightly tell you, Mister Eberhardt. It just come up out of us."

"Could you do it again?"

Tom laughed. "Forty years later on your back porch?—No, sir, I'm afraid I couldn't."

Thaddeus looked away at the sky. "Yes," he said. "Yes—Well, I can tell you, Rossiter, that rebel yell was a terrible sound that day. Yes. Terrible. And you boys were pouring out of the woods with the sun behind you, I'll never forget it—The sun low in the sky—red—and as far as we could see, north or south, a line of you boys, running—making that terrible yell. We had no orders to change front, you understand? We heard later that General Devens had repeatedly asked for a change of front and been refused.—And soon it didn't matter a damn, of course. Our position was completely turned—"

As Thaddeus talked, he forgot his listeners; Sarsfield heard his grandfather's voice soften and fill with emotion. "Dear God," Thaddeus said, "We broke! I kept yelling at the men to stand, but they would not. We weren't soldiers; we were a mass of running men, panic-stricken.—We ran past General Howard, I'll never forget it. It was near Wilderness Church, and he was trying to stem the tide up the turnpike. He had the colors under the stump of the arm he'd lost at Fair Oaks, and tears were streaming down his face, and he kept calling out: 'Stand and form, stand and form!' but the men just ran on right past him. General Schurz formed a line, and it stood, and then it broke.—The men peeled out of the entrenchments—and ran. The rebs were pouring over us like locusts. It was pandemonium, total chaos. Half a dozen times I saw groups of our men try to stand against them, but the rebs simply swept around them, engulfed them. Lord, it was the worst day of my life! I lost a quarter of my men that day." And Thaddeus fell silent.

After a moment Tom, who was looking at his feet, said in a voice so quiet he might have been talking to himself: "Yep, and we was coming on hard, praying for more daylight so we could kill us some more Yankees." Then, looking up, smiling gently, he said: "But you fellers sure could run, Mr. Eberhardt. We had the devil of a time just trying to keep up. And Stonewall coming along behind us saying: 'Press them, boys, press them!'"

Thaddeus laughed in spite of himself. Then he took up the tale: "Ambulances, mules, horses, running men, terrified, screaming their heads off—There was no question of rallying my men; I was just trying to keep them together. They were dumping their knapsacks so they could run faster. Some of them couldn't even bear to take the time to undo the buckles; they cut the straps with a knife!—And damned if we hadn't run all the way back to headquarters. General Hooker himself came out at us, yelling: 'The bayonets! Give them the the bayonets!' We weren't sure at first if he meant the rebels or us! Thank God for those twenty-two guns loaded with double charges of cannister—"

"Twenty-two of them, was they?"

"That's right. All twenty-two guns fired off at once—right in the face of the advancing rebels. Lord, and that finally broke the advance—"

Tom tilted back in his chair, stretched. Then he let the chair fall back onto its four legs and leaned forward toward Thaddeus. "I was running hell for leather, Mr. Eberhardt," he said, "with that—that craziness that comes over you—like you're going to kill or be killed and it don't matter a damn which, your heart plumb banging away in you, and yelling, and just full of life, you know. We knowed we'd licked you boys good, and we was just going to keep on licking you, that's for sure.— And then the good Lord seen fit to put a big rock before me on the ground, and I took me a tumble flat on my face, and just then the very mouth of hell opened up right in front of me.

"I couldn't hear nothing for a long time after. For days my ears was ringing like I had bees in my head. And I looked right. And I looked left. And lo, every poor boy that'd been running along with me was dead."

Thaddeus felt the blood drain from his face. He coughed, looked out to see how his damn fool grandson was coming with his damn fool photograph. Sarsfield was fiddling around with something or other,— shoving a plate into his camera or something or other. Thaddeus sighed and looked back at Tom Rossiter. The two men studied each other for a long time. And still, no one else spoke. "That was a terrible day, Tom," Thaddeus said finally.

"Yes, sir; it was. They say we won that battle, but we lost Jackson that day; and it's always seemed to me that when we lost Jackson, we lost the war.—Yes, sir; it was a terrible day."

"And a worse night. Lord! Did you see the—the woods?—" Thaddeus coughed again, and cleared his throat.

"Yes, sir; I did."

"It was nightfall, and there was a total silence—like, I don't know, Tom, like what you'd expect at the Day of Judgment. And then the full moon rose in the sky—with the smoke of battle before it, big and blood red—"

"I seen it," Tom said; "red like that. I'll never forget that moon as long as I live. And then, as it rose up, it turned all gold from the smoke—"

"And then there was firing," Thaddeus went on, "like the sound of a skirmish or something—"

"Yep," Tom said; "even with my ears ringing and all, I heard that firing."

"And we couldn't make it out. And we kept wondering what it could be. And then one of our pickets came back, and he was crying out that the woods were on fire—" Thaddeus drew a fresh linen handkerchief from his pants pocket and blew his nose on it.

"How many wounded men was in them woods?" Tom asked him. "Did you ever know?"

"Two or three thousand—Lord!—Confederate and Federal both, lying out there under the burning trees."

The two men sat in silence for a while.

"I heard them men in the woods," Tom said.

"We formed into a party," Thaddeus said, "and we left our muskets behind, and we went straight back onto that battlefield. It was entirely deserted. In the distance we could see some rebel infantry; but we were not within their range, so we pressed forward. Then we could hear the roar from the flames coming down on us. The flames—" Thaddeus began, but he could not continue.

"Them boys was crying for water," Tom said. "God have mercy on their souls! And the ones the flames had got to—" He had to stop. He looked out at the day; but he could not see it.

"Well," Thaddeus said, "we hauled out as many as we could—Confederate and Federal both—and then we could no longer face those flames. The rebels fired at us; and then, when they saw what our mission was, they began to cheer for us. And then—oh, Lord! There was nothing we could do, Tom. Nothing! That fire consumed everything— every shrub and sapling, every branch and twig. Lord, Tom, there was *nothing* we could do! And the sound those poor men made when the fire got to them—I couldn't stand it. I'm not ashamed to admit it. I threw myself down on the ground and wept."

"I know, Thaddeus," Tom Rossiter said; "I was one of them rebs cheering you on."

When the two men, as though of one mind, sprang to their feet, each reaching out a hand to the other, Sarsfield took the picture.

9

The day after the Eberhardts' lawn party, Emma asked her father's permission to marry Sarsfield Middleton; and, after only a few seconds reflection, Tom Rossiter granted it. Then Emma did something she had not done since the short-skirted days of her girlhood when all of her aunts had proclaimed her a "romp" and darkly predicted no good end for her: she leapt high into the air with a squeal of joy. Tom, the moment the word "yes" was out of his mouth, began to caution her: "Now, Emma, honey, you listen to me. You got yourself one hard row to hoe." He cautioned her earnestly, and he cautioned her long; he took her down to the river and walked, holding her hand, for several hours while he cautioned her, at times pausing to shake his finger in her face; but nothing he had to say could even faintly dim her delight.

The day after they had given the lawn party, Thaddeus Eberhardt said to his wife: "For once, Mother, you're going to listen to me—and be guided. If Sarsfield wants to marry that pretty little Rossiter girl, that's his business—" Amanda began angrily to respond; but Thaddeus held up his hand to stop her. "No, Mother, this time *you* shall listen to *me*. What the hell did we fight for anyway? One nation, under God—"

"Now, Teddy, don't you go making one of your stump speeches to *me*!"

"Amanda, it ain't a speech—I believe it with all my heart; and if I didn't, what the devil was I doing out there with Stonewall's boys doing their damn level best to kill me?—*That all men are created equal!* And that's the long and the short of it.—And if Sarsfield marries that girl, they'll have children who won't give a hang about who fought on what side of the war—who won't give a hang who was born with a silver spoon—and who grew up feeding chickens. And I'd say it was about high time too!"

Amanda looked at her husband and saw, as she never had before, the man who commanded all the forces of the great Eberhardt business empire; for the first time in their married life, she kept her mouth shut.

Sarsfield and Emma were married in June of 1909, almost exactly a year from the day when he had taken her graduation picture. Upon Sarsfield's insistence, it was a small, quiet ceremony in the new Presbyterian Church on the Island with only the closest members of the respective families in attendance. There were no ushers, no flower girl (Olivia was crushed), no page (Kyle was overjoyed); and the wedding party was made up only of Doctor Arch Kimbell as the best man and Emma's lovely sixteen-year-old niece Katy as the single bridesmaid.

Mrs. Rossiter gladly accepted a gentle, behind-the-scenes guidance from Alice Middleton who took considerable pains to insure that everything was done in the most conservative, tasteful, and time-honored tradition; and, even when the guidance stopped being quite so gentle, Mrs. Rossiter still went along with it, although she said to her daughter: "I swear, that fool woman thinks *she's* the mother of the bride!" Emma wore the indispensable snow-white silk gown with long train, veil, and wreath of maiden-blush roses and orange blossoms; and Mrs. Middleton made it clear to Emma that the orange blossoms were suitable for the ceremony only and must be removed immediately afterward. The old—and, Alice Middleton thought, very pretty—custom of the bride wearing gloves was revived ("Lord save us!" Mrs. Rossiter said to Emma—who replied: "Please, Mama, just let it all go by."); and the ring finger of the left glove was cut so that it could be removed at the right moment. Sarsfield, of course, wore a Prince Albert frock coat and light trousers; if conservative was to be the rule of the day, he thought, then conservative he would be, so, instead of the pale gray gloves that had come recently into favor, he wore white.

Sarsfield asked Emma to pick the location of the honeymoon; "Anywhere you want," he said, hoping she would not pick New York— or Paris.

"You mean it? Anywhere?" He assured her that he meant it. After due consideration, she replied: "Oh, Sarsfield, I know this is going to sound foolish, but—I've always wanted to see Niagara Falls!"

They viewed the falls from the front; and Sarsfield agreed with Emma that it was breath-taking and photographed her with the awesome spectacle behind her. They donned rubber slickers, ventured into the Cave of Winds, and viewed the falls from the back—where it looked like nothing so much as an enormous flowing curtain. Emma had never before stayed in a hotel; and she was always amazed (and not entirely pleased) when they returned to their room to discover that someone had been there in their absence and had tidied up and made the bed. They crossed to the Canadian side so that Emma could say that she had left the United States. Sarsfield took her shopping in Buffalo and bought her frocks and shoes and gloves until she began to feel embarrassed by his extravagance. And, of course, they embarked upon those pleasures shared by all newlyweds. For the first few nights Sarsfield suffered from "nerves"; but, as he kept telling himself, if he knew little of the conjugal act, she knew nothing whatsoever; and she was just as sweet and pliant as he had expected her to be; and so, soon enough, he "got the hang of it." Emma would have rather died than let him know that, as a girl who had grown up around barnyard animals, she knew considerably more about these matters than she let on.

Although she would not be sure of it until some months afterward, Emma was carrying her first child when they returned to Raysburg. They rented a little cottage on Virginia Street on the Island, just a few blocks from the bridge; and Emma spent her days making a home while Sarsfield continued to put in long hours at his business—which was flourishing. Remembering his mother's difficulties, Sarsfield was surprised to find Emma so little incapacitated: she was confined only for the last month. Early in March of 1910, attended at home by Arch Kimbell ("Relax, Sarsfield," he had to keep saying, "I know what I'm doing!"), she gave birth to a little boy. Sarsfield could not have been prouder—or more pleased with himself. They had decided to choose names that had never been used by either of their families, so their son was called Andrew Arthur.

Old Dan Rainey took the grippe and passed away just before Christmas in 1908; he was ninety-six; and he died as quickly and quietly as a baby—"here one day, gone the next," people said. He remembered every Rainey relation in his will; his huge holding of land was broken up; and, after Daniel Rainey, no individual would ever again own such vast acreage in the valley. Sarsfield received a huge tract on the south end of the Island just below the Suspension Bridge.

In the worst heat of the summer of 1909, Amanda woke in the night to find that Thaddeus was not in their bed. Alarmed, she got up to look for him and found him in the drawing room; she could not imagine what he had been doing there: he had never before, in all their married life, risen in the night and ventured off into the house—let alone down into the drawing room. He had turned a chair around to face the wrong way; and then he had sat in it. He had suffered a massive stroke and had lost the use of much of his body. For sometime afterward he could not speak; when he could, his utterances were delivered with painful difficulty. Thaddeus did not appear to know exactly where he was or what had happened to him; from time to time he issued orders for his subordinates at what was obviously the old Raysburg Iron Works, for he was referring to matters that had taken place some forty or fifty years before. He was not expected to live long, but he lingered on into the fall; Sarsfield visited daily, but he always found his grandfather asleep.

In October, early one evening, Thaddeus signaled to his wife; she bent close and heard him mutter: "Tell the old kraut he can keep his basket of apples." She looked into his eyes to see if she could ascertain what he might have meant by that; and she saw that he was dead. Amanda claimed for ever after that Thaddeus had meant General Sigel; she even claimed to remember some wartime anecdote she had heard about the German general and a basket of apples; but Maynard insisted that his father could only have been referring to Karl Eberhardt. Sarsfield braced himself to see Julia again at his grandfather's funeral; but, as it turned out, she was in France.

Thaddeus Eberhardt's estate was worth, depending upon who did the reckoning, between ten and fifteen million; of that he left only twenty-five-hundred dollars to charity—an amount that many saw as niggardly—a display of restrained altruism far from worthy of the position the Eberhardts held in the valley. The will was a masterpiece of the lawyer's art: it contained such a complexity of clauses—so many twists and turns, stipulations, special requirements, codicils and sub-codicils—that Sarsfield, although he pored over a copy for several hours, could never claim to understand it. He was astonished—and moved to tears—to discover that he had received ten thousand dollars in cash and a hundred shares of Raysburg Iron and Steel; he was one of the few grandchildren to be honored by a direct bequest unencumbered by any special stipulations.

Maynard Eberhardt had been left firmly in control of Raysburg Iron and Steel and the over-all business interests of the family; his younger brothers, although neither could challenge Maynard's position, both found themselves millionaires. The daughters, Mathilda and Alice, had what at first appeared to be huge sums at their disposal; but a careful reading of the will made it clear that neither of them could spend a penny of it upon anything beyond what was styled "their immediate, private, and personal needs"—for Thaddeus had made certain that none of his money would flow into the hands of their husbands: George Ebeling and Jack Middleton. "Does this mean my mother can, if she wants, spend twenty thousand dollars on new frocks?" Sarsfield asked.

"That's right," Maynard replied.

"But she can't, for instance—buy a house or invest in anything or give it to anybody?"

"Absolutely not."

Sarsfield read on; he saw that some further money would eventually wend its way down to children, and grandchildren (including himself), and great-grandchildren; in the meantime, a sub-codicil provided for the education of all minors. "Can Kyle and Olivia benefit from this?" Sarsfield asked Maynard.

"Yep," Maynard said; "that's what it's set aside for. Father wanted all the kids to get a proper education. You can see it there—look, right there in that clause.—When it comes to Kyle and Olivia, I'd say you're the trustee of it."

Without bothering to consult his father, Sarsfield immediately withdrew his brother and sister from the Jefferson Grammar School, sent Kyle to the Academy and Olivia to Miss Crawford's. Jack did not say a word about it; Sarsfield wondered if his father even noticed.

Having lost both her husband and her father within a year, Amanda Eberhardt had been deeply stricken—and changed: she had become, to Sarsfield's amazement, a pathetic old lady who wept easily,—one who had suffered too much to hold a grudge against anyone (even against her traitorous daughter). "Poor old Paw," she would say, "I never got over to the Island to see him much in his last years. He'd been around so long, I guess I thought he was just going to be here forever—like the river"; then she would point at the empty chair in which her husband had always sat: "Poor old Teddy, I thought he had more years in him; he was only seventy-two, you know!" and the tears would roll down her cheeks. Sarsfield and Emma brought little Andrew out to visit; and the moment that Amanda saw the tiny, red, sleeping face of her great-grandson, she forgot that she had ever held anything against Emma.

As soon as Sarsfield received his grandfather's bequest, he bought himself a Ford—which made him the first man on the Island to own an automobile. Although he had always been too ashamed to admit it, he had never liked horses (close proximity, too long prolonged, always made him sneeze); and he would not mourn their passing from his life. Within only a month or two of owning it, he could not understand how he had ever managed to live without his Model T: he would rather risk getting his wrist broken by the crank, submit to the teeth-jarring rattle of the ride, and hold himself in constant readiness, as the song had it, to "get out and get under," than to have to jolly along some cantankerous mare with a personality all her own.

In the summer after Andrew was born, Emma found herself once again "in a family way"; her mother said: "Good heavens, Emma Lee, don't you know where they come from by now?" But Emma had always wanted at least two children, maybe more, and she saw nothing at all wrong with having them quickly, while she was still young. On a portion of the land he had inherited from Dan Rainey, Sarsfield built a fine new house, one spacious enough to serve the needs of his growing family. He satisfied his liking for old-fashioned style with Corinthian columns, a belvedere overlooking the river, and a cupola overlooking South Front Street; his appreciation of modern amenities with a sleeping porch, and a bathroom so commodious and gleaming that Emma suggested wryly that they might consider hosting a dinner party in it. By now, the long-promised electrical cable to the Island had been completed; and electrics shone in every room. Sarsfield had a big, new gas range installed, and the latest model of wringer-washer, and a telephone. Emma's home was as good or better than anything she had imagined in her fondest childhood dreams; and, when little Andrew was asleep, she sometimes spent hours of her confinement walking from room to room just looking at everything. Both she and Sarsfield had hoped for a daughter; and their prayers were answered; in May of 1911, Emma gave birth to a little girl; they named her Nancy Ann.

Sarsfield continued to work long hours. All the amateur photographers for miles around now came to J. C. Middleton and Sons (as his business continued to be known) to have their film developed and their prints made, to buy their equipment,—or just to chat with an expert and a professional; Sarsfield, no matter how busy he was, always made

time for them. He was now also preparing all of the color plates used by
the printing trade in the city; and he, moreover, still did portrait work
for all who requested it. He often had to return to the shop after dinner
to keep up with the demands upon his time. He considered hiring an
assistant; but he found, to his surprise, that he had become so careful
with his pennies that he could not bear the thought of paying an additional salary. He was forced, of course, to abandon his work on his own
color process; although sometimes, on Sundays, he found a spare hour
to take a picture for his own pleasure,—for he still felt himself deeply
committed to the development of photography as an art.

By then Sarsfield had formulated a theory based upon his own
experience: that the best photographic work arose from a fusion of the
most intense feeling and the most rational thought—just as photography itself was a fusion of art and science. He had learned that he must
wait behind his camera for that perfect and precise moment when he
would be seized by a powerful certitude, when he would feel, for a
barely discernible fraction of time, that all distinction between himself
and the subject had vanished. Pictures he took at these unpredictable
but unmistakable moments resonated with a mystical fascination for
him; he expended long, painstaking effort to print them properly; and
he returned to view them again and again. He still occasionally won
awards for his work; but he knew that what a man does is what he
becomes;—and he knew what his daily routine was making of him:
each day he became less of an artist and more of a businessman.

Arch Kimbell, just as he had always said he would, had returned to
Raysburg and "hung out his shingle." He could, with his training and
experience, have easily become one of the "society" doctors in town or
limited his practice to high-priced surgery; but he had always wanted to
be a G.P. and serve the common man; he opened his office in an old
building down by the lower market. As soon as it became known that
"the young doc" would never refuse a patient in need, mill-workers and
their families began lining up to see him; he cursed them and vilified
them, called them "thick-headed, superstitious, dumb, dirty, ignorant
peasants"; but he treated them for promises in lieu of payment;—and
he worried about them, and gave them stern lectures, and dragged himself out of bed in the middle of the night to deliver their babies. He
waged a one-man war upon the roaches and bed-bugs that infested the

tenements of South Raysburg and got his picture in *The Times* for his efforts; with a broad grin on his face, he was seen holding up the sulphur candle that "did the trick."

Sarsfield and Arch still made time, every few weeks, to drink a beer or stroll along the river just as they had in the old days. "Marriage seems to be good for you," Arch told his friend; "It's settled you down, given you a sense of direction—"

"Sense of direction!" Sarsfield replied with a laugh, "with a couple kids, it's more like jumping onto a freight train and hanging on for dear life.—But how about you, old man? Isn't it about time you took the plunge?"

"No, not me, not yet," Arch said. "Too many pretty girls in the world."

In recent years Raysburg, like every other middle-sized town in America, had begun to see the rise of "the bachelor girl"—that wondrous phenomenon who had long inhabited the working world of New York or Chicago or Boston. Now she was no longer regarded as a pitiable creature, like Miss Calendene, who had been forced to obtain employment because she had to support her invalid mother; the new working girl was too badly needed as a clerk or a book-keeper or a secretary or a type-writer to be regarded as anything but indispensable for an up-and-coming, go-getter town like Raysburg; she was jaunty, and perky, and bold as brass;—and she was tickled pink to go out with Doctor Arch Kimbell. Every time Sarsfield saw Arch with a girl, she was a different one. "I like 'em all," Arch said with a wink; "but when the right one comes along, I'll know it."

Old Doc Anderson finally died; Sarsfield breathed a sigh of relief and asked Arch to have a look at his mother. "There's not a damned thing wrong with her," Arch told his friend in private; "She's healthy as a horse."

"You're kidding! What about the neurasthenia?"

"Hog-wash. She's in fine shape—could have a few more interests, get a little more exercise—"

"Can you get her off the damn laudanum?"

"Now listen to me, kid. Your mother's been on that stuff for— how long? Ten, fifteen years? It'd be cruel to take it away from her now; and she could probably get it easy enough anyhow. You just let her alone."

So Alice Middleton continued to dream on, day after day, the latest romance in her lap and the eternal river flowing by in the distance like a painted backdrop. Her husband, however, underwent yet another strange transformation.

Jack Middleton had never been the same since his protracted visit to Mrs. Smith's in the spring of 1908. When Jack had turned over the business to his son, his cronies had been amazed; "What's the old devil going to do with himself now?" they asked; and the answer appeared to be that Jack was settling in for a good, long, hard spell of serious, dedicated, and single-minded drinking. He arose at the same early hour each day just as though he had important business awaiting him; he dressed just as elegantly as he always had; he stopped for a shave in the barber shop at the end of the bridge; he visited the Raysburg Stock Exchange and remained there until eleven in the morning; then he repaired to Nolan's and began his day's work; by midnight or one in the morning he would have concluded it.

Jack could no longer be relied upon to get himself home; now a couple of Raysburg's finest had to be delegated to escort him back to the Island and turn him over to Mick O'Hara,—for, left to his own devices, Jack might be found crawling on his hands and knees down the center of Main Street, or, at dawn, sleeping soundly on the patch of lawn in front of the new public library. But, worst of all, Jack was no longer funny; now he sat far too often in dark corners, thinking his own dark thoughts; now he was often seen to leap to his feet at the squeak of a cart-wheel, the sound of a distant Victrola, or the whistle from down on the B 'n' O line; then he would stare about, muttering incomprehensible words to himself, or suddenly flee into the night as though pursued by a demon from hell. Common wisdom had it that "the poor old bastard's got himself one bang-up case of the jim-jams."

When, in 1909, the old mayor, Jim Greer, passed on to his greater reward, the boys gathered in the back room at the Kyle Rainey Club to decide upon his successor. A number of names were mentioned, but none of them "fit the bill"; then Sheriff Emmory, struck by sudden inspiration, said: "How about poor old Jack?" The suggestion was preposterous, ridiculous, and dead right. Jack was persuaded easily enough; his gift for geyser-like oratory returned—along with the old glad-hand and the spring in the step and the sparkle in his black eyes. ("The old man's got nine lives like a cat," Sarsfield told Emma.) Jack stood in the next election and easily swamped the wretched Democrat who had proposed to reform "the whole darned corrupt mess." Within a year or two it had become inconceivable that anyone else could ever be as totally and absolutely and perfectly the mayor of Raysburg, West Virginia, as Jack Middleton.

Sarsfield often remembered what old Dan Rainey used to say: "'Bout the only thing you can count on is that river rolling by." Much of what he had worried about before he had taken over the business and married now seemed to him little more than sheer foolishness; his life consisted of work, and work, and yet more work. The years passed; and he did not know whether he knew Emma any better than he had on the day he had married her. He had learned what she liked and disliked; he could predict what she would do; but he still did not know the innermost recesses of her heart;—but, with two children, such innermost recesses did not seem to count for much. Emma's life consisted of a baby, and baby-bottles and diapers and toys, and then another baby, which made two in diapers at once (good Lord!), and laundry and cleaning and cooking, and then one little one walking, and the other one talking, and both of them in mischief from dawn till dusk. The only people who dropped in regularly were Emma's relatives; Sarsfield was thankful for them: they made life cheerful and friendly and comfortable. Sarsfield and Tom Rossiter became close; they chatted about politics and agreed upon more than either had expected. Sarsfield was always glad to see Emma's mother walk through the door; she brightened their home with her large, garrulous presence. Sarsfield was content enough—when he stopped to think about it; he was sure that Emma must be too.

One Sunday evening in May of 1912, Sarsfield was sitting on the glider on the back porch looking down toward the river; he was too exhausted to move. Sunday was their only day to enjoy anything that resembled a social life; and they had packed in too many activities: church in the morning, and then a big picnic at Emma's parents with a whole "raft" of relatives, and then a visit to the Eberhardt mansion to see Uncle Mayne, Aunt Lou, and Grandmother Eberhardt. They had just returned home; and Sarsfield could not even muster the energy to pick up the morning's paper he had been looking forward to all day. He felt tiny hands pulling at his pants leg, saw the round, bright blue eyes of his little daughter emerge over the line of his knee; "Uh, uh!" she demanded—which he knew meant: "Up, up!" He lifted her onto his lap; she flung her arms around his neck and screamed with delight: "Da-DEE, da-DEE!" As tired as he was, his heart melted; "Who's my girl?" he said, giving her a pat; "Is Nancy my girl?"

He looked down over the sloping lawn and saw that Emma was leading Andrew back from the garden to whence he had escaped at a full run the moment Sarsfield had parked the Ford. "What fer?" the little boy was demanding in his quiet, husky voice that always seemed too deep and mature to be issuing from a child.

"Cat fur to make kitten britches," Emma replied; "Dog pants gone out of style!—Now get on with you." Looking up, she said: "What're you laughing at, Sarsfield Middleton?"

"Oh—just you and Andy," he said, for he would never have admitted to her what he was really laughing at: the sight of his wife in her latest frock. It was not that he found fault with her appearance; quite to the contrary, he thought her quite fetching. What was so funny was the turnabout she had made,—and her short memory. When they had been on their honeymoon, she had stopped to stare at a young lady on the streets of Buffalo; "Good heavens, look at that crazy skirt!" Emma had exclaimed; "You wouldn't get me in something like that if my life depended on it." Now here she was in exactly "something like that," bought to impress the Eberhardts—her very first hobble skirt.

"Say good-night to your daddy," Emma instructed her son.

"Aw shucks," Andrew said, but dutifully added: "G'night, daddy." Emma lifted Nancy from Sarsfield's lap, slung her over one shoulder, and, leading Andrew by one hand, vanished into the house. Sarsfield loved his children; but he heaved a sigh of relief nonetheless. "Goodnight, good-night," he called after them, waving as long as he could see through the screen-door Nancy's little, grinning face looking back over her mother's shoulder.

After a moment, he took up the paper, began to leaf through it. He was struck at once by a political cartoon: the Republican elephant was represented as a child's toy; it was being ripped in half by two little brats in knee-pants, the one labeled "Teddy," the other "Willie," each yelling: "Mine! Mine! Mine!" Although the cartoon must surely have been drawn by a Democrat, it expressed exactly what Sarsfield felt; and he had to smile bitterly to himself. The spectacular rift between Roosevelt and

Taft was for him the most trying and sorrowful public affair in recent
memory: two men who should have been bigger than that, two stalwarts
of the Republican Party (Sarsfield's party!) who should never have
stooped so low—were to be seen "soaking" each other good and proper
every chance they got. To Sarsfield's mind, big Bill Taft had done a perfectly respectable job, a fine job (look at all his anti-trust suits); the only
problem with him was that he was not Roosevelt;—and also to Sarsfield's
mind, there was no doubt who would make the better president: Roosevelt.
But, for the first time in his life, Sarsfield had entertained the radical,
heretical, and thoroughly disturbing notion that Teddy Roosevelt might
be capable of being wrong.

The only beneficiaries of the split in the Republican Party would
be, of course, the Democrats. Who the devil would they nominate?
Why, the old hound dog, Champ Clark, most likely,—or Underwood
(for "the bloody rag" was finally buried, and no one any longer dared to
say: "You can't nominate a Southerner"),—unless they wanted to take
their chances with that "prissy" Woodrow Wilson. A lot of Americans
seemed to want Wilson, Sarsfield could not understand quite why: the
man had never been much of anything but a school master. And a
united Republican Party could beat any of them; but the Republican
Party was not united; and Sarsfield feared for the future.

He laid the paper aside and looked out at the river. He remembered
his days at Harvard (they seemed so long ago!); he had, then, felt himself
intimately involved in the great events of his age; he had experienced
McKinley's death as though the man had been a beloved uncle; he had
stationed himself in Roosevelt's corner throughout every one of the
Colonel's wonderful fights just as though his presence there might be
essential to the outcome. His life was different now; he, like most Americans, still followed the political life of the nation avidly—but with a sense
that he was sitting on the sidelines, as though he were watching a baseball
game; viewed from Raysburg, West Virginia, it all seemed so far away.

Emma returned, settled on the glider next to her husband, and took
up the part of the paper he had not claimed. "What a day!" she said
wearily. They swung gently; she flipped through the pages. "Don't
forget to leave me money for the butcher," she reminded him.

"The butcher? I thought you paid him."

"That was last week. I really do need it, Sarsfield; I don't take the
dollars down and throw 'em in the river, you know."

"I know you don't, Em. You're a good manager."

She smiled at that, then returned to the paper. Yawning with fatigue, he watched the river rolling by. He would, he thought, go to bed early tonight; he could scarcely hold his eyes open.

"Your cousin's got her picture in the paper again," Emma said.

"Which cousin?" Sarsfield asked, although he knew perfectly well which cousin; Julia was a favorite of New York photographers; she was always turning up in the rotogravure section of the Sunday papers—or in *Vogue*.

"The high society one," Emma replied.

"What'd she do now?" Sarsfield asked, feigning only a mild interest.

"She rode a horse," Emma said dryly and handed him the paper.

He was struck by the picture before he could ascertain what event had occasioned it. The horse had reared back, his forefeet clear of the ground; Julia was riding astride, fully in control, one gloved hand holding a crop and the reins, the other waving a tricorn hat in a brilliant gesture of enormous éclat. Her smile was the one he remembered—dazzling as sunlight; she wore a trim, exquisitely tailored riding habit—the last word in chic. She was so gloriously beautiful that she looked more like an artist's idealized rendering than a creature of flesh-and-blood. The caption proclaimed: THIS SUFFRAGETTE'S NO AMAZON! Smaller type below read: "Mrs. Peter Van Gort accepts the applause of the crowd as 10,000 suffragettes march in New York."—"Oh," he thought, "of course she'd want the vote!"

The accompanying article informed him that last Saturday's event had been the largest women's suffrage demonstration yet seen in the United States; women from all classes of society had participated, from factory workers to the brilliant young society matron, Mrs. Van Gort; for the first time at such a demonstration, the crowds lining the streets had appeared to be sympathetic to the cause. And the accompanying editorial (reprinted from *The New York Times*) opined that the situation had become truly dangerous, that women might actually get the vote one day—if men were not "masculine" enough to stop them. Sarsfield looked up from the paper, saw that Emma's eyes were resting upon him; for a moment he could not find a thing to say to her; but then, assuming a tone of jocularity, he asked: "Well, Em, do *you* want the vote?"

"Heaven help me," she replied, smiling slightly, "why would I want the vote? Haven't I got enough else on my mind?"

"I guess you'll get it someday—whether you want it or not," he said after a moment. "Then what'll you do?"

"Why, then I guess I'll vote."

"Will you vote Democrat like your dad or Republican like your husband?" he asked in a tone that would tell her that he was teasing.

"Neither," she answered primly; "I shall vote for the best man."

He threw back his head and laughed at that. "I expect you will," he said.

He took her hand, felt an answering squeeze; they exchanged smiles, then, as though by mutual consent, looked away from each other. "Guess I can get out of this rig," she murmured, rose and walked into the house. He heard the screen-door bang behind her, heard the snap of her heels as she walked briskly in the shortened steps necessitated by the hem of her skirt. He was left alone as a poignant twilight settled over the river; the yellow incandescent lights of down-town twinkling through the blue-gray haze were reflected in the slow-moving water; and he risked another look at the picture of Julia.

Sarsfield and his cousin had exchanged polite notes over the years; she had sent them a twelve-place setting of fine English bone china as a wedding present (Emma had declared it too good to use and put it away at the back of a cupboard); she had sent congratulations and an infant's sterling cup upon the arrival of each of his children. By some quirk of fate, Julia had given birth to her first baby within the week that Emma had given birth to her second—both girls; and Julia had written that she hoped that Nancy Ann and Rosalind Consuelo might someday meet and become friends. Studying the newspaper photo, Sarsfield thought that Julia did not look like a woman who had borne a child only a year before (but then, come to think of it, neither did Emma); Julia's figure was trim as could be—although in the modern style; these days she would have looked peculiar indeed if she had tried to maintain her old turn-of-the-century wasp waist. He wondered what her life was like now—if she still collected Impressionist paintings, if she still read naughty French novels, if she enjoyed being a mother. He wondered what she thought about—if she were happy.

After a time he again laid the paper aside, trimmed and lit a cigar. "Lord," he thought, "things have changed so fast!" He doubted if he ever again in his lifetime would see such enormous and rapid change—automobiles, the long-distance telephone, talking machines, the wireless, the discovery of radium, *human flight*! And then, with no warning at all, his heart swelled with an emotion that was so vast and powerful he gasped aloud. "I went to Harvard!" he thought; "I studied with the great Will James. I danced at the Vanderbilts'. I was invited to the Astors'; and I met old Mrs. Astor herself, and she knew me and even had a few kind words to say to me. I took some of the first color photographs ever made in America. I photographed all the 'debs' that year; and my photographs hang in their homes. There's even a photograph of mine hanging in the Metropolitan Museum of Art. Why, the best I can tell, I took the first color photograph ever done with artificial light in the whole blamed country!" And then he mused about the vast changes he had seen come to America, and about what he had been, and what he had done;—he thought about what he was now, and everything he had achieved;—and suddenly he realized that it was all as trivial as the shifting sands compared to what really mattered. His eyes filled with tears; and he thanked the good Lord for his wondrous luck,—for he had known what few men ever know or can ever hope to know: a single love that was true and fierce and wild and free.

ACKNOWLEDGMENTS AND NOTES

This is a novel, not a history book, and it would be pretentious of me to cite all, or even very many, of my sources, but I feel impelled to cite some of them. Mark Sullivan's wonderful series *Our Times* provided me with an indispensable overview. The newspapers I consulted were the *Wheeling* (West Virginia) *Intelligencer*, *The New York Times*, and the New York *Star*. For women's fashions, I relied upon catalogues, newspaper advertisements, and, most often, *The Designer* magazine. More useful than history books—with their focus upon wars and presidents—were biographies, autobiographies, family histories, journals, travel books, period "sketches," deportment and photography manuals, and works of social and political commentary which ranged from the light-hearted (Peter Finley Dunne and Helen Rowland) to the ponderous (Herbert Croly).

I also read or skimmed a large number of novels written between the 1880s and the teens. I was looking for the elusive flavor of the period; for attitudes, ideas, and preoccupations; for the rhythms and diction of the prose; and for the fictional techniques that were commonly practiced and the structures employed. I helped myself to stock phrases ("Presently the company..."), expressions current at the time, and slang; I do not feel the need to credit these to particular authors any more than I would credit a 1960s novelist with "Far out!" In many instances, however, I did check for general usage in the *Dictionary of American Slang, Second Supplemented Edition*, edited by Wentworth and Flexner, Thomas Y. Crowell Company, New York, 1975, or Eric Partridge's *A Dictionary of Slang and Unconventional English, Eighth Edition*, edited by Paul Beale, Macmillan, New York, 1984.

Early drafts of this book read more like a history of photography than a novel, so I have eliminated all but the broadest outlines of Sarsfield's work in color photography. I feel compelled to add here, however, that he certainly would have been aware of the Lumière brothers' Autochrome process, but he would have found their emulsion far slower than his own, and he would probably have seen the process for what it turned out to be: a dead end. I did not want to try to invent his color process *ex nihilo*, so I have attributed to him methods and inventions (like the "one-shot" camera) that were actually the work of the great American inventor, Frederic E. Ives (for the development of color photography, see Louis Walton Sipley's fascinating *A Half Century of Color*, Macmillan, New York, 1951). I know absolutely nothing, however, about Ives' personal life beyond the sketchy account he gives us in his privately printed *The Autobiography of an Amateur Inventor* (Philadelphia, 1928), and Sarsfield is not intended even remotely to be a portrait of Ives. Sarsfield's demonstration of color mixing to the skeptical printer is based upon the account in Ives' book, pp. 62–63.

Sarsfield's attitudes toward photography are similar (although certainly not identical) to those of Alfred Stieglitz; the most useful of the many books and articles I read about Stieglitz was Sue Davidson Lowe's loving portrait of her "Uncle Al" (*Stieglitz: A Memoir/Biography*, Quartet/Or! Books, London, 1983) and Robert E. Haines' *The Inner Eye of Alfred Stieglitz* (University Press of America, Washington, D.C., 1982). Haines' thoroughly researched and convincing arguments on Stieglitz' aesthetics were an inspiration to me as I created an aesthetic position for Sarsfield.

Anyone the least bit familiar with the geography of the eastern United States will know at once that Raysburg could be only one place; a few novels ago, I created the fictional Raysburg, however, to give myself more room to maneuver and invent without having to be, all of the time, absolutely true to history, and, by now, I've grown to like my partially mythical, partially real town and enjoy going back there. The development of iron and steel manufacturing in the Ohio Valley is far more complicated than I have painted it in this book, and, by the turn of the century, no single individual or company had emerged that dominated the local industry in the way that Thaddeus Eberhardt and Raysburg Iron and Steel do here. Another factor I've ignored is that Raysburg Iron and Steel would have been an independent competing with the leviathan of United States Steel.

"Seacourt"—Henry Eberhardt's "cottage" at Newport—is, of course, fictitious; I have, however, borrowed and amalgamated details from actual

Newport homes of the period. Mrs. John King Van Rensselaer's *Newport Our Social Capital* (J. B. Lippincott, Philadelphia and London, 1905) provided me with lovely details from turn-of-the-century Newport, including the nickname of Julia's electric runabout.

For a general overview of the Civil War, I relied upon Shelby Foote's superb three-volume history; Tom's refusal to attempt the rebel yell forty years after the war is based upon an anecdote recounted by Foote. I invented none of the details of the battle of Chancellorsville; they were culled from a number of sources. The Union officer who tried to save wounded men from the burning woods and wept when he was forced to stop, was not, of course, my fictional character, Thaddeus Eberhardt, but the unnamed major who commanded George F. Williams (see Williams' account in *The American Iliad*, Eisenschiml and Newman, Bobbs-Merrill, 1947).

After I have described courting practices of various social strata in Raysburg and arrive at those I attribute to the Rossiters (brought from the Shenandoah Valley), my debt to Sherwood Anderson is so clear that I feel it only fair to credit him. My view is quite different from his bleak and cheerless one, but his description of young men and women being left alone to drive each other nuts was what inspired me, and my final sentence is a beefed up version of his. His reads: "After a year or two, if the impulse within them became strong and insistent enough, they married." (*Winesburg Ohio*, Boni and Liveright, New York, 1919, pp. 94–95.) Mine reads: "but it was understood that if the desire of the girl for the boy and the boy for the girl became urgent, forceful, painful, *cruel* enough,—then they would marry."

The beautiful young woman on horseback in the 1912 suffragette parade who stopped to have her photograph taken and then, as she galloped back to her place, was applauded by the crowd, was not Julia Van Gort but Inez Milholland. For a good account of the 1912 parade, see Walter Lord's *The Good Years: From 1900 to the First World War*, Harper & Brothers, New York, 1960.

Most women at the turn of the century wore corsets much more formidable than any modern woman would contemplate with any emotion short of horror, but, according to Valerie Steele in her cool and scholarly *Fashion and Eroticism* (Oxford University Press, New York, 1985), it appears that our grandmothers were nowhere near as tight-laced as we tend to imagine them. Julia Eberhardt's passion for extreme tight-lacing is, therefore, an individual quirk and is not meant to be taken as typical. During periods in which corsets were commonly worn, some women apparently fell in love with tight-lacing in a way that a modern writer might describe as becoming addicted; in spite of the discomfort involved, they apparently (as Julia obviously does) found this practice extremely pleasurable; why they did it and the extent to which they took it are questions I have not attempted to address—for the topic, I discovered, is surprisingly contentious. Steele provides a thorough account of the corset in the lives of ordinary women (like Emma Rossiter); David Kunzle's colorful and partisan *Fashion and Fetishism* (Rowman and Littlefield, Totowa, New Jersey, 1980) contains numerous anecdotes of tight-lacing addicts.

The quotation from Theodore Roosevelt that appears before the first half of this book is from a newspaper interview with Oscar K. Davis (quoted in Noel F. Busch's *T.R.: The Story of Theodore Roosevelt and His Influence on Our Times*, Reynal & Company, New York, 1963, pp. 10–11); Teddy, of course, went on to say that what made him different from an ordinary man, however, was that he did "the things that I believe ought to be done. And when I make up my mind to do a thing, I act." Consuelo Vanderbilt Balsan's sad commentary on the persisting influence of childhood comes from her brave and moving autobiography (*The Glitter and the Gold*, Harper & Brothers, New York, 1952, p. 8) and concludes an account of how, in her childhood, "Corporal punishment for minor delinquencies was frequently administered with a riding whip."

The quotation from Diana Vreeland that appears before the second half of this book is from her wonderful autobiography (*D.V.*, Alfred A. Knopf, New York, 1984, p. 194). Vreeland does not fit into the time covered by my book (she's one generation later, roughly contemporaneous with Julia's daughter Rosalind), but, if not from the right time, she's from the right place (New York) and class (upper), and her words are so apt I couldn't resist. Alfred Stieglitz' gnomic comment on his photographic work appears in a letter, dated August 15, 1923, that he wrote to Sherwood Anderson, quoted in Haines, p. 95.

Although all the characters in this book (with the exception of well known historical figures: T. R., McKinley, Taft, Jack Astor and Mrs. Astor, Consuelo Vanderbilt, etc.) are purely fictional and my Raysburg families are not portraits of any real families, I owe a great debt to the old folks in my own family, particularly my grandmother; I often had the eerie experience of finding that Emma or her mother were saying things that my grandmother had said but that, until I wrote them down, I had not known I remembered.

The punctuation system I have used was becoming old-fashioned by the turn of the century; readers who wish to see it in all of its original, highly elaborated glory should look at the work of John Ruskin; with the introduction of only one change (the notion that a long dash always *replaces* rather than *augments* another punctuation mark), this is the system employed by many literary writers (such as Edith Wharton) on into the twenties. I found Professor John G. R. McElroy's *The Structure of English Prose* (Rose Publishing Company, New York, 1890) very helpful for solving problems of style. For spelling and usage I relied largely upon the excellent Funk and Wagnalls *Standard Dictionary of the English Language* (New York and London, 1898).

My editor, Ed Carson, continued to be, as he always has been, a splendid critic and catalyst. I also want to thank my wife, Mary, and my in-laws, Fred and June Skinner, who read this book as it developed and provided advice and encouragement. I owe more than I can say to Fred—he turned a newsman's eye to the manuscript, and, despite my archaic spelling and punctuation, provided a splendid copy edit; he also kindly shared with me his childhood memories of Newport, corrected me when I was not imagining it right, and supplied me with several small, perfect details. I would like to think that there is a bit of his spirit in this book.

The guidance I received from historian Marjory Lang was invaluable; she saved me from making innumerable tiny errors of both fact and nuance and, in one case, prevented me from committing to print a huge and embarrassing howler. Whatever mistakes or solecisms might remain are, of course, my responsibility alone.

While I was doing research for this and later books, I found that my already considerable respect for librarians increased enormously. The staffs of the Harvard University Archives and the Ohio County Public Library were extraordinarily helpful. And I must offer a particularly fervent thanks to the staff of Interlibrary Loans at the University of British Columbia; many of the items I needed were rare, ancient, and obscure, but I quickly received everything I requested.

Finally, I wish to thank the University of British Columbia and the Dean of Arts for a start-up grant for new faculty, which enabled me to do the research required for this book.

Light in the Company of Women is the first of a new series of novels set in my fictional town of Raysburg, West Virginia, at various times from the middle of the nineteenth century to the present; in these books I will, as I have done here, attempt to write in a style inspired by, and similar to, the general style of popular fiction at the time in which the book is set. Some of these novels will continue the story of Sarsfield Middleton and his family.

Keith Maillard
Vancouver, B.C., Canada

May 14, 1991